Praise for *The Great* ..

"*The Great Prince Died* is illuminating for its insight into the moment when a great struggle for human liberation became a tyranny that still threatens the world. Its message is one the free world will ignore at its peril."
—**Selden Rodman,** *New York Times*

"Mr. Wolfe, who served on Trotsky's personal staff in Mexico in 1937, says it has taken him twenty years to develop the necessary 'emotional distance' to write the story . . . A significant novel— significant because of the light it sheds on history, significant because it is an action-packed human drama that is breathtaking."
—**Mildred Zaiman,** *Hartford Courant*

"Here is a novel which burns its way into your mind and your memory. . . . You will not forget it."
—*Newsday*

"Mr. Wolfe has written a political novel, and one of the most striking ever produced by an American author. . . . Victor Rostov (Mr. Wolfe's Trotsky) . . . is a man who, as early as 1904, was predicting dictatorship as the culminating tragedy of Bolshevik-Leninist monotheism. . . . Mr. Wolfe has written such convincing fiction that it may be difficult to remember that history may have happened in some other way."
—**Maurice Dolbier,** *New York Herald Tribune*

"Wolfe . . . has produced one of the major political novels of our time, and a provocative thesis in modern dialectics."
—**Richard McLaughlin,** *Boston Globe*

"Living in a pink stucco fortress near Mexico City with a band of emotionally-driven followers, guarded by Mexican police, Rostov [Trotsky] is aware of the dual role he plays: first, as the enemy, the victim of the Bolshevik regime; second, as a man who holds the horrendous responsibility for having helped to create it. . . . All this is powerfully told in the novel."
—**Robert Kirsch,** *Los Angeles Times*

Biographical Note

Bernard Wolfe (1915–1985) wrote *The Great Prince Died*, the science fiction novel *Limbo*, and helped Mezz Mezzrow write *Really the Blues*. He was raised in New Haven, Connecticut, and attended Yale University. After college he worked in the United States Merchant Marine, and in 1937, he served briefly as secretary to Leon Trotsky during his exile in Mexico. Wolfe was hired as a military correspondent for several science magazines during WWII and began writing fiction after the war. He wrote plays, mainly for television, and published short fiction in *Playboy* and *Esquire*. One of his most well-known novels, *Limbo*, was included in David Pringle's book *Science Fiction: The 100 Best Novels*. His other works include *The Late Risers* (1954), *The Great Prince Died* (1959), *The Magic of Their Singing* (1961), and *Come On Out, Daddy* (1963). In 1955, Mr. Wolfe adapted his novel for an NBC Playhouse drama called *Assassin*. After *The Great Prince Died* went out of print, Mr. Wolfe revised the novel and retitled it *Trotsky Dead*.

THE
GREAT
PRINCE
DIED

A Novel about the Assassination of Trotsky

BERNARD WOLFE

with a New Afterword by
William T. Vollmann

University of Chicago Press
Chicago and London

FOR ARTHUR AND ROSEMARY MIZENER

The University of Chicago Press, Chicago 60637
The University of Chicago Press, Ltd., London
© 1959 by Bernard Wolfe, 1987 by Dolores Michaels
Wolfe and Jordan and Miranda Wolfe
Published originally by Charles Scribner's Sons
University of Chicago Press edition 2015
Printed in the United States of America

22 21 20 19 18 17 16 15   1 2 3 4 5

ISBN: 978-0-226-26064-8 (paper)
ISBN: 978-0-226-26078-5 (e-book)
DOI: 10.728/chicago/9780226260785.001.0001

Library of Congress Cataloging-in-Publication Data

Wolfe, Bernard, 1915–1985, author.
    The great prince died / Bernard Wolfe ; with a new
afterword by William T. Vollmann.
        pages cm
    ISBN 978-0-226-26064-8 (paperback : alkaline
paper) — ISBN 978-0-226-26078-5 (e-book) 1. Trotsky,
Leon, 1879–1940—Fiction. 2. Revolutionaries—Soviet
Union—Fiction. I. Vollmann, William T., writer of
introduction. II. Title.
PS3573.049G74 2015
813'.54—dc23

                                    2014045149

⊛ This paper meets the requirements of ANSI/NISO
Z39.48–1992 (Permanence of Paper).

Politics in a work of literature are like a pistol-shot in the middle of a concert, something loud and vulgar and yet a thing to which it is not possible to refuse one's attention.

We are about to speak of very ugly matters, as to which, for more than one reason, we should like to keep silence; but we are forced to do so in order to come to happenings which are in our province, since they have for their theatre the hearts of our characters.

"But, great God, how did that great Prince die?"

—STENDHAL, *The Charterhouse of Parma*

The HOME of the RUSSIAN EXILES,
Victor and Marisha Rostov,
in Coyoacán, suburb of Mexico City,
in the year 1939.

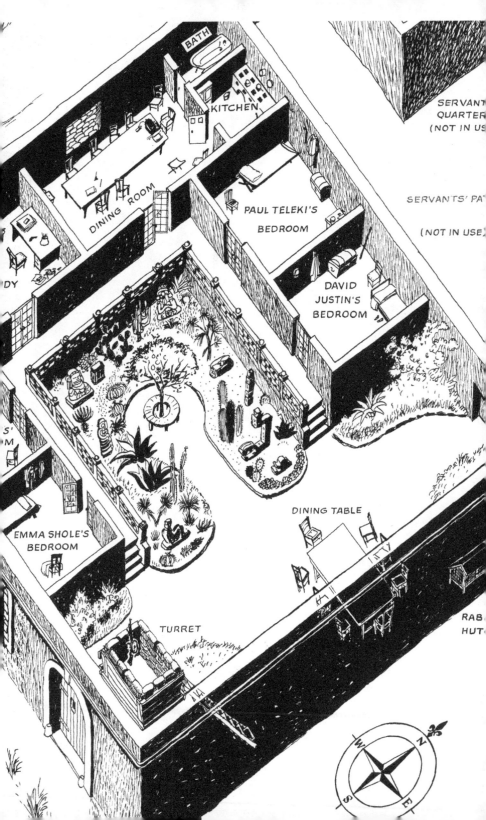

*THE
GREAT
PRINCE
DIED*

❦ DIOSDADO

This noon sun, this hot government. It was, Diosdado considered, a slow wood hammer.

Hit, hit again. In this way it governed.

He was on his back in the parallelogram of shade outside his hut. Without moving head he swung eyes across the overcome neighborhood: his several rows of maize and frijoles, his chickens, his goat, his stacks of rusting headlights and tire rims, the dirt ruts and weed islands of Avenida Londres, the faded pink blue house on the far side of Londres.

One hit, another hit. Surfaces waved up and down under the sun's rapping.

The pink blue house went up and down in sections. Once. Again.

Diosdado shifted his buttocks on the grass, rubbed his sweated neck against the adobe wall, lowered his eyes to his feet. Dust made another skin on them. They swelled and shrank. Wide, the toes were, and spread, and over them, in the tower of the pink blue house, the young man with black hair was piling sandbags. Pistol, as usual, in belt. Lowered one sandbag, another, on Diosdado's hooked toes.

Diosdado hooked the toes more, against these weights.

Feet could hit, too. So doing, to govern. To hammer at the one closest, their owner, with orders, was their way.

He tipped straw hat over eyes. Avenida Londres stretched, rutted, in both directions: empty, smashed. Inside the hut Serafina said in monotone to the kids, "You get the tortillas and no more. Today there are no beans."

Diosdado examined his caked feet: opening mouths with complaints, begging, like kids.

Kids? Small, steady hammers. Similarly, feet. Larger, were his feet, then smaller.

Next to his left foot, the wood guardhouse. On the opposite corner where Londres met Cortés, there outside the pulsing pink blue house. Folded in a chair that leaned against his shack, the sergeant of the policía, the one they called Guillermo, was playing his guitar and singing in a diminished voice. A song about his heart and its pains.

The unpainted shack swelled, shrank. The sergeant did the same, with the same pulse.

Diosdado looked at the sergeant between his dusted feet, two noises, two needs, and thought about Mack truck tires.

It was a distance out, the Coyoacán dump, near the maguey and sugar cane plantations of the open country. Three hours of the morning Diosdado had picked through the tin cans and rusted Ford bodies, looking for a Mack truck tire. These were the best, of just right thickness. No Mack tire. Headlights, rims, axles, steering wheels, but no tire of any type. This was the wonder.

Across in the tower, the young man with the pistol looked down at the singing sergeant, made a face, lowered another bag on Diosdado's toes. Diosdado curled his toes protectively.

Turned eyes again to the bare Avenida Londres. Away, three blocks far, coming from the Insurgentes highway, a figure: the postman. He came along bent, a man being hit from above.

When had he, Diosdado, last received a piece of mail? A year ago. What? He remembered: a paper which unfolded to show a picture of a refrigerator, all white, under it printed words, some words. It was now hanging on the wall inside his hut, which had no electricity, over the stone basin for grinding maize.

Avenida Londres, with its automobile ruts and weed clumps, was no worry now. It would be a worry. Soon, according to the talk, this year, next year, Londres too would be covered over with the tar and its dirt footpaths made cement. Then Cortés. The tar and the cement were coming into Coyoacán, block by block.

This was the shape of the worry. Sun hit on tar and cement, tar and cement hit on feet, feet hit at their owner with complaints. With demands.

The Mack truck tire was now an urgency. But in the entire dump of Coyoacán, where in the usual week five, seven Mack truck tires were thrown by the local bus company, there was to be found not one tire of any type.

This lack, too, was a hammer. On the thoughts, to make them swell and shrink.

The young man with the pistol called down to the sergeant of the policía, "Guillermo, listen, you have to play that thing all the day?" The man of the sandbags did not, then, like music? In the hut Serafina said with the voice on one level, "The tortillas are all. Eat them or eat nothing." The kids mumbled, "Beans, mama, frijoles, some beans?" Across Londres, a sprinkle of laughter from the cops. Two high women's voices mixed in.

Diosdado liked to put questions in the terms of numbers. Considered as fours, as fives, as sevens, otherwise running and escaping things slowed, stood in fixed positions, could be looked at. He applied numbers to the matter of the Mack truck tire:

From one tire, ten and six single soles, eight pairs; in his family were nine, eight needed huaraches, the youngest did not yet walk. Once there were the soles, it took a leather thong across the top, thongs could be cut from old automobile seats or transmission belts, and each was a huarache to silence a complaining foot. One tire, then, was the need of this family of eight walkers, of eight and eight walking feet.

Was there an increase in Coyoacán of feet with the need for huaraches, and therefore a more careful looking in the dump? Hundreds more feet, many?

To be considered that there were not more feet in Coyoacán, only a greater need for the huaraches. With the tar and the cement coming in.

He was not used to thinking in numbers larger than ten; no need, he never had as many as ten units of anything. It took work to think of the ten and six, the eight and eight, units of a thing that were needed to make eight pairs of this same thing, all born from one unit of a different thing. Wasted work, since the beginning unit, the circle of rubber that was mother to good huarache soles as machete was their father, was not to be found.

More laughter. Its source: the wall of the pink blue house stretching away from his right foot. Here were the other cops, all who were not in the guardhouse playing cards, perhaps two tens of them. The girls were with them, as usual, one in a yellow dress, the other in a green striped blouse. The cops were touching the girls on shoulder, on waist, laughing. The girls laughed back, in low notes. The sergeant called to the man in the tower, "It bothers you, Señor Paul? Good, I play with softness."

Why were these policía on duty outside the pink blue house, all day and all night for seven months now; always two tens of policía? If to protect, why did the ones on the inside, when they appeared in the tower, look with anger at their protectors? If to keep them prisoners, why did these same ones come into the tower and give to the policía orders to stop this and that? And why did the policía obey? Cops do not take orders from prisoners and call them señor.

The mailman was a block away. Inside the hut Serafina said with the one note, "Tomorrow, beans. Today, tortillas." In the wired in yard, the three flesh of paper chickens pecked; farther away, tied to his pole, the one goat worked with serious lips over a Chevrolet headlight. The young man in the tower was resting against the sandbags, oiling the trigger of a small machine gun.

These were not prisoners, no. Prisoners do not carry pistols in the belt. Now, a machine gun.

The sergeant was playing his guitar, singing with held in voice. Diosdado wondered if he might go to Mexico City to look in the dumps there for a Mack truck tire. No, Mexico was too far. He did not have fare for the bus, he would have to walk, as he walked to all places, it would take half a day; should he find a tire he would have to roll it, his future shoes, back to Coyoacán along the tars and cements of Insurgentes highway, miles far, his feet bare and full of complaints.

The feet here, the eight and eight feet, the ten and six, would go without the new, thick huaraches for another time. It meant only more walking, to go along the streets where there were not yet tar and cement. This could be done. This was the shape of the situation: sun would govern their routes here and there.

"Guillermo," the young man called from the tower. "Hey, sergeant. Let us have one day without serenades, all right?"

The guitar stopped. Loud laughing from one girl, the other girl. The mailman was coming close.

Diosdado narrowed his eyes, looked at the mailman approaching his left foot, heard the guitar start again very low, wondered which month might bring him another white refrigerator picture to go on the other wall, looked between his feet, two rackets, two beggars, saw the laughing girls, wondered why these two, whores, assuredly whores, were always hanging around the cops, what they found to laugh about all the time. His feet grew large and small. The girls grew small and large. He closed his eyes and was asleep, toes twitching under the sandbags, the digs of the guitar pick, the drip of the gun oil.

CHAPTER I

". . . . one day without serenades, all right?"

Tommygun in one hand, oil can in the other, Paul Teleki leaned on the sandbagged wall and looked down at Sergeant Guillermo. He was not pleased with himself. He had meant to hold in the irritation, the touchiness that was a plague in him now, but his voice had sounded sharp.

From his chair outside the guardhouse Sergeant Guillermo waved lazily. He went on playing until the ballad of regrets was done, then placed the guitar on the ground, composed his hands in his lap and closed his eyes, face up to the sun.

Small range in Guillermo: can't sing, sleep. Paul Teleki looked across Londres at the littered lot opposite. The péon, the one they called Dios, Diosdado, something, was stretched out on the grass alongside his adobe hut, a sun taking corpse with hat over eyes.

Another of limited range. Another easy sleeper. Diosdado, whatever his name was, sometimes hoed the chunked ground between his rows of maize and beans, sometimes carried junk home from the dumps, sometimes honed his machete; otherwise he slept profoundly.

There were lives without distractions. Or abstractions.

The tower Paul Teleki stood in was a new structure. Its wood boards were unweathered, their grain lines still a fresh reddish brown. It was on the Londres side of the villa, in an angle of the high wall, placed so as to command from its twelve-foot elevation a view of both Londres and the intersecting Cortés. The sandbags Paul had been carrying were to reinforce this structure, some to line it, others to build it up, heightening the boarded sides almost to chest level. Paul leaned on these bags, his eyes directed down.

The cops and the girls were in a group below him. The girls had stopped making sounds of laughter but their lips were still open in laughing position as they returned his stare, eyes without questions but unmuted. Paul saw them foreshortened, breasts buoying chins, belly rounds abutting breasts, thin inches of legs below.

8

A block away, to the right, the postman was approaching. The mail pouch a disfiguring hump on his back.

Against the wall below the cops leaned, awkwardly casual, waiting, Paul knew, for him to go away. Both girls, faces still upturned, seemed to be laughing silently at him, their plumped breasts floating the joke. His fingers tightened on the gun, he turned away.

Distractions in breasts. Abstractions behind the laughing lips.

The patio he faced was almost a perfect square in shape. The house itself was made of three joined wings, one along Londres, another at right angles to it along Cortés, the third running back from Cortés parallel to the Londres front; these wings made up three sides of the square, the fourth being a high wall. The house was one story high, its railroad rooms, on all three sides, leading off from a slightly elevated walk. The turret was built over the enclosing wall, at the place where it reached Londres and made a right turn there to meet the house proper. The main entrance, a three-inch-thick planked door, was in this wall, between the house and the corner turret.

The villa's adobe facings, and its extension wall too, were a rain streaked blue, edged with dimming pink. But the original coat of paint had been entirely pink, and it came through the overlay in places, giving the blue stretches a medleyed sunset tint.

This patio was crowded. The area contained by the arms of the villa was a garden, a mass of cactus plants and bright clustered flowers, with here and there, poking up past the spiney flat paddles of the magueys, stone images of Aztec and Mayan deities. In the exact center of this garden was an orange tree, now dotted with ripe fruit; around its base, enclosing a ring of blood petaled flowers, a seat. A bare path ran from the street door to both ends of the elevated walk that jutted out from the house's interior walls; this raised deck was edged with a balustraded balcony. To one side of the street door, a set of crude wooden steps led up to the turret.

Paul Teleki started down these steps carrying his gun and oil can. What had set him off had been the whores, not the music, but seeing emergent breasts, runaway breasts, inches away, light years away, he had spoken against Guillermo's guitar. It was not the unfairness in this that bothered him but what it said about his control, his readiness to be whistled to side targets.

He liked to be as singleminded about the main jobs as a Diosdado was about his hoeing and sleeping.

His targets were beginning to dance and blur.

David Justin appeared from the innermost room, the end room on the inside wing. He stood on the walk as he buttoned his denim shirt and stuck its tails in, yawning and blinking rapidly. He was of medium height, stocky, with short sandy hair and fair skin that seemed recently sunburned. Raising his hand in greeting to Paul, he wiped his forehead, snapped the sweat off his fingers with exaggerated despair.

"You want to feel the sheets on my bed," he said in English.

"No, thanks," Paul said as he reached the ground.

"You could wade in them."

"Some other time." Paul Teleki's English was good but deliberate, the words slightly spaced, as though it still took thought to produce them. He placed his gun and oil can on the turret steps, took out his handkerchief to wipe his fingers. Two of the fingers of his left hand were missing; he carefully patted the stumps. "You didn't sleep any better?"

David Justin shook his head. "Too hot and too noisy." The guitar started up again; he listened until Guillermo's silked voice undertook the words. "Damn them and their concerts. They didn't let up all night." He looked at his wristwatch and shook his head again. "Sorry I overslept. If I could take a sleeping pill—"

"I told you, they slow down the reflexes."

David Justin walked down the five steps from the elevated ramp and stood in the path. He made a boxer's loosening motions with his shoulders, bent to touch the ground several times with his fingers. Straightening up, he rubbed his eyes.

"Then when I do doze off, the least sound wakes me up. This morning a car backfired; before my eyes were open I was on my feet, reaching." He patted the revolver in his belt and gave an embarrassed laugh. "Took me twenty seconds to find it. It was under the pillow."

"I've told you, hang your holster on the bedpost! Put the gun in it! What do you think I gave you the holster for?" Paul Teleki's anger went before the words were out: a Justin could not be blamed for the way he handled guns, it was the bulked breasts over flowing summer cottons he was fuming at still. "Give it another week. Plain silence'll wake you up, it does the worst backfiring."

"And plays the biggest guitars?" David Justin's shirt was already soaked through with sweat. He pulled its front away from his body. "That's the trouble with walls, you know, Paul: everything on the outside sounds serious. Especially the silence." He was approaching the turret steps, for the first time he noticed the machine gun. He stooped to pick it up. "You got it!"

"Emma brought it this morning." David weighed the gun as he might a baby, crouched to point it at an imaginary target in the orange tree. Paul reached for the weapon. "I don't suppose you've ever handled one of these."

"I was in the R.O.T.C. in college." Paul seemed puzzled. "That's a military training program. But I was with an artillery unit. I'm very good with a six-inch howitzer."

"This is all the howitzer we'll get." Paul put the gun back on the steps. "Maybe we'll arrange some target practice."

David Justin pointed up at the sandbagged walls of the turret. "Going up fast. . . . Wish I could help more—I've had to spend my watches working on the translation, I'm way behind. The press releases take too damn much time." David went to the pile of sandbags lying against the wall and lifted one experimentally. "These things are *heavy.*"

Paul took the bag from his hands, got another from the pile, and carried both to the foot of the steps. "When things get hot you can say to the bullets in your five different languages, please go away. Maybe they'll work better than sandbags." He disliked himself intensely for venting his bad humor at the wrong, the irrelevant, target again. He indicated the turret. "Get up there, will you?"

David climbed up. He reached over and took the bags offered by Paul, as he placed them in position he looked out across Londres. "What do you know. Diosdado is finally getting a letter. The postman's over there waking him up."

"Maybe it's his invitation to the Presidential ball."

"Or a summons for moving the city dump into his yard. Or a 1911 goat tax that just caught up with him." David patted the sandbags flat. "There's a man who obviously doesn't belong to anything more specific than the human race. He never has dealings with any institution known to man. He worries me, Paul. Seriously. I've tried to talk to him, it's impossible." David leaned over to look into the street. "They're back." He seemed surprised. "Those women. Hanging around in broad daylight now."

"The cops like a nip; we give them cognac. If they like women."

"What if they liked hashish? Vacations on the Riviera? I see those two every time I'm on night duty, last night too. We don't even know who they are."

"What's the mystery?" Paul was going for more bags. "They're a couple of whores, from that yellow apartment house down on the next block."

"How do you know so much about them?"

"My learned eyes."

"If that's what they are, all the more reason to get rid of them. One word to Ortega—"

"All the less reason. Take away guitars, cognac, whores, a cop's eyes close. A cop with his eyes closed—no cop at all."

David took two more bags from Paul's hands and hoisted them into position. "I'll try to make my peace with cop physiology." He scanned the street again. "The postman's coming over, I think. Yes."

Paul immediately took a position at the door, stood there expectantly. In a moment the doorbell rang loudly.

"Señor Paul! Paul!" Guillermo called from the other side. "Special delivery!"

Paul pulled the hinged lid back from a small peephole in the door. He looked out into the sergeant's fleshy face and wide black eyes. "You can bring it in." He looked up to David. "Time to unveil the electrical wonders." He placed his finger on a buzzer set in the wall and pressed it. The door swung open.

Guillermo stepped in, staged astonishment on his face.

"Bueno, Señor Paul, Señor David." He examined the buzzer, put his finger on it delicately, with scientist's investigating touch. "Hey, this is a good thing. I like it." He shut the door and buzzed it open, repeated the operation. "Very good, yes. You make this yourselfs?" He was looking at Paul with a too wide smile.

"Where's the letter?" Paul Teleki said.

"A door is nice this way. You look in the face, you like the face, you push quick." Guillermo illustrated, opening the peephole then buzzing the door. "I like to put button on my wife, here." He patted his left buttock. "I say to her, woman, I have big hunger, bring food. I push, she jump. Ah, Señor Paul? You put the button on my wife? No little door in the head, though. I know what is in this woman's head." He pointed to the sandbags against the wall. "A whole big bunch of sandbags. To throw at me, naturally."

"The letter, Guillermo. The letter."

Guillermo offered the red and blue striped envelope. Paul took it, looked at its face, nodded. "New York." He tore it open and unfolded the inside sheet. "Same story: they want to send more guards." David had come down the steps. Paul gave him the letter, pointing to a room in the far corner of the house on the Cortés side. "He's in the study with Emma."

David Justin went off, carrying the letter.

Guillermo was now studying the turret with dramatic admiration. "You work very much with the bags."

"We look for the house with the highest walls, then we make them higher." Paul had picked up the machine gun and was wiping its barrel with his handkerchief. "Some like avocados; we like walls."

"And the turret." Guillermo took from his shirt pocket a package of Elegantes, offered one to Paul, was refused, lit one for himself and sucked in sweet smoke with an appreciative sound. "And the little door in the big door. Now the machine gun."

Paul's face clouded: "They're not to keep *you* out, sergeant. Only those who might get by you. While your muchachos entertain the muchachas." Again the substitute targets. He was not angry with the police, either: you cope with a physiology; but if you pretend such anger do you begin with cops and switch in the middle to the muchachas, the putas?

Guillermo had come to attention. His face was composed. "The bad ones do not get in here, señor, unless over my dead body." There was the metal of dignity somewhere in back of the soft syllables.

"They've gotten into other places. Sometimes over bodies."

Guillermo considered this information, his eyes steady on Paul. He snapped into good humor. "Nothing to worry, Paul. If we are all dead, you got enough sand in those bag to bury each and everybody!"

"Then who'll play the guitar at our funeral?"

"My wife! You put special button on her fat behind to make her to play!"

"Who's going to push *that* button?"

"Make it to go by himself! You think I want some damn stranger to push my woman in the behind? A man of a name I do not know, to upfeel my wife?"

Guillermo began to laugh. Against his will, face muscles fighting the concession, Paul Teleki began to laugh with him.

David Justin was back in the patio. He came down from the raised walk and headed for the door.

"I better to go back to the boys," Guillermo said, not moving. He had his eyes on a wall shelf that was crowded with bottles.

"Oh, no you don't," Paul said. "I gave you one on Saturday."

Guillermo turned to the nearing David Justin a fact finding face: "You know how high is here in Distrito Federal, Señor David? At the least, 7,500 feet: you stand up, your head bump on the moon spots. In the sun, oh, nice; very friendly and nice. Only in the nights, no sun, the boys they get cold." He wrapped his arms around his thick torso and imitated a man shivering. "Cold like on Popocatepetl. Even with the serape."

Paul Teleki made a sighing sound. He took a bottle from the shelf and handed it to the sergeant. "All right. Go sit on Popocatepetl. Take the cognac for central heating."

"Not for the taste!" Guillermo said fast. "Only for the cold! If I see one muchacho who lick the lips with this stuff, I knock his lips off! Million thanks, Señor Paul! A kindness!"

Paul buzzed the door open, Guillermo touched the buzzer with his admiring air.

"I know, I know," Paul said, "it's a nice thing, you like it, you like all our things." He took Guillermo's arm and steered him through the door. In the splashes of sun outside he caught a glimpse of tawned legs in high pumps, a smear of yellow, a patch of green in stripes, over fleshed breasts in bold rise. He shut the door quickly and turned back to David. "The Old Man read the letter?"

"He's dictating an answer now." Paul's face tightened in irony that David caught. "What do you think he'll say?"

Paul Teleki was sure what should be said: we need a lot of men here, a lot of guns. Because this pretty pastel house is an eyesore and a pestilence, it invites attack as ants invite stepping on. Out there, on the free side of the wall, the come and go as you like side, they are enemies or potential enemies, cops, postmen, Diosdados, green and yellow putas in high, taunt heels. None of this could be said to Justin, the translator. During Justin's almost four weeks here they had had this discussion several times, always leading nowhere. Justin, the trust all translator, contended that Teleki, the sullen arsenal, was a phenomenon: the whole human race the enemy? Paul would answer to this, yes, precisely so, your enemy as well as mine; David would conclude with a belittling shrug, share and share alike. Impossible to tell this translator there was one rule about walls, stay on your side and fraternize with nobody on the other side, no matter how end of the world boring it gets at three in the cold morning, no matter how the whores giggle: respect the wall; how to mention Justin's lapping with the eyes at those sluts in their French heels? Justin would raise shoulders and answer, off with the faucets in my mouth, you're the politburo in this house.

Paul Teleki started up the turret steps. In a moment he turned and said, "V.R.'s a general who's gotten used to working without an army." He entered the turret and surveyed the street. "Love's in bloom: the ladies are going home with two of our cops. Correction: four cops. Two more right behind. Standing room only today." He faced about as though pulled and directed himself again to David Justin: "*I'm* the only army he can live with. And he's souring on me. What *can* he say? Hand up those bags, will you?"

". . . . and David Justin is working out very well. More guards would mean a comic-opera existence, we would be bumping into each other in every room. Use your limited funds, I beg you, dear friends, for your publishing and agitational work. There is where our first responsibility lies: to expose the Neanderthal's crimes before the eyes of the world. With best fraternal wishes, etcetera, etcetera."

V.R., the Old Man, Victor Rostov, paced the study as he dictated, making the words march smart as he marched, voice strong and purposed, eyes patrolling the bare wooden floor. He was solid, free of lax flesh; he was dressed in house slippers, loose tweed pants, a straight hanging French peasant jacket of light blue linen; as he executed his about-faces he smoothed his silvering thick hair, stroked his mustache and clipped Van Dyck. He moved with review precision, ten brisk strides to the wall, ten back. The room was barren, except for a few leather bottomed peasant chairs and a very large bright yellow wooden desk piled with manuscripts and newspaper clippings.

The one window in the room, facing on Cortés, was blocked off with a solid wall of sandbags. Sunlight stained the area immediately around the French doors that gave on the patio, but the interior of the room was in shadow. To make up for the lack of natural light, a naked electric bulb, suspended by its cord from the ceiling, was lit.

Emma, at the desk with pencil still poised over pad, kept her editorial eyes on V.R. He came over to her. "You don't agree with my answer?"

"Answer? Or evasion?"

"Think: they can raise an army if they want. Does it matter whether we have one David Justin or twenty? We only multiply the targets."

"While *they* mobilize their army—"

"*We* mobilize public opinion. You've seen today's *El Machete?*" V.R. picked up a newspaper from the desk and ran an index finger across the streamer. *"ROSTOV PLOTS TO ASSASSINATE SOVIET LEADERS . . . . COUNTER-REVOLUTIONARY'S ROLE AS HITLER AGENT REVEALED."* His fingers let the paper drop as though to avoid contamination. "Why do they print this nonsense? They won't dare move against me until the public is prepared, you see? I'm trying to reach the public too."

Emma's face softened. She was slightly angular, her bones prominent; in relaxation her small features had a pale prettiness.

"I know how you feel. Behind walls, never out of sight of people. You need space, you'd like a planet to yourself. But you were always such a fighter. Now. . . ."

"You think I've come this far in order to raise my palms to the sky like an old Talmudist and say, so be it, it is written?" He held hands out, palms up, in a parody of ghetto hopelessness; her face eased further into a reluctant smile. "No. But don't expect an old Red Army commander to rally his decimated troops at the enemy's *strongest* point." He pulled a chair close to Emma and sat, leaning toward her. "Emma. Marisha's concerned about you."

The smile faded from her face. She became absorbed in her stenographer's pad. "It's nothing. I've told you, I've been sleeping badly."

"If you sleep badly it can't be nothing. You've lost weight."

"Oh, ever since the first warnings I've been—tense. That's all it is. Otherwise we're getting along fine, really, really." She looked up at him and lowered her eyes quickly. With a jerking take of breath she put her pad on the desk. "I'm a bad liar. We're *not* getting along. There's a wall between us ten feet thick. Jacques says it's because of the strain we're all under. I wonder."

"Maybe you *should* leave here, Emma. You and Jacques."

"In the revolution your men didn't run from you. Especially before a battle."

'Emma: there's no army to run from. Only a few stragglers in a forgotten suburb. I wish I knew Jacques better." He turned to see the clock on the wall. "Almost noon; no Ortega. I thought the lure was juicy enough today."

"Maybe he hasn't seen the morning papers." She stood, began to make order on the desk. "When do we get to the Kronstadt chapter?"

"Let's get George Bass out of the way first." He pursed his lips and fingered his pointed beard. "The Neanderthals have priority."

"V.R. At least—if Ortega wants to increase the police guard, don't oppose it."

"If that's what he wants, he won't consult me." He rose too. "Can you get that letter done right away? It should go out today."

She nodded in her serious way. V.R. put his hands on her shoulders and looked with a smile into her large eyes: "You won't go home?" She shook her head emphatically. "All right. I won't order you to abandon your advance post at the typewriter. We'll talk about this wall that's bothering you, Marisha wants to, I know. You mustn't worry, Emma. There are ways to bring down the most stubborn walls, trust an old campaigner."

CHAPTER II

General Ortega's black Buick slowed down to make the turn from the Insurgentes highway into the dirt corrugations of Avenida Londres. Three blocks away, down the lines of pastel residences, the stucco villas of the well-off newcomers, the adobe walled and tile roofed low houses of the older and less moneyed natives, he could see the raw wood guardhouse outside the Rostov place: the one oblong of tension in this yawning suburb. Would it help to paint it? No good. Could the rifles of the police be painted to look like golf clubs, flower pots? Dress the police themselves in artists' smocks? The car, though going slow, bumped and weaved as it proceeded along Londres. "Faster, man, faster," General Ortega said with a curtness to the driver. Though he could not blame the driver for the gouged road or, more to the point, the headlines. The headlines, not the road, were responsible for his snappishness. On General Ortega's knee was the morning edition of *Las Novedades*. The words rose to his eyes with the bulked insult: *ROSTOV: MEXICO OVERRUN WITH FOREIGN AGENTS*. The fifth such article in as many days. This one going beyond the others, which had been bad enough. Time for a showdown with Señor Victor Rostov, not only his, the Chief of Secret Police's, honor was at stake, but that of a government. Showdown, yes. But after which provisos and to what end? Such a man could not be muzzled, perhaps should not. And still. How many more front page insults?

General Ortega was a shoulders back, cut square man, with a body discipline surprising in one past sixty. He was so addicted to the idea of an ordered self, so shunned the loose touch, that he wore his braided cap evenly on his head, not tilted one millimeter. Though he disliked any show of emotion, feeling that eruptions from the inside were a gaudiness and an interference, he was now biting his lower lip to the point of hurt. "Never mind the road, faster," he said again to the driver and was instantaneously sorry. No sense to prodding a subordinate because of a prodding headline. But five prods at *him* in as many days.

On the block before the Rostovs', on the opposite side, a glare yellow apartment house. General Ortega noticed, without putting his full mind to the sight, that two young women were mounting the steps here, showy women, yellow blouse, green striped dress. Prostitutes? In this suburb? Not likely. Family neighborhood, modest means, no base for two such, General Ortega thought and in the thinking dismissing the women to consider again the headline.

But some houses down Londres from this house he saw a more noteworthy thing. Policemen. Four. They were standing rigidly at the side of the road, in a line. As the Buick came alongside they as one raised their arms in salute.

Four? From the Rostov detachment, certainly. Few others on duty in the area.

For a bothersome moment he considered whether these four might have some involvement with the two flashy women. No. It would mean the women were prostitutes. No base, etc.

What, then, were the men doing away from their posts? Investigating something? Running a routine errand? Four? A thing to ask of Sergeant Guillermo. It would not hurt to check this, he thought, studying the headline.

When the Buick drove up to the Rostov villa all the police there were on their feet too, at attention. Sergeant Guillermo stood with them, his guitar out of sight in the guardhouse; he, like the four on the next block, had seen the Buick turning into Londres from Insurgentes. He stepped forward smartly and opened the car door.

General Ortega was frowning as he got out. There was a vacant, anesthetized feeling in his abdomen: he had just sighted the péon on the grass across the way. Under Madero, the general's men had been just such péons, with cartridge belts over the loose cottons, but his uniform had not been a signal for them to run or turn to stone. This uniform had then been a passport to their thoughts. They had opened their minds to him, a man like others under the fitted khakis. Now the barefooted and cotton draped moved away at the sight of him, fearing blows, fearing orders, either or both. Sometimes actually plotting against him; he had in his pocket a letter from the manager of his plantation warning him to expect new hostile moves from the péons in the district. The sight of one of these bottom people always, now, reminded him of the Madero marches, the free and open talk back and forth in those shared days, and brought him this gone dead feeling in the stomach.

They had stormed the cities, even the city of cities, this capital. Now the cities were storming them. As the streets were macadamed and the bright villas sprouted, their scratchy lots and adobe huts had to be overrun and they themselves driven back into the remoter country.

This sleeping one too would be paved and zoned and suburbed out by the growing city he had once held in his hands unused to holdings. He would go quietly, back to the vacant perimeters, to the less coveted backlands, eyes trained on the ground, holding his few chickens by the feet upside down and leading his goat, saying nothing to those in uniform who were the pushing, shoving city.

But sometimes they did not go. Sometimes they decided to stand their ground, even when nobody was pushing them, and push the owners of the ground. Even those who were their friends and had fought in the days of trouble on their side. The plantation manager's letter said: "They want everything and every inch that has your name on it; eventually they will want your name, too."

This was General Ortega's thought as he looked across at the sleeping Diosdado. So he frowned, feeling a prisoner inside his tailored tans.

Guillermo did not know that the turning down of his chief's mouth had been caused by Diosdado and the feelings he stirred. Uneasy about the absence of his four men, afraid the General had seen these men, Guillermo said while still at salute:

"Strangers have been seen a block from here, my general. On the street past Londres. I have sent four men to investigate."

"Good, good," General Ortega said. He was still regarding the péon's unmoving figure. "The neighborhood must be watched. But your men are not to leave their posts at will." Now he turned to look at the turret and his lips curved again; he had not been here since the structure had gone up. "Very professional. They have even left spaces between some bags for gun muzzles." He addressed Guillermo: "Open the door."

"It is not possible, my general. The door is now permanently locked, as I have reported. It can be opened only by a button from the inside. As I have reported."

"Yes." The general had forgotten. How many stacks of paper could one man memorize? "Then tell them to push the button."

Guillermo went at once to the door. General Ortega was close behind him. Guillermo rang the bell, waited, rang again. Several times General Ortega slapped his folded newspaper against his thigh, biting on his lip; the peephole in the door opened and Paul Teleki's face appeared.

"Yes, general?"

"My business is with Señor Rostov."

"I'll tell him you're here."

"Be good enough to open this door. *Now.*"

Sounds from inside: Victor Rostov calling, "Who is it?", Paul Teleki answering, "Ortega. In a big hurry," Victor Rostov saying, "Quickly, quickly." There was a sound of buzzing. The door swung open, General Ortega stepped through.

"Fortifications, electrified doors," he said. "Yes. I see. The villa is becoming a fortress." He considered Paul Teleki. "You seem to believe that my police are your first enemies."

Paul Teleki made an upward and forward movement with his shoulders. "No, sir. Just that we're our first friends."

General Ortega noticed the figure to one side, over by the turret steps. "You are David Justin?"

"Yes," David said.

"And what is your work to be here? To interfere with the police too?"

"He'll behave himself, general," Paul Teleki said. "He's fresh from a university, he's a student of Romance languages and howitzers. In that order."

"Remember: you are a guest of my government," General Ortega said to David. "I expect you to cooperate with the police assigned to this house."

V.R. had come out of the study. He proceeded quickly along the walk until he reached its beginning, stopped and nodded formally. "I was expecting you."

"Because of this?" General Ortega held up his folded paper. "I begin to wonder whether you write statements or beautifully composed fantasies."

"Fantasies, yes; with documented footnotes. Will you come in?"

V.R. stood aside to let General Ortega come by him on the walk. Together they went to the study and entered it. General Ortega took a seat near the French doors, V.R. placed himself at the desk.

"Your circle is expanding," General Ortega said.

"David Justin? On the other side, at least ten agents have entered your city in a month's time. That's where the population trends are interesting."

It was a matter of finding openings. There would be a sparring. "Justin, please. I would like to know about him."

V.R. batted the air with one hand, repelling flies, irrelevancies. "My friends in New York wanted to send a man who knows about guns. I insisted on a translator, no more. The boy won't ravage your country with his Royale portable." He held up the copy of *El Machete* so that his visitor could see the headline. "What about these slanders? *They* don't interest you?"

"We are used to hot words, this is a hot country. Justin, Justin is the serious matter." The general held out his own paper. "With each story you publish in the papers about foreign agents coming here, you hold my police up to more ridicule. Each time you bring in a private guard you are saying that Ortega and his men are imbeciles, incapable of doing their job."

"I have the greatest respect for you and your department, General Ortega. But this is a sunny, thin-atmosphered place, events here take place in the daylight. How well are you equipped to deal with shadows and night crawlers?"

General Ortega turned in his chair to look meaningfully at the sandbagged window. "Not much of our famous daylight gets in *here.*" He shifted again and studied Victor Rostov. A largesse, a melodrama of a man, yes. With a hold on his emotional masses: still the air of the remodeler of continents, the orator general exhorting his country's rag wrapped rubbish into army swarms. Only this one out of hand, unmilitary thing about him, the carelessly spilling gray locks over the massive head. In all this bulking control, one touch of the runaway. Artist's mane on parade body: was there under this one surface discord a corresponding inner discord? "Señor: I would be glad to arrest these 'shadows.' Only give me their names and addresses."

"I've given names in my articles: based on reports from responsible labor leaders in Barcelona and Paris."

"Many names. But the addresses?" General Ortega opened his paper flat and began to read. "Here, a specific case. George Bass. Middle forties. American. Thin, wiry, average height, thick black hair, speaks several languages. Bass, you say, entered Mexico during the past month. No one named George Bass has crossed our borders in the past *year.*"

V.R. turned the fingers of his hand back and forth as though rotating a faucet.

"I can assure you no one named George Bass has crossed any border in the past two decades. But he's a tireless traveler. Common sense must tell you something's up, general. Overnight the press campaign against me becomes an epidemic: *somebody* has to be behind it. An expert."

General Ortega became aware of the teeth forcing down into his lip. He pressed his lips shut.

"Your enemies, you say, will mobilize whole battalions to kill one man. Here in Coyoacán, behind these walls, unable to take one step in the world: what danger are you to them?"

V.R. stood and walked, tight postured, only the hair a slackness, to the doors. He looked out into the patio simmering with sun. "He has killed all the old ones. I'm the only one left; he regrets that. And I speak out against him for his crimes: the sell-out of Spain, the Moscow Trials, the purges, the liquidation of his officers' corps, now, with war so close. At this moment, while he attacks me as a Hitler agent, he has Molotov in Berlin, negotiating behind the scenes for a deal with Hitler; I've been exposing this too. I call for a workers' party of many tendencies, a workers' state of many parties: he wants the whole world genuflecting to him. And consider: I'm a Jew, a cosmopolitan, an intellectual. I speak other languages, I'm at home with other peoples, I write literately. *He* remains the surly Georgian peasant burrowing in his native mud." His fingers found a wandering strand of hair and pressed it down at his temple. "Yes, general. He'll have to kill me. He must kill all the old ones whose universe is not one of mud and vodka bacchanals."

"You start with political abstractions, you end with personal ones."

"Murder is a personal business." V.R. turned and came back to the desk, stood facing the other. "You know that I had a son? Removed from politics, a scientist; he remained in Moscow; killed two years ago, in the purge of '37. Today I take politics more personally than I used to."

"I repeat, señor: give me something tangible to work with."

V.R. sat at his desk and lifted a bulky typescript as though to weigh it. "Six pounds worth of tangibility. My biography of the Georgian mud worm."

"It will be a contribution to literature, I am sure."

V.R.'s smoky blue eyes hardened. He spoke forcefully, with ringing strength in the words; back on crude platforms, thundering at one hundred thousand rag bundles. "*They* take my writings as more than literature. Their agents have more than once broken into my vaults, not as literary critics. But my biggest records are stored in another vault. Here." He tapped his wide forehead. Above, disturbed by the vigorous movements of the head, the mass of hair shifted. "He'd like to empty this vault too. It's a little late, the book is almost done."

"Do I understand you correctly, sir: you believe he will send his armies after a manuscript?"

"When George Bass's gunmen come, they'll be after these pages as well as their author."

General Ortega stood up. With a gesture of it is useless he slipped his newspaper into the pocket of his tunic. "I would be more impressed, señor, if you would establish that the man you call George Bass exists elsewhere than *in* those pages. What, please, is his address?"

V.R. rose too. There was the slow beginning of a smile on his face. "You'll find him in Mexico City, general. If your eyes become adjusted to the dark." The smile took on depth. "I propose a division of labor: I give the names of these shadows, your men track down their addresses; fair enough?"

With outstretched hand V.R. indicated that General Ortega was to precede him through the exit. They walked together into the patio and stood in the sun, the general leaning against the pink balustrade of the ramp.

It had not gone well. Issues evaded, oversteppings sidestepped. General Ortega remembered yet another irritation that called for exploring.

"The young lady who works here, Señorita Sholes. What is her relationship with Jacques Masson?"

"They're friends."

"That has occurred to me: they occupy the same suite in the Molinas Hotel. Is Masson simply the girl's lover, or your political associate?"

V.R. waved his hand impatiently. "Emma visited us several times in Europe. Two years ago, in Paris, she met Masson; he was a Belgian active in our circle there. When we were expelled from Norway they followed us here."

"The girl is with you every day. Masson, according to our records, has been in your home only three times, for minutes at a time."

"He's busy with his affairs, I suppose. He exports cottons and ceramic products to Europe: an entirely legitimate business."

In the walled corner of the patio Teleki and Justin were carrying more bags toward the turret, from a nearby room, the one next to the study, came the sound of fast typing. General Ortega's face grew grimmer. The sandbags were a provocation, the words coming from the typewriter were provocations, to make, no doubt, insulting headlines for tomorrow.

"And a profitable one," General Ortega said. "He spends freely in the restaurants and cafés."

"He's said to be a clever trader." V.R. was now arranging the calipered point of his goatee. "General, why these questions? What has Masson to do with me?"

"That is what I want to determine. The girl would not be living with a man who did not share her politics. If this man is politically with you, why does he not visit you?"

"Ah. You suspect he's doing undercover work for me? Set your mind at rest, general, he's not working for me in any capacity. I know very well the conditions of my asylum here, I would not think of violating them by usurping your functions."

The clack of typewriter stopped. There were back and forth voices from Emma Sholes' room, women's voices. Emma came into the patio followed by Marisha Rostov, a small, frail woman with gold glint, gray shot hair. The two descended into the garden and walked slowly to the orange tree, talking. V.R. and General Ortega went toward the garden too.

"Good afternoon, General Ortega," Marisha said. Her lips trembled, imparting an unsteadiness to her voice: the words had vibrating edges. "Is there something wrong?"

The general's eyes were on V.R. as he spoke the words to her: "A routine matter, señora. I am reinforcing the police guard."

V.R.'s eyebrows went up. Beyond that, no reaction. But Marisha looked concerned. As she spoke she too looked to her husband: "Is there a particular reason for this measure?"

"It is only a precaution," General Ortega said. "Because of the new attacks on Señor Rostov in the Communist press. And—to supplement Señor Teleki's sandbags."

"It is thoughtful of you. . . ." Marisha's voice was shakier. "I regret that we must be so much trouble. . . ."

"Political asylum was once an honored concept," General Ortega said simply. "There are few asylums left, and the prisons multiply. You are welcome here, señora." He held out his hand to each of them, bowing formally. "Señora. Señorita. Señor Rostov. I must go."

Each in turn said a polite goodbye.

As General Ortega walked to the door, where Paul Teleki was waiting to let him out, he felt, absurdly, that his military cap had slipped badly to one side. He raised his hand to the visor, was surprised to find it still in dead center and perfectly level. Then what had tilted? His intentions?

When Paul Teleki opened the door for him he concentrated with unplanned seriousness on the bodyguard's eyes and said, "You were careful with your wiring, young man? You would not want to press your magic button and see the turret turn upside down." Teleki was astonished. "The sandbags will drop and muss your hair."

Going for his car, General Ortega was furious with himself because he could not determine why he had said the nonsensical words.

"What did he want?" Paul Teleki said.

"He's increasing the guard." V.R. was absorbed with the wall buzzer, his fingers running along the wire that led from it to the door frame. "You waste your talents, Paul. If you must play with wires and batteries, make a toaster." He turned to see Paul's dissatisfied face. "We can't accept their hospitality and refuse their protection."

"We *can* get more people inside the house. What did you write New York?"

"Their proposals make no sense. Even as arithmetic."

"Not if they want to send more like him." Paul's thumb jerked to indicate David Justin, who was working in the turret. "But four reliable men with these"—he kicked the machine gun with his toe—"and able to use them. . . ."

V.R. went over to look at the gun. "You've bought another antique? Plant it in the garden with the failing Quetzalcoatls." He stood more erect. He spoke with extraordinary force: "The question's closed, Paul. Do you understand? I don't want them here."

"There was a time when you wanted millions with you."

"Times change. . . . I don't want Emma here. I don't want that boy here. I don't want *you* here." V.R.'s voice dimmed. "I'd like Marisha to leave, if there were a way to make her go. You are all useless here, and each rusted gun you bring in is useless. To have company now—is an obscenity." He became aware that the women under the orange tree were looking in his direction, his features unknotted but his voice continued serious. "I'm not my own man any more. I've become a prize in the contest, a trophy."

"Even to your followers?"

A moment went by. It seemed V.R. would not answer. Then he said through his air of light conversation, "Followers oblige you to wear the same face and postures all the time, Paul, like a statue. Those Quetzalcoatls—grinning down the centuries—their faces must get very tired. . . . Once the situation was more open."

"When did it begin to close, V.R.? When did the contempt for guns start—Kronstadt?"

"You have Kronstadt very much on your mind these days."

"Because you have. You haven't started the chapter yet?"

"Soon, soon. I've left a space in the manuscript for it. At the moment there's George Bass to write about."

He put conciliatory fingers on Paul's arm, then walked away along the enclosing wall. At the corner of the patio, where the inner wing of the house ended, was a wood cage with compartments in it, faced with wire mesh. The rabbits in these cubicles stirred ears and still walked at his approach. From a basket under the hutch he took some lettuce leaves and began to feed the animals through the wire, and as he did so he brushed back the thick hair along his temples and turned to smile at Emma and Marisha.

David Justin came down from the tower. "Any news?"

"Ortega's stationing more men here," Paul said, all his attention on V.R.

"Oh? I guess the Old Man's articles finally got under his skin."

"Or the turret. The sandbags. The peephole." Paul saw V.R.'s easy smile to the women, the turn back to the rabbits, the drop of mobile features away from fun. The general emanating confidence to troops while he retreats behind his temples into hopelessness. Truth the big program, small lies its one by one planks?

"Whatever the reason, we'll have more men."

"To keep an eye on." Paul found himself clamping teeth on words that came up in a boil: "You won't grow up? You refuse? We're nice enough to give you a wall: cringe behind it like the rest of us! Can't you get it through your translator's head that every new person drawn this way is another danger? Every new cop, every new whore with the tits hanging out! Yes, I've seen your mouth watering, Justin. We're under siege and you've got your mind on whoring expeditions. Keep your thoughts and hands to yourself! That's what our wall means. Trust nobody, cops, whores, nobody. . . ."

V.R. went on feeding the rabbits and smiling toward the women under the orange tree.

CHAPTER III

The fir woods of the Desert of the Lions were far behind. The dust powdered green Packard was well past Cuicuilco, where the earth has lost its green skins and is down to rock ribs and chalk gristle; it was now on the veering climb into the mountains, on the road to Dinamos. George Bass was at the wheel, fingers hooked stiff, eyes narrow to follow the road. He drove sitting forward, inches of space between his shoulders and the back rest, as though the motor powered him independently of the car: small man, in his middle forties, with cropped black hair. Large agitations inside him produced small surface ados, shiftings in the lip corners, double time blinking, unfunctional tocks in the fingertips.

"But suppose she calls?" It was the passenger speaking, a younger man, tall and tight in flesh; he sat with a clothes model's posed immobility in his expensive summer linens, only his eyes and the hollows of his long face active. He looked ahead toward the staggered roundings of this long range. His hands were on his knee with the fingertips pressed hard together. "She probably will call. I won't be home."

"That's a crime?"

"I always come back to the apartment around noon for a nap." The younger man's English was precise, with the exactitudes that come from study. "She knows that. Sometimes she calls."

"So she'll call."

"If I don't answer she'll be asking me questions all night."

George Bass did not look away from the road but his eyes quickened with humor. "You don't give her other things to think about nights? You with your talents?" The younger man smoothed the sharp crease in his trousers. "If she wants to know why you didn't take your beauty nap today, improvise something. Something brilliant. Like, today you weren't sleepy."

The younger man looked at his watch. "We've been on the road over an hour."

"Easy, Tomás, easy. It's not far. You just can't go fast in these mountains."

Silence. The car shouldered left, then right, as the road negotiated the hard rises. "George, be reasonable. Suppose Emma gets back to the apartment before me? She'll think all kinds of things."

"You told her you had an appointment. Well, the appointment kept you. These cosmic problems can be handled." He was rotating the wheel with test jerks, overshooting by a fraction each time and then hurriedly compensating. He rolled to a stop and pulled out the hand brake, leaned back for the first time and stretched his shoulders. "This damn wheel's too stiff, I keep telling you. You'd better take over, my shoulders get too tight."

Masson got out and walked around to take the driver's seat. George Bass slid to the right and pointed to the sequenced humpings beyond the deep valley, ranges stacked in card pack order, fuzzing into the distance.

"You never did like to drive," Masson said as he started the motor. He was least of all interested in what he was saying. "People like you usually do."

"People like me? People like me like to control a situation, all its parts. Driving, you control your own car but not the others, not the road." He looked out the window again. "I don't like driving and I don't like mountains. Never did. You know what's wrong with mountains? They scale a man down. You should bring your intense Emma up here. Be as good for her nerves as you're bad for them." He had to be joking but his face was blank.

"Is it good for Cándida's nerves?"

"Her health's improved since you saw her last. A visit from you should be another tonic." The younger man made no response except to increase the car's speed. "I thought you'd like spending an afternoon with momma, on her home grounds for a change. You haven't seen much of her lately."

"Emma might take it into her head to come home in the *afternoon*, she sometimes does that. If she doesn't find me—"

"Tomás, Tomás. If that girl goes anywhere this afternoon you can adjust your story to it. If she steps out of that house in any direction, you'll know."

"How?"

"Because I'll know. I'll get a call on Cándida's phone."

"From?"

"We have friends in the neighborhood. They keep an eye on the house, inside and out."

Masson sat up at this. He looked sharply at the other man. "You even see through walls."

"Some people were made to build walls, some to see through them: division of labor."

For a while they drove without talking. The tree growth was getting thick, the drops beyond the road sheerer; edge of coolness coming into the air, even under this blaze of sun. Finally Masson said, "How does it stand with Cándida?"

"All that's out of my hands. I'll tell you this, they're impressed by the way you've been handling things. Keep it up and I don't think you have to worry about Cándida."

"Can't you tell me *yet* why they ordered her back?"

"Tomás, do your job, get it out of the way, and don't ask questions. This'll be over soon enough. If it comes out all right, if they're satisfied, they'll probably drop the charges altogether and you won't have to bother your head again about the matter."

"I've a right to know what the charges are. After two years—"

"That's not for you to say."

But the young man sat up again and looked at Bass with harder eyes. "You said—did I understand you? You said it'll be over soon enough. Does that mean—"

George Bass nodded. "It looks good. Teleki had us stopped for a while, he's too smart. The new one, Justin, he's wet behind the ears, he can be used." Bass gave Masson an appraising look. "Tell me, how is it with you and the girl?"

"I've followed instructions."

"I want details now." The playfully lazed tone was gone. "You made it strong? She's really worried?"

"You said to act upset, make scenes. It wasn't hard."

"Did the subject of your going there come up?"

"She's half mentioned it twice this past week. I led up to it, as you told me to do, but she was the one who said the words. George. What do I do if she *does* invite me out?"

George Bass answered with a measured blandness, watching the other. "Accept. You're to start paying your respects, you see? Now you become a fixture in that house."

Masson had one hand free of the wheel, resting on his knee. The long fingers of this hand rose without destination. "You never said I'd have to go there. It won't work."

"It's up to you to make it work. You're very masterful with the girls, young fellow. Coax her to say the right lines, you'll get your engraved invitation."

"Of course I can get into the house, it's all been set up; but once I'm there the whole thing will explode in our faces. I'll slip up somewhere, one word, one gesture. . . ."

"A fine actor like you? For close to two years you've convinced that girl you adore her, all of her, from head to foot. In the most convincing way; by the Stanislavski method. A girl you wouldn't spit at, ordinarily. I've got faith in you. You'll act it through, Tomás."

When Masson spoke it seemed to be to himself: "You do some acting too. You always said I'd never have to go near the place. You meant the opposite. . . . Two years. A very great number of nights. You want more still."

"The girl and the nights were the background work, Tomás. To set things up. You'd let all that hard work go to waste?"

They were almost at the ten thousand-foot level, it was chilly, but the younger man's forehead was sequinned with sweat. He brought out a handkerchief and patted his face. "I won't do it. I can't go there. It's been bad enough—"

"You'll do it." The drop in George Bass's voice to the tone of mild reportage brought the younger man's head around. "Say no and they'll call her back in twenty-four hours. And she'll go."

Masson put his handkerchief back in his pocket. "Oh, yes," he said. "The famous charges. So I must give you my life and more." He kicked the accelerator, the car jumped forward. "That's why we're taking this trip? You've got to blackmail me into the next shit?"

"What do you know about these things?" George Bass said evenly. "You never had a purpose in your life, just bigmouth wants." He reached out to tap Masson twice on the knee. "Relax, will you, for God's sake? Don't see everything as a plot. I thought you'd like to see momma, I really did."

". . . . would you shoot?"

The woman was sitting under the sundeck that butted from the house's front, knitting. This was a country house built on the lines of a lodge, a weekend retreat, its stucco walls sectioned with rough split logs. Well up on the side of the slope, overseen by molar crags, it had perhaps a half acre of cleared land around it, enclosed by a high wall of columnar torch cacti. Those patches of the grounds which had not gone to weed were spilling with bright flowers, the remnants of a garden. Everywhere outside the wall, at spots inching over this wall, the forest with its undergrowth of green sponge mass.

The woman was well over sixty. Her black and still alive hair was pulled into a bun, she was dressed in black, there was a black rebozo loose around her shoulders. She seemed scraped of flesh: the long axe edge nose was all bone, the eyes were tube ends in a setting of bone, the lips were thin dark strips unsupported by inner pulp. She was unusually tall, she seemed by ordering her high chin higher to have willed herself inches past her normal height, pulling all curves into up and down lines.

The man, in his early thirties, stocky, band muscled, wore a Basque pullover and a beret. He was sitting on the edge of a buffet table dangling his leg.

The woman kept her eyes on her quick fingers, she might have been addressing her fingers. "Well: would you?"

"Hypotheses. Who shoots at hypotheses?"

"If it were more? Picture it: I take it in my mind to escape. I run into the forest, I am running to the police to tell them everything. In a moment I will be gone for good. Will you shoot?"

"You won't run and I won't shoot."

Now she looked at him. Her enormous eyes were amused, though the rest of her Goya hewn face was at rest. "This shows what you are. You are a coward, Ramón. If I were the one to guard and you the guarded, and if you tried to run, I would shoot. Whether you run as reality or as hypothesis."

"I would not run in any form because my orders would say not to run. You respect your orders too." He pointed at the strip of wool she was knitting. "What will it be, another rebozo? You talk of shooting people and you knit your soft squares."

"I will have seven rebozos instead of six. This is what is left for some makers of history to make." Her voice was touched with nasal music, not masculine but pitched below the expected woman's range and with more substance than her elongated body promised. "Two years ago I was taking Barcelonas from people."

"You do this well. This talent I did not expect in you."

"I learned to do this from my mother, I have done no knitting in forty years. If you asked, I could not say how to do it, but my fingers get it done without consulting me. As your fingers should shoot when situations ask for it, without consulting you."

"They did not learn to shoot from a momma and they do not always ask for consultations." He reached for a stubby cigar in his rear trouser pocket; he had trouble pulling it free because of the revolver there. He wetted the whiff's end with his lips, bit the tip off, lit it with a wax match. "Listen, Cándida. When they told me to leave Barcelona, I was glad, things were bad there. When they said, here's your ticket to Mexico, go there and help George—better still. But when George said, watch the woman, that's your first job, you can believe me, I wasn't happy." He drew on the cigar too energetically, its coal sparked. "I tried to get out of it."

"I am nothing, after Barcelona. The Moors are not all over me. Here you sit and smoke cigars."

"I, all of us from Barcelona, have much respect for you."

"For my talent to invite charges?"

"For what I saw you do myself, and other things. There are stories. They say the worst jobs went to you, and you did them well."

She let the knitting drop to her lap. "The worst ones? The worst is that of Tomás."

Ramón waved his cigar impatiently. "To live in nice hotels and stick pins in a girl? Besides, it's time he went to work. At home his talent was for the red wine and the whores, that was his work."

"He fought at Madrid."

"You forced him to go."

"He went."

"For three weeks. A vacation of three weeks from the whorehouses. He gets the scratch on the arm and announces himself a totally disabled. He went to the Madrid front not to save Madrid, only a small portion of his pretty face."

She ran her bone of finger over the lumped lines in the rebozo. She nodded. "He lived with me but he kept his filths from me. Sometimes I heard the stories."

He rolled the cigar between his fingers, studying it. "He kicks and fools a girl, what he always did for nothing, and does this now on salary. No, my respect is for you, not Tomás."

She replied to this with a violence that caught him off balance: "And where is the respect for yourself! A man who apologizes for the dirty jobs he has to do? Who asks from the prisoner soft words to take away his guilts? Did you ask Paul Teleki for benediction when you made fires in his skin? I could run and you would not find the conviction to pull the trigger: you have an impotence and you call it respect! Be my enemy; it is more honest; you will have better thoughts of yourself!" The fire went out of her. She bent her head and began to knit again. "It was bad in Barcelona when you left?"

"Bombs from the air every afternoon: you can tell the time by them. The moneyed ones wait with open arms for the Moors. Many Falangists walk the streets at night, shooting down those known to be against the Falange. Every night, dozens of new bodies. We had to get out, those of us who had the way."

"Many did not have the way."

"They become the corpses at night."

Her lips became thinner still. "Hypothesis: which is worse? To receive the crucial bullet in an alley of Barcelona or in a corridor of the Lubianka cellars?" His head went up. "Choose: to die fighting in the streets of your own city, or digging for coal and gold with other slaves of a freezing Siberian labor camp?"

"Cándida. Leave it. Many who were taken there had a hard time, yes, but we can't know the story. Speak in this way, there will be more charges."

"And I will go as the others went? You had respect for these others, too. They were your adored leaders, you remember? If they had dropped with a Falangist bullet in Spain you would talk of them now with reverence; they drop with bullets of another color, delivered equally in the back, in your never wrong Russia and you forget your respect, you try to forget their names. Spare me your respect until the giver is a man, with balls."

"They know what they are doing over there. Stop to believe this and you believe nothing." He tapped his cigar until the long white ash came loose. "You and Tomás had the best of it. George let you leave Barcelona before it was bad. Where did you go? No bullets and camps in Paris."

"We lost a generation of friends in the land of our friends. We heard the roll call of the dead every day in Paris and it spoiled Paris for us."

"Because you said certain things of this. They heard of your words and they brought charges."

"Fool!" Her eyes were fierce. "If I had licked all boots and spoken only Presidium slogans they would have made the charges still! Not for me but for Tomás. They know where he is soft." She examined the rebozo with contempt, threw it on the table. "This was why they sent us to Paris. Not for holidays, because there was in Paris an Emma Sholes who needed a lover and Tomás was the best candidate. The charges were to make Tomás a willing lover."

"Abuser. When isn't he willing, when there's a girl to abuse?"

"No paychecks can pay for this he has to do. And this—he has yet to do." She saw him raise his wristwatch. "It is past noon."

He took a pair of binoculars from the table. "George says he made this thing, did you hear him? Why would he play with magnifying glasses? A man who prides himself on seeing so much." He put the instrument to his eyes and looked down to the road that bisected the valley. "There: the Packard, I think."

"Mother, you're all right?"

"Intact."

The Packard was parked in the drive close by the house. They were standing near it, he holding both her hands.

At the house, under the sundeck, George Bass was opening a large carton which Ramón had just brought from inside.

"Have they said more about your situation?"

"You thought they would?" Her voice was cold.

"George told me something today." He dropped his voice and began to speak rapidly, his eyes on Bass. "Now I must go to Coyoacán. Every day. If I refuse, you're to be sent—"

Her head jerked: "You? He said why?"

"No."

"I will make him say."

They approached the house. Bass had removed several policemen's uniforms from the carton and was holding one up for inspection. Ramón said to him, "Derdergo was careful about the sizes." He slipped into the jacket Bass held out and placed a colonel's peaked cap on his head. He walked over to the window to see his reflection. "What are your orders, my chief?" he said with a snapped salute.

"My orders are, next time get at least a general's outfit. You want to be a lousy colonel all your life?"

Ramón laughed but Bass's face remained impassive. Ramón took off the jacket and placed it back in the crate, then piled the other uniforms in. "There are a dozen, of all shapes and sizes. As you said."

"It was hard?"

"No problem, Antonio, Derdergo, the comrade who went to the store, is himself a lieutenant in the San Angel station. He told the clerk they were for the men of his station."

Cándida and Masson came up. "You give Tomás new orders?" Cándida said in English.

"They're the old orders expanded," George Bass said.

"He must become now a house guest there? This is not the old orders."

"He was supposed to be everything to the girl, wasn't he? Now he becomes everything: companion in work as well as bed. She's nervous about him, you know. This should calm her down." Bass turned coolly to Masson. "But this is the thing: you've got to nail down the invitation and in the next couple of days."

"It is more than to calm the girl," Cándida said.

"If you're so anxious to get the girl calm, why did I have to stir her up in the first place?"

"So now you can calm her," George Bass said. "Could you calm somebody who's already calm?"

"He was to have no part in the attack," Cándida said.

"It's for your own protection," Ramón said to Masson.

"Can't you see that?" George Bass said. He walked to a metal chair and sat down. "A man who's *in* a house being shot up obviously can't have anything to do with the shooting."

"Who *cares* if they suspect me?" Masson was insistent. "Once the thing's done I can get out of the country in a few hours. Wasn't that the plan?"

"If you want the attack to work," Ramón said, "better be there."

Cándida looked keenly at Ramón, then at George Bass. "Yes. This is what it was leading to, all of it."

"It's this fellow Justin, you see?" Bass said reassuringly. "We've been waiting for a patsy like him to come into the picture. We want you to look him over."

"I thought you had people out there who see through walls."

"It can't hurt to have another pair of eyes *inside*." Bass looked speculatively at Masson, his head tipped. "Also, you've got to be at the door with Justin when our tea party begins."

"You can't expect *me* to open the door?"

"You a doorman? We wouldn't give you such a humiliating assignment. No, Justin will open for us. He doesn't know which side is up. But just in case he balks, in case he needs a little moral support. . . ."

Masson's fingers dug for the sunglasses in his breast pocket; he slid them over his eyes; he said with deliberation, "No. Absolutely no, George. Enough is enough. I can't have anything to do with those people."

George Bass stood up. "Your happy hotel life's over, my friend. Cándida, you have five minutes to knock some sense into him."

Cándida stared at Bass. She nodded, but not in agreement. "Good. Let us go inside and discuss what is sense."

Masson followed his mother's tall figure through the door. The front room was large, furnished with wooden tables of gay colors and leather seats.

She said immediately: "And you are surprised? Think: did he need you only to stand by and report on Emma, when so many others were reporting? Think, for once: why did he wish you to drive that girl half crazy? Only to keep her from getting suspicious? Only that? . . . While you were saying your first sugary words to the girl, there in that Paris café, George was already looking ahead two years to this moment. You know how we work, you know reserve forces are sometimes used."

"What does he really have in mind for me? You know how he thinks. Does he expect *me*—"

"I am in his custody now, not his confidence." Her face lost its frozen quality, her voice became less stern. "He may have no plans. Perhaps he only wants you to report what goes on in the house."

"He knows everything about that house. Mother, what about *you*? What's *your* situation now?"

"The same," she said indifferently. "They still say they want me back in Moscow, they still keep me here in the Dinamos mountains. The discrepancy between what they say and what they do is apparently lost on you."

"*What* do they want you for? You still don't know?"

"Ramón has a loose mouth. He talks. Or perhaps it is that George has told him to talk. . . . It seems that in Paris I said angry things about their terror, I was denounced." Her blue lips came close to a smile. "It seems my remarks showed Rostovite deviations. . . . It suits them to threaten me; to get to you."

He walked to the end of the room, came back. "If I obey you won't be sent there? They'll drop the charges?"

"Bass assures me of it. I care nothing, one way or the other; how many times must I tell you that?"

"You must care! I care!"

"You 'care' about everything. You were a child who should never have been trusted with a mother: have your eyes once left me since you opened them? If you had not camped in my shadow, Bass would never have seen a weakness in you he could exploit."

"You *agree* with what Bass is doing!"

She came suddenly to life. She took hold of his arm with both hands: "With his objectives, yes! Not with his choice of personnel! Chico, chico! If you had been *hard*, he would have had to find his weakling somewhere else!"

Masson pulled away. "It's definite? If I obey you won't have to go?"

"This is not your concern! You must not—"

"I must. I must. Because of you I must do everything they tell me. Just as you do everything they tell you. We're both trapped."

"No. There is a difference." He had turned from her; at the cramped passion in her voice he swung around. "*I* do not obey them out of fear. You think it would not take courage, to go there?"

"It will take courage," he said softly, "to go to Coyoacán, my mother."

The power seemed to leave her body, her head went low. "Chico, you must not worry. Bass may only be trying to make sure the attack goes well."

He did not even hear. "We *are* trapped. Both of us. You by your politics, but at least you picked them. I by my important hard-core mother; I had no choice in mothers. How can we live freely and breathe freely? We have mothers. I *must* do this, little mother of mine. Because of you."

"Because of yourself! Because of what you are. And what you are *not.*"

"What about the things *you* are not, mother? Have you ever thought of *them?* So many things. A pot washer; a diaper changer; an unspectacular housewife never brought up on charges by *anybody.*"

He stood looking at her in a fury. The phone rang; George Bass came in quickly, followed by Ramón.

"Answer it," Bass said to Ramón.

Ramón took the receiver. "Yes?" He listened for some seconds, said "Moment," and handed the phone to Bass. "For you. The girls."

"Yes?" Bass said in Spanish into the phone. "At what time?" He waited again. "All right. Return there, both of you. Make sure you are seen, this is the important. Even if Ortega comes again; especially if he does. If anything else comes up, call the other number in three hours." He hung up and addressed himself to Masson: "Emma left fifteen minutes ago. She took the bus into town."

"She may look for me at the apartment," Masson said dully.

"Then you will explain why your business kept you out of the apartment."

"I *have* to get back there. Please, George. I'm the one who has to deal with her. If I'm away too long I'll never hear the end of it."

"Your job is to shake *her;* why are *you* so shaky?" George Bass looked expectantly at the younger man. "We have some business to settle here first. Well? You've thought it over?"

"I'll do what you ask. Just let me get back."

Bass clapped his hands twice, sharply. "Good! Good! The boy obeys his momma, it shows good upbringing."

"Do we need these obscene jokes?" Cándida said. "He is obeying the terror *against* his mother. Because he has not the strength to disobey."

"That's pretty admirable too," Bass said. "Not all sons would be so solicitous about their mommas."

"No. Not all." Her blue lips hardly moved with the words.

"Interesting paradox," Bass said to Ramón. "A lad does his duty because of tender feelings about his momma; momma resents it. She'd like him to have more 'official' motives, imagine."

"Our movement produces some upside down people," Ramón said without humor, keeping his eyes away from Cándida.

"That's good, of course," Bass said. "We need such people to turn the *world* upside down." He took a step toward Masson. "Cheer up, boy! The attack will work. All you'll do out there is have a few meals; get us the dope on young Justin; and back him up on the big night. Ramón, where's that package?" Ramón picked up a parcel from the corner desk and brought it over. Bass pulled the strings off, from the unfolded paper he lifted a raincoat. "Swanky, isn't it? How about that stitchwork? It's the latest thing from Rome, I picked it out myself, I know how fussy you are about clothes." He handed the garment to Masson. "Take it along each time you go there. I want them to get used to it."

"What for?" Masson said.

"Who knows? It might rain." Bass drew a thin manuscript from his side pocket and held it out. "Here's another prop. An article about the GPU plot against Rostov. An exposé." Masson looked bewildered. "Don't worry, we've put no trade secrets in it, it's just a rehash of the stuff Rostov's been publishing in the papers. I must say, he's made some pretty good guesses."

"What do I do with this?"

"Today or tomorrow, mention it to Emma. Casually, no fuss. Just to get it established—say you're working hard on it and you're stuck. Plant the idea in her head that it ought to be shown to the big man but let her think the idea came from *her*."

"It'll make you an important fellow out there," Ramón said.

"And? If she wants to show it to Rostov?"

"For now, stall," Bass said. "Tell her you want to work it over some more. Another thing: how many keys are there to the luggage compartment of your car?"

"Just one. It's out in the car."

"Emma doesn't have one? You're sure?" Masson shook his head. "All right, then. I'll take that key from you. When we go out."

Masson lowered his head, rubbed his temples with the fingers of both hands. "When will the attack be?"

"Isn't it clear? The first night you can arrange to be there late, maybe sleeping over, and Justin's on the night watch." George Bass slapped the young man on the shoulder. "Relax, Tomás! You'll come out of it without a scratch! Ramón's boys'll be firing a good three feet over your charmed head!"

Masson hunched away from the hand. "Can we go now?" he said, ignoring all his environment but the figured blue tiles on the floor.

CHAPTER IV

". . . . cops, whores, nobody."

Paul Teleki at last ran out of words. David Justin had been listening with mouth open.

At this moment Guillermo on the other side of the wall began to strum his guitar again and sing subduedly of his heart and its shatterings.

"This is a total partnership to keep the world out," Paul said absently, as though he had lost the thread. "Not a line of work for a sociable fellow who welcomes company and likes to be liked."

"You know who has those whores on his mind? You more than anybody."

David Justin turned his back and walked across the patio, to the place where V.R. was feeding the caged rabbits. V.R. looked up; instantly, too automatically, his face brightened.

"So, David? You're getting adjusted to our exotic landscape?"

"It's more—intense than I'd expected."

David looked toward the garden as he spoke. He was actually observing the two women, for whom V.R.'s smile was clearly meant, but the movement of his head drew V.R.'s attention to the maguey plants and the pocked statues scattered among them. V.R. walked the few feet to the beginning of the garden, a lettuce leaf still in his hand, and patted the head of a crumble faced Inca deity in maximum grimace.

"Quetzalcoatl was noted for his intense expressions," V.R. said. "He took his work seriously. You have to when you're convinced you were born the father of all your people including your ancestors. . . . We rent this villa from an archeologist, you know, a specialist in pre-Columbian civilizations. He's left no room for Old Bolsheviks among his shards."

"It's a long way from the Kremlin."

"We Marxists are in the prediction business. We predict the tumbling centuries, predict them well. But we're obliged, like others, to live in moments; nobody predicts *them,* that's the trouble. One moment you thunder manifestoes from the Kremlin, the next, you're feeding insipid rabbits under a histrionic sun. With mummy grins among the magueys. Speak out against a Georgian primitive: Quetzalcoatls and sandbags. We're in the prediction business and we're perpetually surprised."

"I want to tell you." David Justin hesitated. "I heard what you said to Paul. I—think I understand what you mean about wanting to be alone."

"Of course you'd understand. You're an American." Marisha was looking toward them, V.R. waved the lettuce leaf at her. "Americans huddle together and shout slogans about the sacred sense of privacy. Don't take offense, young man. You come of an extraordinary people. We'll all have to learn from them how to cultivate individuality while running in the pack. As they learn; *if* they learn."

"I'm sorry I had to be forced on you. I'll try to stay out of the way."

"You should go home, David. I'll try to arrange it. In the meantime, feel welcome here; it's not a personal matter." The blue eyes under the tumbled hair became inquisitive. "You volunteered for this? Why? You were bored with your language studies?"

"Languages seem beside the point," David said uncomfortably, "when nobody's talking to anybody else in the world."

"So you applied for a job as bodyguard. You decided you had the equipment."

V.R.'s tone was not unkind but the young man flushed. "My concerns were more on my mind than my qualifications. I don't know if I can explain. The Moors were storming Madrid; the unemployed were storming New York relief offices; in our Columbia seminar rooms what were we storming? The images of Baudelaire. The rhetoric of Rimbaud. I began to feel plugged out."

"From French poetry to Marx? You've come into politics through the back door."

"I suppose I was looking for a guiding hand. At least, that's what I thought I was doing."

"And you found—others looking for the guiding hand."

"Maybe I *ran* into politics. Maybe it was a desertion, I couldn't say. But I still feel plugged out."

"Some book-bloated men," V.R. said, "even intelligent ones, desert the lecture hall just to be out in the streets for a while. Those who stay too long in small rooms, and who have restless natures to begin with, develop a strong romanticism about the streets; but claustrophobia is a bad reason for turning to public life. The streets are not so gay a place. They are for people who have no other place to go."

"I'm with you in this fight," David said very seriously. "I haven't any reservations, though I wonder. . . . While I'm here, I'll do my job." He ran his tongue over his lips; this next thing was harder to say. "V.R., about the Kronstadt chapter. I've had the people in Paris look up the old White Guardist papers, all of them: the quotes just aren't there. Not the ones you want, anyway."

"We'll manage, David. In any case, I can't get to the chapter right away." V.R. noticed Paul staring down from the turret. "Paul's giving you a bad time?"

"He thinks I'm too trusting."

V.R. laughed. "That means: for once he wants to try the experiment of trusting the world himself and doesn't dare. Too large a dose of underground life can make a man burn to negate himself."

"How can you keep a concept of the underground in a place like this? There's too much sun."

"True. Undergrounds don't last in the tropics, the sun creeps in everywhere. Result? In these steamy latitudes revolutions tend to become outings." V.R.'s smile broadened and not all of it was for the women. "Don't be confused by Paul's exterior. That crust," and he pointed to the turret surrounding Paul Teleki, "hides a most thermodynamic heart, as those sandbags try to shut out the sun."

"Is he tired of me? Is it as banal as that? He—insists he still loves me. But he says it with—such a rage. It's. . . ." Emma Sholes was close to tears. She tensed for better control. "We sleep in the same bed but we're strangers. Sometimes he's gone all evening. . . ."

"He has his business," Marisha Rostov said in her unmoored voice.

"He always used to tell me when it was business. . . . He's so *mechanical* with me now. He—makes love to me—like a machine. . . . I'm—an assignment, you'd think, a chore. . . ."

Marisha looked up at the oranges in the tree. "We know so little about him."

"This morning, before I left, he told me not to take the car, he had to drive somewhere. I asked in a perfectly friendly way what his appointment was about. He was so furious—I thought he was going to hit me." Marisha's face was pained, her hands rose as though to push away these confidences. But Emma was not to be stopped. "He shouted at me, terrible things. He knows the fate of the world doesn't depend on his buying and selling bolts of cloth and dishware, he said. But if he has a woman around who's always implying that his work is silly and trivial, it makes him feel—emasculated." Marisha turned her head away. She adjusted the loosely knitted wool shawl that was always over her thin shoulders; from the corner of the patio V.R. waved a lettuce leaf and smiled at her, she smiled back. "Last night, when I went to bed—I asked him to join me. I had to *ask;* several times. He came, finally. He—began to make love to me. Then, without a word—he stopped. . . . Went into the next room and closed the door. . . ."

"These things are not to repeat, Emma."

"Emasculated! Why did he use a word like that? Why? . . . I've never belittled him or made fun of his work. . . ."

"Perhaps," Marisha said in her delicate voice, dropped almost to whisper, "perhaps he feels that, compared to your work with Victor, his work *is* trivial. We have often seen this in well-to-do sympathizers, Emma. They humble themselves before Victor in a terrible way, to do penance for what they consider their insignificance. . . . Jacques may be attributing to you something he feels himself."

Emma's face livened. "That's just it, Marisha! I think that's the whole point! I have a life of my own out here, there's no place in it for him. He said as much this morning. . . ."

V.R. had left the rabbit cage and was moving toward the elevated walk. He clapped his hands. "To work!" he said. "I'm ready to dictate, Emma."

"Can you come here, Victor?" Marisha said. Her husband made a turn and came along the path into the garden. "Victor, we were talking—about Jacques. Emma thinks he feels himself excluded from her life. He has so little time with her."

"Easily remedied," V.R. said. "Let Emma come here less often."

"I'm coming every day," Emma said stubbornly, "at least until the book's finished." She kept eager eyes on V.R.; there was an idea working in her. "Isn't there another way? I wonder—couldn't he spend some time with me *here?*"

"You've asked him before," Marisha said doubtfully.

"He felt he had no right to take up V.R.'s time—as a tourist. V.R.

—couldn't we give him something to do? He's awfully good with languages. Couldn't he help David?"

V.R. stroked his beard several times. He was aware of Marisha's eyes on him, their sober regard, as he said slowly: "He won't come as a tourist? Good. Tell him to come as a colleague. There's work enough for all."

Marisha was searching in the pocket of her dress. She brought out a very small shell container. "Victor, your pills. Will you excuse us, Emma?"

She stood and waited for V.R. He made a gesture of humorous resignation. "You see? When there's a major crisis, men cut cunningly into the mind's anatomy, women reach for their pillboxes."

He followed Marisha to the walk and on into the study. Emma stirred on the garden seat, looked up at the ripe oranges, started to count them with raised finger, glanced over at the turret. Paul was in the turret, David down below. She rose and walked to their corner. "David, V.R.'s talking about asking Jacques out here to help. . . ."

Paul called down, "How is he at carrying sandbags?"

Emma ignored him. "If he comes, please, David, find something for him to do. It's important to me. Couldn't he help with the translating?"

"The chapters *are* piling up," David said. "If the Old Man says it's all right—sure."

Out in the street Guillermo's guitar grew bolder. The accompanying voice went into indifferent glides, telling a story of this or that heart broken past mending.

Paul Teleki came down two of the turret steps. "There's too much traffic in and out of here as it is."

"It's V.R.'s decision, isn't it?" David Justin said.

"Sure: to make things cozier for *her*. To smooth things out for the lovebirds." Paul came down two more steps. "You know the trouble with you political window shoppers, Emma? You work at changing the world only in the slack seasons. You'd like to make your upheavals from nine to five, and keep the evenings free for the nightclubs. When in your lives do you sink over your heads, all the way, in an outside commitment? With no nights or seasons off?"

"You don't *need* a personal life," Emma flared. "You take politics so personally, it's your career and your wife and family."

Paul nodded vigorously, over agreeing. "That's why I've become

so good at it. And *that's* why the Old Man is alive today. No, I don't
have a personal life. You know the last time I had a woman? Five
weeks ago. Know who it was? The barefooted girl who brings the
fresh fish, the one with the bad skin. I had a ten minute fling with
her in back of the fish stall in the market place. She thinks I'm a big
man around here, the chief porter and gardener." He came down
some more steps. "The last time I was in a nightclub was in Budapest. In 1933. They had a gypsy violinist with all his front teeth
missing."

Emma's anger was spent. "I shouldn't have said what I did."

Guillermo's guitar picked up life; several of the police began to
sing along in dips and flattings. Paul jumped from the stairs in a
burst of energy. "Listen, Emma, is Jacques as good a dancer as they
say? That's something I've got a lot of respect for. I'd like to be able
to do a nice double-jointed rumba. It must be a good feeling, to
make your hips go like jelly and the hell with the eyes on you."

He grabbed Emma by the waist and began a hopping dance, forcing her to go along with his deliberately clumsy movements. His
elbows flapped, his knees were bent.

"Come on, Paul," Emma said. She struggled to free herself but
he held on. "Stop it, now."

"Show me those steps, will you, Emma? Show me how Jacques
makes his elegant Belgian hips go. I want to learn, really." He was
making grotesque offtime jumps and skips, dragging her along. "I'll
study hard. When I'm very good I'll take you dancing in all the velvet clubs. We'll make a fine team, Emma. The rumba will be my
career and my family. You'll be my big velvet rumba. Teach me,
Emma. Is this the way?"

Emma made a furious wrenching movement and managed to
break away. She stood perfectly still. When she was this angry, small
bulges appeared at the corners of her mouth and there was a multi-
plication of creases under her eyes, in her forehead.

"All the same," she said, "Jacques will come, if the Old Man
wants, and you'll keep your sneers to yourself. There are human
beings left in the world, no matter what you've become."

V.R. filled a glass with water from the desk carafe and swallowed
the pills Marisha had given him. He went to the window and pressed

two of the sandbags apart until there was a small aperture. A thin cylinder of sunlight bolted into the room.

V.R. bent to see through the hole. On the far side of Cortés a figure in white cottons was walking slowly, a board across his shoulders from which hung two wooden buckets.

"We discuss problems of personnel and take our stomach pills," he said, "and our neighbor, the péon, goes to the well for more water. We need sandbags to fill up our windows, he needs water for his goat and his maize. You see? Everybody's busy in the world."

"Is it wise?" Marisha said. "A man we hardly know?"

"We *do* know something about him. When he came here, Paul wrote to Paris for a full report."

"You never told me that."

"It was nothing to bother you with. He made quite a good impression in our study circle there."

"Is it surprising? Emma would not take up with a man who was opposed to us. Still, is it wise to have him here now?"

V.R. turned to face her. "Where's the danger? A man who wanted to make trouble for us wouldn't be *avoiding* us. That's what he's been doing for months."

"I am not thinking of danger; only peace of mind. Feeling closed in as you do, why invite still another person into the house? One you are uncomfortable with?"

"Oh, I suppose I seemed reserved with him. It wasn't anything; in this confined life I've withdrawn from everyone, even Paul."

'But not from me." She smoothed the hair on his temple.

"Not from you, Marisha. And still I would like to send you away. . . . What's your reservation about Jacques? There is something else, isn't there?"

"He does not seem sympathetic to me," Marisha said slowly. "He —fidgets. There is something funny about his laugh."

"Come, a laugh is *supposed* to be funny. Let Emma pick her own mate, it's democratic procedure. Besides, it will make things better for her."

"To the extent that she will permit them to be better. When have we seen her without trouble?"

"She may not have much capacity for happiness. It's her prerogative." V.R. picked up the manuscript from the desk and ran his thumb over the page edges, watching them flip. "It's almost done, you know. Kronstadt, and finis." He put the manuscript away. "It won't be a great hardship to let her come with Jacques until the book is out of the way. It's a matter of two or three weeks at the most, if the Kronstadt chapter goes well. I think she'll be ready to go then; she'll have seen that having the fellow with her around the clock doesn't work miracles. What do you say? Shall we try it?"

Marisha stood in silence, running her fingers over the pile of manuscript. "If the Kronstadt chapter goes well," she said. V.R. looked at her sharply. She snapped shut the pillbox in her hand, slipped it into her pocket. She nodded, her face serious.

V.R. patted her shoulder and went to the French doors. In the far corner of the patio he saw Emma standing stiffly, hands on hips, looking at Paul. "Emma," he called. "In the study, please."

Emma turned, hurried up the walk and into the room where the Rostovs were waiting.

"Invite your young man," V.R. said. "We'll find ways to keep him busy."

Emma's eyes filled with tears. "Thank you. Thank you both." She made a quick move toward the telephone on the desk. "I'd like to call him, he should be home. May I?" V.R. nodded. She lifted the receiver and dialed. "Molinas? Señor Masson, four six two. Please." She stood, waiting.

"We'll break this 'wall' between you," V.R. said with a smile. He had gone to the window and was looking through the space between the bags again: across the way he saw Diosdado returning, bent under the weight of the filled water buckets, stepping carefully on the hot dirt path as though his feet were sore. "Let me tell you an old military law: there's no wall that can't be breached, with the right explosives."

Marisha looked quickly at her husband, his smile remained constant.

Emma went on holding the phone, the smile disintegrating on her face.

CHAPTER V

Past nine; the garage on Avenida Juárez, three blocks west of the Alameda, was deserted. He parked the Packard in the driveway and climbed out, nodding to the attendant. A few steps away he stopped short and turned to signal the man. "Listen, take a look at the steering wheel, it feels a little tight to me."

When he got to the street he considered the folded raincoat on his arm and said to it suddenly, "Speaks through my mouth? Makes his headquarters in my mouth?"

To see directives in chitchat.

Everything to Bass's tastes. Each thing for Bass.

To *him* the tension in the wheel was just right.

He went east on Juárez, the raincoat over his arm. It was his intention to turn into Revillagigedo, toward the hotel, but he passed that street and continued on toward the Alameda. At the corner of Luis Moya he cut over to the park to enter the cross path running back from the command posed statue of Benito Juárez. Couples on the benches, arms locked, talking low with heads together. Home: Emma; heads to come together and legs to lock, tonight he had to service her to make up for last night; put off going home.

Outside the Palacio de Bellas Artes the signs announced Chávez conducting at a concert of regional folk dances. Tonight. He was tempted to go in, the image of Emma, too thin thighs parted, eyes begging, body of small endowments offered as tin cup, was sharp in his thoughts. But he turned and made his way back through the park, he saw also the accusations colonizing in her eyes. The raincoat was stiff on his arm, its new poplin rustled. He felt the crackling papers of Bass's manuscript in his jacket pocket.

That house being expertly strangled with Italian coats and concocted manuscripts and luggage compartment keys.

That girl being chased and whipped by her hungry legs.

And he? Pushed by a black rock of a mother?

Suppose the machine guns worked. The headlines of the next day, taking the skin of happenings for their deepest meat, would shout,

ROSTOV CUT DOWN BY HIS ENEMIES. Wrong. Rostov was to be cut down by black mothers and asking legs and by those they held tight. To see laws and issues where there were only organisms wanting to eat their way along but held by the feet?

Who made history? People who arranged black legs and asking mothers in neat patterns.

Through their lieutenants: who instruct garage mechanics to loosen a steering wheel when the wheel does not feel tight to them.

He passed a couple embracing on a bench and he saw, spread on a bed, the essence of reception, the ultimate in entrapment, ache too far down for law or issue to reach, the open for pillaging body of the waiting Emma. Home: Emma, waiting.

The gathering up of mothers and legs in neat patterns was not a matter of law or issue to George Bass. It was a need and a satisfaction. When the patterns worked and closed steel teeth on the proper eating along organism, George Bass looked like he had dined well.

What was the trap that held George Bass, who grouped legs and mothers in workable formations? A need to arrange the traps for others and call the results on the public surface—the working out of law, the upflowering of issue. "History"; the public face given to private dining.

What kind of history had been written last night? Not the kind to get into history books. The girl, trapped by her legs, had called from her bed, come, please, come, now, to the son in the next room, his eyes on the mother in the mountains with guard over her. The son had come, taken his place in the trap of legs, because he had orders and his mother was under guard in her trap of ideology and the girl was to be catered to as well as made nervous. But the son could not go through the motions of the sly pleasuring because his eyes were fixed too singlemindedly on the guarded mother whom he was to see the next day after so many weeks of not seeing, and the image of the trap of the mother made it too much to stay and pretend a fuck within the trap of the needy legs. So the son had with quick toss disengaged himself from the legs and gone back into the next room where he could sit and look undistractedly at the trapped mother whom he was to see the next day and whom he dreaded to see though it was a need, as it is always a need for organisms in their moments away from the traps to eat their way along, eat unselectively at the world as it comes. So the girl had stayed in her abandoned bed with her emptied legs, full of her untended needs that went deeper than all laws and issues and sobbing half the night in a total let unknown to the laws of the larger issues. Where in history books was there room for this night history? For it was history, a private determination of public spectacles. This unplanned and unprogrammed disengagement, this ritual of revulsion enacted twenty-four hours ago on the histrionic dark bed, had very probably written the exit lines for Victor Rostov. Because the son had too abruptly snapped the girl's legs shut, the girl would almost certainly open Rostov's door for him and insist he come in. With raincoat and baggage of Bass.

ROSTOV CUT DOWN BY HIS ENEMIES?

No. Rostov cut down by girl laying welcome mats before the fortress to guarantee her own cried for pelvic visitations.

With this sentence forming in his mind he came back to the statue of Juárez.

Question, what the headlines and histories would say about Jacques Masson. Be a minor footnote to the issue and laws at best. Different ways it could be worded. Also present in the villa that night was Jacques Masson, close friend of the household. Tomás Baeza de Rivera, alias Jacques Masson, conspirator, underling, who helped set up the plot. The mysterious figure, Masson by alias, origins unknown, connections unknown. . . . Which?

Jacques Masson, intimate of the Rostov circle, Tomás Baeza de Rivera, agent cunningly planted in the besieged house—what did it matter how they identified him?—made his escape during the mass assault.

Or: was cut down like the others by the machine guns.

It could take that form.

Whatever the wording, the words would be George Bass's. Who, unknown to headline writers and historians, inched obscurely back and forth under the ideologies and played with legs and mothers nobody saw.

Wording was up to Bass.

Up to Bass whether Ramón's boys fired a good three feet over the son's charmed head or aimed for the head.

This decision and the reasons for it, like the reasons for the raincoat and the false script, whatever they were, would appear nowhere under the headlines, nowhere in the margins of any history book. They all preferred to see laws and issues.

Everything to Bass's tastes. Each thing for Bass.

But there were those over Bass. Traps supervising traps.

He was back at the corner of Revillagigedo. This time he turned and walked south. On the second block he came to the Molinas, a small residential hotel with a simple canvas marquee. Entering, he told himself that the thing was not to go at her any more, he could only stop it if he did not start it; cautioning himself this way, he let the elevator boy take him to the fourth floor. At the door of 462 he stopped, key in hand, and listened. The radio was on, three voices singing in close harmony about a heart that had lost its reason, corazón deprived of razón; a spectacular guitar thrum in the background. No more going at her, then. Hold it from the beginning, when it can be held. He turned the key in the lock and opened the door.

Emma was standing near the window, one of his raw silk shirts in her hand. She was setting the living room in order; wearing toreador pants; wrong for her narrow ass and skimped legs, the thin paisley silk bunched in back for lack of filling.

"You're late."

"My appointment kept me."

He walked across the room and dropped his coat on the sofa.

"I tried to call you this afternoon." She was asking for openings.

"I couldn't get back for my nap today. When did you get in?"

"Before five. Victor had a letter he wanted mailed so I left early. I was hoping you'd be back."

"Now you see: I'm back."

The afternoon paper was on the desk. He picked it up and seated himself in the easy chair. Without checking he knew she was looking hesitantly at him; the grim mood of the night and the morning now in pieces.

"Jacques," she said, "I'm glad you're here. I want to tell you something." He looked up with no expression. "We've had a bad time of it lately, all right. I'm not blaming you, I can understand how you'd feel shut out. But chico!" Why had he ever told her he liked to be called that? Too much wine one slowed night. "Chico, listen!

That's all over with!" Her hands were locked in front of her, the shirt still hanging from them. Locked, of course, so that they would not go out on begging expeditions to him before they knew they were welcome; her angers could not last because her wants were too strong. "I talked to Victor and Marisha: they want you to come out and work with us! Every day, if you can make it!"

You could get her to speak all filths and call them her own, if you catered the full amount to her yawning legs.

She stood with her hands in prayer.

"I'm honored." He did not move.

"They've got something exciting for you to do. David wants you to work on the translation!"

He remained cool: "Wonderful. I've been wanting to get a look at the manuscript." He turned a page of the paper and dropped his eyes to it.

Emma, he knew, was standing with the crushed look, the help me look. He gave her no help. After a moment she began to move around the room.

"This place is a mess," she said after a lapse. "I've tried to tell you before, you can't leave things around for the maids to pick up. They're overworked as it is, they never know where things go." He turned another page of the paper as she went to the closet to hang up his clothes. "I'd like to meet your mother. I could tell her a couple of things about her spoiled son."

He dropped the paper. He sat up. "Did you say something about my mother?"

The harsh tone confused her. To crush this one it took feathers. "I only said I'd like to meet her sometime. . . . She did a good job of spoiling you. . . . I could tell her about *that*. . . ." In retreat, but trying to land small counter blows as she ran.

"She'd be less than fascinated. She never had much taste for female chatter." He went back to his paper.

"Was that such a terrible thing to say?" Now the wronged note. "I didn't *insult* her. . . . Jacques. *Why* are you so *damned* touchy?"

He turned another page and bent his head. She shrugged and went back to her work. Crossing to the sofa, she saw the raincoat. "You've bought a coat! Handsome, Italian, isn't it?" The singers on the radio were now harmonizing, in minor lilts, about the ranchería in the mountains where life is uninterruptedly good. "What's this? I've never seen one of these before."

His head went up. She was looking at something on the coat lining, just under the armhole. He jumped up and pulled the coat from her hands, examined the spot she had been pointing to. "I don't know what it is. Some sort of loop." It was a narrow strip of material, sewn there by an amateur hand. He went to the closet to put away the coat. "It's just a coat, that's all. There's nothing remarkable about it."

"I didn't *say* it was remarkable," she said helplessly. "Just that there was that funny loop."

"You seem to hold the theory that everything was put in the world as a subject for small talk." This was no longer functional, of course: the needed invitation had come; still he attacked, there was no way to stop. "Weren't you and silence ever introduced?"

She forced herself to draw a semblance of a line: "Don't speak to me like that, Jacques. I'm not going to ask you again, don't take that tone with me." He gave her a look of put on exasperation, feeling his face was far away and on drill. He felt nothing, nothing but the sure knowledge that he could break any rebellion in her by parting her legs, her thin legs. Resigned to the inevitability of the bed ritual for this night, sure of its healing magic, he was careless about bruising her in the preliminaries; perhaps he drew out the preliminaries in order to bruise her the more. "It's strange you should buy a raincoat now. The weather's been so beautiful."

"Go ahead," he said, spacing and weighting the words. "Read significance into everything. Chatter away."

Emma let herself down into the corner of the sofa. "It makes no sense. None. Something's awfully wrong, Jacques. You're not the man I fell in love with. You're a complete stranger I wake up to find trespassing in my bed. Somebody who doesn't even *like* me."

Close to saying, your legs never speak the word trespasser, he replied mechanically, "My feelings haven't changed but your demands certainly have. You need tender loving care twenty-four hours a day, feeding on demand. *You're* the spoiled child, Emma."

"What do I ask of you? To be loved: is that a crime? You act as though I'm trying to take your valuables at the point of a gun."

"Can't you grow up? Grown people understand there are serious matters to be faced, too." He knew the paradox in what he was about to say before he said it. So many times he had said the pushing reverse to women, women he was after and who held back: admit you have a body that wants to break the penal codes and I'll make it sing. "You can't make love around the clock."

Her face reddened as from a slap. "I wasn't talking about love making and you know it. Not that there's been much of that, lately, but that's not what I meant. *What* serious matters do you have on your mind? You used to tell me when something was worrying you, now *I'm* the one shut out; by *you*."

A retreat that cost major effort: "I'm worried about the Rostovs, for one thing. If the Old Man's information is right, the big attack could come at any time."

"It may not be a big attack."

"I don't know *what* it may or may not be! I'm only guessing."

"I'm worried too. I don't take it out by being nasty with you."

Hesitating, he felt the manuscript in his pocket: easy way out of this, it could be built to. "There's something else. They'll only tolerate me out there."

"That's absurd, Jacques! They *like* you."

"No, no. Paul hates the sight of me, he's always making snide remarks about tourists. The Rostovs don't really approve of me either; she looks at me queerly, he's so—formal."

"They both respect you, they really do. Paul's a problem, I know. I'll talk to him."

"No, don't interfere. I'll be a tourist, they know it and I know it."

She raised both hands to him hopelessly. "Jacques: what do you want me to *do*? Tell me, *what more* can I do?"

The building was done: "I'll confess something. I've been feeling so ineffectual, I've been trying to write an article. For the labor press in Brussels."

"A political article?" She was startled.

"About the Old Man's situation. I studied journalism in Brussels, didn't I ever tell you? Before I came to the movement. I used to write for the labor papers." Of course: she was astonished back to hope. The moment she cooked an anger it looked for excuses to run. He pulled the script from his pocket. "This is what's on my mind, if you must know. I want it to be good, to make people take notice, but it just isn't coming."

She came over to him and took the typed pages. She read a bit on the first page, glanced quickly at the remainder. "But it's fine, Jacques! It looks just fine! You've managed to get all the facts about the GPU's methods in, it's really impressive!"

"No, it's not right, just a lot of words. Maybe I've lost my touch, I don't know." He felt the lack of expression on his face but it was too much work to put something there. "I wish there were somebody I could get a professional opinion from."

"Why not V.R.?"

How well she learned her lines and never knew their source. "I can't take up his time with my scribblings." He could master his scripts too.

"He'd be pleased! And if there *is* some small thing wrong with it, I'm sure there's not, but if there is, he'll locate it in two minutes!"

He forced his face to show doubt: all right, George? "I'll work on it some more. I want to get it in the best shape I can, then maybe I can bother him with it."

She studied the script a moment more, intensely pleased. A big bone this time. Finally she put the typed pages on the desk and went on with her work. "I'm ashamed of myself. There I was thinking black thoughts about you." She was at the closet, hanging up one of his sweaters; her eye was caught by something on the shelf. She reached for it. "Remember this?"

"What?" He was seated and busy with his paper again.

"The axe." She came around in front of him and held it out. "You said I couldn't be a real mountain climber without a climber's axe."

This took trying: "*You* said all you wanted was to climb the god-damned Alps, not chop them into ice cubes."

"It was a wonderful, wonderful week. I woke up for the first time in my life." She sank to her knees and pressed her cheek against him: she had found the way to insinuate her legs. "Every girl ought to have an alarm clock like you. With that nonpareil Swiss movement."

He let his fingers move over her hair. "Spanish movement's more like it. . . . I mean, I'm starting to feel like a Spaniard, a Latin, down here. . . ."

"Olé. . . . Oh, you must have had a lot of women. . . ."

"You can't eat at the same restaurant all the time." Her weight going away. "Till you find the one Cordon Bleu place, that is." Her weight coming back.

She raised her head tentatively as she snuggled closer. "Chico. You don't have to go out again?"

"No." Lazily.

"You've eaten?"

"Not yet."

"If you want something sent up. . . ."

"There's time." But he made no move. She sat on her heels, waiting; he let her wait. On the radio two male voices were singing about the mysterious lady of Monterrey who would not take her black veil off.

She decided to fill the gap with nostalgia: "That day at the Café de Flore. The first day. When you asked me to go to Switzerland, just like that, twenty minutes after we were introduced, how I blushed. I've never been so red in my life."

"Your face looked like it was bleeding all over."

"I'm used to revolutionary directness, comrade dear. But I'd never been propositioned so—two fistedly."

"You loved it." How long could it be drawn out? She fell helplessly into the word play because she knew its terminal point.

"No. Not then." She was thoughtful. "It sounded as though you didn't really want me to come but were taunting me, to see me squirm. But you intrigued me too. A man who went skiing one minute and quoted *Das Kapital* the next! I was offended. And pleased."

"Frightened, too."

"I'd had such rotten luck with men. Chico, I didn't know what a body was for. I'd tried, too often, but I'd never been had, not once. Maybe it was my fault. But nobody could *touch* me, for all the trying." She rubbed her cheek along his sleeve. "You can do anything you want with me; everything. I don't care." Still waiting for some initiative from him while her words took their own. He stayed slumped in the chair. "Jacques. What—happened last night?"

"Last night? When?"

"When you—left me."

"After I came to bed I realized I was in a bad mood. It wasn't anything to do with you."

Painful for her: "It wasn't—I didn't do anything wrong? You weren't displeased with me?"

"I wasn't displeased." There was still time to stop it but he let it come: "Though you were so insistent. You kept asking, *begging*. You oughtn't to do that, you know. I don't like women to beg." There he managed to hold it.

But she was too far into her own thoughts to be struck by his. "I can't stand the feeling of being inadequate, Jacques. Not after what I've had with you, after it's been so good. When you withdraw from me. . . So abruptly. . . ."

"Drop the subject, Emma. I've told you what it was. I didn't like your begging tone, but that wasn't it."

"But—if you had things on your mind. . . . They shouldn't be there any more. . . ."

"What is it now?"

"You know what I'm trying to say."

"Why don't I want to touch you *now?*" Weight away. "Is that it?"

"Don't be angry, chico." Weight back. "I'm not accusing you or anything, but after so long. . . . If I'm not attractive to you. . . ." Her lips kept moving after she was out of words.

He waited a long time. It was still possible to keep it within bounds, with a big effort. As though from a distance he heard his iced voice saying: "You do like rough treatment. All right. You know what you are? An addict. You've made an addiction of me. You were in a freeze. Nothing could reach you. The men you went to bed with, they couldn't do anything for you; ice to ice? *I* broke the trance you were in. *I* serviced you well. You found out what an orgasm is, you went wild. Since then you can't get enough of me. Your legs won't close for a minute."

She had jerked away. Her hands were at her reddening cheeks. "Don't."

"You think a man likes to have women coming at him like that? With tin cups in their eyes?" He knew what he would pay for this but that was not the point. What mattered now was to bring the dirty bones out, all he was forced to throw her way, and name them one by one. "Is that your idea of what a man wants, this incessant begging and begging: gimme, gimme, gimme? But we have to be nice to them, the poor beggars in their nylons and heats, don't we? It's the Christian spirit." He had been over nice to the other one; everything for her; she sat rigid in black clothes and black face, eyes saying their loud no, refusing the gifts.

"Jacques," Emma whispered. "Don't say those things."

He was playing with the ice axe, tapping its sharp end against the floor tiles. "All right. The lady has her craving again. The ladies always have their cravings. Wake them up. Wake them up." The other, the one in black, was not to be awakened. Given everything, she asked for nothing, had no thanks for the lavish offerings. "You've only to ask, to beg. We can't let you go begging in the streets."

She was whimpering now. "You mustn't. . . . I only want you to love me. . . ."

He leaned forward and took her by the shoulders. "Of *course* I love you. Don't you *know* I love you? I *love* you, Emma. You *are* attractive to me. I *need* you, I *want* you, I *love* you. Since you beg so nicely."

He bent her backwards until her thin shoulders were on the floor. He leaned over, his body pinning hers against the tiles as she fought. "No. . . ."

"Yes, Emma." He got her hands over her head and pressed both wrists to the floor with the axe. With his free hand he worked at her blouse. She fought. "Since you have an addiction."

Her body stopped its lashings. Her eyes were closed. She began to moan. "Love me, chico. Please. Please."

"I'll show you how I love you, Emma. How I've always loved you. I'll love you. Open your legs, I'll tend to your nerves and your needs."

"Everything. . . . I wanted. . . ."

"I know. You wanted. You needed. You *begged*." He ripped the blouse back from her shoulders, down to expose the pathetic buds of breasts. The buttons from the blouse flew off and clicked against the tiles as they rolled. He pushed the axe away, it made a scraping noise across the tiles. I was happy in Oaxaca, I knew a good girl in Oaxaca, the milky voice on the radio sang.

Sobbing: "Everything. . . . Please. . . ." Her fingers in convulsion made hooks on his back as Tomás Baeza de Rivera bent over. "You're hurting me. . . ."

❧DIOSDADO

Three days since the visit of the postman. Diosdado's life had become complicated. First, the matter of the envelope brought by the postman. In it no picture of a refrigerator, no picture of anything, only a paper with words on it.

Serafina stood now in the door of the hut, holding the envelope in one hand and the paper in the other, while he squatted on the ground and sharpened his machete with a piece of lava stone. He was always putting the envelope away in its resting place, she was always taking it out to look at it.

The kids crawled in circles around the goat, pulling first at its beard, then at its tail.

"A letter, and for you," Serafina said. "This I believe."

"The look of a letter, yes. The words of a letter. It is for me or it is not for me."

"The postman says it is for you if he brings it to you."

"This is the word of the postman."

"He says what is not true?"

"He wears the uniform, woman. He says what the government wishes him to say. His uniform is of the government."

"For the government he brings you a letter which is not for you?"

"The thought of the government is not to understand, woman. The government thinks in a way to fool you and in this way to benefit from you. Probably they bring me a letter of another so at a later time they can say this Diosdado has things which are not his things."

"This you cannot know. For this, you must know what is in the letter and from where it comes."

"I know the place from where it comes." He stood, clamping the machete under his arm, and pointed to the printing and embossed seal on the letterhead. "These are the marks of the government. Those who write this are ones in uniform, with thoughts against us."

"You do not know the words and you know this? Diosdado, do

this for me, go to the square, to the man in the white coat, the man of the medicines."

"I am not sick. This letter is not a sickness."

"It is not for the medicines. He is a man who reads. He is known to read letters for many who cannot read."

"When I have a letter I wish him to read I will go to this man. I do not go now because I do not wish him to read this letter."

"If he does not read it we continue not to know what is in it."

"Woman, I know what is in it, it is from the government and the government writes only when it wishes a thing, the house of a man, his land, his money, his goat. I do not wish the government to have my things and so I do not wish the man in the white coat to read the letter."

"If the letter is not for you but another?"

"The man in the white coat will believe I have stolen it from the true owner and he will tell the policía in the city hall I am a thief. Leave the letter in its place, woman. Let it rest and let me rest."

"The letter does not please you. Why do you not burn it or feed it to the goat and so to finish it?"

"Woman, this on the top means it is of the government. If it is for me or for another it is the property of the government and it is against the laws to destroy such property. For this they can do much against you."

He took the letter from Serafina, ran his calloused finger over its embossments, folded it carefully and slipped it back into its envelope. Going into the hut, he placed the envelope in its proper place, out of sight behind the picture of the all white refrigerator which was pegged to the adobe wall. On one side of this picture an old model Enfield rifle was hung, on the other, a well polished guitar.

Serafina came in and went to the stone bowl, to begin grinding the maize. The tortillas toasting on the adobe top of the oven were done on one side, she turned them.

Diosdado went outside and squatted again. He resumed the honing of his machete.

This machete was his most important single possession. His arm. With it he cut huarache soles from truck tires when there were tires. With it, too, he hoed the ground between his rows of maize and beans, sliced thongs from automobile seats and transmission belts, sharpened a pole for the goat or flattened tin cans to be placed on the roof of his hut and held with heavy stones.

He had had the machete for twice ten and eight years, since the times with Madero. With Madero, he had used the machete for other things. In the sweaty spring of 1910, on a mountain pass over Durango, he had cut off the head of a man with face and look close to his own but wearing the uniform of the Díaz government troops. This man, a sentinel, had looked surprised, with a very large surprise, as Diosdado came fast from behind the tree with machete already in motion toward the neck; many times afterwards Diosdado wondered how long the look had remained on the man's face on the trip to the ground.

This sentinel had had strapped to his back two objects, one, a rifle, two, a guitar. These were now on the wall of the hut, near to the picture of the refrigerator.

The kids were still running around the goat, pulling at him. It was to be noticed that two of the older ones ran with a certain limp, delicately, toe favoring, their feet were sore from the pavings on the nearby streets where they went to look for pieces of wood and thrown out furniture.

Without huaraches they would very soon be unable to walk along the paved streets to look for things to pick up.

This would not be good. It was on the paved streets of the richer houses that the best things were to be found, in quantity.

Diosdado continued to sharpen his machete. His eyes went back to the green Packard touring car parked on Londres directly in front of his lot.

The Packard was the second complication in his life. It raised questions. For three days, for hours each day, it had been parked in this place. As he sharpened his machete he studied it for long minutes each day.

This was his calculation. If the Mack truck tire was not to be found, and this was the case, each morning he looked in the dump, another tire of another type had to be found. But in the dump were no tires of any type. This green car had five new looking tires, four on the wheels, another attached to the back.

In the absence of a used Mack tire, a new Packard tire was to be considered. The new Packard tire was of a fair thickness.

The man who owned these tires, more than he needed, would have to lose one, yes, but not to the world, not in general. It would have to be lost in particular, to Diosdado.

Diosdado studied the Packard, then the policía across the street. There was also the matter of the policía.

"Woman," he said loudly, "you make the beans today?"

"Today the tortillas," Serafina said. "Tomorrow the beans."

"Today the both. Wrap many tortillas around many beans, all the beans you have."

"To use tomorrow's beans with today's tortillas?"

"It will be a good thing. You will have the money to buy more beans."

In a few minutes she came out with an earthenware bowl. It was full of beans wrapped in tortillas. The kids, seeing this, forgot the goat they were tormenting and ran to her. Diosdado waved them off: "Not for you, not this time. These are for the policía on the street."

"Before I feed the policía with the food of my little ones," Serafina said, "I feed the goat."

"Go, woman. Offer to sell them the tortillas with beans. They have nothing to do and they are always hungry, they will buy. With their money you can buy food for four days instead of two."

"If there is money," she said, "it must be for the huaraches. The little ones can go no more in these streets."

"Go. There will be huaraches also."

"Is this possible? From one bowl of tortillas, enough money for so many huaraches?"

"From these tortillas," he said, working carefully at the tip of the machete, "will come the huaraches, but not from the money from the tortillas. There will be the huaraches and there will be equally the money. Only to be certain that when you speak with these policía you are with the back to the wall and they look at you with the back to me. Do this now, woman."

She turned and walked across Londres carrying her bowl. Very soon she was with back to the wall of the pink blue house and the policía were in a half circle around her, joking with her and buying tortillas.

Diosdado went to the rear of the yard and picked out a blueish automobile headlight from a pile of junk there. He smashed it with several blows of the machete, selected some of the slivers and put them in his breast pocket.

He stood and walked several slow steps toward the street. He squatted at a place close by the hen yard and worked at his machete.

Later he was closer to the street, squatting, honing.

Soon he was at the street, almost on the street, still squatting, still honing. Close, inches from his face, was the Packard. The right front tire, almost new, of the green Packard.

Diosdado rubbed the machete slowly back and forth over the soft lava stone, the steel tip going closer with each sweep to the tire.

With one eye Diosdado watched the policía grouped around his wife, so many uniforms, eating and talking.

The tip of the machete went into the side of the tire, drew back, went in again, over and over, while Diosdado watched the eating and talking uniforms.

CHAPTER VI

"It came in the morning mail," Paul Teleki said. "The whole issue's devoted to Kronstadt."

"The new Gold Rush," V.R. said. "A Klondike of I-told-you-so's in Kronstadt now."

"The lead editorial's addressed to you."

"I'm not flattered. We know these people: they propose to move mountains with pen knives."

V.R. stood in his dark bedroom in the Londres wing of the house. He had eased apart two of the sandbags filling the window recess; with avid eye he looked out into the stunned street. (The island city of Kronstadt had been this hushed, this storyless, after the bombardments and final assault; with cakings of blood laced ice instead of the mere bland bleach of sun.) Paul Teleki stood in the doorway, holding in his hand the socialist magazine from Paris, *Monde Ouvrier:* low-assay humanism being mined out of Kronstadt now: those who can't do, dig: with toy picks. (In *his* hand that mud skied March twilight as he led the first troops across the iced over Finland Bay toward the Kronstadt garrison, his command car left behind on the mainland, on the Oranienbaum waterfront, had been the badly typed last petition of the garrison sailors: surrender terms refused, demands reiterated, negotiations requested; behind him no negotiators with briefcases: white sheeted troops with rifles and mortars.)

"The editorial's called, *BACK TO THE CALENDAR, COMRADE ROSTOV! A SLIGHT CONFUSION OF DATES*. Shall I read you the key paragraphs?"

"They're professional mourners, Paul. All spectacles offend these career spectators. . . . But read. Since you're in a reading mood."

Paul opened the magazine and began with insistent voice (his compulsions were multiplying):

> *"With the slashing prose we expect from him Victor Rostov is proving, in the articles and releases that pour from his refuge in Coyoacán, that Stalinism is less a philosophy of government*

67

than an orgy in which the revolution, voraciously, with loud smacking of the lips, eats its own. Rostov's pen puts most épées to shame; the diagnosis is masterful. One of the truly brilliant minds of the Old Bolshevik leadership cadre, he falters only when he tries to define where and when the revolution's self-consumption began. . . ."

V.R. was squinting to see the street. The péon neighbor's wife, she of the bare feet and neutral face, wearing her mantilla of absenteeism, had crossed over to the police shack, carrying in hold accustomed hands a bowl of rolled tortillas. (As humanists carry their chalices of caught tears.) Now out of sight; several policemen standing near the corner, immediately to the right of this window, evidently talking to the woman as they handed her coins and took the food; others could be heard. (Nobody talked at Kronstadt after the massacre: nobody ate: eyes avoided eyes.)

". . . . Rostov would seem to be suggesting that Bolshevism's hunger for the flesh of its own corpus appeared only in 1936–37, with the trials and mass purges, or in 1934, with the Kremlin-instigated Kirov assassination and the repressions in its wake, or in 1931–34, with the liquidation of five million anti-collectivist peasants, or at the very earliest in 1927–29, with Stalin's consolidation of power and his expulsion of the Left and Right Oppositions from the party and the government bureaucracy. We reply: study your calendar, comrade! You have overlooked 1921. . . ."

Paul stopped. Waiting for a show of anger over the taunting date? With his annotator eyes? V.R. continued to look out.

Masson's nodular voice from the patio: "I hear we're to start at ten-thirty. Are the motorcycles here?"

Sergeant Guillermo's more musical voice, trained to put aside urgency: "The motorcycles. The car as well."

Ahead, running toward the Coyoacán square and the city hall (where Cortés the conquistador had made headquarters after *his* massacre: had they talked and eaten after *that* one?), a portion of Calle Cortés; down it, just past the péon's maize plants, several motorcycles and a blue police sedan. Closer, around the corner on

Avenida Londres, Jacques Masson's green Packard. (At Oranienbaum the general's command car had been a Dusenburg. Khaki
drab. As the general was climbing from it to lead the march across
the ice to Kronstadt a shell from the fortress burst directly ahead,
lifting one sheeted Red Army soldier over the hood with gymnast's
grace; his red running gray brain matter splatted over the wind-
shield, the larger bits unaccountably pulsing.) The péon, senselessly,
was in a squat just behind the front wheel of the Packard, half his
face hidden; a minute ago he had been close by his chicken coop,
working over his machete. (Péon: pawn: he lived barefooted on a
chess board—what hand moved him here and there? What perverse
hand had reached in to move the péons at Kronstadt?) The tip of
his heavy blade (to dig out what Kronstadts? all the damp-eyed digging in those mildews now) came into sight, disappeared again; still
stroking it with his stone.

Paul resumed:

> *"Does your memory need refreshing? Very well: 1921 was the*
> *year detachments of the Red Army marched from Petrograd*
> *along the Bay of Finland, to Kronstadt, and there annihilated the*
> *allegedly mutinous sailors of the garrison. Kronstadt is especially*
> *interesting because the 15,000 men devoured there were not*
> *White Guardists or Allied interventionists (these had been pul-*
> *verized in the civil war just concluded) but heroic revolutionaries*
> *who had fought with and under the Bolsheviks against the coun-*
> *ter-revolutionary armies; they were the proletarian vanguard.*
> *Why is Comrade Rostov's memory so conveniently blank about*
> *all the years before 1927? Because he desperately needs to iden-*
> *tify the revolution's cannibalism with the regime of Stalin, who*
> *in 1921 was nowhere to be found in the Bolshevik leading coun-*
> *cils? Has Victor Ros—"*

"Nothing new here. Old bones rattling." V.R. said this without
turning.

"There's more. You have to hear this."

"No: you have to read it. . . . These gentlemen don't like omelets: world, reconstitute the eggs!"

"They're asking whether you didn't use some bad eggs."

David Justin's less than programmatic voice, hesitant with scholarship: "How do we work it? The motorcycles go first?"

Emma, factual and disapproving of the facts: "They'll lead the way, Paul says. Three of them. We go with Jacques, Guillermo and his men follow in the police car."

V.R.'s neck felt the strain of holding still. He rubbed it, smoothed back his runaway hair as he looked across to the partly hidden péon. V.R. had these last days taken to staring for long minutes into the street, making sure that he himself was unobserved; the most trivial sights, the péon picking through his junk piles, the police turning their guitars, a burro being flicked along with its load of faggots, the postman sleepwalking by, were Lucullan feasts to his eyes, he craved the evidences of protoplasm about its minor businesses. He was not pleased with this voyeurism. A veteran of twenty prisons, he knew that the inmate has, for dignity's and sanity's sake, to make his peace with the patios, the prison's, the mind's; but expecting the oncoming Basses (the sailors had expected negotiators behind the general: *there* was expectation) his eyes ached for the vision of a péon or a burro emptied of purpose, free to come and go, with no horizons farther than the shuffling feet. (The sailors had longed for generals carrying olive branches? The dialectic has its limits: no such interpenetration of opposites!)

Paul's voice ground on:

> *"Has Victor Rostov developed this total amnesia about Kronstadt because the decision to liquidate the sailors was put through by Lenin and—Rostov; and because the punitive army was led by none other than—Rostov? Back to the calendar, comrade! The revolution developed its indiscriminate hunger pains very early; Bolshevism became a cannibal practically at birth. It is Victor Rostov who could give us the most authentic eyewitness account of its first orgiastic feedings. . . ."*

Paul paused again. Expectant silence.

Masson's voice from the patio, apologetic but barbed: "Here's the stuff V.R. dictated this morning. I just finished the translation."

Emma's voice, cooled by choice and too businesslike: "I'll give it to him."

(Lovers with such a wall between them?)

"Will Paul want me to drive?"

"Ask him."

(Were they in love with each other or with the wall?)

Harshly: "I thought I'd ask you."

(For the sandbags between armed lovers, what peepholes!)

"Paul doesn't tell anybody the full arrangements in advance; it's a precaution. Can we put this basket in the luggage compartment?"

"There's no room, it's filled with my samples. Better put it in Guillermo's car."

To the right, the police were finishing the tortillas and wiping their lips with their sleeves. The péon woman came back into sight, moving away from the wall until her face was almost directly in front of the window and turned in profile. A face that belonged in the patio with the pieces of statuary: a façade of stone in which nothing moved; sandbagged with immunity; two apertures for eyes but did she look through them? The eyes were there, black and too full but opaqued with indifference, turning back the world's overtures; having seen too much over the centuries (whole villages felled by Cortés' crossbows: fortresses demolished by friends?) to register anything. (Nothing expected, nothing seen. Sailors expected briefcases; saw mortars.)

She walked to the left. Across the way, her husband had moved back from the Packard, he was on his heels now alongside his chicken yard; still going at the machete. The woman's bowl was empty. Held by the last chatted words of the police, accepting them as she accepted days and fleas, absorbing them with skin alone, responding to lip movements more than understood sounds (if the buzzings about Kronstadt—where is there a humanist with lung power?—could be taken this absentee way!), she finally nodded twice, made her frieze of a face nod, and started back to her hut. The husband was now some distance from the chickens, still at work on the machete.

Marisha, with words that fluttered at their edges (was nothing still inside her now?): "The sandwiches are ready. Will you see to the basket?"

Emma, thawed: "I'll take care of it. Are the forks and paper cups packed?"

"One thing more," Paul said. "There's a footnote. It's the main thing." Something (the momentum of malice?) carrying his recital along:

> "Another fascinating date has slipped Rostov's mind: 1904. Long before the seizure of power there were those who grasped that in the Bolshevik cry for one-partyism there was the promise, no, the guarantee, of a Stalin. Listen to these words of warning, thundered by a clear-eyed critic in 1904—1904!—against Bolshevik-Leninist monolithism: 'The party must substitute itself for the working class; then the party caucus for the party; then the Central Committee for the caucus; and finally a dictator substitutes himself for the Central Committee.' An incredible forerunner, word for word, of the charges Rostov is making today against Stalin, yes? (As well as a beautifully succinct description of what happened at Kronstadt.) And formulated long before anybody heard of Stalin, long before 1921, long before the seizure of power, even—against the first signs of Lenin's steel-trap mentality! Who was the remarkable prophet who, in 1904, when Lenin was only a feeble voice in a far-away London rooming house, already saw the lineaments of carnivorous Stalinism in Bolshevik centralism? Yes, yes—Victor Rostov!!!"

Now V.R. turned.

"Two decades late and from the sidelines! Can they make history? No: they heckle history!"

Paul's eyes were wide with heckling as he approached V.R. to hand over the magazine. He said (compelling because compulsive): "It's the fifth such attack this month."

"You take the career pallbearers too seriously, dear Paul. We've heard this before: the wordy humanism of the unemployed."

(But in Coyoacán, pinned behind his sandbags, the generalísimo too is unemployed: Paul's eyes were saying it.)

"They've got to be answered, V.R. You've got to get that chapter done."

"I dictated the first section this morning. Jacques's done the translation, I mean to read it to you at the picnic. You'll contain yourself till then?"

Paul left the room. V.R. went back to the window. The péon's wife was with him now, the man was on his feet, running his finger testingly across the edge of his blade. The woman handed him something: the proceeds from the sale of her tortillas: he went through the motions of counting, put the coins in his breast pocket, walked over to the coop and lifted an outraged chicken by its feet. The woman began to talk seriously to him, shaking her head. Abandoning the goat they had been tormenting, the barefooted children rushed over to dance comically around their parents, pointing to the chicken and hooting. The péon placed the chicken against the door frame of his hut, with a quick movement of the machete sliced the head off. The children danced, hoorayed, began to play catch with the severed head. Handing the decapitated bird to his wife, the péon bent again to wipe his blade clean with a handful of earth. Face blank, eyes undeviatingly down, in the péon's attitude of foot scholarship.

From the right, coming with linked arms across Londres toward the police, two smiling girls, one in yellow dress, one in green striped blouse.

Parade of small epics out there: unheroic simmer Paul, bodyguard, and he, body guarded, were now farthest spectators to; yet ideologically it was their one concern. What they built programs for, drafted theses for, this world of the lively picayune, these day maneuvers and flea circuses—past their touch: the sandbags only memorialized the gulf.

(No gulfs allowed the sailors. Tried to push the nagging world back from their fortress walls; it had swarmed over the walls firing broadsides.)

V.R. stepped back from the window with a quick shake of the head. To permit himself such a string of insipidities: sink now into the humanist mildews?

His neck hurt from the strain of holding position. He rubbed it again, brushed back his hair at the temples.

Sound of hands clapped sharply.

"Victor," Marisha called unsteadily from the patio. "Victor, are you ready to go?"

"Listen to this." George Bass was at the Hotel Reforma, calling from a phone booth outside the men's lavatory. As he talked he kept his eyes on the man across the foyer, a Mexican Air Force major who stood before a mirror working over his oiled hair with cat petting strokes. "Just made my morning call to the girls. The people are going on a picnic. T. heard about it yesterday but they didn't tell him the details and he couldn't ask. The girls just now found out where to—the woods near San Juan Teotihuacán, where the pyramids are, some place where there's a small petrified forest. Half of the cops are going, T. too, he's taking the main party in his car. Here's an idea worth trying. It might, just might, accomplish something. Here's what you do. Around Teotihuacán the government has been taking over some big estates and cutting them up for the péons. Get out there as fast as you can, they're leaving any minute. Circulate around among the péons, the ones with fincas, let them know this foreigner is in their area with armed bandits, some even in uniform. Tell them this foreigner with the beard—"

Avenida Londres was postcard still. Not even breeze to worry the few weed outcroppings. Standing in the road, wayward upright, Paul Teleki made his last check of the convoy: three motorcycle police, the Packard, the police sedan, three more motorcycles, yes. Sedan filled with policemen, Guillermo at the wheel. Jacques and David up front in the Packard; behind them, flanked by the women, V.R., plaid linen cap clamped on hair, blue handkerchief held over face: ordinary tourist blowing ordinary nose. Paul always insisted on the handkerchief.

A block away a white something detached itself from the stalled scene. It moved; Paul's hand went toward the gun in his belt, dropped. The péon Diosdado, sitting on his heels at the roadside, hands busy in the weeds.

Guillermo signaled readiness with a lift of his head. Paul nodded and walked around quickly to take his place next to David in the Packard. He wagged his finger at Masson. "Let's go."

"What's the route?"

"Follow the motorcycles, the cops know the way."

"We're staying off the main roads?" David said.

"Until we're in the country."

The sound of the Packard's fussing starter was cue for the cycle engines to turn over. Paul stuck his hand out the window and made a circling movement, Guillermo answered with two beeps of his horn. The forward cycles began to roll, Masson accelerated, the cortege was on its way.

They passed the bent figure of Diosdado: he had two large mushrooms in his hand and was rummaging in the weeds for more. On through the intersection, the car hesitating as its wheels bucked the road's corrugations. An explosion. The Packard lurched to the right, Masson braked hard.

The forward cycles stopped dead. Behind, the police car shivered to a halt.

"Marvelous, a flat," Paul said.

"Don't see how," Masson said.

They both got out to see. David remained in the car with the machine gun on his lap where Paul had slipped it.

The right front tire was completely collapsed.

"This is how you check things," Paul said.

"There was nothing to check! I got a new set of tires three weeks ago."

Guillermo came running up. "Tire? Nice hell of a thing." He bent toward the wheel, held still; he stared. "What? Ah?" A figure in white was there in front of him, on its knees, running quick hands over the tire's surface. "You have business here? You think to find mushrooms on tires?"

Diosdado did not look up. His hands went on exploring. In a moment he held out a palm to show several jagged pieces of pale blue glass.

"These dirt roads," Masson said. "You don't know what you pick up."

"Where's the spare?" Paul said.

"Around in back."

Paul reached inside to the dashboard and pulled the ignition key out. He examined the keys on the ring.

"What do you want?" Masson said.

"The compartment key, the luggage compartment key."

"The luggage. . . . No, the tire's not inside, no, it's over the door."

"And the tools?"

"No—the compartment's full of cups and saucers, serapes—"

"Serapes? What?"

"My samples. The things I buy and sell." Masson reached for the keys. "The tools, they're here, under the driver's seat."

David raised himself up, lifting the seat cushion under him; from the storage space below, Masson brought out a lug wrench and a jack.

"Is it bad?" Marisha said from the back.

"We have to change the tire," Paul said.

"No piecemeal reforms!" V.R. said through the handkerchief. He was in holiday spirit. His voice through the handkerchief was prankish. "Change the car!"

"Change your mind," Paul said. "We could forget the car and go home." V.R. looked steadily at Paul. "Good. We'll change the tire."

Paul followed Masson to the rear; there, standing by the spare, was Diosdado, mushroom stems protruding from the open front of his shirt.

"He say he is a very good one with the tires," Guillermo said.

Masson held out the tools. "Let him. I'll pay him for it."

Diosdado went to work with the wrench. In less than a minute he had the wheel disengaged from its bolts and was rolling it forward. It took him little time to get the front end of the chassis jacked up and the old wheel removed.

"You can see it wasn't my fault," Masson said. "You run over glass on these roads and never know it."

"Get out your serapes. We'll take a nap," Paul said. "Get the cups and saucers, we'll have tea."

The new wheel was in place, the jack removed. Diosdado stood with the old one resting against his knees, looking at Masson.

"What's he waiting for?" Masson said to Guillermo. "It goes in back, in back, on the door."

Diosdado spoke for the first time, in Spanish, his voice muted, his face adjunct to fact: "This one—no more good, boss. The holes in many places."

"What's he saying?"

"I see what is in his mind, " Guillermo said. "He think, the tire is finish for the car but for him it has some importance. These ones, they make from the old tires the huaraches and other things."

"Tire—no more good, boss." Diosdado regarded a spot somewhere ahead of his feet.

"How will he get it off the rim? I need the wheel, I—" Before Guillermo was through translating the péon was reaching for the machete at his belt. He held it up, making digging motions. "All right. Tell him to be quick. He can take the tire and—"

"We're wasting time," Paul said. He addressed Diosdado in Spanish: "Take the tire, also the wheel, the two together. Tonight we bring the car back. Then to return the wheel."

Paul handed him the nuts belonging to the spare. Diosdado took them. "I do this, boss." He looked at the weeds. "I am satisfied to have the tire, boss." Masson put two silver pesos in his hand. His eyes widened; he studied the coins, weighed them in his crusted fingers. "Many thanks, boss." He raised his eyes to look at V.R. in the back seat. "That the sick one is well soon. That the boss has health." He started to roll the wheel down the street, stepping carefully around the hot rocks and sharp weeds.

"He always sees V.R. with a handkerchief to his nose," David said. "Handkerchief means sick."

"With no diseases he knows." Paul took his seat in the car. "To him we're a source of rubber."

CHAPTER VII

Highway almost empty. Good road. Ramón was heading northeast to San Juan Teotihuacán, making seventy. Entrusting car to eyes and hands, mind working back to the telephone talk. This new approach, fincas, péons, foreigners with beards, armed bandits: improvisations. Bad. Two years to put Plan A (himself) and Plan B (Tomás the turd) in position. Thought and work behind them. Last-minute shifts because of last-minute picnics? Need elasticity, absolutely. Within larger strategies, room for the moment's tactical maneuvers, certainly. But this, this of fincas, beards, no plan there. Jabs, guesswork. George not one for quick changes. Making it up. Until Spain. New situation in Spain: armies. Used to small apparatuses, selected cadres: suddenly, armies. Relief to have a mass force, luxury. Man could be less clever. Do the job with muscle. In Spain, sometimes, George tended to the mass approach. Hit out hard, overwhelm with numbers. This, now, of the péons and fincas? Mass approach. Surprise attack. Weight of numbers. Muscle. Péons might be set in motion; maybe; not led millimeter by millimeter. Such a last-minute army? A gamble. Small chance of getting Rostov with cops and Teleki there. Maybe George did not expect to get Rostov? Had said: it might accomplish something. Something? If not the main job on Rostov, what? Hard to follow George's thinking. Always seven steps ahead of everybody. Getting too careless? Possible. Might be little off balance. Himself getting in trouble back home? Possible. Stories, small signs in the air. Better not to be one of the big ones. Cándida: big one: faced charges. George bigger one still: rumors of charges. Rostov? None bigger. One of the revolution's top ones. Man on top of his century. Head not worth a peseta today. This afternoon could face his last charges. Before committee of péons not knowing his name. To the right, far off, puncturing the overhead blues, pyramids of Teotihuacán. Pointed tops: rooms of sacrifice there. Where men used to face charges. Charged with being wanted by sun god, the boss, without delay; hearts pulled out and dropped, still pumping, on fires. Country hereabouts still smelled of baking flesh. Tickling in his nose. Pungent plateau dust. He sneezed twice. Smelling, almost, the still pumping hearts as they sizzled. Could he know the smell? Dust in nose reminding him: dark twists coming up from Teleki's hand as the flesh smoked, the kitchen smell of it. Sneezed then too, from the smell. Probably all flesh gave off same smell when it cooked. Bad, letting that be done to Teleki that afternoon outside Madrid. No sun god waiting for Paul Teleki. George wrong that time. Cándida wrong. There, draw the line, when possible. Meant, maybe, George getting impatient. Maybe Moscow sun god getting impatient for George, there were rumors. Town of San Juan Teotihuacán, flat and unambitious under the sun, up ahead. Squeezed down houses the wash color of work shirts. He drove off the road, parked by some palms, pulled his jacket off. Underneath, péon cottons, rough, itched; on the feet, huaraches of tire rubber, heavy. He patted the gun at his waist under the knotted tails of his shirt, sneezed twice, began to walk, going over the key phrases, foreigner with beard, armed bandits, etc.

They went this way and that through the back roads, past Churubusco, close by Ixtapalapa and Villa Madero, skirting the city limits until they were at the Shrine of Our Lady of Guadalupe; here they turned into the main highway that ran straight northeast, the route Cortés had taken in his retreat after the bloody noche triste, to Teotihuacán. V.R. lowered his handkerchief, Paul saw the movement in the rear view mirror.

"Better stay covered," he said without turning.

"Surprised you didn't sandbag the back seat," David said.

"Is it likely George Bass is making the educational tour to the pyramids?" V.R. said.

"He'll go to the moon if he knows you're going," Paul said.

"With this entirely unique headgear," V.R. said, pulling the scoop visored cap over his eyes, "my destination could very well be the moon. Next trip find me something less conspicuous to wear. A babushka—an Eskimo kayak."

"Can't you get it through your head we're on a picnic, not a funeral?" Emma said.

"You haven't heard about the leaping transformation of a thing into its opposite?" Paul said. "Read up on the dialectic laws."

"Paul," Marisha said, "it is a sunny day. Take it on its own merits."

V.R. said to Marisha: "Mexico, Mexico has a distinct smell. What does it remind you of—bread baking, dried wood shavings, burnt sugar? It's as hard to pin down as a GPU agent."

"Smells like a GPU agent," Paul said. "Like George Bass."

"I remember the museums," Marisha said, her voice searching for a level to rest on. "During the revolution—when I was with the commission to safeguard the museums. This is like—old documents disintegrating in a museum vault."

"You know sunshine can be an insult? Sunshine insults me." Paul shifted his feet, being careful not to disturb the machine gun on the floor. "Raises bad smells—a little like rotting cider, some tainted lobster, a touch of moldy leather: a whiff of the crematorium. More or less George Bass's smell."

"You know his smell?" David said.

"I smelled him once. Near Madrid."

"Inches away," Marisha said.

"It was more my smell than his," Paul said. "George Bass concentrates an insulting amount of sunshine on people's skins. He stirs up a strong fragrance of sautéed flesh in other people and some of it sticks to him."

"You're giving us a marvelous appetite for this picnic," Emma said.

They had passed through the town of San Juan Teotihuacán. On the right, a distance from the highway, the terraced pyramids came into view. Granite bullied into system; no easy yields of curve; these ratio'd lifts, echoing each other in slashing plane and severe slope, might have been designed as a veto to the haphazardness in all the trees and hills around.

"What price neatness!" V.R. was sitting forward to see better. "A Platonic city: the Toltecs thought with a slide rule and lived by the caliper. . . . Are we stopping?"

"It's not on the itinerary," Paul said.

"I told you I wanted to see the pyramids."

"Somebody might recognize you."

"Then I'll carry out an unprecedented tactical maneuver: I'll get back in the car." Paul gave no answer. "Jacques, pull up here. Tell the police we're making a detour."

"Didn't you hear?" Paul said. "Pull up so we can see the sights, Jacques. What's the matter, your head full of invoices?"

"Always we worked the land. Always others had the profit of it. What did we own? Nothing, neither the land nor the profit. Listen to me, friends. We waited. There is the waiting of centuries on our faces. Now some of us, a few, finish with the waiting. We begin, some of us, to have the land and the profit of it. The land is in our names and gives a meaning to our names. Some do not like this. They wish us to go back to the waiting. They wish all the land of all the world for themselves. They come from places far away, from over the seas, to take our land. If we give up our land, our one property, what happens? We become nothing again, our names are empty and without meaning. This man comes to our homes, one who does not belong here, a man with the name of a foreigner and the face of a foreigner and the beard of a foreigner, one who does not speak our language and cares nothing for us unknowns. If we allow this foreigner with the beard to march here with his arms and his fat bandits? If he robs us of our fincas and our names—"

The cars were parked in the shadow of the largest pyramid, the women stayed behind. As soon as the others were gone Emma turned to Marisha and said, "Paul's going out of his mind! He won't let up!"

"*You* attack Jacques too."

"I? I haven't said two words to him since Friday."

"You attack with silence, with your eyes. I wonder: why are you angry with Paul? Because he puts into words what you only think? . . . You said the trouble came from your being apart; now you are together. . . . Paul is a problem, I know."

"That's his profession."

"Can we blame him? The full burden of our security is on him, only him. . . . Jacques is doing good work. Victor is pleased with his translations. But if we must choose between him and Paul. . . ."

"Then—shall I tell him to go?"

"Emma—be honest with yourself. The question is, should *you* go."

"Oh. . . . Victor spoke to me again. Yesterday. . . . It's such a mess. I can't go home alone, after all I've written my family about Jacques. But how can I bring Jacques? They'd see in a minute what a travesty our relationship is."

"It is a travesty here."

"I know that. I know it. That's why I can't make a move in any direction, why I can't think straight any more. . . . It's hopeless. Of course. I'll have to face it. The moment Victor finishes the book —I'll go."

"The book may take some time."

"Hasn't he told you? He started on the Kronstadt chapter this morning."

"It may take weeks—you should not wait that long. . . . There is no way to control Paul any more."

"All right. I'll go in a week. Even if Victor isn't finished. . . . Can Jacques work with us a few more days?"

"Of course. When will you tell him?"

"The first chance I get. . . . Oh—tonight. When we get home."

"Good. You will feel better."

"Marisha. David will be leaving soon; Victor's already written to New York about it. There'll be only Paul—"

"He may go too; his career as an unwanted doorman is almost over. He has such an appetite now for things far from politics; he has never had the experience of being naive. . . ."

"I've never had the experience of being anything else. . . . With Paul gone you'll have nobody but the police."

"We broke with a police state; we had to end in the company of police. . . . This is not your concern, Emma. It is what Victor wants. . . . Things will be better for you in Chicago, depend on it. Once you settle there you will forget what has happened."

"Things were bad before I knew Jacques; they're bad now, they'll be bad in Chicago. About Jacques, for the rest of my life I'm going to be cursed with total recall." Absentmindedly Emma rubbed the bluish streaks on her upper arm.

"Those marks, Emma. I have wanted to ask—did you have—"

"I was rummaging in our closet, something heavy, an Alpine axe, fell off the shelf. . . ."

"You have them on both arms. . . ."

"I fell, too. . . . It's nothing. . . ."

Noon; too early for sightseers. They moved across the immense paved plazas of the ghost city with the police fanned out about them in alert pairs. From the Moon Pyramid they advanced to that of Quetzalcoatl the Plumed, marveling at the corbeled arches, the bas-reliefs, the alfresco murals, the glyphic designs, the calendrical pictographs, the face-sprouting steles, the snapping jaguar mouths in undeviating rows everywhere: here had been a court presided over by the T-square. They stopped to finger basalt altars and cyclopean monuments crawling with snakes and birds, snake-birds, boas tufted and padded with feathers, ferocity packaged in down; they crossed handball courts with stone rings jutting from the walls, where young men had reveled in muscle for muscle's sake, act for once torn away from aim; finally they stood at the foot of the greatest structure, the Sun Pyramid, rising in massive slopes and precise setbacks to a sacrificial temple, ringed with palaces, almost two hundred feet up.

"Skyscrapers before Christ?" David said. "They had all the space they needed."

"They had geographic space," V.R. said. "A need for social space made them go up."

He was reveling in his freedom of movement. He had been taking long steps, swinging his arms in delight, as though to remind himself that there were no confining walls about; his pace was so quick that the others had trouble keeping up. Now, his cheeks infiltrated with lively color, emphasizing his words with tosses of head and sweeps of hand, he began to talk about the ancient peoples who had built and rebuilt this city.

The clue to these Toltec-Olmec settlements, he said, was their mortality rate. Fantastic labors went into them; they were abandoned over and over. Monuments to permanence with an average life span less than that of a man: how could it be? The answer was —eyestrain. The incredible myopia of a class. These city-states had been theocracies, ruled over by priests and nobles who needed to put the riffraff behind—rather, under. Why the upward trending? The theocrats (among the Mayans, at least) called themselves the *almehenob,* those who have fathers and mothers, and the *halac uinicil,* the true men, the real things. The thoughts of such exalted ones must turn to monoliths—with themselves in residence on top. They trace themselves up, through soaring genealogies, up, up, back to the sun, the most noteworthy and exalted object in their ken and, therefore, their progenitor; they whip the nameless refuse into building mighty pyramids, then mount the pyramids to elude the refuse who have no kin in the sky. Do they imagine they will see more from their lofty heights? Nonsense. Raised so high, staring straight into papa sun, blinded by the sun, a man must find his vision going. But the theocrats insisted on going up and looking up; became, literally, the raised on high, the uppermost, the tops; then, united with light and the source of light, went blind. They wanted this blindness. They needed it. Overhead, a dazzling ancestral Oneness. But below? Signs of a seething anarchy: the threat of all unities flying apart. What were these signs? First, the absolute bankruptcy of their agriculture. Each city-state relied for its sustenance, its life blood, on the surrounding farms. But these people used the primitive slash-and-burn method of cultivating the land: clear the timber, burn away the stumps and undergrowth, plant and plant again. Without rest or renewal, the maize and frijole farms were quickly exhausted. So these people built permanent cities, cities for the ages, and abandoned them every two or three decades: they had not bothered to make their food supply permanent. There were other troubles, too. The slaves sweated to erect these massive cities, sweated to scratch crops out of the decaying soil; always under whiplash, they grumbled and plotted, from time to time rose in revolt. So, when the pyramid cities were not conquered by a suicidal agriculture, they were toppled by the forgotten worms around the base, the despised burrowers and haulers, those without pasts and names, the false men. Worse yet. If ruinous farming and insurrectionary slaves did not finish the cities, there was a third danger. Invasions from the north. Those lofty theocrats, with eyes forever raised, saw neither the hopelessness of their agronomy, nor the stirrings among their slaves, nor even the Chichimec barbarians, the Dog People, who came down in wave after wave to overrun this wide plateau. When they were not slaughtered on the spot they had to run away and start all over, every few years. All because they would not, could not, look down. Because, when they did deign to look down, their clouded eyes saw only an undistinguished blur there, an unappetizing gray mass, nothing worth the attention. The only immutable thing about a monolith is the immutable law governing its demise. What was that law? That those who rise to the apex can't see the base; that the base will rise up one day, not seen until the last minute, and destroy the apex. If the theocrats had looked down and seen, truly seen? They could have invented plowing tools and fertilizing systems to save the land, satisfied the simple needs of the slaves, built defenses against the marauding Dog People. What did they invent, these blind priest-nobles? Plowshares, soil conditioners? No. Better strains of maize, barricades? Hardly. Only calendars, the most accurate the world has known. They had taken refuge from statesmanship in mathematics. Was it not clear where the priesthood's obsession with numbers mysticism came from? From terror—terror of the swarming Manyness down below. The multiplicity of moving things down there made them feel that they themselves were in danger of flying apart. (As pyramid perchers always do: why do they give themselves boastful names like Stalin, Steel, if not to ward off, by verbal magic, the fear that they may become scattered rubble? Monolithism— the craving of the fragmented! The One Party universe—a dream of multiple personalities!) So the priest-nobles staked out space and calibrated time, to prove the heavens are ruled by the intercalary ratios: all because the scum below was so many headed and uncontainable. Number was magical because it could rule, subdue, order the cosmos; the most magical number was One. Was there not a perfect shining One holding sway over all? Were they not one with this prime One? These pyramids were temples devoted to the number One, that soothing, placating figure, sum of the apex dwellers, regal negation of the Manyness below. People will dive so deep into the skies and dream such dreams of neatness to hide from the signs of multiplex anarchy in the streets—

"You said all that once before," Paul broke in. "1904. You wrote a whole book in 1904 on the theme of monoliths and myopia—for Lenin's attention."

V.R.'s eyes narrowed. Troubled by the quick tension, Masson stepped in to say mildly: "Can slaves storm pyramids by themselves? They need bold leaders to guide them up—a party—"

"The Bolshevik party?" Paul said.

"Yes—exactly. The One fist through which the Many can strike. V.R. joined the Bolsheviks in 1917 to help build it—"

"In 1904," Paul said in his deliberate monotone, "V.R. was suggesting—insisting—that Bolshevism was only a new monolith to take the place of the old."

"Not under Lenin," Masson said weakly. "V.R. came to see that. If he could join Lenin in 1917—it shows—he saw the Bolsheviks were not the danger. . . . Later, with the Stalinist degeneration. . . ."

"V.R. predicted the degeneration in 1904. Under Lenin, not Stalin."

David's eyes were pleading with Paul to stop as he said: "Another law governing monoliths. They always take the pyramidal form— really big ones, anyhow."

V.R. continued to look at Paul for a taut moment; he relaxed finally, as though to postpone the showdown, and turned to David.

"They can't be cylinders. Out of the question." He spoke with less zest now, more mechanically. "If they're as broad at the top as at the bottom they're topheavy. For stability's sake, the elite must whittle its monolith to a pinpoint, just large enough to accommodate itself."

"And its terrors," David said.

"Of course," V.R. said. "When the masses begin to move, they can only move up: they'll storm the top by sheer weight of numbers."

"Storm it, yes," Paul said. "Stay there, no. There's no room for a crowd."

"You're proposing another law?" David said. "The Many will take the apex; only the One can set up housekeeping there?"

"That's valuable real estate up there, the party wants it for itself. First the party, then the party caucus, then the Central Committee, then the boss of the Central Commitee—"

"I can propose a couple of laws myself," David said, talking fast, aware of V.R.'s sober, set face close by. "One, the apex must constantly whittle away at the base: to control the Many, of whom there are far too many. And the corollary: chop away too much of the base, the apex will fall. It's tricky."

"Stalin whittles and whittles," Paul said. "Does he show any signs of falling? The hell he does."

"Originally he had a hundred and seventy million bottomdogs," David said. "No pyramid needs that broad a base."

"Give it a few million bureaucrats for props—back them up with guns—the pyramid's damned steady. Besides, Stalin's smarter than the Toltecs. The higher he goes, the more he looks down. Comrade

Number One follows events and trends on street level and keeps them going his way."

"True enough," David said. "When the slaves get restive he wipes out a few million. When farm production fails he sends out corps of tractors and truckloads of seed to the collectives. When the Dog People begin to bark on his borders, he expands the Red Army."

"And at all signs of trouble, no matter what, he sends out more Basses. To break up the restless slaves within and the agitating Dog People without. He looks down—he sees far. No myopia in Josef Dzugashvili Steel's twenty-twenty pig eyes." Paul moved away from the group to look at a jaguar head snapping out from a frieze on the pyramid's wall. "Can it be that all regimes are pyramids? Forever gnawing at their bases?" He ran his finger over the jaguar's stone fangs, then turned to look at V.R. "The suppression of Kronstadt has been called a gnawing."

"At the base of the regime?" V.R. said slowly. "Or at those who were trying to undermine the base?"

"The sailors said," Paul continued, "that they only wanted the state structure they'd been promised. And that they'd fought for— more than most."

"They wanted all hundred and seventy million of their countrymen rushed to the apex," V.R. said, "all at once. It was not only impossible—it was the surest way to make the whole structure collapse of its own weight."

"Then we're at an architectural impasse." Paul rested his elbow against the jaguar head. "Bottomdogs will always resent being on the bottom. Peak people, being sensible engineers, will never invite them up: must consider the laws of gravity: peak needs a base. One class struggle's built into all history—foundation versus peak."

"That will be true," V.R. said, "for as long as societies are monolithic pyramids: the strongest argument against monolithism I know. We Bolsheviks did not want to perpetuate the pyramidal society: we'd inherited it from Tsarism, we had to take it over and gradually, bit by bit, transform it into its opposite, first, by building an economy of abundance out of the Tsarist ruins, second, by dissolving the old rigidities and inequities—in that order. Such a job takes time: one foot after the other. The sailors wouldn't wait. They wanted rich cream before the cow was milked—before we had fodder for the cow—before there was a cow! But we couldn't retire and let the pyramid be pulled down until we had a horizontal, airier, more viable structure to put in its place. Our aim was—the ultimate withering away of the pyramid; a stateless society. The sailors wanted a glorious overnight withering. We had to stop their premature attacks on the pyramid—in the interest of abolishing pyramids altogether. We did what we had to do. Do you understand? For once—drop this easy game of lamentation and face the dirty facts of government in a bankrupt, starving country! It had to be done; we did it; tears only blur the picture!"

V.R. had begun his long speech quietly, with almost a professorial tone; toward the end his voice had taken on a charged platform ring, eerie here among the forgotten handball courts and depopulated geometers' mounds.

Paul walked to Masson with lips bent into an approximation of a smile. "Tell me: what's at the base of your personal pyramid, the rumba dancer or the after-hours master builder? Will the rumba dancer chisel away the builder or the builder the rumba dancer? Which—"

"You've got to stop this," Masson said. "It's intolerable, the way you—"

"Look! Look up there!" David said suddenly. "Oh, there's a thing to see!"

He had his head back, he was staring up at the summit of the Sun Pyramid. A figure had appeared there, a man dressed all in white, garments flapping in the breeze: unmistakably a péon, with the trademark bagginess in blouse and trousers. An attendant, assigned to the area to pick up cigarette butts and discarded Coca-Cola bottles? A field hand from the neighboring fincas, come to study the blood-patina'd altar on which his ancestors, the unreal things, the ungenuine articles, without blood line but rich in expendable blood, had been flayed and skinned to please the carnivorous Sun God? The man, ridiculously small and frail, stood on the edge of the highest terrace, outside the topmost temple, slightly crouched, head down; both hands motionless at his crotch. Directly below him, on the long slope that cut down to the next terrace, a dark stain was spreading over the weathered gray stone.

"This happens on monoliths too!" David's face was turning red, his throat was choked. "You see? For a thousand years they haul the great blocks, carve their friezes and gargoyles, chisel their orderly glyphs and pictographs! What mathematical hymns they threw up to the magnificent One! Why, do you know, there's a fine observatory inside each and every one of these pyramids? Yes, yes! Designed with peepholes that focus on all the astronomical guidelines, dead on the lines of sight along the azimuth of the meridian— everything lined up neat as pie with the heaven's exact signposts! They measure, ratio, caliper, they cunningly compute angles and proportions echoing the unities of space and time—and behold! Presto chango! In the end the nobody—the bum who hauled the stones to the top and was ground to bits at the base, had his heart yanked out of his butchered thorax to feed the sacrificial fires—the worm, the eternal bottomdog—he's on top, on the uppermost point, one inch from the sun that never condescended to spawn him: taking Number One's post: making number one! Who said the base can't become the apex? Relief—relief at last!" He bent over and began to laugh hysterically, holding his sides. "The only true man, the only real thing left! The last *halac uinicil,* in the micturating person! The world's—his toilet bowl!"

Yards away, Sergeant Guillermo and his men were looking up, stains of smile spreading over their faces.

CHAPTER VIII

Miles off the Teotihuacán highway, close by a country road, ran a thin stream dotted with rocks; beyond it the land dropped away more than twenty feet to form a hollow laced over with stunted, skew branched trees. These, in contrast to the vivid evergreens on the higher ground, had no foliage, no fruits or flowers; shoots from a time before history, they had been old and stone smooth when the Toltecs first saw them. Their nobby surfaces, stripped of bark before alphabets were invented, were a sateened silver, crosshatched with lines of crystallization; they had been partially petrified during some inundation, then lifted into the open again by erosions and land shifts. Denuded and desapped trunks, bulged like snakes engorging objects bigger than themselves, striped with peristaltic ridges, made senseless detours sideways and down, throwing out a fuzz of branches as they went; these ciliated themselves in turn with jointed, witch claw twigs. A garden of complicated driftwood pieces, upended for a practical joke: ossified fingers spiraling, twining, fusing—a rhizomic hysteria fixed at its high point. Coiling through this growth, undestinated as smoke, were thumb thick lianas, green and crusty of bark, throwing out on all sides enormous orchids, many over a foot long. Above, kiting in casual arcs, several vultures. Butterflies everywhere: an atmosphere of eyelids.

The cars and motorcycles were parked alongside the road. Crossing the river had been easy, thanks to the many stepping stones. Along the edge of the silicified wood the picnic things were laid out; the police had taken positions, two by two, along the river. While Marisha and Emma busied themselves with the food V.R. unpacked his nets and summoned the younger men to the stream: it was to be a butterfly hunt.

V.R. had recovered his outing mood. As he knelt to remove shoes and turn up trouser bottoms he said, "Subtle tactics, gentlemen! Anticipate the enemy! Butterfly tracking is a continuation of politics by other means; we follow Clausewitz against the insects."

David was studying the patchwork clouds of butterflies over the water. "Funny: the layer as a whole seems to be rippling but standing still; it's an illusion. Concentrate on any one individual and you see that, though he seems to be going here and there aimlessly, he's steadily trending downstream. With the prevailing wind, I suppose."

"Precisely. As a class they're stuck in one spot; as individuals they've full social mobility."

"We've no designs on the class?"

"None. We're out to bag a few individuals—the more distinguished ones."

"What's the plan of action?" David said.

"You frighten them upstream; they run down this way—along their regular line of march—into my net." V.R. stood and distributed the loose string nets. "Don't try to catch them, just create a commotion. I want them to be looking over their shoulders, so to speak, as they approach." The others moved off upstream, V.R. began to wade in. When he had steadied himself on a large stone he looked around and saw that only David and Masson were in the water. "Paul! No! They're thickest over the water, can't you see?"

Paul had been slouching on the bank, machine gun under one arm, butterfly net in his other hand, taking perfunctory swipes at the insects. "No good Marxist goes after individuals," he called back. "I'd rather stand to one side and see them as a class."

"Into the river!" V.R.'s crackling voice came back. "On holidays —we're bourgeois individualists!"

Paul shrugged. He placed his machine gun on the ground, removed his shoes and rolled his trousers, waded out to a large rock. David and Masson were already stationed on rocks farther downstream, swinging their nets over their heads in vigorous circles.

"We'll take hostages," Paul said. Nobody heard. He was talking to the air. "Our terms? Unconditional surrender." He began to make halfhearted passes with his net, a flick to the left, a flop to the right.

"Harder, harder!" V.R. called. "Proletarian boldness will carry the day!" With each shout he made another scoop with his net into the speckled air. "They're staggered, Paul! They never expected this pincers movement!"

Paul thought, as he moved his net mechanically back and forth:

true. What good would it have done them if they had expected it? The fortress had been built on an island, to guard the western bay approach to Petrograd. When the Bolshevik guns, at V.R.'s signal, opened fire from mainland positions north, south, and east, the Kronstadt artillery could not effectively counter: most of it was fixed to fire west and only west. No fortress is constructed to answer a bombardment from its own trusted rear. Had V.R. boomed out his triumph that day when his shells hit the stuck to one spot pigeons on Kronstadt, the distinguished and the undistinguished alike, as he was booming now, playing Red Army, playing Kronstadt, playing mobile man in the world with the panicked butterflies?

"Look at them go!" David shouted. "We're routing the spectrum!" The batting of nets was throwing the butterflies into a frenzy, they heaved in one mass like gauze. "Got them on the run! Take that! That! What do you mean by painting our air?"

Something was happening with Masson. He had hold of the slender pole of his net with both hands, he was wielding it with full strength as though it was a baseball bat, chopping. "They think they just have to be pretty," he said, loud enough for Paul to hear. It was not said with humor. There was an excess of purpose in his movement: he was not trying to frighten the insects but to annihilate them, his face was shining with sweat. "Dance and dance," he said. "Won't tighten the wheel." As he swung hard, over and over, the crushed butterflies dropped to the water and fluttered helplessly.

"You're slaughtering them!" David yelled. "Jacques! What's the sense—"

"Wants them to lockstep a little!" It was Paul; his voice pitched high with some wildness. "Sober up and get to work!"

Paul's shout made David freeze. He looked upstream with a worried face. Masson would not stop, he was slashing harder at the butterflies; face knotted, he said, "Come and go, the wheel's not loose," and swung again.

From downstream V.R. called in his fullest headquarters voice, general imitating generals, the Clausewitz in him capering, "Gentlemen, charge! The enemy's regrouping his forces!" But David went on staring at Paul.

"Pretty boy murders butterflies for being too pretty!" Paul continued, hardly aware of what he was saying, just needing to make noise. "For not having loose wheels! No middle class pampering for him, the hard life, he's—"

Carried away, he forgot he was standing on a rock. He went forward, his foot slipped, he fell splay armed into the stream.

David relaxed. He began to laugh.

The quick violent movement and the splash seemed to bring Masson to his senses; he dropped his hands to his sides and stood motionless, breathing hard, watching Paul.

When Paul got to his feet he was soaked as high as his chest.

Marisha had come to the water's edge. She clapped her hands.

"Lunch!" she announced. "Come, everybody!" She saw Paul standing confused in the water. "Paul! Butterflies, not fish! The butterflies are not in the water!"

The men plodded their way to the bank. V.R. had a cellophane bag in his hand, filled with beating butterflies; he held it up with satisfaction.

"Fine specimens," he said. "Two or three I haven't seen before."

"They don't like being singled out," David said. "They give every indication of wanting to sink back into their class."

"The curse of distinction: to be pursued by the trophy hunters." V.R. smiled at Paul. "Only one casualty in our War of the Butterflies? Not too bad. What were you shouting? I couldn't hear."

Paul gave no answer. He had not heard. A hideous chain of thoughts was banging fast through his head: and politics is a continuation of war by other means; politics is the dramatically marked one separated from his adopted class, standing downstream with net raised high while we, the undistinguished, the underlings, do our best, by calculated yells, by making commotions, to stampede the whole class into his net; what do we truly know about the operation except that if we make effective enough commotions the net holder, distinct in his distinctions, will think well of us the indistinct?; and if we get worried about the operation and try to call off the stampede it may be too late: while we face west the shells will come at us from the east: Kronstadt?

"He was saying," David volunteered, "that butterflies don't know how to lockstep. Something like that." His eyes stayed on Masson.

"It was a quotation," Paul said. "From an obscure source."

"Someone was killing them," V.R. said. "The river was full of them. That wasn't necessary."

"Me, I'm afraid," Masson said. He was still panting a little. "I'm not very good at this."

"You're very good at it," Paul said. He was bent over, wringing out his trousers. "You can even tell when their wheels are or aren't loose."

". . . . Our people had clashed with armies; now they were in a mood to dicker with storekeepers. The grocery still casts a longer shadow over human affairs than the parliaments; when Stalin began his drive for power he knew how to make himself grocer to the nation. . . . Thus Kronstadt. If in 1917–1918 the Kronstadt sailors stood considerably higher than the average level of the Red Army and formed the framework of its first detachments as well as the framework of the Soviet regime in many districts, by 1921 a great percentage of the garrison's personnel consisted of raw and colorless recruits. These were not forged-in-battle proletarians. They were the youngest and least conscious throw-offs of the backward peasantry, exaggerating in themselves all the weaknesses which overwhelm the oppressed when they are exhausted and hungry: heterogeneity, insufficiency of culture, narrowness of world outlook. Most of the reliable worker-leaders were gone, either killed at the front or dispatched to far off provinces as Soviet organizers; those who remained were elbowed aside. The garrison, as I had ample opportunity to see for myself during visits just before the mutiny, was overrun with completely demoralized elements wearing showy bellbottom pants and sporty haircuts: petty black market speculators of the sort known as sack-carriers, hoarders, adventurers, self-aggrandizers, not to mention the anti-Soviet Lettish and Esthonian and Finnish volunteers —in short, every kind of riffraff, dandified and well fed, the limp gray sediments that are left of the oppressed when the tide of revolution falls back. . . . What happened at Kronstadt? Two things. The few revolutionary workers, drunk with their class successes in the civil war, wanted the moon on pumpernickel; they* *were a vanguard of firebrands behind whom the army had vanished. As for the backward peasant and lumpen elements who now overshadowed them, the back alley dealers in bolts of cotton and sacks of wheat, they wished only to enrich themselves and loosen the hold of the new proletarian regime on their profiteering lives. From this confused two-class composition of the garrison city came the twofold character of the mutineers' demands: seemingly ultra-revolutionary (secret ballot, open electioneering, free Soviets, less discipline, equal rations, general amnesty) and regressive (proprietary rights for small landholders and household craftsmen, free trade, immediate new elections, the Soviets without the Bolsheviks, Constituent Assembly). The workers were only naive and over-eager in their anarchist dream of diluting the centralized power. The reactionary peasants, dreaming of bourgeois restoration, were criminal in their insistence on feasts when starvation diets were the order of the day. And it was the peasants who were predominantly in control of the garrison, hiding their counter-revolutionary aspirations behind the confused workers. The brackish country elements had overwhelmed the spirited town elements at Kronstadt. . . . What could the Bolsheviks do? They were obliged to keep state power concentrated in their hands as a solemn trust until such time as the masses could fill their bellies again, rouse themselves from their dull gray lethargy, and think once more of politics. Kronstadt was, despite its tattered proletarian cover, a direct petty-bourgeois adventurist plot against that power; the White Guardist generals were waiting for just such an excuse to strike again; Kronstadt had to be put down with absolute firmness. Did this 'monolithic' suppression create a precedent which made it easier for Stalin to crush all oppositionists when he began to consolidate his personal dictatorship? No doubt. But if the Kronstadters had not, as part of their underhanded drive for bourgeois restoration, removed themselves by force from the Bolshevik corpus, there would have been no suppression—and no precedent. The sailors, both the bourgeois-minded peasants and the gulled workers, contributed much to the fashioning of the monolith up which Stalin climbed, strewing groceries as he went. . . . No moral effluvia from the humanists over this terrible circumstance! These rummagers in the byways of politics, these petty pickpockets of history, are too busy weeping over their 'purest of the pure' heroes—those dandies with flashy haircuts, elegant pants, and hoarded grain to sell at a profiteer's price—that pathetic dull gray mass. . . ."*

Lunch was done with. They were grouped around V.R. on a blanket figured with lozenges and Greek frets echoing the pyramid ornamentations. Finished with his reading, V.R. put the typed pages down and said to Masson, "Fine translation. You agree with the analysis?"

"Certainly. Every word." Masson's finger was tracing over the blanket's gray geometries. "I just wonder: can you overlook the personal element? I mean—Stalin put hungers before slogans." He looked up at V.R. and away again. "They show up in soviets—as in beds. . . ." He was immediately appalled by the words he had just heard coming from his mouth; he glanced around to see if he had offended. Emma lowered her head over the mangoes she was peeling and slicing into a plate.

Holding his displeasure V.R. said, "But a country can't be run as though it were a bedroom. The dilemma of politics. . . ."

"Something bothers me," David said. "The references to groceries—grubbing—the atmosphere of pettiness. . . . What's petty about hungry people wanting a square meal?"

"Correction: wanting to smash the proletarian regime for it—when the whole nation was one soup line."

"Some people deny there were such radical class changes at Kronstadt. But suppose it's so. This sounds as though you *blame* the Russians for getting tired of heroics. . . . Gray sediment—dull gray mass—how do you outlaw neurology? When nerves get strained they need a rest."

"That's why people *start* revolutions; their nerves have been mangled by the *old* regime. But lay down your weapons too soon—close your eyes and dream of banquets—you'll wake to find a new regime staffed by banqueting George Basses. They're even worse on the nervous system, I assure you."

"What about Jacques' idea? Chase the petty appetites from the front door, they may sneak in the back."

"The first law of revolution is: post a twenty-four hour guard at *both* doors."

"Stalin got in—the *front* way. With all his appetites."

"Revolution's not a trade: it's handled by amateurs who make it up as they go along. We didn't know much about organizing our guards." V.R. smiled at Paul. "Besides, Paul wasn't there to advise us; we were low on sandbags. And we didn't know how many George Basses were at the door; both doors."

"Speaking of appetites," David said, "what do you suppose a man like George Bass is after?"

"Bass reduces statesmanship to a problem in ballistics: the ideal Stalin man. His hungers, I suspect, have little to do with congresses —or bedrooms. Maybe what he hungers for—is to manipulate *other* people's hungers." V.R. watched Masson's finger going like a pointer over the precise rhomboids woven into the blanket. "I met him once or twice—in Moscow, in 1925. He came to us with an American trade union delegation. A man who took an inordinate pride in being undistinguished, I thought; he flaunted his ordinariness. Whatever was verbal bored him. While the other American unionists made speeches, drafted programs, he inconspicuously met and married the sister of one of Stalin's closest friends, a heavy industry planner. Stalin was hard at work building his machine, he needed reliable lieutenants; Bass never went back to America, not openly, at least. No doubt he dropped out of visible party life entirely. I was told later he went to a GPU school, learned the fine art of juggling false passports. . . . What does George Bass hunger for? To look like the dullest, grayest Bass ever born; and, from the shadows, to make the dull and the gray hop to his tune. Stalin provided him with the tune —and the orchestra."

"A man like Bass has his needs taken care of every minute," David said.

"The fruits of his labors keep falling into his mouth. Stalin's a good provider."

"Suppose there are no fruits? Suppose a cause has no chance of taking hold in your lifetime—why join it? Why work for a thing you'll never see, grasp, smell?"

Paul had been sitting quietly to one side. He spoke up: "You don't think we stand a chance?"

"Be honest: do you?" David shook his head as he spoke. "At most there are twenty thousand of us in the world."

"I don't count noses to find out where I stand. I'm here because I've got no place else to go. What're *you* doing here?"

"A few weeks ago," David said slowly, "I'd have had a pat answer. I'd have said: I grew up in a bad depression; the people I knew were having a hard time, including my family; I *had* to become a rebel."

"You had a fellowship at your university," V.R. said. "A teaching job was waiting. There was openness in your life."

"All right: my indignations were more complicated than I thought."

"And maybe preceded your thought?" Paul said. "You're an intellectual: you gather belligerencies in your swaddling clothes and ideological covers for them in your academic gown. If you're talking about how the personal sneaks into the political. . . ."

"Did *your* belligerencies spring full grown from the stately brow of Karl Marx?" David said. "But why argue the point: yes, at seven I was plotting against my second-grade teacher, at ten, against my scoutmaster. My one note was anger. Maybe I had all along to be against: the grownups, at first. Then I took on the capitalists. . . . Later that wasn't enough, I must have been a glutton, I had to join those who were taking on Stalin too. What's my real program? To do battle with everything and everybody outside my own skin?" He was talking now to V.R. "Still: do motives have to be traced all the way back? Isn't the world pushed ahead by rebels—whatever pushes *them?*"

"The world needs a push now and then," V.R. said. "But those who have too much need to push—don't always know which way is ahead. The exercise may be more important to them than the direction: ideology becomes the tail to muscle. . . . Why the burst of metaphysics?"

Paul said: "He's thinking: he may die and he can't find a good enough reason."

"Is there one?" David seemed almost to be speaking to the grass.

"Intellectuals look for it too hard, it's their occupational disease."

Emma looked up from the mangoes she was preparing. "What would your reason be? Force of habit?"

"You should go home, David," V.R. said. "You're here for the wrong, personal reasons."

"More than the others?" David said intently.

"More nakedly than the others."

Marisha was helping Emma arrange the pulpy orange fruit slices. "The mangoes are good," she said. "The ripest I have seen." She set the platter down. All of them helped themselves but Masson; Paul held the platter out with a comic waiter's flourish, Masson shook his head.

"Afraid of getting spots on your shirt?" Paul said.

"I'm not hungry," Masson said.

"There's a technique for eating mangoes with an imported silk shirt: put on your imported raincoat."

"I told you, I don't want any." Masson appealed mutely to Emma, she looked the other way.

"A hungry man like you. . . . What's *your* idea, Jacques? Why *should* anybody in his right mind spend his life working for a new world he's sure he'll never see?"

"Stalin's crimes have to be exposed. For the record, if nothing else."

"Who's to benefit from the record? Posterity?"

"If not your contemporaries, then posterity, yes. The truth has to catch on sometime."

"You tell pretty lies, Jacques." Masson was startled enough to sit up. "Nobody does anything for posterity. That's like saying you drink champagne and go to nightclubs for the sake of your grandchildren. Perfect your rumba for the benefit of generations unborn."

"It's not hopeless for us. If we expose Stalin effectively—who knows. . . ."

"But you're not counting on it." Paul reached over to finger Masson's sports shirt. "That's why you wear silk next to your skin." Masson pulled away. "You want a little softness *now:* in case things don't work out later. . . ."

"No," V.R. said. "Certainly we can't hide our faces and motives behind posterity. Stalin claims he's working for posterity too."

"What made *you* a fighter, V.R.?" In his eagerness David gulped down a mango section unchewed. "Some writers say that—at first— you wanted to oppose your family."

"They want to psychologize away a whole revolution: downgrade history to an adolescent indulgence. They look so hard for the spectral father figures in the wings that they overlook the very live Tsar on stage. . . . Isn't there a law in science to the effect that you must exhaust the very near causes of an event before you reach for the ones infinitely remote?"

"But finally," David said, "the infinitely remote may be needed to make sense of the very near."

"When I was fourteen," V.R. said, "I organized the workers on my father's farms. I led a strike. Why? Not simply to make trouble for my father. My family was quite well off, yes, but we all had acute hungers in those days, even those of us who ate well. We hungered for a Russia that was not all mud huts and boredom: for complexity, for ferment. . . . And what we wanted seemed within reach."

"Yet some reach and others don't. That's a fact no political theory can explain."

"Politics doesn't make people reach. But politics is made by the reachers. . . . We turned to the workers. They had to be our fingers."

"We have the advantage over you young people," Marisha said. "We *have* held our new world in our hands."

"And now that it's been snatched away and made a nightmare," V.R. said, "we reach again. Why? You can develop quite a hunger for continuity too." His tone became lighter. "There's a saying that a man spends his first thirty-five years manufacturing his premises and the next thirty-five years trying to keep them from looking too ridiculous."

"But if the recipe for Bolshevism was yours . . ." David said. "If it could produce a Stalin . . ."

"Bolshevism does not produce Stalins!" V.R.'s voice had reverted to its platform manner. "Does the healthy body produce the cancer that consumes it? Say rather that Bolshevism did not *prevent* the appearance of its own cancer: in that sense, and that sense alone, the recipe was faulty. I'm looking now for the wrong or missing ingredient, looking very hard. That's a hunger too. . . . But Kronstadt tells us nothing about Stalinism—unless it is that people who can see no farther than their own bellies will make a cesspool of the brightest dream." He crooked his finger at Paul. "You've asked a thousand times about the Kronstadt chapter. Now you've heard the first part: your opinion?"

Paul examined the slice of mango in his palm. He closed his fist slowly on it until the juice began to run out.

"I'm no longer qualified to have one. I feel very gray and dull these days." V.R.'s concentrated blue eyes did not waver in their inquisition. "You insist? All right. We talk like hungry people trying to castigate the hungry. Can you make a hierarchy of hungers? Past a certain point of intensity they're all the same. What's our hunger? For continuity? Maybe: continuity of push—because we're so horribly idle and—*pushed*. Our program says we must push and we've got nothing to push, no part of the world volunteers to be trundled by our expert hands into the sweet bye and bye. It's we who are dull and gray and unemployed! Now we even jog the Kronstadters in their graves! *Our* ideology's becoming the wagging tail of *our* atrophied muscle! *They* couldn't see farther than their bellies? *We* can't see farther than our unemployed formulas! We're smothered too! By a dull gray mass—of formulas. The Kronstadters were alive! Then they were dead! No formula can fully hold that." He placed his smeared hand on the ground and systematically moved it back and forth to wipe the palm. "Your chapter? Brilliant discussion— of everything but Kronstadt."

"Suppose they arrest you?" He sat lower on the bench and tipped the high peaked sombrero over his eyes. The two women on either side of him listened with intent faces. "We have to consider the possibility. It could happen. Certainly." He looked across the Coyoacán square to the market stalls on the far side. "A chance we have to take. I want you out on the street every minute, both of you. Don't go back to the apartment except to call in your reports or when Marcos gives you a signal." He was dressed like a prosperous planter just in from the country: striped vaquero pants, heavy heeled boots, falling loose around his waist a Cuban guayabera shirt with generous lengthwise pleats. He was studying the faded city hall building, there past the stalls. "Get seen. Get seen. What if Ortega does get wise and take you in? What have you got to worry about?" That old wreck of a building, he thought, was where Cortés made his headquarters. After the sad night, noche triste, after the slaughter of his soldiers. When he'd come back and given the business to Moctezuma's whooping gang. Here he sat with silver spurs on an inlaid desk and told the beat down Indians what to do. "If they throw you in jail just stick to your story: you're a couple of pleasure ladies, never heard of politics, never heard of Rostovs. Above all: never heard of me. That clear? Not a word about me. That *could* get you in trouble. Real trouble." It occurred to him: both these girls were Indian, maybe not one hundred percent but in good part. And looking at the moment pretty beat down. "How long could they hold you? Not for a day. What could be the charges? This town's full of pleasure ladies. Anyhow, we'll put up bail inside of an hour, we'll get you our best lawyers. Ah. This is all talk. Ortega may never look twice at you." Funny thing. He himself wouldn't take the inlaidest desk in the fanciest city hall if they handed it to him on French toast. "Now go on back there. They'll be back from the country sometime this afternoon. Hang around, get seen, it's important, never mind why." He, George Bass, much preferred to sit on an unobtrusive park bench and in a low voice tell the Indians what to do. No silver spurs, no. But less sad nights, noches muy tristes, that way.

CHAPTER IX

V.R. was taking a nap on the blanket. Next to him Marisha sat, fixing the captured butterflies in alcohol and pinning them to the leaves of a specimen book. The police were grouped near the river, singing mellow and driftingly as Guillermo thumbed his insinuating guitar.

Paul and David were off near the corner of the petrified wood. Emma and Masson walked without aim in the opposite direction, scrupulously not touching.

"I'd like to strangle the son of a bitch," Masson said.

"He speaks highly of you, too."

"You know what he just said to me? Things may be getting rough; if he were a tourist he'd start making his travel reservations."

"He's got a right to be jumpy. He's the responsible one."

"Does he have to take it out on his friends?"

"Oh, he doesn't question our loyalty, only our competence: is he so far off?"

"Let him get some facts before he judges."

"You can get tough—with women. We'll see how you do with George Bass."

Masson put his hand under her elbow, she moved her arm away. "Emma. You can't go on avoiding me."

"I can try. . . . I've finally discovered the secret of your charm, Jacques. You make love to a woman as though you were hitting her. To prove your point—sometimes you *do* hit her."

"I don't mean to hurt you, chica. But—you sort of invite it, you know."

"And you're so ready to oblige. . . . It's been dawning on me: most of my life I've had a shamefaced tangent of a feeling that sex is something violent, brutish. A little—foul. Men sensed this in me, I suppose. They went out of their way to show me I was wrong: as though I wanted demonstrations in good manners. They were all sugar and spice; they never touched me. . . . You decided to give me what I really asked for. . . . The other night—you gave me an overdose. . . ."

He made an annoyed gesture with his long fingers. "Let's forget it. We've both been nervous and out of control." Her face stayed dead. He started again with a softer tone, the testiness gone, pleading. "Chica, why did I start coming out to Coyoacán? So that we could be together. Now we're farther apart than ever. I can't live like this, with a block of ice between us. If I can't get any warmth, any sympathy from you. . . . I can take almost anything, even Paul and his attacks, if I only know you're with me. . . ." His voice dropped lower still, took on the caressingness of the background guitar. "These last nights—by myself on the sofa—my hands sweated for you. They keep remembering. . . . Can't you remember the good part? Put that night out of your mind. . . . Chica. . . ."

She evaded his reaching hand again. "This time I'm making it my business to remember."

His face went hard. "That's a nice useless piece of information." He dropped his outstretched hand. "That's what you called me over here to say?"

"Not quite. Look, you've got to come home with me tonight. I don't care what appointments you've got: break them. . . . Oh, it's not what you think. Oh, no. I've enough black-and-blue marks to last me a while, thank you. A lifetime. . . . There's something we must talk over."

"What's it about?"

"I'll tell you tonight. Until then, stay away from me."

V.R. lay on his back, eyes closed.

He thought: could it have started there?

Could it—"it"—Paul's annotator eyes providing the quotation marks—then have started at Kronstadt?

That was to assume "it"—(the general's shadow pacifism)—did exist and had its queasy career in time. (General who develops allergy to weapons? Balloonist-agoraphobe.) But perhaps—(things in this less either-or than both-and world having such a thirst to be impregnated with their own negations: dung can sprout roses)— perhaps the revolutionary general might from the beginning have

carried in his depths a revulsion with the tools of his trade: a
malaise like a traveling silt, sometimes surfacing (the other day:
"No more guns here, Paul; plant your antiquarian's piece with
the Quetzalcoatls"), sometimes sinking to lend negative tinge to
thoughts coming through (1904, and many times again before 1917:
"Politically I am with you and not the Mensheviks, Comrade Lenin;
certainly, proletarian insurrection, a clean socialist sweep from top
to bottom, is the first need; but organizationally I must and do
draw the line: will it remain a true revolution of the masses if all
its instruments and arms are in the iron hand of one centralized
party checked only by itself if at all?")? Here (under the bougainvilleas, three days ago) a fury over a rusted machine pistol, there
(in the emigré garrets of London and Vienna three overflowing decades ago) a wariness with Vladimir Ilyitch's grimness, hardness,
dryness; two symptoms—(with a third, Kronstadt, in the middle?)
—of the same recurring "it"? If symptoms (two, or three), then
of what? The Assisan in the Bolshevik? (The fireman in the incendiary?) But the sainted Francis with the sweet and universally offered smile (humanist's smile: inverted sob) does not make needed
insurrections; too busy binding the wounded to pry loose the regimes that wound. (And plagued even so by a chronic shortage of
bandages.) But if "it" was truly there and did after all get out of
hand with Kronstadt (overtensed muscle going slack)? It would
mean the revolutionary general had sickened of the challenge of regimes; warrior (history's prod) sentimentalized down to the wispy
dimensions of a bandage maker (history's mop). No. They had
marched on Kronstadt not to kill. (In face of danger some animals
eat their young.) Rather to preserve. (Yet some animals eat their
offspring as a tic, only because their jaws will not stop working.)
No tendency to tears had developed at Kronstadt. (Tears put out
no fires, dissolve no regimes.) Yet immediately after Kronstadt he
had retreated from the Commissariat of War, abandoning the army
for purely administrative posts (ah, the balm of paper!); in the
six years from Kronstadt to his banishment he had not again
touched a weapon nor issued a command to those who continued to
make their careers with weapons. (Many did continue!) Why the
sudden preference (thirst?) for production charts on steel ingots
and statistical dossiers on rolling stock? (Did not Lenin, seeing the

firebrand retreating into the filing cabinets, the general shrinking to bookkeeper, observe in his Last Will and Testament that *Rostov is too much attracted by the purely administrative side of affairs?*) Something had assuredly happened at Kronstadt. Silts had shifted. (A depth become a surface?) The monkish Franciscan, disguised in administrator's sack suit (Bolshevik variant of sack cloth?) coming out in the general? (The narcosis of paper!) Impossible to say what "it" was. (What inspires balloonist with agoraphobia?) A thirst for negation?

Sun.

Square meals of sun for everybody.

Equal rations of sun for all neurones.

Under the loose orange lakes of his eyelids white crushed butterflies riding. (Sheeted soldiers creeping.) Coalescing into one stopped péon honing machete over squawking chicken: making urine down pyramid: eyes directed groundward. (What's up but theocrat's private sun?) Micturating and honing péon too makes programs. (Man program-making animal.) Programs of his dull gray feet. (No expectations but from his feet.) Péon election to remain alien to everything on far side of skin. (In face of total scorn gaze goes down and in.) Not a looker; the looked at. (World keeps an eye on its raw materials.) To him world spells a big No. (Only his feet say Yes or Maybe.) What could stick of protoplasm with inturned and atrophied eyes know of those who make vocation of looking? (Fixated on genitals and machete that are his world and his answer to the world.) Of sailors at fortress crenelations watching their own viva'd general advancing on them over the ice? (Of stalled generals in barricaded bedrooms scanning for Basses in the open stretches a step and a lifetime away?) Péon, career alien, files blade and relieves bladder while regarding his toes. (Expectation the mother of looking: expects nothing but days and fleas: a duplication of now.)

But sun!

Glaring everywhere, expecting nothing.

Spendthrift sun!

Florid wastrel centralism.

Hot now that duplicates itself: its career.

Behind no sandbags.

Given choice of executioners? (Who is, save the suicide?) Given choice, sailors might have voted for phantom Basses as against too-real Red Army soldiers in white sheets. (Taste for the tangible a cultivated taste.) Would have been wrong: certain debt is owed friend turned opponent who offers surrender terms, comes for you by day and in the open, wears a face. (Luxury that disappears from the newer, subtler wars: the tangible executioner.) No, no, nothing had started at Kronstadt. (Had something ended: expectation?) Omelets require the breaking of eggs. (So said Lenin, insurrection's Escoffier.) But had Vladimir Ilyitch not insisted that the omelet be made by one chef and that all, including sailors, eat whether they liked the recipe or not? (Assuming that a breaking of eggs by itself insures a palatable omelet: what if some were bad?) Yet the general in recoil from generalship (and forced gastrologies: no stomach for them?) had before returning to Oranienburg, to his khaki command Dusenburg, closed his eyes to shut out the sight of haphazardly angled bodies on the ice. (Broken like eggs; poisoned by the omelet?) Guns had been necessary at Kronstadt. (Dreaming sailors wanted an anarchy in the kitchen of state, a nation of chefs.) Shutting of eyes had likewise been necessary in that landscape of limbs hardening in odd gestures of dance and petition. (What poseurs were corpses.) Nothing to be expected in an abattoir, his eyes had refused to look. (Even at his own feet and hands; neither expecting nor wanting more of him.)

Sun expects nothing.

Recognizes no hierarchies of hungers.

Hungers for no continuities.

Worries not which direction is ahead.

Knows no aheads. Just moment's everywheres.

Is. Spills.

Machetes get sharp eventually. (As regimes get hungry?) In what direction will they strike when ready? (Will cannibal regime eat itself from bottom up or from top down?) Fatal flaw in social planning: impossible to know which way péon will move with his machete. (As individual péon cannot know where regime will begin to cannibalize; nor can the general-administrator, for that matter.) Useless to consult the péon; he does not know either, he knows least of all. (Nor can regimes be quizzed as to *their* eating habits;

they can't see beyond their own bellies; *they* don't know.) Péon
planlessly empties bladder and sharpens knife, awaiting the arrival
of an impulse. (As regimes sharpen their teeth.) When tired of
crouching under the ignored sun he will spring; in direction that's
convenient. (Regimes snap, now at péons, now at sailors; now at
generals.) Péons go into convulsion when they finally move. (Unlike
regimes: too deliberate to spasm.) Their thrashings can neither be
anticipated nor regulated. (And the regime's gnashings?) Péon:
work horse for the world's dirty work. (Protoplasmic stockpile of
the nations.) Leashed all his life to the wheels and handles and
weights of man's enterprises: at the last moment lifts up his head
and goes dervish. (Heaved and spun by his own long-stalled motors.)
Then is unleashable: scum that settles on humanity's bottom rather
than chance it at the top, when on the rare occasions it decides—
(whether for breath of air or just to commote)—to swim for the
top—(*there's* a traveling silt!)—will, when it erupts on the surface,
explode without law, making a hash—(no omelet!)—of the plans
lovingly drawn by those—(the omelet makers)—who seek to direct
all explosions. (Contradiction to begin with: to draw up codes of
behavior for explosions?) Every revolution has its wild ones. (Péons
too long immobilized and so, when set in motion, moved easily to
total activity, convulsion.) But convulsions spend themselves, governments endure. (Why regime must win out over single machete.)
Péons stormed cities. (The plumpest chickens, the shiniest pyramids.) Then their generals become bureau heads—(therefore anti-
machete, anti-storm)—calling péons comrade rather than scum—
(an improvement?)—began, in the interests of stabilizing the new
regime—(can government be founded on spasm?)—to brush away
the péon nuisance, the péon swarm, the péon reminder of the wild
to themselves who, having called out the wildness—(having ridden
on its back into power)—now felt obliged to put it again in harness.
(The maddening point at which program maker becomes harness
maker!) Man the program *and* harness maker! (Program equals
harness?)

Sun knows nor comrade nor scum.

Banquets of heatlight for all.

Spew of hot groceries in all directions.

No missing ingredients in sunshine.

Smile that goes everywhere! Unrationed skywide omelet! Without push.

Centrifugal bonanza of omelet!

Unself-centered centralism!

Unsentimental Assisan sun!

Bestowing self on all péons and generals but the sandbagged.

Revolution's dilemma: individual rebels may sputter and go out, power must be held steadily. (Sporadicism, seasonality, spasm, the luxury of single men, not governments.) At the end of insurrection, government again. (Time for steadying and settling.) Flailing gives way to institution. (Anarchy authors authority.) But while government may try to be of all, or of a great many, it can never, clearly, include all or even many, there being room for only a given—(by whom? by *whom?*)—number in the bureaus. (Precious real estate on pyramid's apex!) *From each according to his ability, to each according to his need?* (The phrasing Marx's, the visionary wish old as mankind.) But on the day after the taking of power the péons' first need is for specialists to do the paper work for them. (Standing on thresholds of newly reconstituted bureaus with hands outstretched, spokesmen of the riotous outdoors become a nuisance to the orderly indoors.) At this dialectically tricky point what had been rebel's fist—(all ability)—becomes beggar's laxly cupped hand —(all need). There is not enough to fill all, or even many, hands. (And too many hands spoil the filing cabinet.) Eternal paradox of the One (office) and the Many (péons massed dully-grayly in the doorway). Pushed, the Mexican péons went, back to the micturation and honing. (Desk theocrats push hard.) Pushed, the Russian péons did not always go. (Kronstadt!) Holding to their one ability, the ability to shout out, at the tops of their lungs, their needs. (Kronstadt.) They will not always turn and walk; thus the necessity for guns. (And the vileness of guns: Kronstadt, Kronstadt.) Thus the contempt for guns? (Chapter that must be written, impossible chapter to write.) Thus eyes lose their expectations of the world: hungers are accepted as housemates. (Most impossible hunger: for the omelet that requires no breaking of eggs and yet is palatable.) What hungers now wracked the agape young Paul Teleki? (A hunger for hungers?)

Banquets of sun!

(Paul greedy for all banquets.)

In sun's froth no decrees against neurology, no good reasons for dying.

(Paul, emerging from underground, blinking under sun, discovering neurones, losing reasons for dying.)

Paul: must go.

(Sun! Infinitely remote, nearest cause of all!)

Paul must be told to go.

(Where can deposed general, reduced to dull gray protoplasm by sun, go? Back to dull, gray, sandbagged underground.)

Paul must be made to go.

"Christ, Paul, *will* you cut it out? Riding him and riding him."

"Import-export man ought to export himself. Besides, he's anti-butterfly."

"You always massage your hand when you're angry?"

"Oh—my hand gets angrier than I do. Have to calm it down."

"In the car, when you talked about smelling Bass—you were doing it. Did Bass—have something to do with your missing fingers?"

"He threw some light on my hands and their mischief once."

"All right, it's your business. . . . What've you really got against Jacques?"

"You see his face when we were in the river? Man's a maniac: he'd fire 88's at gnats. Working up major rages about butterflies—because their wheels aren't loose! Because their wheels aren't loose!"

"You work up major rages about whores. Because their hips *are* loose. . . . Is it Emma you're after?"

"She's not my dish. She only intrigues me because I bore her. Know *why* I bore her? Because a soft worrier like me doesn't promise any big kicks where it hurts most. I'm a hoarder. Save my biggest kicks for myself. . . . But that son of a bitch of a dry goods salesman has all the comforts. My nose stays pressed against the window. . . ."

"You keep taking pokes at me, too."

"Get a Roumanian for a friend you don't need any enemies. . . . We've got a house full of Roumanians! Just dropped by to say hello: fighting the good fight while they wait for the ballrooms to open."

"That may go for Jacques."

"Not you? The five Romance languages're *your* ballroom; you'll run back to them when politics gets too grimy. As Jacques'll go back to his invoices and cafés, Emma to her search for the bedroom grail. . . . You're hobbyists. Politics is your hobby. You shop around for your sensations. Give me exporters who export around the clock, seven-day-a-week nymphomaniacs—enthusiasts. People who commit themselves to one thing and relinquish the outs."

"Bass relinquishes the outs."

"And I respect him. He's a worker."

"What do you work at, Paul?"

"Me? Isolation. Even there I'm a failure: I've always got company."

"You want me to go home, don't you?"

"The Old Man wrote New York about it yesterday. At my urging."

"You'll protect him by yourself?"

"You tourists may have thrown yourself into his fight for the moment but you keep the back door open, to beat it when you've had enough. That's the door George Bass will come through. If you get out—maybe I can close it. . . ."

"How wholeheartedly are *you* committed to V.R., Paul? You've begun to needle him about everything."

"My prerogative, friend. Sign your life over to another man—you've the right to tear his masks off. Maybe the duty."

"Maybe the need."

"Maybe the need."

The police had left their posts. They were sitting on the river bank eating their lunches, sunning themselves as they listened to Guillermo's fussing guitar. Paul had sent David to the southern corner of the wood while he himself took position at the northern end.

He had removed his still damp pants and hung them on a tree branch; butterflies conducted poking examinations about this large gabardine bird that hovered but would not fly. Paul sat on the ground in his shorts, tommygun across his lap, looking now at the huge orchids springing from the dead trees, now at Masson stretched on his raincoat near the river. Those senseless lunges at butterflies! Because their wheels were not something or other! Low comedy words: code worth breaking, it held the key to this dancer. What would this dancer really like to hit? Him, Teleki? A Teleki, for all his digs, was nothing to a Masson. Something deeper eating at him: Emma? A fury in his bowels about Emma, for sure. That love match was exposed high-tension wires: couldn't lash out at Emma, lashed out at butterflies? What did wheels loose or not loose have to do with Emma, Masson's big bug about Emma? No code for those key words. What did loose hips have to do with whores, his, Teleki's, fury against the whores? For he was furious with the sunshine too. Furious with everything that moved on the far side of the sandbags. Masson would have to go. Would have to be arranged, and quickly.

At the moment he thought this Paul heard a crackling in the sunken wood. He was on his feet and reaching for his trousers before he realized the irrelevance of this reflex modesty, the danger was not of being seen bareass but of being killed bareass; he stopped and raised his tommygun on the ready.

White shapes moving in the wood. They came closer: men dressed in white cottons. They emerged from the tangle of trees to stand in an unmoving group below Paul, fifteen péons in péon pajamas, some carrying machetes, some rifles. They stood and looked up at him on the rise as at locusts.

Plaster casts of tension over his arms and legs. He wished, absurdly, aware of the absurdity, that he had his pants on. Péons who held heads up and looked: it smelled of trouble; he felt, almost wistfully, that he could deal with it if he had his pants on.

They stood and looked up. Their weapons stayed, dead limbs, at their sides.

Through the strain Paul felt something else. A thawing or the promise of it. The final absurdity: relief, a young pleasure to see something gelled solid from the hints in the sparkled air and the rumors from around the corner—there, space taking, visible.

Praying, and numbed with the knowledge that he could generate such prayers, that it be the enemy. In a flicking illumination, much too much light being thrown on his hands, he saw: one of his central hungers was now for confrontations.

"Good day." He was surprised by the degree of welcome in his voice.

One of the men, the oldest, took a step forward.

"The one of the beard is here?"

Yes, we have beards in stock! A gross? What color?

"If he is?"

"It is said this man is here."

Who blabbed? The vultures?

"Perhaps you will tell me: by whom?"

The butterflies, those rumor mongers?

"This is not the important. We come to talk with the one of the beard."

"You will talk—or the rifles and machetes?"

"We talk as we talk. We ask that you stand aside."

"Lay your weapons down—I will take you to this man. I regret it but you cannot pass with your weapons."

Vultures angling down the blue, blue sky, butterflies twitching along.

"You will lay your gun down?"

"This I cannot do." Eyes fixed on the spokesman, Paul felt the large black birds' diagonal drops on his scalp, it tingled. He took a calculated chance, looked around quickly. No stir in that direction: guitar playing, butterfly pinning, blanket napping—these armed men were too low in the hollow to be seen from the riverside. "This gun fires many bullets very fast. Do not make me use it."

The deadened faces showed no anger, no interest.

"Can you shoot all?" the leader said. "Those who remain—"

"By the river are many police, with guns."

"Police? The bandit soldiers of your bandit leader."

Paul felt the hairs on the back of his neck moving. Very slowly, very gently, he slid his thumb along the gun to push the safety catch down.

"Police of your government, from the capital. Your president wishes to protect this man." Paul jerked his head again: the cops were still in a circle, singing. "You were told we come here for something? What?"

"This man comes with his own army and many guns to take our land. This we know."

Péons with land? Paul saw now that their huaraches were woven leather ones, their straw hats new and of some quality, they had bandanas of lively color above their shirts: men who could buy things in stores. Péons become small farmers, suddenly plugged into the world: suddenly with something to lose. Paul's finger curled around the gun's trigger.

"This man takes no land from the poor. In his own country he took land from the rich, only from them, and gave it to the poor, only to them." True, all of it true: but the word Kronstadt was a circling buzzard over the carcass of his fine words. "The police will come. They will speak as I speak." Trigger finger stiff and screaming for ease, he lifted his head and called as loudly as he could, aware of the shiver in his voice: "Sergeant! We have visitors! Guillermo! Bring your men!"

His finger would do it. The finger begged for permission. But the enemy had evaporated again. George Bass had crawled over the countryside, casting no shadow under this contamination of a sun, and left his droppings. These men were not Bass, only carriers of his droppings and not even conscious of it. Confrontation? Only a chance meeting of proxies. His finger was an aching hook on the trigger and he was praying that they would not raise their weapons.

The spokesman elevated one hand, his empty one. He pointed to the left and to the right. At the signal the men began to step sideways: bad to be a compact group if there was shooting; they spread out to form a spaced line. Faces saying nothing but eyes alive.

They stood motionless again. Paul stood motionless.

"We are not your enemies," Paul said. "Those who rob and kill the péons wish this man dead." But Kronstadt! But Kronstadt! The vultures made their relentless arcs back to '21. "This is their trick. If you kill this man you save them work. We carry guns against these people and no others. The police will tell you."

Straining for a sign of movement from behind.

"They are false police," the leader said. "They pretend to be of the capital but they are of Jalisco."

Caw! Caw! Jalisco!

Movement at his back: police on both sides, Guillermo rushing to him with guitar and drawn automatic. The sergeant stopped at the edge of the hollow and looked down in amazement.

"What do you do here, friends?"

"We look for the man of the beard," the spokesman said evenly.

Guillermo stared.

"For what?"

"He comes for our land."

Guillermo's eyes bulged.

"Land? Señor Rostov—your land?" He seemed not to believe; then he smiled. "Go home, friends. We come to visit the pyramids, to catch butterflies by the river, only that. In one hour we go and this is the end. The señor wishes no thing of yours."

"You wear the uniform to deceive. You are of Jalisco. You are the army of him who steals the land."

Guillermo's face colored. His heavy cheeks moved while the rest of his face turned stiff.

"Jalisco? What is this of Jalisco? Man, we are the police of the Distrito Federal!" he bellowed. "Listen! You understand what I say? Police of the Coyoacán station of the Distrito Federal! If one comes to take your land, even one small frijole from your land, we shoot him ourselves, we, we will shoot this pig! Some piece of shit without a name comes to you and tells you such shit and you—"

"Sergeant."

All heads swiveled.

It was V.R., no butterfly hunter now but a man summoning himself to maximum, arriving with quick stride at the edge of the hollow. Behind him, Marisha, Emma, Masson.

"Have your men stand back." Guillermo looked puzzled. "Tell them, please. I'll talk to these people."

For over a decade he had been firing mere words at an enemy continents away: field marshal trivialized to suburb pamphleteer. For the first time since he had been evicted from events he was confronting live men, had within reach a blooded situation. He was burning with the need to take hold of it, with his hands alone; to hurl himself at faces rather than dictaphones. His voice was again the voice of the Red Army commander, with fine steel in it, and his blue command eyes were fierce.

Guillermo nodded to his men. They stepped back.

V.R. went to the edge of the hollow and looked down. His lips moved in the hunt for words. He knew only a smattering of Spanish from the newspapers but he had to find the words to make these faces go mobile.

"You speak—of land," he began. "You, your fathers—fight and die—with Zapata, with Pancho Villa, with Madero—for land. For much time—no land—as before. Now—some places—the government takes ranches—gives land to péons—a few. Land is good. You say—not lose land. Good! This is good! This is—right! The land is—your name—your address in the world—your future! The man who puts hand on it—that man—steals your name—your address. You have the right—the duty—to destroy this man. This is—my first belief in life!"

Addressing himself, as once to soviets and Winter Palace mobs, to dead faces, dead trees; only the butterflies and buzzards moved. V.R. walked down the slope. He stopped three feet from the old man and with a quick movement pulled off the silly visored hat, as though it cramped thoughts with hair. Words! Where were the words that would free his tongue and let his visions come out as more than travelogues? He let the hat drop. Butterflies swooped to it.

Paul moved down to one side of V.R. His tommygun stayed poised but the feel of it was an abomination: the blue coldness of corpses. With no purpose formed he became aware of a fantastically bloated, upcupping purple orchid that sprang toward V.R.'s face from a green crawler coiled around a tree; without design he pulled it from its stem with his free hand and let his thumb stroke its thigh soft, vulva agreeable petals. The butterfly fragility of the flower counterbalanced the dead cold metal weighting his other hand and lessened his nausea. But he went on watching these men.

"I ask—one thing," V.R. said to the leader's macadam face. "Are you—true men? Now—do the—bad works of others—and know not that you do this—no, you are not true men! You are—animal! Burro! This is—the way of—burro. Put from you—the orders they speak in your ears—take the orders from inside—look with your own eyes! Listen to the drivers of mules—you are no more than mules! Mules do not own the land—they work for others! To deserve the land—be your own boss! You value—the name—the address—that come from the land? Then—have the free minds

—to go with the names and the addresses! I am—all my life—with those—who have the wish and the dignity—to stop to be burro! You take the land—stop now to take the orders! Learn this! Learn when—to make the ear deaf!"

Without the connective tissues of grammar and syntax, couched for the greater part not in true Spanish but in Spanish-sounding cognates for French and Italian words, it was not much of a speech in content. But the string of ragged commonplaces had been pulled from a hat of utmost feeling. The eloquence was in the hands and eyes, the square body gathered for evocation. A voltage of presence hammered through and around the trivial words.

Incredibly, as it had so many hundreds of times at steppe encampments and in convention halls, it found its mark.

(Once, once only, Paul thought, had the magnetism failed. The oratorical thunder had reached all the way from the Smolny Institute in Petrograd to the island of Kronstadt. The very walls of the fortress had shivered. The péon-sailors had remained deaf, rifles to their shoulders.)

In the faces the farmers turned to each other were large questions. The leader continued to regard V.R. for an examining moment, then wheeled about to see his comrades. Nothing was said between them, eyes simply interrogated eyes, while V.R. stood before them pushing his spilled gray hair into place. But when the leader turned again he no longer seemed to be convinced of anything, only tired; the rifle in his hand was a burden.

"My name is Rostov—Victor Rostov," V.R. said more quietly. "I live—Avenida Londres—Coyoacán—south of the City of Mexico. I wish you—to know the truth about me. Send to your president —ask if I am, yes or no, a guest in this country—and friend to the péon—all my life. Ask if in my life—I take land from the péon— or from the rich who drive the péon. If you find—one word from me not true—my home—is open to you. What questions you have— I answer. If you wish to know—why one comes among you—and tells you lies—I try to tell you the reasons for this—and show you the places—to find—if my reasons are true. Do not take my words for truth. Take the words—of no man! There is—at your back— no more whip—no more driver!"

The leader bent his head once, slowly.

"You do not wish to take our fincas," he said. "Good. Then another, the one who came here today, wishes to take from us more: our thoughts. Our people have a long history of being burros. We will not go back that way." He slung his rifle under his arm, pointed down. The vultures made derisive high sounds overhead. "I wish you a good day in the country. That you enjoy the pyramids and the butterflies."

His voice was courteous, grave. He did not smile, no light came into his features, but his tone was that of the unobtrusive host.

Warmth rose in V.R.'s face. He brushed back his thick hair with a sweep of both hands. The hand he held out was taken, undemonstratively.

"For these good words—thank you," V.R. said with great affection. "Come to see me in my house—bring your friends. We talk. This—for me—a privilege, señor."

The man bowed slightly. He turned and beckoned to his comrades. They began to file into the wood.

"Well done, Victor," Emma said from the top of the rise. "Oh, well done." She was close to tears but there was overriding pride in her voice.

"Olé!" Guillermo called out excitedly. "Magnífico! Olé!"

Spontaneously all the police began to applaud, hoisting their rifles high in the air with each exclamation: "Olé! Olé, Señor Rostov! Olé!"

V.R. was climbing energetically up the slope. He went to Marisha and took her hands.

"You see, Marisha?" he said joyfully. "When we talk to honest people—when they let us talk to the world—Bass doesn't have it all his own way!"

But it was not over yet. Guillermo had swung his guitar into position; as the shouts of his men died away he began to thump syncopated chords from the strings, laughing out loud in precise tempo.

The departing farmers stopped, the leader turned around and considered the sergeant.

He made a motion. He wanted Guillermo to come down.

Guillermo stopped playing immediately. Automatic again in hand, he scrambled down the incline.

The two men entered into a discussion involving much dramatic movement of eyebrows, shoulders, hands, elbows. The voices became passionate. Isolated phrases reached Paul: man, no; countryman, yes, yes; this is not the way; I tell you, the tapatío; but in Jalisco we; too many strings too fast; no, countryman; man, yes, listen.

At a high point in the debate Guillermo raised the guitar again and insistently struck a series of chords.

The old farmer shook his head. He snatched the guitar from Guillermo and played other chords, looser, softer, less bodied.

Guillermo described indignant negatives with both hands. He took the guitar back and repeated his chords with still more vigor.

They continued to argue back and forth for another time: slow, slow, friend; countryman, fast; no, fellow; absolutely, man.

The old man said a final sober word. Guillermo shook his head. The old man turned his back and followed his party into the wood; white cottons could be seen moving between the agony postured trees. The diminishing sound of twigs being cracked; they were gone.

Guillermo made his way up the hill.

"What was that all about?" Paul said.

"This man is crazy!" Guillermo almost shouted. His face was red again. "He is not only bigshot owner of land, he is big critic of the music, this one!" He moved his fingers over the strings of the guitar, thrumming the same tune he had been playing before but with less enthusiasm now, the sparkle gone. "He say, I play tapatío too fast and with bad chords, like one of Jalisco. I say to him, Jarabe tapatío is of Jalisco and must be play like those of Jalisco. He say no, here on plains of Distrito Federal they know how to make my dance better, more slow, the right way, with more chord, more like Sandunga! See?" He illustrated, playing the same number in the slow tempo of a dirge and making a face. "He call this what he play tapatío but is no tapatío, is song for the bowel movement!"

"You were arguing as though your life depended on it."

"My life, Señor Paul? No, no—yours!" He was completely serious. "Yes! They hear before, when I play Jarabe, and they know I am of Jalisco. Is true! I come from there it is five year now. Then you say, these men here, they are of police of Distrito Federal. The farmers think, if we are police from Distrito Federal why we play Jarabe like those of Jalisco? This prove to them we are false police, therefore bandits from far away—you understand this? So you are lie. So they are make up mind to kill you—only we come too quick. I apologize, Señor Paul. You to be full of bullets because I play Jarabe certain nice way? No, man! I do not like to see you kill by music critic!"

The others were at the blankets packing. His pants back on, Paul stood guard at the wood's edge looking up at the maneuvering vultures.

Magnificent, yes. Olé. Oh, well done. But if the general had to talk to the world of honest people about Kronstadt, where some péons, finished with the burro life, had decided never again to be burros? Who had told the ex-burros of Kronstadt to accept no orders, believe nobody, trust only in themselves? If Bass had put the vulture word Kronstadt in the farmers' mouths? If the farmers had stepped out, rifles and machetes raised, and spoken to the general the one unanswerable word: Kronstadt? As in the bombed-out church basement near Madrid, not much more than two years ago, men with hands tied behind their backs had looked straight at him, Paul Teleki, and screamed the word for which there was no answer.

The vultures cawed. Saying Olé to each other? Saying Kronstadt.

Frigid gun barrel in one hand, skin tender orchid in the other. Suddenly he howled.

He heaved the flower to the ground.

He hopped around, making snapping movements with the hand as though to throw off leeches.

Inch-long red ants swarming over his fingers. Biting. Crawling. Biting.

The pain, it was like the head to foot stings he had gotten once from a jellyfish in the Bosporus, like—focused sunlight boring smoky holes in his skin there near Madrid: he thought he heard Ramón sneeze again, twice.

He dropped to his knees, snapping the fingers. He pounded his hand on the ground, first the palm, then the back, until the ants were crushed or knocked off. He crowded the fingers in his mouth and bit on them hard, to drown the uninvited pain with another, more supportable because self-inflicted.

Crouching, he saw a vile thing.

The vultures had stayed on: maybe there was carrion deep in the wood, maybe a wounded forest animal was in hiding and the birds had caught the scent. Now, as Paul made sounds of hurt and flung his arm about furiously, he looked up and saw that one of the elbowy dead trees was grimed with vultures. They held to the branches in close military lines, black burlesque judges. They were looking steadily at him.

Too much!

After 48 sleepless hours spent in planning this picnic—flat tires, pyramid detours, Bass's long rat paw propelling finca péons through woods, Masson massacring butterflies and ranting about loose wheels —now stinking bird magistrates in session, echoing roped men in Madrid cellars, jeering down at him with their Kronstadts, Kronstadts!

Picnic? Picnic of abuse!

And his hand hurt. Under this epidemic of sun. Sun could sting too. Sun had once, outside Madrid, eaten his hand like an army of ants.

He was sure he heard Ramón sneeze twice, loudly.

All right! Rage in him he could not contain.

"Loose or not loose!" he shouted.

Positioning himself on his knees, raising the tommygun.

"So much shoe polish! Dare to judge!"

Taking aim, even as he heard the alarmed voices from the river, Guillermo's, V.R.'s too, asking what was it, was he all right, rising to his feet, taking careful aim.

"Pickpockets! Dull black mass to hell!"

Impossible hurt in his hand as his finger, needful on its own, pressed the trigger, spraying the branches and the black filths at attention on the branches.

Frantic phlegming and wing beating. But only half the birds got away, the others dropped by twos, by fives, as he moved the spitting pipe back and forth; exulting in it, for once meeting the world on his own terms as V.R. in his moment of glory just past had met it on his; but not with pale words, with hard bullets, the conclusive forensics to still the last questions.

He kept on firing, from left to right, back again.

He did not stop until the gun's circular drum was empty. The shouts were louder behind him, he paid no attention. He was weeping but not with soft sentiment, not as humanist, out of a fury big and blinding as the sun.

He threw the tommygun from him. He sat down and curled his arms around his knees; he was suddenly calm, as after a prolonged steam bath, and dry in his gut, cold as gunstock steel.

He sat that way for a time.

They were behind him, around him, speaking in blurts:

"Are you all right?"

"What happened?"

"Paul, Paul, are you all right?"

The voices stopped. They were all studying the ground, the litter of black vilifications. Aniline red running over black feathers; some of the birds were still alive, wings going flight nostalgic at the ground, bead eyes open, faces grinning grim toward the smiling uninvolved sun.

The others were silent. A void of shock around the ossified dull gray trees; butterflies made bright traffic through it.

Paul held his hand up. There were raised red splotches on the skin. New ones on top of the old ones.

"Been bitten. Big ants, red."

Marisha: "Alcohol, I will get the alcohol." She ran off.

David bending over. Paul felt his hand being taken delicately.

David: "I wet my handkerchief in the river before, it's still damp. Here."

Moist, cool something being wrapped around the hand.

David: "I've read about those little bastards. Pancho Villa used to bury prisoners in the ground up to their necks and pour molasses over them; the ants cut a living head down to bone in minutes."

"You don't understand," Paul heard himself say. "The orchid was so soft. They came out of the orchid."

The foulest thing of all, of course.

Marisha hurrying up. Cool, cool alcohol pouring.

Emma at last, in a small voice, pointing to the still flapping vultures: "Why? Paul, why?"

When he looked up it was not to Emma, his eyes, with a strategy of their own, searched out Masson and held him. Aware again of how much his hand was hurting and absolutely, icily desperate, he said: "Would butterflies do?"

"You've got to," V.R. said. "Get off by yourself."

They were heading back to Mexico City along the Teotihuacán highway.

"They say Lake Patzcuaro is very pleasant," Marisha said.

"Two weeks?" Paul said. He rubbed his injured hand. "How can I?"

"You make yourself too indispensable," V.R. said. "We have David and Emma; now Jacques. And the police count for something."

"Today's plot didn't work," Paul said. "They're already planning another."

"Plots take time," V.R. said. "You won't consider a vacation now? Good: we'll table the matter. Can't you at least take one night off?"

"Go into town tonight," Emma said. "Take the whole night: why not?"

"Who'll stand guard?"

"One night won't kill me," David said. "If you don't think that's safe—why can't Emma and Jacques stay with me?"

"We certainly can," Emma said. "You really need some time to yourself, Paul. Go to a nightclub, act a little silly, remind yourself that triviality's no crime. Dance! Even that! Do your famous rumba!" She leaned forward to Masson. Her voice chilled. "You can stay, can't you?"

"The whole night?" Masson said.

"Yes. Paul shouldn't feel there's a deadline."

"I—think I can do it. Yes. I'll just make a phone call from the house. . . . I have to get word from a wholesaler about some goods I've ordered."

"It's settled!" V.R. said. "Tonight Paul becomes a student of the rumba." He laughed. "On our staff we have the world's foremost assassin of butterflies and the new world's champion in the mass liquidation of buzzards: and both are addicts of the rumba! Your distinguished names will be in the history books, gentlemen! The outstanding dancers and fauna exterminators of our time! What do you say to that?"

Kronstadt.

Kronstadt must be said over and over to that and everything. The extermination of our time.

But Paul looked left to the pyramids, stark on the enduring plateau where retreating conquistadors had trailed their blood, and held his tongue.

CHAPTER X

Cough drops? No. Keys? Not likely.
What was the so special thing in Bass's pocket?
Ramón was trying once more to guess.

They were in the curtained back room of the Cantina de los Tres Quetzales, a workingmen's bar just north of the Plaza Comonfort and La Lagunilla, the Thieves' Market. Bass was drinking a gaseosa, Ramón a Moctezuma pale ale. Bass's right hand stayed in his jacket pocket, as usual, moving, as usual.

Over what? Not sugar cubes for horses or gum drops for toddlers. What, then? No telling. Metal cigarette container designed so thumb pressure on the side would release from the flip-up end a .22-caliber bullet? Possible: the commissariat technicians supplied such things. Or: silver fountain pen whose top discharged cyanide pellets when the clip was turned? Also standard equipment on the upper echelons. (Ramón remembered: George had given him one when he was sent to Ceuta to do the job on that colonel, what was his name, Ocho, Ochoa: worked fine.) Maybe derringer with electrical silencer? They too existed. Hard to say but no matter. Forever stroking it, whatever it was: drinking, talking, going down the street, he held to it as a holy man to beads. Announcing to the world there was something of note in his pocket, something worth investigating. And professionals, George repeatedly said, work hard to show the world they're not worth a second look. Lapse you would least expect from George, otherwise a hawk for details. Not a problem, of course. It did not so much worry Ramón as amuse him: then even George Bass had a style that was not all maneuvers. A waywardness in neat George Bass too. Getting more nervous? Sensing the bad and worsening trouble back home? Whatever: the hand burrowed and burrowed. It always delighted Ramón to see the upstart in a disciplined man: the Spanish anarchist in him? Even him, who had in Spain made a career of shooting anarchists? How the hand went on its own picnics. A drunk, a squirrel.

"Where the hell is he?" Ramón said.

"Something must have held him up."

"They've been back from Teotihuacán an hour. He should at least have called."

"They may be busy on another release. About today's doings."

"Too bad it didn't work. I did my best, George."

"I keep telling you: it did work."

"How? How? When I got through talking over a dozen of them left San Juan with their guns; they looked like they meant business. But the cops must have held them off."

"Or Teleki."

"That's what I'm saying—there couldn't have been any gunplay. I told you what the girls told Marcos: the whole party came back and not one was even scratched."

"Who was after scratches? The thing was to call attention to the girls. Ortega's *got* to pick them up now."

"George. My head is thick. You're saying what I did out there can get the girls arrested: I don't see how but all right. At least tell me this: how does it help if the girls *are* arrested?"

Bass sipped his carbonated drink. "Why would we expose our people out there? We failed at Teotihuacán—have to start from scratch—need more information—take chances—that's what I want them to think. That way *they* won't be so careful."

"But they'll know we're active."

"Tomás has to push it: tomorrow or the next day at the latest he's got to fix it so he stays the night there, I don't care how. . . . We've got the advantage now; three days from now it'll be gone."

"It may not be so easy for Tomás to arrange."

"Our mission is not to make things easy for Mr. Tomás."

"He knows it. He doesn't like us for it."

"It's not our objective to make him like us, either. . . . Everything's in order at your end?"

"Everything. The boys are standing by, the guns are all packed away, we did it Saturday night. . . . I don't like that part of it."

"It's the safest place. You'll be riding out there in three crowded cars, any one of them might be stopped: if the men were carrying an arsenal. . . . Don't worry about the guns! I'm the only one who's got a key."

"Another thing. Tomás. How can you trust this piece of nothing? If he doesn't do his job on the door—"

"He'll do it. He's very good on the alphabet, he knows after A comes B."

"Does he know B is his lordship and nobody else? You think he's figured out about the raincoat and the manuscript?"

"Maybe he hasn't faced it consciously. He doesn't like to look dreck in the face. But he's not stupid."

"If he guesses the meaning of Plan B even two feet below his brains, he'll do his job on the door. Good."

The wall phone rang. Ramón jumped up and went to answer it: "Yes?" He listened, his eyes opened. "I will tell him!" He hung up and said excitedly, "George, you're a magician! That was Marcos. The girls just came back to their apartment—under arrest! Five cops and Ortega with them. Marcos says it was funny, two of the arresting cops have been screwing the girls for days, their steadiest customers! Ortega searched the place himself. Five minutes ago he took Rosa and Sovietina off to jail."

"Marcos wasn't caught?"

"He saw the cops coming and hid upstairs in his own room."

"You see the moves? See? You make your mouth go a little in San Juan Teotihuacán: a few hours later, in Coyoacán, two girls get picked up. Cause, effect!" Bass spoke with satisfaction. "You—you said it didn't work, you dumbhead!"

The phone rang again. Ramón took the receiver. "Yes?" He stiffened. "Yes. . . . Ah. Tonight? . . . *Tonight?*" He listened again, lips moving from side to side in sucking motions. He nodded at Bass, gesturing with his thumb at the receiver and forming the word tonight with his lips. Bass stood. His head made vigorous dips in answer. "Good. We can make the delivery, count on it."

Bass's hand worked agitatedly inside his pocket. The moment Ramón hung up he said: "Him!"

"He's sleeping over—"

"Tell me his exact words."

"Staying with friends—won't be coming into town—wishes to know if his shipment will go out tonight."

"That's it. Word for word—"

"There was something else. . . . One of his business associates has been called away. Impossible to say when the man will return. He may not be on hand for the delivery either."

"The name? The name?"

"Peter Contrarios."

Bass seemed staggered. "Teleki? A bonus like that?"

"It's code?"

"I see what's happened. They feel so good about showing us up at Teotihuacán, Teleki's taking the night off! Justin on the door, Teleki nowhere in the house—it's beautiful. . . ."

"Now—if only Tomás can handle Justin. . . ."

"He will. . . ." Bass took his hand from his pocket and began to talk in systematic spurts. "There's not much time. . . . Send word to the boys. . . . Check the cars. . . . We'll meet at the assembly point. . . . Want to go over everything one last time before you start. . . ."

They arrived home before five. At six General Ortega was at the door demanding to see Señor Rostov. As soon as he entered the study he said without preliminaries, "You found more than pyramids in Teotihuacán." His attitude was a compound of outrage and satisfaction.

"You've heard about our adventures?" V.R. said lightly.

"Sergeant Guillermo stayed in Teotihuacán to investigate. He telephoned me. . . . The man who stirred up the farmers was gone, of course. We have a description: he may be a Spaniard. We also know that he arrived in the area forty minutes before you did. *Before*. . . . This poses a question—"

"How does Bass get advance notices of my movements?"

General Ortega nodded. "Your people do not have loose mouths, presumably. Then it had to be my men who talked. But to whom? And when? Señor Teleki told them the destination only this morning. . . . I have been in Coyoacán for the past two hours, looking into this. There *is* a plot against you. I have made some arrests."

"Congratulations! The shadows begin to take on substance!"

"My prisoners are women, two of them. Some of my men were intimate with them and answered questions about your household. . . . The women admit only to being prostitutes."

"Prostitutes who do research into my affairs?"

"And give themselves for nothing. They even bought the men presents, costly ones."

"Have you identified them?"

"In part. We will do better. . . . Both were recently in Loyalist Spain. One was a clerk and translator in an unofficial GPU prison. The other worked as courier for a foreign operative—one of his names was said to be George Bass."

"But there's no sign of Bass."

"A man rented the apartment for these two. The landlord remembers him: a foreigner, in his forties, thin, nervous, dark."

"And elusive. . . . Your police work has been impeccable." V.R. stood up. "You talk about Bass—you're somehow offended with *me*."

"Sir—when you attack the GPU—are you not somewhat in the position of an outraged parent who disowns his own delinquent son?"

"You graft strange fruits on my family tree."

"With your approval, at your urging, the Bolshevik regime built the secret police. And did you not, you personally, turn over the final Kronstadt repressions to the secret police? Today—forgive me—you are like a man who has started a riot and then cries for protection from the law. This offends my sense of logic, señor."

"Three days ago you would not believe the GPU exists. Today. . . ." V.R. looked sharply at the general. "You were, if I understand correctly, with Madero's armies?" General Ortega inclined his head. "And after?"

"I retired to my ranch."

"The moment the fighting stopped—you retired? When did you return to public life?"

"Only when Rubén Viedma became president. He is my old comrade-in-arms; he insisted I was needed; the government bureaus were full of corrupt people, he wanted a man he could trust to head the secret police. I accepted against all my instincts." General Ortega rose. "My biography is not at issue, señor."

"But it is! You made a revolution—then left for the country? You'd create a new society and abandon it next minute to the political winds—before it's secure? Sheer dilettantism, general. If you'd remained to help build the new state machinery, including the very necessary machinery of secret police—if you'd helped in *that* less spectacular and sometimes dirty work. . . ."

"My work was to help crush the vicious police of the old regime, not to help create their successors."

"Unusual policeman! You despise police states—and the police."

"This is the reason President Viedma insisted I be Chief of Secret Police. He did not want a policeman who enjoyed his work. . . . I felt at home in the army; things were aboveboard. Shall I tell you something? I grit my teeth when I go to my office now."

"We in Russia accepted the transfer from army to office."

"Carrying your machine guns."

"A new state is administered with guns. Until its enemies put away *theirs.*"

"But if the new police look exactly like the old? All policemen have a tendency to look alike."

"Then it's our fault, for not giving the new police new faces."

"How? By plastic surgery?"

"No; the surgery must be more than skin deep. Don't laugh. There's a first time for everything."

"Those who make a *career* of law and order—under any regime, old or new—are invariably the most lawless: imposing limits on others, knowing none for themselves. . . . I am a soldier. I am used to straightforward weapons. The policeman fights his suspect by stripping his moral clothes from him; he attacks from the safe side of a desk—with dossiers. . . . A vile thing, that two men should be placed in such a humiliating cat-and-mouse relationship. Humiliating to *both* parties."

"And it's not vile that two men should fire bullets at each other across a no-man's-land?"

"Less so—both have bullets. . . . Very good: Stalin could not have come to power without first taking over the GPU. You have written this yourself. What you have *not* written is that you and the other Bolsheviks perfected the GPU apparatus for Stalin to take over. Kronstadt was one of its training grounds."

"Revolutions spend themselves and recoil, general. The Russian people had exhausted themselves in their struggle; the workers of more advanced countries did not come to their aid. That was the disaster. Our one hope and perspective was the revolution in perma-

nence: proceeding to the full proletarian-socialist stage in our country, then sweeping into Central and Western Europe. We had banked
on the German and Polish workers, among others, to take over their
own governments and help our prostrate country. No help came:
reaction; apathy; the need for a vigilant police. . . . If you want
guarantees, don't try to make history; invest in three percent bonds."

"The paradox remains. Your protective apparatus turned on its
founding fathers and killed them off one by one. Now it comes for
you; even through the Teotihuacán woods. Perhaps you gave it too
healthy an appetite?" He pointed to the sandbags in the window.
"You refuse to be a dilettante. Here—locked out of the history you
made—what are you *not* a dilettante at?"

V.R. smiled. "Think of Stalin at this moment, cowering in the
Kremlin, wondering which of his handpicked guards will turn and
fire the fatal shot. *He* knows what it means to be cramped! He feels
more like a condemned man than I do! I have friends I can trust."

"Your enemies are more numerous."

"But three days ago you would not acknowledge them; now you
see them under every carpet!"

"And in some closets. . . . Your arguments, taken separately, are
brilliant, señor. But one flaw runs through them all."

"The flaws in men of action, general, are especially visible to those
who retire to the country."

"I am back in the city now. . . . The new regime must be on
guard, you say? Agreed. But—an arm needs exercise. A police arm
needs very much exercise. If the enemy does not provide it, the arm
will turn in other directions: Kronstadt."

"I seem to have stimulated your reading."

"I read many statements on Kronstadt, yes—but not *your* statement. I wait for it from week to week."

"I'm writing it now. . . . General, were there no Kronstadts in
your revolution?"

"I never exterminated my own men."

"How could you! You ran from power the moment you had it,
so others less squeamish would do the job for you! You were back
in your safe gardens; but Madero stayed. And the péons stayed:
they had no gardens to retire to! When the péons who had brought
Madero to power asked for land, did he give them land—or urge

caution, order, gradualism, law, respect for property rights? And when some péons, tired of waiting for the right papers, took the land: were they not driven off? . . . Villa and Zapata—they liked the musty smell of offices no more than you did; they went home to the country too. But they left behind an army of bureaucrats. Bureaucrats who did not hesitate to silence the péons when they shouted their needs too loudly; with bullets when necessary. . . . Yes, yes, your wild ones were put down, too. Those who go on fighting when the revolution's over, out of sheer inertia, or because they've learned no other trade—they have to be stopped, the revolution at a certain point applies its brakes and says enough. You helped to set a terrible bloody mechanism in motion. Then, from a distance, your back nicely turned, safe in your vegetable patch, you pretended an esthetic dismay with brakes! Not good enough, general! Can you leave a nasty job in the middle? This dilettantism shows more callousness about human lives than a thousand Kronstadts!"

"I was not a dilettante in my vegetable garden, señor. I grew much needed vegetables. And even developed new ones: I was an agronomist, first and foremost."

"But you deserted your vegetables for a time. . . . You wanted the nice taste of rebellion. The joy of a thoughtless hitting out at the fathers. But when you had to take the next step—to become a thoughtful father yourself and accept the headaches that go with fatherhood—when you had to see your own children rise up against you. . . ." V.R. shaped the underside of his beard with the backs of his fingers. "Our goal was and remains the anarchist condition, yes. A withering away of all fathers, all authority. But it could not be the first business on the agenda, as the Kronstadters thought, the best worker elements, at least. To live without regulation and not go amuck, men have to be transformed: a longterm business. Our immediate assignment was the transformation of society to make possible the new breed of self-regulated men. We accepted it. We accepted all the braking it entailed. Society had to be made to crawl before men could walk. And the Kronstadters, the worker militants among them, wanted to run: they had to be stopped."

"From 1904 to 1917 Lenin was the Bolshevik father: you were the favorite son in rebellion against him. In 1917—did you become mature enough to supplant the father—or did you only collapse like a helpless child in his arms?"

"The Bolsheviks in that year adopted my program: full, immediate, proletarian-socialist revolution—the permanent revolution. They were the only ones who did. Did I join Lenin—or did he join me?"

"Lenin came around to you politically. But you—you went all the way over to him *organizationally.* He accepted your program of proletarian revolution; you accepted his concept of hard one-party centralism." General Ortega drummed his fingers over the thick manuscript on the desk. "The collapse was yours; it is not socialism that is crushing Russia and coming after you now in Mexico, but— bloodthirsty centralism. It was not socialism that destroyed the Kronstadt sailors, but centralism. . . . The moment you trained the guns of centralism on Kronstadt, you lost your moral right to fight the end-product of centralism, Stalin."

"Sir: when you retired from the revolution to the country, did you not lose your moral right to question those who do not retire?"

V.R. was leaning toward the general, his eyes hard and unblinking. Ortega stared back; his lips thinned. "The police who associated with the prostitutes have been replaced. The new men are from my headquarters staff, they will be reliable." His voice was passionless and functional. "I was not led to the women by my powers of deductions alone. An anonymous letter came in my mail yesterday: here—a photostatic copy." He drew a folded sheet of paper from his tunic and handed it to V.R.

V.R. opened up the letter and read aloud the typewritten lines: *"Two women live at 178 Avenida Londres, Coyoacán. Their behavior is worth looking into. They are very good friends with the police guarding Victor Rostov. They entertain some of them in their apartment all hours of the night. Are they only admirers of the handsome police? Or are they more in love with the interesting pieces of information that can be obtained from the police when they are made drunk enough?"* That was all. No signature, no salutation.

"You have no idea who sent this?"

"We have not been able to trace it."

"A person of keen intuitions, whoever it is. . . . So, general. You're beginning to see the shadows. It should make you—a better policeman."

"And a more discontented one."

V.R. stood politely at the door, waiting for his visitor to precede him into the patio. Just outside, on the walk, Paul Teleki and David Justin were standing; obviously they had been listening. Paul had changed his slacks and sweater for a suit and a tie.

General Ortega went straight to Paul. "You must have seen these women. Why did you not report them to me?"

"Don't you remember, general? You don't like me to interfere in police affairs."

"You did not report the matter to Señor Rostov either."

"I had no evidence. Do you prefer charges against women for having big breasts? Anyway, I assumed that any close associate of your police must have a sterling character."

"Thank you for what you've done," V.R. said to General Ortega quickly. "It is extremely important to us." He said to David: "See the general to the door, please."

"You're going back to town, general?" Paul said.

"I am."

"Perhaps I can ride with you?"

"If you wish."

"Thank you. I'll be along in a moment."

David followed the general toward the door.

"Why didn't you tell me about the women?" V.R. said.

"Would you have accepted more guards—or prepared another statement for the press?"

V.R. watched the general go out the door. He shifted his eyes to Paul. "Go into town and enjoy yourself, Paul. Have your holiday. Tomorrow we will have our long postponed serious talk."

"About my future?"

"Your future; my past; and present arrangements." V.R. clapped his hands and called out loud: "Emma! Jacques! Marisha! David! In the study, please!"

The women came into the patio from the kitchen; Masson hurried up from the garden, followed by David. V.R.'s grim air left him, he was suddenly brisk.

"Good news! Two GPU women have been arrested for bribing our policemen!"

An uneasy looking back and forth.

"Bass is still free?" Marisha said uncertainly.

"This makes it harder for him!"

"Are these the girls I've seen outside?" Emma said. "There's something funny about this. They were so open about it, I never suspected. . . ."

"Lately they carried billboards," Paul said.

"Did stripteases," David said.

"You mean," Masson said, "they *wanted* to be caught?" He seemed astonished.

David was frowning. "Ortega found out about them from an anonymous letter." He considered Paul. "Who informed on them? Who stood to gain?"

"Who cares?" Paul said. "They no longer need their whores; they're set, they throw us a bone to put us off—that's all we need to know. Right, dialectician?" But the ironic question was addressed to Masson, not David.

"What?" Masson said. "Ah, who can tell how those people think?"

V.R. put his arm around Marisha. "First they bungle things at Teotihuacán, now this—they're in retreat for the moment! They've given us some real ammunition at last! What do you say to that interpretation?"

"What can I say?" Marisha said in her slight quaver. "That it is better to hear than Paul's."

"Gentlemen," V.R. said, "tomorrow's release has been written for us. We've hard facts to talk about for a change! After dinner— to work!"

"I'll stay if you want," Paul said.

"No, no. Emma and Jacques can handle it."

"V.R.," David said, "can I see that photostat?" He took the paper from V.R.'s hand and bent over it.

"A very good evening to everybody," Paul said. "I'm off to see the sights."

"Pretend you never heard of politics and have a good time," Marisha said.

Paul thanked her, made a mock bow to all and went off to the door. V.R. walked along with him. Paul reached for the wall buzzer, hesitated.

"I don't have to pretend," he said, puzzled. "That's it. Politics is forgetting it ever heard of *me*. I'm losing my political hold on things. I can't *think* politically any more. Something—personal—is rising up in me and pushing all the other things out. I take everything personally now."

"Kronstadt too?"

"Even that. It makes my head spin. To take things personally— you need some training in how to be a person. We have no schools for that. . . . Victor. I'm going to pieces. I've no idea what it is. It's Kronstadt and it's more than Kronstadt. I have serious differences with you—I'm losing my politics, you're holding on to yours with both hands—but that's no excuse. I don't get anywhere by badgering everybody. . . . I'm sorry. Nobody appointed me the head voice of conscience to the world. . . . I don't even have the vocabulary for that line of work. . . ."

"It doesn't have to be settled tonight." V.R. patted the younger man's arm. "Go into town. Get drunk if it suits you. Put your face close to something without a handkerchief over it. Remind yourself that a good part of the world is simply indifferent to you: it can be refreshing."

The Buick bumped along Avenida Londres toward Insurgentes. They sat silently in the back. When the car turned into the highway the general sat up straight, nodded emphatically, and said, "Today's picnic—a complicated affair. Yes, I begin to see. Incredible! So many Basses to deal with—and yet! His biggest struggle—to the death, yes, literally—is with *you!*"

"General," Paul said with irritation, "Stalin is the one who isn't pleased with Rostov's program. I *agree* with it."

"Do you? Even with his program for picnics and tours?" The annoyance went from Paul's face; he looked confused. "Look here. When you called me two days ago to ask for the motorcycle escort, you spoke of this picnic with a cold fury. You're against these outings! You've been against them from the beginning!"

"We have our differences about how to run the house; of course. Petty details."

"Not so petty. . . . Hear me out! For months I have been considering the problem of Paul Teleki: an angry man, chronically angry—why? I have asked myself the question many times. Now I see! Your anger is not really against the police, the outsiders, the general world you cannot manipulate. First and foremost it is against—Victor Rostov! That part of the world closest to you, that you can command and manipulate least of all! You wish to bury him alive: he goes on picnics!"

"Each point of view is understandable."

"But not why they stay together under the same roof. . . . Your household has two aspects. Come, you know that the externals can be looked after by my police; some may be incompetents, some can be seduced by clever and well-subsidized women, but with twenty of them on the street your house is safe—from *outside* attack. The problem, then, is *inside* your walls. If the door opens there is danger, if it remains shut you are secure. But the door is operated from the inside, you have seen to that. That door is the uncontrollable factor. It is operated—by Señor Rostov—his whims!"

Paul ran his fingernails along the window pane. "I repeat: temperamental frictions. Victor's simply a man who's been in shackles too long, he needs to stretch and look around. He's lonely, he feels cut off. It's only natural. Much as I feel obliged to fight it."

"Lonely! Cut off! Themes of trashy novels and soap operas, young man! Victor Rostov *chose* the career of loneliness; great public figures do. If butterflies and pyramids were his first need. . . . Did he mope about like a self-pitying character from a potboiler serial when he was in the Tsar's prisons, in Siberian exile? He asks for this isolation today as he did under the Tsar: he did not have to undertake a total struggle with Stalin! No, Señor Teleki. He is a brilliant man but not a sentimental man. Sentimental clichés are not his gasoline. He least of all can feel himself mistreated by events. He is not a dilettante as a prisoner. . . ."

"What are you saying? That he doesn't want to live?"

General Ortega drew from his side pocket a slim volume. He opened it. "I become a great reader. I have been studying a volume of Bolshevik reminiscences by the old Commissar of Education, Lunacharsky—*Revolutionary Silhouettes*—you know it? Here—quite an interesting passage I have marked. . . ." He found the place and began to read: *"For work in political groups Rostov seemed little fitted, but in the ocean of historic events . . . only his favorable side came to the front. . . . Lenin never looks at himself, never glances in the mirror of history, never even thinks of what posterity will say to him—simply does his work. . . .* A trifle naive, that, but no matter. . . . *Rostov often looks at himself. Rostov treasures his historic role, and would undoubtedly be ready to make any personal sacrifice, not by any means excluding the sacrifice of his life, in order to remain in the memory of mankind with the halo of a genuine revolutionary leader. . . .*" He closed the book and set it on his lap. "He looks all the time into the mirror of history now. It is being shattered before his eyes, and his face with it. Kronstadt is only one of the stones."

For some time Paul was quiet, watching the villas rush by. "If that is so," he said at last, "why doesn't he get rid of me?"

"Can you say that he will not, eventually?" General Ortega returned the volume to his pocket. "In the meantime: three days ago you received a letter from your friends in New York, proposing that several more guards be sent to you. Men who are good with guns. Señor Rostov refused."

"Because of you!"

"I would let them come if he insisted, he knows that. . . . There is also the question of Justin. Your friends wished to send a real bodyguard. Señor Rostov insisted on—a translator."

"We needed one. Badly."

"You could have had both. Is it not clear: the man you protect has outlawed guns in his house? . . . He keeps *you,* yes. For the time being. He must make a certain minimum show of defending himself—before the world, before his friends, most of all before himself. But he makes a mockery of this defense. He runs more and more to the pyramids and the butterflies. . . . You are in a constant conspiracy against him—to guard him in spite of himself. . . . This most professional of public men has become a dilettante —at staying alive!"

"You keep using that word."

"I have come to see: this is a drama of dilettantes pretending to be professionals. On all sides." The general dropped his gaze to his fingers and his voice became blurred and slower. "But do not deceive yourself that it is easy to run a large experimental ranch. To develop seven improved varieties of the mescal plant, and a longer lasting mango fruit too, takes work. Not to mention the very promising H-strain maize. Contributions can be made in different ways. In a sense politics is an offshoot of vegetables." His head jerked up, he looked startled. "Excuse me. I was thinking of something else."

"Let's assume you're right. *Why* would Victor want to die? Where's the sense to it, after such a life?"

"To keep the meanings and shapes of that life from exploding in his face, perhaps. . . . Look here: Stalinism is a fever and a holocaust, as much so as Nazism. When Hitler set up his Gestapo he patterned it exactly after the GPU, he could find no better model: I read that in one of Señor Rostov's books just last week. But Rostov was himself one of the founders of the Cheka, out of which grew the GPU. Unless he can prove, absolutely, beyond the shadow of a doubt, that there is no line of blood that leads straight from Kronstadt to Stalin—from centralism to absolutism—his whole life work is in question. He cannot find the proofs!"

"Are you in a good position to be so critical of secret police?"

"The best," General Ortega smiled without amusement. "I am a dilettante policeman."

"Have you heard this saying?" Paul said as though to himself. "A man spends his first thirty-five years forming his premises, his next thirty-five trying to keep them from looking too ridiculous?"

"A clever observation. No, I have not heard it."

"Somebody was saying it recently. He may have made it up."

They were approaching the downtown area. At the Cuauhtemoc statue the chauffeur turned from Insurgentes into the garden-ramped Paseo de la Reforma; ahead the traffic circle with the figure of Columbus rising over it could be seen.

"Where would you like me to drop you?" General Ortega said.

"Plaza de la Reforma, anywhere around the Plaza will be fine," Paul said distractedly. "So: Rostov chases butterflies—my blood pressure goes up? That's your theory?"

"Señor Rostov is a dilettante as a ward. That makes you, does it not—a dilettante of a guardian."

"Tell me: who do you think wrote that anonymous letter about the whores?"

General Ortega looked at him with a composed face. "Not Bass."

"Why do you say that?"

"Bass wanted the women arrested. But he had other ways to bring them to our attention. That was the only reason for the Teotihuacán business, of course."

"Of course. Then who wrote the letter?"

"Someone—who has a thirst for happenings? Who is fed up with impasses? . . . Let me ask *you* something: when do you think Bass will try again? Try seriously?"

"There was an apparent failure at Teotihuacán. The whores have apparently been taken by surprise. This suggests a delay; all signs point to their needing time. . . . So I would say soon. Very soon."

"Yes," General Ortega said. "Yes, I think it will be very soon now. Strange. A few days ago I questioned that they were here. Now I feel them behind every tree." He spoke to the driver, the car pulled up across from the bright lights of the Hotel Reforma. "Your corner, Señor Teleki. It has been an illuminating talk."

Paul moved forward on the seat. "You're right, of course: everything depends on the door being opened. How do you think they'll manage that?"

"The door opens only one way, señor—from the inside."

"If your police keep all traffic away—"

"Your people insist on a certain traffic. . . ."

"Yes," Paul said slowly. "Too much traffic; too many dilettantes. That's what makes my blood boil. That most of all."

He climbed out of the car and shut the door. General Ortega leaned toward the open window.

"The traffic?" he said. "You are not angry about the traffic. You are not really angry with Señor Rostov, finally. What you find intolerable now is—yourself. Señor Rostov has one profession today: suicide. To be bodyguard to a dedicated suicide—what does this say about *your* profession?"

"What's the profession of a Chief of Police? Philosopher?"

"I was made Secret Police Chief precisely because of this softness. This perhaps dilettante inclination to thought."

"Thanks for the very soft and thoughtful ride." Paul turned to go.

"May I ask," General Ortega called, "where you are going?"

"I'm off to be a dilettante tourist."

❧ DIOSDADO

He did not know how automobiles run but he knew how they are put together. When he took them apart in the Coyoacán dump it was not enough to remove the tires, the lights, the seats, the transmission belt and other usables. Also important was to look in the places to keep the things: many excellent articles were sometimes left there, eyeglass cases, oil cans, maps, jacks, sun tan lotions, pens, pencils, books, magazines, shoe laces, bathing suits. Articles which could be sold to the secondhand dealers of the stalls of the market place.

But the places to keep the things were sometimes locked. It was necessary to know how to open the locks.

He knew the tricks of the locks. He carried in the pocket of his shirt the strong wire and the thin piece of metal.

Now, approaching the green Packard on Avenida Londres, rolling the wheel that was to be returned, he was aware of the wire and the metal pick in his pocket. Slipping the wheel on the bolts, beginning to place the nuts on the bolts, watching carefully the policía across the street, he felt these objects making suggestions against his chest.

The Packard had returned over an hour ago.

The sick one with the handkerchief always to his nose had gone fast with his friends into the pink blue house.

The police were back in the wood shack, talking.

To the west the dropping sun made paint of the sky.

Against his chest the wire and metal, making loud suggestions. Under his hands, behind the wheel he was making tight, the place to keep the things, without a doubt locked.

His fingers felt for the handle.

Tried to turn it.

Locked.

He was interested in this locked place. This morning, when the tire made a noise, when he was standing in the street waiting for permission to change the tire, he had heard the talk between the two men of the pink blue house. The tall and not happy one, with eyes that did not stay in one direction, who always drove the Packard. The smaller one, of the black hair and the machine gun, who sounded like the boss. They talked in another language but they pointed in their talk to this locked place. The word serapes had been spoken several times. Not serape. Serapes.

Diosdado had a serape for the nights of cold or the days of rain, a man needs only one. But there were those in the market stalls who sold serapes. Therefore bought them.

He had no bad thoughts against the tall one with eyes that walked. This one gave him the tire and also the money. But there were perhaps many serapes in the locked place. If many, the tall one could give away one serape and not suffer from it: a man needs only one serape.

Saying this to himself, watching the policía though with head down, he took the loud wire and the noisy metal from his pocket. His hands went to the lock and worked fast.

He twisted the handle. It turned, the door came open.

Looking across to the guardhouse, head down, he lifted the door a small way.

Bending lower, he put one hand in.

Blankets. Many blankets.

Good, thick wool.

Of so many one would not be missed.

His hand began to fold one blanket into a bundle.

Inside the blanket something hard and cold.

Metal.

Heavy.

His hand pulled the hard and heavy something free of the blanket and he bent to look.

Machine gun.

His hand felt in the other blankets. Hard and heavy objects in them.

Many blankets, each wrapped over a machine gun.

He had no thought to take a machine gun. True, machine guns

were worth much and there were many. But at the market stalls was none who might buy and sell machine guns.

He pulled the top blanket away from its gun and lowered it to the ground.

Slowly, watching the policía, he pushed the door shut and turned the handle.

The lock snapped and was locked.

Head low, eyes on the policía, he bent and folded the blanket. His shirt was open, he was able to get the blanket around his waist under the shirt. He was able to button the shirt.

He finished tightening the wheel. Saying to himself: Serafina was against the chicken?

Walking without haste, not to his hut but along Cortés toward the market place, studying his feet, feeling the blanket rough but friendly against his skin, he added numbers. From the sale of the tortillas with frijoles, one peso and some centavos; for the changing of the tire, two pesos; for the blanket he was about to sell, at the least three pesos. A total of six pesos and some centavos.

And this was not to consider the tire, which, being new, except for the few machete holes of no importance, was in itself worth much.

And Serafina had been against the chicken?

A day was good, a day of feasts, a day for chicken, when it brought one automobile tire and no more.

Months since he had had in his pocket the sum of six and some pesos.

All this because he had pushed his machete in the tire of the Packard and made the tire to be bad. A thing for which on other days they would put a man in jail. Today, for spoiling the tire, there fell into his pocket six some pesos and also the tire: good wages not to be understood.

A day for chicken, clearly.

With some of the money he would buy rice at the market, it would be a day of rice with chicken for all in his house. The little ones had not had chicken for some months, the youngest, never. They danced to see the head come off the chicken. Chicken they liked better than candy.

Was the chicken more wages for spoiling the tire? For something. For things not understood. But are there not things not to be understood but only tasted?

Who can understand a chicken?

Serafina, woman, the rice with chicken tastes good.

CHAPTER XI

Panning shot of a massive building topped by a lit-up Soviet star. The newsreel commentator spoke out in doomsday basso:

". . . . Commissariat of Foreign Affairs—Kremlin Square—headquarters of Vyacheslav M. Molotov. But—for the past ten days— Russia's kewpie-faced Foreign Minister has not been seen here. His whereabouts are unknown. The mystery of the week! Where—is— Molotov?"

Dissolve. A more ornate building. Rising above it an all elbows shining swastika.

". . . . The Reichschancellery—Unter den Linden—Berlin. This week intense activity here at the hub of Nazi diplomacy. Jackbooted S.S. troops patrol the area. . . . Rumors this week are flying thick and fast across Europe. From Oslo to Lisbon they whisper—Molotov is in Berlin! Meeting secretly with monocle-wearing Nazi Foreign Minister Joachim von Ribbentrop!"

Cut to a low adobe villa on a sleepy street. Wooden shack in front of it. Police standing about in groups.

"Today—in far-off Coyoacán—from his carefully guarded villa— lion-maned Victor Rostov growls defiance at his old enemy Stalin. His charge—Stalin is preparing a pact with Hitler! A Nazi-Soviet Pact—against the West!"

Wide pan from villa to deserted street. View of the hut on the corner opposite, a Packard touring car parked outside it. The camera held for a moment on a péon bent over in the nearby vegetable patch, hoeing with his machete between stalks of maize. The péon looked toward the camera with a messageless face.

Cut to interior garden of villa. Victor Rostov standing erect and tumble-haired by an orange tree. Speaking ringingly:

"Naive people will say that the coming rapprochement between Stalin and Hitler makes an enigma of the Moscow Trials. No: it is the logical end-product of those Trials! Those judicial frame-ups— impossible amalgams, naming me time after time as the chief Hitlerite conspirator—were needed—to prepare the Russian people and the world for this rapprochement! The shocking idea had to be introduced first as a plague—then as a national policy! Stalin had to kill his opponents—on the grounds that they were Hitler agents—before he could consummate his treacherous union with Hitler—without opposition! I am the only one left who can speak out against this crime with the authority of the revolution. He will have to kill me too. . . ."

The commentator, in Armaggedon tones:

". . . . Strange, strange political winds whistling through the diplomatic back alleys of uneasy Europe this week! Devious and disturbing are the rumors that fly around the globe—as murky as the dark Russian soul itself!"

This was the Teatro Cine, on San Juan de Letran. In the last row of the almost deserted orchestra, close by the aisle, George Bass shifted in his seat and made a noise in his nose. He was wearing a dense beard and mustache, his hand moved steadily in his jacket pocket.

Murky Russian soul! Chestnut time!

News with a mold on it. Word circulating for months through the apparatus of important doings between Molotov and von Ribbentrop; talk of it in Madrid as far back as '37; even said that Stalin stopped the Spanish revolution dead in its tracks to give him better bargaining power with Hitler: so he could say to Hitler: "See? You don't have to worry about *me* making revolutionary troubles in the world: the anarchists and socialists and Rostovites stirred things up in Spain, my people stamped them out: you can do business with me." Some in position to know claimed Stalin had been after Hitler for this understanding since 1934. Hitler played cozy about the first overtures. Wanted to be shown what was in it for him. Now he saw: his side was winning in Spain. But the liberals never saw. Too busy applauding Stalin for his Popular Front sweetness and light in Spain. Now the Pact was world-shaking news to them.

The Popular Rear! Surprised by everything they help prepare and sell.

A pleasure to listen to this Rostov, after the drools from liberal do-goods and see-nothings. A trained and sophisticated political mind. Went to the foundations of a matter. Of course. Trials were needed before the Pact. Idea of agreement with Hitler a jolt. Had to introduce it in stages: first as plot. After that, no novelty or shock power to the idea. Coming from the regime itself, officially, will be palatable. Can the regime be anti-regime, Rostovite? It *kills* Rostovites! (The inflexible ones who might make beside the point moralizing noises when the Pact comes.) Rostov working with Hitler must be in Hitler's pocket. Stalin working with Hitler must have Hitler in *his* pocket. All the badness in the idea pinned to Rostovites. Rostovites wiped out—idea remains, minus its badness. Pea-brained fellow travelers! Loved the Trials, sold them to a doubting world. Travel with anything that moves fast and makes enough noise but always five steps behind. Pact would show up the Trials for what they were. Thereby showing up the liberal bootlickers who supported the Trials, supported everything that came from the progressive above and with the stamp of left authority, for what *they* were. Rub their snouts in the facts for once.

Murky soul of the ass kissers!

Deal with Hitler necessary. To turn his appetites toward the West; in any case, to gain time. More there? The strong joining the strong? Maybe that too. As it should be. The West going down the drain. Nazism and sovietism the emergent powers. Poles apart? Mostly in the propaganda. Maybe just coming at the same idea from opposite directions. Seeds of socialism in these Nazis: National *Socialism*—not an accident, that wording. Stalin planning toward an end, many ends. These liberal idiots swamped by systematic thinking. Never understand the power game: paint pretty brotherhood pictures in the sky and blabber about deviousness and dark souls down below. Lot of fellow travelers stuck too hard on heroic politics to be thrown off even by rigged Trials and engineered Spanish defeats. Pact would throw more of them off. Good thing. Clear the air.

Bass was bored. He twisted and turned in his seat, stretched his fingers in his pocket. He had not come here to listen to some grammar school hash of politics. *The Hardening Trees* was playing in this Teatro. He was fond of American gangster movies. Also, it was said this particular movie was such a hit with Stalin he had it run off two or three times a week in the Kremlin.

Bass hated politics mixed in with his amusements. Party had made deep inroads into the arts in New York, London, Paris. Many plays in those cities nowadays filled with the arise ye downtrodden sentiment. When in those cities he never went to see such tripe shows. Long ago he'd had a belly full of the talk. What a relief to sink down from the open party, the talkers, into the apparat, the doers. Who manipulated the party from below without the talkers even knowing. Like the Mexican party. Did the windbags of the party in Mexico City know why they were until today splashing big headlines and spouting loud speeches about Victor Rostov the Hitlerite agent? And why, starting today, exactly today, they would be making headlines and speeches about Rostov the agent of American imperialism's redbaiting Dies Committee? They did not. Had their excuse to talk, that was enough. But they talked for one reason—because George Bass, through certain quiet channels, told them to talk. To build up the right atmosphere for tonight, George Bass's night. Their talk was needed to keep attention away from the green Packard parked on Avenida Londres, where the péon chopped up the ground with his machete. Tonight, in Coyoacán, they would make a better base for Molotov in Berlin—*they:* not the loudmouths, the quiet workers of the quiet apparat. Was it the loudmouths of the party who maneuvered the green Packard into position?

The movie was beginning. He sat up straight, his hand rested in his pocket.

A highway gas station and hash joint in the New Mexico desert. Interesting location. Promised action.

Truck driver over coffee mug: "Looks to me like Russia's got the whole world on the run. Know why? Those people are making new things, a whole lot of them! What're we doing over here? Trying to keep our old things going—oiling, patching, wiping off the rust. . . ."

The hell! Two-bit messages from gangster stories now.

Bass's mind wandered. He thought of Molotov in Berlin. Agreement would go through, no question. Number One set on it. If it wasn't near would they be so anxious to close the book on Rostov? And substitute the Dies Committee line for the Hitler line? Rostov had to be shut up before the deal was made public. Could make a racket about it. . . . Pact would mean interesting shifts in the apparat work. Already signs of it. Until last year good part of the work was counter-Gestapo. In the last months, with Spain finished, an easing up on the Gestapo. First, Spain laid away, second, GPU letting up in Gestapo's direction: Hitler bound to be impressed. More to follow. Pact would mean collaboration between GPU and Gestapo in some areas. Sharing of information. Exchange of prisoners. (Already started, it was said.) Division of labor on mutual anti-West projects. Nothing alarming in that. Who had the GPU's rich experience in handling the Gestapo? GPU would run rings around them. Gestapo people often hotheads, drum beaters. Not a blowhard in the GPU: organizers, people with cool heads who did the job. Would lead the Gestapo around by the nose. Be a vacation, after Spain, after Coyoacán—

First truck driver: "I'll tell you something else: they've cut out crime in Russia too. You know how? By cutting out the thing that makes crime—greed—the gimmes!"

George Bass winced. It made his false whiskers tickle his face. Wetwash ideas! No crime in the fatherland? And the countrywide purges and trials? Fire drills? And the fifteen million in punitive labor camps? Picnickers? Exactly a hundred and seventy million greeds in Russia. Where there's a person there's a greed. But organize the greeds—mesh each man's into the next one's—weed out those solo types who won't mesh—

Tweedy-bummy Leslie Howard had come on. Beat down poet type. Eating pie and drinking coffee. Talking to the young Bette Davis waitress.

Down-in-the-soul Howard: "Am I searching for something? I— I guess I am. Something that an intelligent man could believe is worth feeling for—and dying for."

Bass grunted. Getting more and more idiotic. What was worth dying for? Death, only death worth dying for. Poetic people always looking for something to die poetically and promptly for. If not Russia, universal suffrage, campaigns against the tse-tse, euthanasia —poetry. Did they really want a new world or were they only set on getting out of the world altogether? Using the one as dressing on the other? Even Rostov. Even him. Big soft poet element in him. What was he dying for tonight? Because he let the wrong Packards park outside his house. There were ways to keep the Packards at a distance. If the will was there. . . .

George Bass had seen interviews with candidates for the apparat. Had conducted some himself. When they questioned candidates in the Commissariat the big point was always: why do you want to work in the secret cadres? If the people began to run at the mouth about their visions of a greedless new order and their willingness to give their lives for same—they got thrown out. Fast. The apparat needed levelheaded people who wouldn't blow up in a pinch. Those emotional ones who dealt in slogans and exclamations could blow up any time.

Bass remembered what he had himself answered to the key question, that crucial day in 1925 in the Deputy Commissar's office: "Why do I want to transfer from the open party? When I work I like to see results. The more I see of open politics the more I realize it's more than anything a big debating society and the people in it amateur noise makers. The professionals in this world today work with more quiet. The people coming to the top all over, today, they're the managers. Right now the biggest need, if you ask me, is for good managers underneath, out of sight—to set things up for the right managers on top. I like the feeling of being a professional, in any line of work." He'd started at the GPU training academy the next morning.

Some gangster movie! Full of talking poets!

He took his hand from his pocket. In it was a large convex disc of glass with a brass ring around it. With the other hand he began to move a fine emery cloth over the glass in steady counterclockwise sweeps.

No action in this talk opera until talky Howard got his poet ass out of the way. All right: then the big question for tonight. Question he'd come to the movie house to mull over. Ramón's boys had instructions to fire three feet over Tomás's head. Instructions could be changed.

Three feet up, Tomás stays snothead Tomás.

Three feet down, Tomás is a chop suey.

Temptation, a big temptation, he thought as he polished the glass with precise movements.

Tomás the shit. One slick and hot head.

That one had something worth dying for. His damn greed for momma and momma's scalp both.

Paul Teleki had reasoned that a Police Chief's car would not be followed. The few times he'd taken a bus or cab into town he'd had the feeling there was someone close behind; the idea of another person usurping his footsteps, a stranger linked to him only by a commonality of footsteps, drove him wild—the ascetic by choice wants no camp followers to his few limping revels. Because they are revels? Or because they limp?

When he left General Ortega he caught a cab at the Plaza de la Reforma and drove to a point near the Zócalo Cathedral, on Monte de Piedad. Another cab took him to the Funeral Flower Market on Hidalgo, just back of the Alameda; a third, to the Follies Bergère building off Plaza Garibaldi. Going from there on foot, checking sidewalk traffic by its store window reflections, he got back to Juárez and entered Sanborn's resturant. It was too early for Mexican diners but the place was filled with American tourists, nobody gave him a second look as he picked his way through.

In the men's room he took from his pocket a wide, bristly mustache and pasted it with care across his lip. On his head he stretched a black beret. Seeing himself in the mirror stripped of his usual distinctions, leveled to the class of nonentities, one more bit of barbering and tailoring, nameless and therefore eligible for all transactions, he felt his heart speed up. With a change of face he sensed possibilities swing open; it made him feverish, he was not used to expectation.

Nobody looked at him when he walked out. He was set loose from all eyes: it affected him as both a sedational tonic and a loud shout in his ears. He was tense as he went past the Teatro Cine— *The Hardening Trees* announced on the marquee: enough of calcified forests for one day!—then east along Emiliano Zapata, then back past the ruins of the old Aztec pyramid across from the Museum and the National Palace. Soon, without planning it, he was in the slums of the Old City to the north.

He let the curbs direct his feet: at the end of the night there would be a girl, there would have to be a girl, but no whores, no C.O.D. spasms; telling himself that, he found he was turning into the Organo, the Street of the Everythings, going past the cribs over whose split doors the whores leaned with breasts spilling, some with pastepot smiles, some not bothering to smile but talking up their prices and pretties in bored voices, street peddlers hawking penny wares.

"Want something good, sonny?"

"Man, come in, it is nice here."

"Two pesos, you have a big party."

"Everything you like."

A Hindu woman with a caste mark on her forehead said, "Here, man, you want to be kissed all over?"

A heavy young mulatto ran her fingers up his arm and half sang, "Look, how big," pulling her loose camisole down to expose perfect coffee breasts: "All for you, boy, take it, take it"—he jerked away as though slapped.

Had enough of harpies in ideologies.

Ideologies with tinted claws and lipstick.

Offering slogans as ready breasts. Saying, take, take, all for you.

No resales tonight. Glaze of thumbprints on them. He would rather have the fish-stall girl with the bad skin, aromatic with red snapper, who admired him because she was sure, though he had never said so, that he was the number one porter in a Londres house and thus a man with position and a future.

She at least *tried* to see him. Not her fault if she got him confused with somebody else.

Politics makes strange bedfellows: would he ever in life, if choosing freely, be in the same room with a Masson, an Emma, even a David; even a Victor Rostov? Who never saw him, only his membership card?

Beds make stranger bedfellows: no whores tonight. He wanted, begged for, the sign of one uncalculated impulse in the world toward him. For once to be neither customer nor target: simply a focus and a power to draw and a source of responses.

Then why walk down the block of mouths, breasts, thighs, vaginas by the barrelful, wholesale, in packinghouse lots: where quantity was most reluctant to make the leaping transformation to quality, sluggish maneuver to free impulse?

To prove to himself again what an incorrigible target he was. How the world made him no true offers.

They called, whistled, clawed for his jacket, his pants, the salesladies, the programs, and he threw off their hands and began to trot, his less principled groin telling him no, his over meticulous mouth twisting with the bad taste of this concupiscence that haggled. Heart racing now: threads of sweat twining down around the false mustache, as though its unrooted hairs were themselves sweating with this nausea.

He turned into the first cantina he saw, a blue walled workers' bar with a zinc counter. He drank down a beer in one swallow and signaled for another. He was calmer now, and within the calm more endline hollow. Looking out through a side window he saw a crowd down the block, grouped around a crude structure with loose canvas sides and a domed canvas top. What was it, he asked the bartender.

"The carpa," the man said.

What?

"The carpa? A tent put in the street. A tent for the shows— clowns, jokes, music. Our good clowns come from the neighborhood carpas. Cantinflas comes from them."

A vaudeville! Be a target for a vaudeville.

He paid for his drinks and went out to pick his way along in the street crowds. At the entrance of the tent he paid the twenty centavos demanded by the fat lady cashier and went through the canvas flaps.

It was a hothouse inside. Rows of low benches ran down to a stage consisting of a few loose planks over wooden horses; Paul maneuvered through the people in the aisle and squeezed into a seat in the second row. Up on the stage, the boards creaking and shifting with their beat, was a trio playing guitars and singing in fuzzed minors:

> *Mañana me voy, mañana,*
> *Mañana me voy de aquí,*
> *Y el consuelo que me queda*
> *Es que yo no me voy sin ti.*

Tomorrow I'm going, tomorrow! But where? My consolation is that I won't be going without you! Who're you?

Bottles of pulque and tequila were being passed through the audience from one careless hand to another. The people buzzed, catcalled, laughed. Men in soiled white jackets went up and down the aisles selling frosted cakes, tacos, ices on sticks, lengths of sugar cane, roated squash seeds, pineapple chunks sprinkled with red sugar, fried earthworms, refrescos, tamarind and Jamaican flower infusions, papaya juice. The atmosphere suggested a village festival more than a professional performance.

The audience began to clap loudly. There were enthusiastic cries: "Oliviero!" "You dig well, man!" "Lend me your shovel, Oliviero!"

The singers were gone. Now a speck of a man, all bones, his hair a thick tangle over his eyes, wisps of mustaches parenthesizing his lips, was coming on the stage. A péon. One more péon. He dragged his bare heels; caught under one arm was a large shovel; the thing that he was carrying horizontally was not a barber's pole but the stiff body of a girl, nude except for a pair of high-heeled shoes and painted from head to foot with wide, diagonal, red and yellow stripes. The expression on the man's face, as the crowd shouted to him about his shovel and his digging, suggested that the inconceivable had for once happened in his péon world, a surprise; the eyes bulged as they stared down at the rigid body chiefly because there could be a sight left in the world to make eyes bulge. He set the girl on her feet; she stood with body upheld but head drooping, an Indian girl, ample in hip, narrow-shouldered, with small but high breasts, the legs skimpy and a little bowed. Her eyes looked out toward Paul without blinking, there was nothing in her face but the acceptance of a minute's slowness.

The man was a head shorter than the girl. He circled her toy soldier body, looking it up and down, his lips narrowed in hard thought. He put his ear to a breast and listened; he looked into both her ears, nibbled at one of her fingers, tried to turn her nose as he would a knob. The crowd seemed familiar with this routine. As the man's bewilderment grew, as his eyebrows fluttered more and more elaborately, they called: "It is a tree, Oliviero! Climb up!" "No, man, it is a bureau! Open the drawers!" A cambion, an autobus, Oliviero, can't you see? Pay your fare and take a seat!"

Another figure stepped from the wing, a sag stomached man in a policeman's uniform. The péon was galvanized. He hastily took a position in front of the girl, made himself taller and shorter, squirmed left and right in a ridiculous attempt to hide the striped body. The policeman stopped and stared at him. The péon looked elaborately innocent, half asleep.

He suddenly realized he still had the shovel under his arm.

He had an overpowering need to show it was anything but a shovel. He placed its edge on the ground and, legs nonchalantly crossed, tried to sit on the handle as though it was a chair; he slipped off. He raised it to his chest and fingered it as though it was a guitar, making twanging noises through his closed lips. His beseeching eyes said to the policeman: No? The policeman's fierce face came back: No.

The péon stooped as though sitting at a table. He held his hands up as though they contained a bowl, blew on the bowl as though it was full of hot soup, raised the big shovel as though it was a spoon and began to eat noisily with it, his wide eyes on the policeman. The policeman's face did not relax.

"What have you got there?" the policeman said, pointing to the nude girl.

"Where, boss?"

"Behind you."

"There is nothing behind me but my behind, boss."

"If you had a behind that looked like that you would be a rich man. You could open a business."

"I am a friend to the police, boss. If you like to kiss my behind you can do it for free."

The crowd bawled its delight.

"Come on, man! What is it?"

The péon turned around to look. He jumped. His face was a study in astonishment.

"How do I know, boss? A bureau, a tree. Ah, I know. An autobus." His eyes lit up, he examined the girl with new interest. "Yes, boss, that is it, it must be an autobus. I wonder how many passengers an autobus like this can carry?"

The crowd was ecstatic.

The policeman raised the péon's shovel and looked at it suspiciously.

"You have been digging."

"Sure, boss. I cannot go up so I must go down. I am waiting for the government to give me some land but before I get the land I will be under it. Before I move in I want to see that it is comfortable down there and does not leak."

"Where did you dig up this—this thing?"

"Across the street from the National Palace, boss, in the ruins of the Aztecs." The whine in his voice was subtly, indefinably overdone, behind it was the jeering suggestion that anything taken seriously is wildly funny, not the thing but the sobriety over it. "Some relatives of mine once owned that real estate."

"Burro, you do not know it is forbidden to dig in old ruins and take out national treasure?"

The péon poked the girl's buttock unbelievingly.

"This is national treasure, boss?" He whistled. "Then I know some houses on Organo Street where there is a lot of national treasure. The whole national treasury must be there on Organo Street." He put the shovel behind him. "I know what the law says, boss. I study the law. When I want something that tastes good, I find out where the law says not to dig and there I dig. The law is very helpful to a man like me, boss. It is better than a map."

"And this is what your shovel found under the stones?"

"Yes, boss. But I think this is not a stone." The péon pressed his whole face against the girl's stomach, licked the girl's skin, put a finger to the body and tasted it testingly. "No, boss, it is not a stone, this is definite. If I had a pyramid made out of such stones I would be the next president of the Republic of Mexico."

The crowd roared. The girl stood motionless, awkward on her high heels, staring straight into the audience. Paul had the weird impression that her eyes were directed at him, only him.

The policeman hit the péon over the head with a fat rubber club. The crowd roared again.

"What is it? Tell me, you. When a man steals a thing it is his duty to know what it is."

"How do I know, boss? Ask my shovel, it was my shovel that found this thing." He held the shovel up and addressed it in a whisper, then put his head close as though to listen; he nodded several times. "The shovel says it would have to dig very far into this thing to know what it is. If you give it permission to dig for twenty-four hours it will make a full report." He pretended that the shovel was speaking again. He held his ear close. "The shovel says this thing is not a stone but it looks a little ruined. It has a hole in it."

The péon tickled the girl's navel wonderingly. The policeman walloped him again.

"Maybe you will tell me this is Quetzalcoatl?"

The clown leaned over to look at the girl's pubic hair; the crowd howled; over the man's head the girl seemed to be looking straight at Paul.

"It could be Quetzalcoatl," the péon said reflectively. "Quetzalcoatl has the plumes. This thing has certain plumes. Very nice."

"Quetzalcoatl is the serpent with the plumes of the bird, burro. Here there are plumes but no serpent."

"I could donate a serpent to the plumes, boss. We péons, we have no land but we have very good serpents, that is our total goods. If I put my serpent with these plumes, boss, then tell me, in your opinion will this thing be Quetzalcoatl?"

The policeman whacked him on the head.

"If you do not confess what this is I will arrest you for stealing."

"Boss," the péon said, scratching his head, "the judge will ask, what did Oliviero steal, and you will say, Oliviero stole—maybe an autobus, maybe the Bank of Mexico. Then the judge will hit you over the head with the rubber hammer."

"Maybe it is the Bank of Mexico."

The péon went around in back of the girl, bent low and looked up at her.

"Excuse me, boss, with your permission, if this is the Bank of Mexico it would please me to make a deposit." Wild laughter in the audience. "But I do not think this is a bank. If it is a bank, why are there no police to guard the entrance?" Still on his knees, he looked up with an enormous new thought stretching his eyes. "Listen, boss, you think the police are inside? Where there is a door the police like very much to go inside, especially if there is gold in the vaults."

The spectators were slapping each other on the back and choking in their glee. The policeman began to whack the péon, over and over.

"Tell me what it is, you! I order you!"

The péon began an investigation of the girl part by part, listening, fingering, smelling, tasting. Wobbling a little on her heels but never changing her pose, she looked down—into Paul's eyes.

"This is a hard question, boss. Here it has two pillows attached, yet it cannot be a bed. Does a bed wink at you? Also it needs a shave, boss. No, absolutely not, a bed does not need a shave. Where is there a bed that grows a beard?" He raised his eyes to the audience and looked thoughtful. "There is also the one in Coyoacán who grows a beard. Is he a bed? No. He is a Row-stowf."

Paul half rose in his seat. He could not believe that he had heard right. But the audience was howling and crying out, "Veec-tor Row-stowf! Veec-tor Row-stowf!"

The girl's eyes were boring into Paul's eyes.

"Well, stupid?" the policeman said. "What are you going to do with this government property?"

"Boss, the important people of the government have many of these treasures. They do not know what to do with them, they put these nice things in the museum. Oliviero would like to have this one, just this one, while he waits for his finca from the government. Until he gets his finca, this will be Oliviero's finca."

"If I give you this you will not ask for anything more?"

"No more, boss. I will even vote and pay some taxes. I will put this in writing. I will learn to write so I can put it in writing."

"You will take care of your finca? You must not damage government property."

"Oh, I will not damage this finca, boss, I promise. I will water it every day, many times a day, to keep it in good condition and soft. I will turn it over every day with my hoe. I will plant many things in it, yes."

"And what else?"

"I will sleep on it like a bed, and open it like a bureau, and spend it like a treasury, and ride it like an autobus."

"And what else?"

"I will put my serpent with its quetzal feathers and call it Quetzalcoatl. My serpent is all I have in this world, until now it is my one finca, yet I am a nice fellow, I will give my one serpent to its little feathers, many times a day. This is a promise, boss. I would not fool the government." He bent over, placed his ear against the girl's abdomen, listened intently. "Only I would ask that the government withdraw its forces. Please, boss, do me this favor, get the police out of my finca. I wish to have my little house to myself." He looked at the girl's middle and began to yell threateningly: "Hey! Come out of there! Go home to your own fincas! What kind of a patrol is that?"

The men on the benches were convulsed. The girl shifted from one uncertain foot to the other, her face a mask, her eyes refusing to budge from Paul.

"Take it, stupid," the policeman said. "But remember, this is all you get. All the other treasures belong to the government, you understand?"

Oliviero put his shovel back under his arm and picked the naked girl up, holding her stiff body sideways. She seemed like a manikin being carried off. He stared down at her generous buttocks.

"I understand, boss." The péon twitched his lips, making his long stringy mustaches flap. "Absolutely, boss. I see that this national treasure has four pillows, not two, this is a very nice treasure, I can get a nice rest on this treasure, thank you, boss, many thanks, and my serpent thanks you too, boss, and I promise you this, those quetzal feathers will thank you too, boss. I am a better farmer than those of the government, I know what to do with a nice little finca like this, I go to start my plowing now, right away, ten million thanks, boss."

He began to shuffle off. The girl, rigid in his arms, kept her eyes fixed on Paul. The crowd went wild. Everywhere in the tent people were laughing hysterically, clapping their hands.

The policeman ran after the péon and pulled the shovel from under his arm. The péon disappeared in the wing. The policeman looked at the shovel and said with wonder, "The Aztec ruins? Why should those péons and bums have all the nice feathers?" Licking his lips, face lit up with anticipation, he placed the shovel on his shoulder and hurried off. The crowd screamed and whistled.

The singing trio came back on the stage and began another number. A ballad with feeling: you have crucified me already, might as well drive the last nails in. Paul pushed along the jammed aisle past the vendors and out to the open air, cooler now with the evening breeze. He inhaled several times, deeply. He remembered the girl as she was being carried off, stiff as a board, studying him.

He stayed near the tent, searching the faces of the people as they straggled out. It was several minutes before he saw her—she stepped through a fold in the rear of the tent, dressed in a long loose skirt and a blouse, still wearing the high heeled pumps. She went to lean against a nearby wall and eat the taco in her hand as she looked about: the world was now her vaudeville.

Paul went over to her.

"Even when the national treasure is covered it looks and looks. Why were you looking at me?"

She gave him hardly a glance as she bit into the crisp taco.

"The others laugh—you look angry: a face that stays by itself."

"It is not so amusing to me, what people do for a living."

"To make people laugh is my living. You would want to get me fired?"

"You do not enjoy what you do. Are there not other jobs?"

"This is not the worst thing. The pay is more than in other places."

"Other places? The houses?"

Her face came to life: her eyes burned.

"I sell the looks because I do not wish to sell the touch! Never have I taken one centavo from a man for those things, in or out of the houses! Go. Think what you think, man. I live as I live."

"What is your body worth to you?"

"More than a man can pay! Some must make their own fincas. My body is mine."

"Then," he said, surprised at himself, "You please me. Much. I want to have you. You will go to a hotel with me?"

The taco crunched again between her teeth.

"I please you. Much. When you learn there is no charge."

"Listen, girl!" His hand was quivering as it reached into his pocket, slipped a bill from the roll there, held it out for her to see. "You think I care for the money? I am not a rich man but the money is nothing to me! With this twenty pesos I could buy five girls on Organo Street tonight. Come with me and when we are alone, before I touch you, I will put a match to this bill and burn it before your eyes: that is how much your body is worth to me if you take no money for it!"

There was more than anger in her eyes now.

"I am not a whore," she said. "But I am not a wife either. What you look for is a wife."

"No, no, no," he said. "I'm married. I married too young, before I knew what a wife was. I married a program, you understand?" To her puzzled eyes he said, "She just ran away, the bitch! Without leaving a goodbye note!" Then he was babbling: "Listen! We could go well together. You, you are taken for a body without a head— I, I have lost my darling of a program, I am now a head without a body! You see how we fit? Together we make a person. . . ." He took hold of her wrist with strength. "I want you. Would you like me to burn fifty pesos, a hundred? I will burn them! You, you should know what it is to live too high on a stage! Laughs from the whole world at a distance are not enough!"

He was not pretending. Above the stripteaser's thickening instrument was a face with a prerhetorical oneness, at least a face that could be taken for that, beginning to fade, maybe, the lipstick on a little crooked, the teeth dulled by too many cheap cigarettes, traces of the red and yellow stripes still on the skin, but in the black eyes that took a stand and the strong upslanting cheeks still marks of the ancestors who walked straight and did not make their living from snickers; and now that the acknowledgment of him, of his presence there in three dimensions, was starting to grow up in her eyes he was wild with desire for this bowlegged tacos eater, one of the two million Aztecs hanging irrelevantly on in these Distrito Federal plains, who was still experimenting with her French heels.

"You talk as one who is also in the vaudeville."

"I do not take my clothes off. I put on costumes, one over the other—but they laugh at me, too."

"You wish only to take off your clothes? This you can do with any whore on Organo Street. It will cost one peso more."

"She has seen too many; to her they are all one."

"You wish to be seen? Send her a photograph."

"I will look like the one who came at two o'clock and the one who will come at four."

"How did you see me in the carpa when you looked at my body without clothes?"

"As one who was not at home as a zebra. As one who looked like a foreigner in her own city."

"But you did not laugh? Maybe because your head is too full of feelings for yourself: this is a sickness."

"You do not laugh at yourself when the others laugh. Is this a sickness too?" He leaned closer and increased his pressure on her wrist. "Come with me!"

She threw away the last bit of the taco.

"You look, I think, for the things that are not in yourself. Will you find them in a woman?"

"I will not make fun of your body!"

Her fingers were greasy; she licked them, rubbed them across her cotton skirt.

"What you look for, can a woman have? A woman is a plain and ordinary thing, like a man."

"Come with me."

She licked her fingers again.

"All you do not find in the rest of the world you look for in a woman? You think this nice thing to make the skies like firecrackers is five centimeters inside me? For one minute you see a national treasure in my thick body—this pleases me, because I know that in me is about thirty centavos, nothing more. Come with me, man. Come and be disappointed. What else do I have to do until the next show? Come and see how empty is the bank. . . ."

CHAPTER XII

"George does not go with you?"

"Does he leave his bed when there is rough work?"

"I know. He draws the diagrams. You pull the triggers."

"Each has his specialty. George draws well." The hood of the car was up. Ramón was pouring gasoline into the feed spout from a large tin. He finished, set the can down, and looked at Cándida. Under the two bare bulbs that lit the patio outside the country house her elongated face was a structure of crowded planes, like a thin yellow crystal with many facets. "And I pull the triggers well."

"You are in charge tonight?"

He wiped his hands on a rag. "I. Not Tomás. I." He looked up at the ink spot clouds in the sky and nodded. "A dark night. Made to order. No doubt George arranged this through his contacts too." He raised his head and called toward the house, "Marcos! You hear me? Bring the box with the uniforms!"

"I want to know, Ramón. What are your instructions about Tomás?"

"To pat his pretty head and give him a lollipop! Not one thing more. How many times must you hear it?"

Marcos, a small and slope shouldered man, came from the house carrying a heavy carton. "They are all here, Ramón. Twelve. Where do you want them?"

"Put them in the back, on the floor."

"I know how George thinks," the woman went on. "He says what is Tomás after tonight but a nuisance? . . . Listen to me, Ramón! He is my son! I am a proud woman, you know this, but I am begging: you see. Do not harm him!"

Marcos had put away the carton. He stood beside the car. Ramón addressed him: "If I leave now I can go slow and get there on time." He opened the door and got into the driver's seat. "Watch her and watch too how you behave. Give her disrespect and you will pay for it. If it goes well I should be back by sunrise." Now he looked straight at Cándida. "Pray that Tomás does his job on the door, woman. If he opens the door he will be all right."

"If George gives you new instructions? He has a taste for neatness. To get rid of the evidence with the corpse. . . ."

"Then pray that George is not too neat tonight."

"If he gives you instructions you will do it."

"I do not give the orders, Cándida. I take them."

"You see! You allow for the possibility. You have thought: there is a certain chance George will decide to finish Tomás too. You have been preparing yourself for it in your mind. If it comes you are ready to—"

But the motor was turning and Ramón put his foot on the accelerator.

There was no need for the expense of a hotel, she said. Her room was two blocks away. She had an hour and a half before she must be back for the next show at the carpa. They would go to her room. If he had to know how much was in the bank these were her banking hours.

As they walked along he said abruptly, "Why does Oliviero make jokes about the man with the beard, the man in Coyoacán?"

"He is in the papers, true?"

"To be in the papers is funny? That by itself, the name, not what you say?" He thought about it for a time. "You mean: those mentioned in the papers are funny to those who are not in the papers?"

"Man," she said in a puzzled tone, "think: if they put our pictures in the papers they would have to leave empty spaces underneath. They have no words for us."

"So you laugh at Victor Rostov. Do you laugh also at your president?"

"Equally."

"And Jesus Christ Our Lord?"

"Equally."

"And Quetzalcoatl?"

"Equally. All who are in the papers."

"And Josef Stalin?"

"Ta-leen?" she said, faltering.

Certainly she could not read and so knew only the names she heard from others, the pictures she saw. She would know about Coyoacán, half an hour away; but about the Kremlin?

"In the tent," he said, "they laugh at you, too."

"Also at Oliviero."

"No. They laugh with Oliviero. They laugh at you."

"But all of us laugh together at the big ones with the pictures in the papers. This is the biggest laughing."

He was withered with a shapeless pity but he wanted this big middled, bowlegged, serious faced girl still more.

She led him into an old stone building, through the small courtyard, up three flights of steps to a tiny room. A lumpy cot and an unpainted bureau. One large window: outside it a postage stamp balcony with grillework.

"This is where you laugh?"

"Here. I get it all out of my face here. So in the carpa I can keep my face serious."

Undressing, an Elegante slanting from her lips, she answered his questions. Born, Guadalajara. Father a tree cutter in the mahogany forests. Killed with Zapata when she was three. Mother already dead of the bad lungs. Sent to Mexico City to her aunt who sold flowers in the Funeral Flower Market. Aunt died when girl was fourteen, of the worms from bad pork. Worked as scullery maid, as ladies' room attendant in second class tourist hotel, as chargirl in some fancy houses. Sold all of herself but her body. Why? Body her goods, her bank balance: every person needs one thing he can give away. Danced in nude chorus line of Teatro Rojo: looks without touches. But her figure not of the best. Becoming heavier around the middle. After some years could make money only by showing body in the neighborhood carpas and sometimes in small vaudeville troupes touring the villages. Not once in her life did the touch go with the look. She did not believe in private property: why, when she had not one gram of any property? Nevertheless her body remained her private property.

Sitting on the edge of the bed as she finished this recital, down now to her coarse cotton slip, bare legs casually crossed, she seemed not to know or not to care that the smileless, earth hued face behind her Elegante was spokesman for two million Aztecs on this plain who had survived all Cortéses and bad lungs and bad porks.

Then with a swift lift of her arms she raised the slip over her head and the enduring aborigine was zebra. The slanting red and yellow stripes were still on her body. She saw how he was staring and said from behind the cigarette:

"My property, yes. With or without the stripes."

He did not move.

"Can I wash all over between the shows? I clean only the face, arms and legs. It is all right, man. It will not come off."

As he was removing his own clothes he reminded himself of his assignment for this night: to put his face close to something. It had not been specified that there be no circus stripes on it.

"It does not come off," she repeated. She was stretched out, a traffic sign, a barber's pole, a roll of holiday bunting against the mussed sheets. Her eyes were closed. Her small striped breasts rose strongly with her breathing. She held her arms out for him and said, "We make our own Quetzalcoatl! This is our one news! This is what the papers do not print about us! We make our own good Quetzalcoatl!" She actually said it. It was no Organo Street obscenity. It was her love talk.

As he leaned over the riot of stripes he thought: get close to some one thing with no handkerchief over the face: the night's assignment.

But as he lay down beside her he remembered with a chill—the mustache on his face not his own.

He was very careful in kissing her, as she whispered with closed eyes about the good Quetzalcoatls; he was afraid the mustache might come off on her soft moving lip.

Things picking up. Glass-lipped Humphrey Bogart had swaggered in the roadside cafe with his gang. A con fresh from a prison break. Wild man with a machine gun. Ten corpses behind him on the streets of Kansas City.

Trigger Bogart: "I'm only going to tell you one time, ladies and gents—you make one wrong move and you're going to be a lot of very dead citizens. My boys here—they pack a lot of iron and they ain't delicate about using it."

George Bass laughed out loud.

He doted on these hoodlum, tough guy, private eye, gun-fighter, solo-go movies. He took them for the truest comedy.

The toughs kept their hands menacingly in their pockets—in the pockets were always real .45's. How could they know you could get the same effect exactly, and breaking no laws, with a simple piece of optical glass? Imagination is the luxury goods.

Talk-talk Howard: "Massacre is around the corner. . . . I will be among those killed in—inaction. . . ."

George Bass laughed again. The poets were always scared shitless by the hard faced fellows with hands in pockets.

Hand-finishing telescopic lenses had been his one hobby for close to ten years. When in the big cities with time to kill he did not look up any party loudmouths; he dropped around to the local planetarium. He liked New York most of all because the fine Hayden Planetarium was there. At the Hayden he attended meetings of the amateur skywatchers. Not for the watching. To work with them in the making of homemade telescopes.

The lens he was polishing now in his pocket would be the best he had ever made. A fine plano-convex achromat ocular.

Once the optical instrument was finished he lost interest. He was bored by what could be seen through telescopes. If the stars looked slightly larger, so what?

Bass felt about optical apparatus as he did about a party apparatus: interesting to build from year to year a piece of working machinery but after it was done why keep sighting through it? He had caught his glimpse of the future. Settled. Now to get on with the building of more and more tools to bring the far things closer. Keeping both eyes on tomorrow only made a man absentminded, his hands got careless. So Bass worked hard on the telescopes when he had free hours: shaped glass discs into beautifully precise curvatures, ground fine brass cylinders to high tolerances, marked calibration bands with loving care, weighted tripods delicately, enjoying the way all parts fitted. The organization part was to his liking. When he finished a telescope he gave it away to the first interested person and started on another. Let the poets do the stargazing. Pie in the sky gazing.

Carborundum-eye Bogart, chewing on cigar: "What'd you say you write, pal? Po-tree? Pomes? You put up your pomes against the bullets from this machine gun and we'll see how you make out. . . ."

These were the best comedies! The wild misunderstanding in them of the true nature of hardness.

Assume each man by himself can be real hard, brass hard, glass hard. An unlikelihood, flesh and feelings being so soft and without puncture-proofing—look at young Tomás!—but all right: assume it. The total hardness of two hard guys is more than the total hardness of one. One Bogart alone has to get squashed because there are always two other Bogarts to see the value of joint action—brass tube within brass tube, one tripod leg with another tripod leg—and gang up on the first one, the solo bum. The lie of the movies: do-it-yourself. The assumption that it, everything, can be done with one skinful of labor force and no more organization than your own two fists. The one bum's winning out is the central joke, the fantasy. It was Bass's theory that these movies were meant as satires.

Sneery Bogart: "Keep 'em covered, Nels. . . . The first one that moves, blast him. . . ."

Bass shook with laughter. 1922 was his eye-opener. Hacking twelve hours a night in Philadelphia. One early morning a fare climbs in and gives an address in the suburbs. The cab noses into the dark street, the fare sticks a gun in his neck and says hand over the receipts. He felt no Bogart calm. He was hardened up like a forest. The thought came to him: oh, no, no man can do this alone, you need extra arms and legs, a larger body to sink in, a warm big body with no nerves to sing and dance at crucial moments. He saw the whole thing in a second: two hardnesses, a man with another man, a man with a gun, have to win out against one man, no matter how hard. And he, George Bass, never made any pretenses to be hard. He was, rather, neat, leaning to order; he'd had ambitions to go to night school and be a bookkeeper.

He joined the union drive. The idea of a lot of them together was right to him. With his gifts for getting things working together he was pretty soon head of the drive, a full time organizer. His own fists were seldom involved in the street fighting: he mapped the strategies from a desk in the union hall. Later, the party: organization carried a step further. They recognized his talents when he got to Moscow with the trade union delegation in '25; also it didn't hurt that he married Sophia, they called that more of his organizing talent but they were wrong, he really liked the girl, still, being married to a Presidium alternate's sister didn't hurt. He never came back to the States as Henry Deinker. Henry Deinker died there in the GPU academy. He was still the same soft party but now he had the extra arms and legs. All he carried in his pocket was a piece of glass.

Tired-of-breathing Howard: "I will consider it a disservice if you spare me, sir. Perhaps you don't understand—in shooting me you'd be a law enforcement officer—carrying out the one law of existence —the elimination of the unfit. . . ."

Happy-to-please Bogart: "That's one law I don't want to break. . . . Give me the high sign when you're ready to join the big majority. . . . I'll make it nice and quick. . . ."

There: the poet finding his something worth dying for: dying. Asking for it. Begging for it!

Tomás was begging for it.

George Bass rubbed the glass circle on his lap carefully, evenly.

Tomás would be a dead weight after tonight—assuming tonight went smoothly—but it had to.

Some nastiness in Tomás. The reliables were family men. This little snot had no feeling for family life. Momma was his one thought and family. The way he treated anything in skirts! The piggish thing about him was not what he was doing to Emma but— that he liked it. And added his own touches. He had to do it to some girl. Could not say straight out to the world and himself that a man is fundamentally tapioca—and therefore simply be pudding and nice with a woman. He had no claim to live. Be a courtesy to Emma to lower the machine guns three feet.

To share the same bed for two years with a girl—without the first friendly feelings for her? Who worth breathing could do it?

But—if something went wrong tonight? Things set up just so: but if they missed?

After A comes B. Tomás was B.

They knew all about B in the center. They had approved Bass's plan to set B up. They considered B the necessary collateral for A.

If A did not work and Bass had eliminated B—the center would have a possible strong case against Bass.

There were maybe those in the center who would welcome a case against Bass. Who were looking for it. There were indications. If it came to B this boy was automatically kaput. That was built into B. The biggest thing in favor of B.

He liked parts that were of good material and worked well together. But sometimes you have to work with these flawed, balky materials, full of soft spots. The whole world could not be perfect brass tubes and perfect glass lenses.

The dirtiest of jobs called for the dirtiest types. The one thing that kept the organization from being perfectly smooth, absolutely hard.

George Bass was genuinely fond of his blond, dimply Sophia back in Moscow, she was his one pillow in life, and so he was inclined to be a little sentimental about women and their treatment. He could not stand the joy a Tomás took in kicking an Emma.

Ready-to-meet-his-Maker Howard: "I'm an anachronism—I'd like that for my epitaph: *He came on all the scenes too late.* . . . I'm ready to die now—for freedom. Freedom from consciousness. . . . Any time you say, liberator. . . ."

George Bass laughed as he stood up, ready for his meeting with Ramón and his men. The lens was back in his pocket, his hand touching it. He walked toward the entrance.

Commutation of sentence for the tough with women Mr. B.

One and Only Sarah

Report from the front. (In front of what—ourselves?) When you saw me off at Penn Station last month I had purposes, directions, definitions. Now . . . Am I the translator here? Of a book that won't get finished. V.R. can't write the crucial chapter. All the quotes you and the others dug out for us confound his point. . . . Am I a guard? Not a welcome one. V.R. receives visitors in private, demands blithe excursions to the country. We were on a butterfly hunt today; fifteen péons with guns came for the Old Man. He talked them out of it but it was close. . . . The taunt in all this is as bad as the threat.

David Justin was sitting under the orange tree, writing on a pad across his knee. He put his pen down and listened. V.R.'s shadow crossed and recrossed the closed French doors of the study: pacing as he dictated in his acoustical-chamber voice the new press statement about Teotihuacán—"behind those duped farmers the sure hand of George Bass and behind Bass the even surer"—and the two whores—"overseeing these ladies of easy virtue is no ordinary procurer but." From the dining room adjoining the study, the sound of staccato typing, a spasm of key impacts, a pause: Jacques working on another chapter.

It had showered during the late afternoon, the orange tree was still shedding drops. On Avenida Londres the ruts were rivulets populated with the outsized frogs that swarmed up from the nearby stream during every rain: walkers hereabouts after a downpour could expect to step on their bodies, slimed and squirmy as cowflops. A chorus of self-heavy rasps: and behind this massed sound a burrowing, a crawling, too many events in night preparation.

David bent over his pad:

> *I've written you about Teleki. He and the Old Man are at complete cross purposes now. Paul wants absolute security, V.R. wants—who knows?—to be absolutely alone. Listen to this. A few days before I came V.R. secretly ordered a car with a chauffeur. The car drove up; V.R. dashed out without a word and rode off. Paul and Sergeant Guillermo found him a half hour later—in the Palacio de Bellas Artes, in the front seat of a box overlooking the stage, listening to an all-Beethoven concert! (See Lenin: "I can't listen to Beethoven. He makes me weep and there's no time for weeping.") V.R. didn't have even the usual handkerchief over his face. Some idiot in the orchestra spotted him and jumped up, pulling a gun (many carry guns here) and screaming "Abajo Rostov! Abajo el Hitleristo!" He was already taking aim. Paul and the cops sprinted down the aisle but they were nowhere near. It was the blowtop's neighbors who saved the day. They began to yell "Arriba Rostov! Arriba El Viejo!"—not for political reasons, just to be hospitable to a guest in their country—and jumped on the lunatic. . . . Is it just that the Old Man has an enormous appetite for life, all the more so when he's so boxed in? Then*

why the pall of last-minutism, looming deadlines, over his "open house" policy and his "afternoons in the country"? He's after more than Beethoven and butterflies. This is the appetite of the condemned man eating the hearty breakfast. But who condemned him with such finality? If he let Paul put into effect a few simple security rules he'd stand a chance of stopping Bass. . . .

Loud talking from the cops on the street side of the wall: "Timoteo said she went at it like a rabbit!" "The one in yellow?" "No, man! The one with stripes, the green stripes!" "Like a rabbit? Ya-ee." "Like a tornado, he said!" "Man, Timoteo got nice presents too!" "I heard: a silk shirt and a case for the cigarettes." "He can wear the silk shirt and smoke the cigarettes when he looks for a new job." "Man, he will stay in the department." "Sure. They will put him on the beat or he will direct traffic again, no more!" "A tornado? He said that? Ay-ee!" "Better than a rabbit, man!"

So I've been going through the old texts again. Looking for the person V.R. was before he grew his full carapace of politics. His autobiography steers carefully around the personal matters, of course; to hear him tell it he was sired by a manifesto and weaned on a thesis. But less slanted memoirs from the early days help to fill in the picture. They suggest that at age seventeen V.R. was more, much more than a political machine. That, in fact, he despised the political and other mechanisms that take the place of people. . . . At fourteen he stirs up a strike against his father. For political reasons? But the muzhiks on his father's farms were treated rather better than was the rule in the Southern Ukraine. What did he have against his father? The man's existence? Maybe he pushes against parents simply because they're there? He can't stand any weight of authority. At the slightest pressure from on high, at the first sign of walls to limit his movements, he begins to thrash about and swing his arms wildly: The usual claustrophobia of the teens, disguised as good works. (I know all the symptoms: all I have to do is close my eyes and remember.) I'm not saying poor muzhiks aren't to be sympathized with. But when the sympathy is an excuse to let the fists fly; when the need of the fists for action is the starting point. . . . He goes to school in Nikolayev. Here he begins to take big pokes at his teachers. What lowly muzhiks is he espousing in these brave stands? The poor don't benefit, he just gets himself expelled.

He meets some radical workers and students. He joins their secret study group. He begins to organize the South Russian Workers' Union. He comes in contact for the first time with Marxism and—is appalled. His young stomach churns. Why? Because Marxism represents the same rigidity, stoniness, dogmatism, refusal to budge that he always saw in his parents? . . .

He becomes a Narodnik. What was so attractive to a rebellious teen-ager in the naive, romantic, half-socialist and half-anarchist ideas of these ardent populists? The Narodniks hated stifling authority and the trampling pressures from above too! They wanted —openness, fluidity, elbow room. Their slogan—Land and Liberty. (Were the first slogans of the Kronstadt sailors in 1921 very different?) Many of them scorned the Marxist belief that each man is a product of anonymous social and economic forces: they insisted on a subjectivist approach to things, argued the primacy of the "critical mind" and the individual will over groups, forces, impersonal trends. All this must have been meat and drink to an authority-rejecting young firebrand. He wanted no part of determinism, the psychological sort of parents, the social sort of history, or the theoretical sort of the Marxists. Away with restraints! Down with all pressures, molds, conditioners, mechanisms, straitjackets, walls! You see that programs are a matter of taste, too. . . .

There's a girl in the Nikolayev study group, somewhat older than V.R.—Marisha Shvigalovskaya, fugitive from the top aristocracy, schoolteacher, a devoted Marxist. Over and over she says to the seventeen-year-old Victor, already the "most determined and most pitilessly sarcastic controversialist" of the circle: "How on earth can a person who thinks he is logical be contented with a headful of vague idealistic emotions?" Over and over he answers: "How on earth can a young girl so full of life stand that dry, narrow, impractical stuff! This fine Marxism of yours is a doctrine for shopkeepers and traders!" Is it entirely beside the point to remember that Victor's father was something of a shopkeeper and very much the trader: a man whose being was pre-

sided over by the economics of daily life and the statistical drama of the world market?

Here's a scene that haunts me. The Nikolayev rebels arrange a little New Year's party in a gardener's hut close by an orchard. Victor sends an intermediary to make sure that Marisha Shvigalovskaya will come. She says no: Victor is too belligerent, humiliates her, reduces her to tears. The intermediary insists that Victor is sorry for the way he's behaved, that actually he's coming around to the Marxist view; he wants Marisha at the party so that he can make it up to her. The girl finally agrees. . . . The party is under way. A bottle of wine is opened, glasses are filled. Victor announces, to everybody's astonishment and Marisha's considerable relief, that he's been won over to Marxism. Toasts are drunk to the workers' emancipation, to the crushing of Tsarist despotism. It comes Victor's turn to propose a toast. He rises, looks squarely at Marisha with a peculiar glint in his eye, holds up his glass and shouts: "A curse upon all Marxists, upon those who want to bring dryness and hardness into all the relations of life!" Marisha runs out weeping; she never wants to see this brute again. Two years later, of course, Victor and Marisha are exiled in Siberia; comrades in Marxism now, and married. . . .

Movement on the enclosing wall. Furry ovals inching. The tarántulas that nested somewhere on the property, out on their nocturnal expeditions; what dark assignments led them on this creeping and probing through the bright bougainvilleas? Tarántulas behind magenta petals: carnivorous red ants in great orchids: GPU whores in sunny suburbs: the assassins of Mr. Bass in—what? In a situation of total falsehood what façade can be taken as a true representation of its insides? Crawling and burrowing everywhere.

He went from populism to Marxism. But only to undertake his fourteen-year-long struggle against Lenin's variety of Marxism—Bolshevism. What repelled him in the Bolsheviks? His book against Lenin, Our Political Tasks—*written when he was twenty-three!—is more than a tract against programmatic centralism. Dancing across all the sharp political dissections is the old Nikolayev populist-anarchist rebel in love—(apparently)—with space, with fluidity, with sparkle, with bold subjectivity—the parent-smasher now caught up in a nausea with the sternest and least wavering parents of all, the Lenins. What he could not stand in Bolshevism, finally—we have his own word for it—was its bone dryness and steel hardness. . . .*

In 1917 he embraces the Bolsheviks with both arms. In 1921 he becomes very hard and dry himself. With the Kronstadt sailors. Who are in love—(apparently)—with space, fluidity, sparkle. . . .

Was he a soft young man who in 1917 finally learned to be hard? That's what he says in his autobiography, to explain his going over to the Bolsheviks.

But could he have been a falsely hard one who couldn't keep up the pretense and finally reverted to his true softness?

I don't know. I don't know. Was there a conformist deep in the heart of this parent-smasher? Were the fists at fourteen such a lie?

He flung away parents, Tsars, all walls and restraints!

Then he reachced so needfully for the Lenins! There was a steeliness!

All I know is that he formulated as his prime contribution the theory of permanent revolution—and could not maintain his own stand against the hards and drys.

At seventeen, back in Nikolayev, he proudly informed Marisha Shvigalovskaya that his one enemy was narrowness. But look at how he narrowed himself over the decades! At first he was against Marxism. Then, against the narrow corruption of Marxism—Leninism. Then, against the narrow corruption of Leninism—Stalinism.

Maybe he's narrowed down his target so much that there's no way to hit it?

Is the only way out of this trap—down?

Parent-smashing, finally, is an inadequate program. No permanence. Too hard to keep up indefinitely. The more you smash, the more you're tempted to cave in.

He must stay alive, of course. He's the only one remaining who can speak out from the left, from the workers' side, against the Stalinist blight. (By becoming the dupes of Stalin's Popular Front in Spain, France and other places, the socialist and anarchist leaders have forfeited their right to speak.) Once he goes there won't be another such voice for decades. There is a way to keep him alive. Tell this to our friends in New York. They must round up a half dozen real guards, tough fellows from the unions who know how to handle guns, and send them down here immediately, whether V.R. wants them or not. Let them station themselves outside the house, to reinforce the cops, if V.R. won't let them in. Another thing. V.R. must be made to see that, if he insists on having visitors, he must never receive anybody, even the most transparently friendly person, without having a third party present, an armed guard. Let V.R. fulminate against these "intolerable restraints" all he wants. He's accepted hateful restraints before, with less cause. I've come to see that Paul's right. The program here has to be one of total paranoia.

As for me? I'll be coming home soon. V.R. has asked for my recall and I'm not fighting it. I've a confession. I've suddenly realized that I don't know how to make a true and permanent revolution, one that doesn't simply turn up the conformist undersides of flaming rebels, install them in absolute power, and stop there. I don't know how to make a revolution that won't simply substitute one set of restraints for another. That's not a happy thing to admit about yourself, in times when the world needs the deepest and broadest shakeups. I have only one consolation. Nobody else seems to know how to turn the trick either. V.R. least of all.

There's one thing I do know, and well. I know how to teach the Romance languages. I know how to translate nineteenth century French romantic poetry into more than passable English. I may as well accept a few walls and restraints myself and learn to live within the area of my competence: I'm going back to graduate school to get my degree, I've already written them about it. Then I won't change the world. But neither will I have any Kronstadts to disturb my sleep. I'll listen to Beethoven when I want to.

Dear, dear Sarah: marriage is a silly bourgeois convention, all right—but can you stretch a point and marry a future university instructor? I'll tell you my reasons: I'd like, for comfort's sake, to reduce the roster of our enemies to the minimum. Comfort

can be a program too—not the worst. I don't think the institu-
tion of wedlock is an enemy worth a lifetime's battle. Especially
when you can't win. If it's easier to live in the world with a cer-
tain symbolic slip of paper than without it, I say—let's acquire
the paper and get on with the main business. Conformism? I'm
learning that conformism can be the occupational disease of the
fulltime rebel too. I don't want to make a constant and profes-
sional show of muscle in areas where it doesn't count, and where
the enemy can't be budged, and where the only issue can be—
headaches for the showoff. . . . Down with all narrowness, my
one and true love! I want to marry you. Start looking for a larger
apartment, will you? Let's both be very soft and yield most ful-
somely to each other: that's a kind of collapse which, whether
it changes one molecule in the world or not, can only have good
consequences. It will at least change us; and we're a not insignifi-
cant part of the world, I insist. Parent-smashing? But maybe you
can just turn your back on the parents and walk away, with an
occasional smile over the shoulder and even a friendly wave.
Maybe you can even go back and visit the old folks once in a
while. I have a revolutionary new program for getting past the
need to smash parents: become a parent. . . . No Kronstadts
between us, all right? No centralism in our family. I will try to
be very undry and unhard with you.

Emma Scholes came out from the study. Directly behind her was
V.R., clapping his hands and calling, "Jacques! Come here a moment, please!"

The sound of typing stopped. Masson hurried from the dining
room.

"You look tired," V.R. said. "Your eyes are bloodshot."

"Just strain. . . . You've finished?"

V.R. handed him some typewritten sheets. "Tomorrow's release—
a strong one! Can you translate it tonight?"

"I'll get on it right away."

"Fine. Tomorrow, first thing, Emma can type the copies and
bring them in to the newspapers."

Emma and Masson remained on the walk; V.R. came down the
steps and walked over to David.

"We're literary tonight. . . . What are you writing?"

"Just a letter." David put his pad aside and stood.

"You were very quiet coming home from the picnic, and all through dinner. . . . What's wrong?"

"You—I understand you've written New York about me."

"The letter was complimentary: I said your considerable talents are being wasted here."

"That's not what's bothering me. . . . V.R.—I've no right to say this—"

"Translation: you have every right, and intend to say it."

"Revolutionists—aren't we as conformist as the status quo people? We stick to readymade ideas—we're afraid to see them tampered with. . . ."

"Tampering as a program? . . . Some ideas are good as they stand."

"*If* they stand. . . . Most scientific theories worthy of the name get updated over the years: how much re-examination of Marxism has there been since Marx?"

"You want change for the sake of change?"

"No, but . . . Maybe there's a deep submissiveness in us? Under the manufactured toughness—mush? I wonder if leaders, especially rebel leaders, don't sense a leeching, a hanging-on in their followers —and hate them a little for it? Maybe—because it echoes something in *them?*"

"Leaders sometimes suffer from submissiveness, certainly. They have so often to submit to their *followers.* . . ."

"Seriously. . . . Haven't you ever felt your supporters, even the biggest fist shakers, are a little like suckers feeding on you? We can cover it with all the nice words, fraternity, solidarity, comradeship, brotherhood, mutuality—"

"You'd like every man alive to be without precedents? David, David! The world in which everybody can be his own model is a long way off—unfortunately. Most people—if they can't look back— need to look up."

"Until their necks begin to hurt. . . . For a long time you were an enemy of this looking up—"

"Until I myself reached a certain elevation?"

David became busy picking a loose button from his denim shirt.

"I think I see why you have such regard for Paul. He's almost as strongwilled as you are."

"A sad theory: we love most those we're incompatible with!"

"What makes for the incompatibility? The loved ones look too much like ourselves. . . . You loved the Kronstadt sailors. . . ."

V.R. reached up to touch a plump orange over his head. "Oh, yes. They were special. The closest ones of all." His voice had lost its teasing edge. "My aides at the front. The guards at my apartment. They followed me through the streets, I often visited them at the garrison. . . ."

"They reminded you of yourself—before you became a Bolshevik?"

V.R. picked the orange and held it to his nose. "Would you have had me revert to childhood—to please those who wouldn't grow up?" He began to peel the orange. "What was that business with Paul and the vultures?"

David looked toward the walk, where Emma and Masson stood talking. Masson was leaning close to the girl, head nodding, hand making short chopping motions; Emma's face was frozen.

"Have you seen how Jacques looks at women? To him they're things to be manipulated and maneuvered around—*objects*. . . . Paul hates him."

"That's no reason to shoot vultures. . . . Jacques has his limitations; he's not a towering human being. Still—Paul goes to such lengths. . . ."

"There's something dirty about that fellow. Marisha said to me tonight—soft things have something to fear from this man. . . ."

"His personality has sharp edges, yes. . . We can't cross examine our people as to their sentiments towards butterflies!"

"With personalities—maybe the first causes are the infinitely remote. . . ."

"We work for a world in which personality will flower; but we've no time now for personalities. . . ." V.R. was tired after his long evening's work. He stretched his neck, massaged the tendons with his fingertips. He began to eat the orange. "What do you think is really wrong with Paul?"

"I keep remembering a line from Rimbaud: *It seemed to me that to every creature several other lives were due.*"

"Of course. He's now against his will making an inventory of the other lives. All those not his." V.R. delicately spat orange seeds into his palm. "Here's a thing. . . . Over the years many young comrades have come to live with me. Most of them made trouble: my young friends wish to become sterner jailers in my life than the Tsar's police or Stalin's GPU ever were. They can't wait to pile up the sandbags around me. . . . The sons taking a certain disguised pleasure in policing the father, maybe?"

"They throw themselves at your feet: what else can they do but try to hobble them? They've got to get even with your feet somehow. For being there. For being so inviting."

"And you? You're joining this conspiracy against feet?"

"No: I just want to go home, to the things I know about. But Paul—"

"When they leave me, young comrades often drop out of politics. Why? Disappointment with me because I'm not a more malleable and doddering old patriarch? They're fighting the wrong class struggle if they insist on throwing up their barricades between the young and the old. That way—politics *is* overwhelmed by the personal."

"Didn't you conduct your first class struggles along age lines?"

"I was a rebel as a young man confronting the elders. Forgive me if I remain a bit of a rebel as the elder confronting the young. . . . I told you I like consistency."

"Look, V.R. Whatever Paul's motives, no matter what personal things set him against you—the security measures he wants are in your interest. What happened at Teotihuacán this afternoon—"

"No!" With surprising force V.R. flung his handful of seeds down on the head of a stone Quetzalcoatl. "He disapproves, he fumes—and he stays on. Why does he stay? He's got full mobility, if he wants to use it. . . . Security's *not* what he's after, clearly!"

"What he's privately after doesn't alter things. Stalin's first enemy obviously ought to take good care of himself. . . ."

"Face it, young man! All that can happen to the maximum security experts in my house is—they'll go with me! I'm prepared for what comes—it's the consequence of my entirely deliberate actions over a lifetime. *My* actions—*my* consequences—I'll have no spurious sharing of them with outsiders!"

David took a step backward. His mouth was open.

"You've worked this hard to build a political movement—you speak of your followers as outsiders?"

"They share my ideas—there the sharing stops! The next thing, if it's to come, is my own property! Have I made it clear? Here I become the true monopolist—my death is my own private property. . . ." His hair was shaking loose with the strong sweeps of his head. "What happened to my son? They did not give him his own death. They gave him mine. . . . I'll have no more proxies." He saw that Masson and Emma were looking down at him with troubled expressions; he lowered his voice. "Go back to school, David. It's where you belong. You'll find your Romance languages more tractable than I can be now." He took a step toward the house.

David said too loudly: "Another man in your position might say: the consequence of my quite deliberate life is that now—I must stay alive."

"You mean: it's what I owe the sailors?"

"What you owe the sailors. To live—and to stand against new Kronstadts."

"First one must define the old."

"I think you owe that to the sailors too. . . . An analysis that goes deeper than bellbottom pants and sporty haircuts. . . ."

V.R. had taken another step away. He turned now to look sharply at David. He said one thing more:

"So your program becomes tampering. . . . You're truly concerned about Paul? Then try to make him leave with you. Good night."

Still straightbacked after the long and exhausting day, his step still energetic, V.R. climbed to his bedroom and went inside.

Masson and Emma were whispering; he pushing, she holding back.

David went to the door and opened the peephole; he stood there taking deep breaths; his skin was damp. Outside the police were still chatting: "I could have had a bite of that cake. Only Wednesday Timoteo asked me to go to their apartment with him." "You were invited?" "Man, the one in yellow said she liked me! She sent me the invitation." "Too bad! She would have shown you how the fast rabbit does it!"

A cab drew up in front of the house. Sergeant Guillermo stepped out quickly from the guardhouse and went to his position at the door; Paul climbed from the cab, not sloppy or unsteady but drunk to the point of too cautious movement.

David buzzed the door open. He waited until Paul was inside; then he said urgently, "Why did you write that letter to Ortega?"

"For God's sake," Masson said mechanically, "what's the mystery?" He was watching Paul come through the door. "Paul? This early? He wasn't supposed to. . . . Well? You won't tell me?"

"This isn't the time to discuss it," Emma said.

"You said we had to talk. It's not my fault we couldn't go back to town. . . . Get it over with, will you?"

"You really want me to?"

"Yes. I don't like to play games."

"All right. . . . I've decided to go home."

"Chicago?" She nodded. "But—that's impossible, Emma. I've got my business here, everything. . . ."

"Nobody's asking you to come."

"You'd go alone? For a visit?" He went on watching Paul. "I thought he'd be spending the night in town. . . . Might be a good idea. You could use a change."

"This is for good." He showed no reaction. "At least where you're concerned," she said more loudly. "If I do leave again it won't be to come back to you." He nodded but without comprehension, his eyes directed toward the door. "It's over with us: is that plain enough? It's been over for a long time, I've just been too much of a coward to admit it."

He finally heard. He looked at her. "Emma. . . . You can't mean it. . . . No matter what troubles we've had. . . ."

"You've been a good provider, Jacques—of troubles. . . . Maybe all this talk is academic: Bass may move before I do. You've checked your gun?"

Masson patted his coat pocket and nodded. Emma opened her handbag, took out a small automatic, pulled the clip and hit it shut again.

"I've been doing target practice in the back yard with David," she said. "My aim's getting better."

"Don't dramatize, Emma. That's what you're doing with this talk about leaving. . . ."

She pushed his hand away and raised the sleeve of her dress.

"Marisha was asking about these bruises. Would you like to tell her the story? Would you, Jacques?"

"Put all that out of your head, *please*. I'll try as hard as I can to be better to you, what more can I say?" Clumsily he tried to put his arm around her waist. "It's the wrong time to quarrel. There's no room for these indulgences."

"I learned something about you the other night. You weren't being a man. You're a parody of a man."

"Lower your voice! They can hear!"

"A man can be forceful, yes, urgent, yes. But you were—sadistic. I wondered, after: what kind of a man gets violent with women? A real man can afford to be a little—easy. Soft, even. If you have to demonstrate your muscles all the time—doesn't that mean you're unsure of them? . . . Oh, you *look* like a man, yes. It's all looks." Masson raised his hand with its palm toward her. "*Now* am I belittling you? *Emasculating* you?" He made a quick move toward her, caught himself. "Hit me again. Prove you're a man." He held his hand in the air. His face muscles were rippling.

'Stop, will you. They sit and say no and no. Can't you stop?"

She was standing with breasts pushed forward, breathing hard, defiant.

Then all the hardness seemed to drop out of her body. She visibly shrank, her lips lost their set cast and began to quiver.

"Chico, chico," she groaned, "why do you destroy us? Why destroy our love, why?" As her body crumbled she moved toward him and threw her arms around him, pressed her cheek to his chest. "Oh, chico. . . . Be good to me. . . ."

He stood stiffly, patting her head with one hand, raising the other behind her to see his wristwatch. The free hand went down and felt for the gun in his pocket. He looked again toward the door.

"They're watching," he said. "Go to sleep. It's late."

She straightened up and moved back to see his face: it was blank. Her shoulders sagged.

"All right." She hesitated. "Jacques. . . . If you would. . . ."

"I can't. You know that. I've got the release to work on."

"Why'd you write it?" David repeated.

"At it again," Paul said, his mouth loose.

"What? You've written anonymous letters to Ortega before?"

"They, they at it again. Not me. They." Paul made an inconclusive circling motion with his finger.

"The cops? I'll tell them to shut up if you want."

"The cops make pretty music with their gossip as with their guitars and we should all be grateful for their unfailing esthetic note in the midst of all this—whatever it is. No. The they who are at it again is *them*." This time he pointed with jerking approximations toward Masson and Emma. "They haven't learned to mingle, those two. Minkle. Meegle. Mingle." He fumbled with a cigarette, accepted David's offered light. "I mingled tonight, Davie. I went to bed with a zebra. She had red and yellow stripes. Exactly thirty centavos in the bank." He gestured toward the elevated walk again. "Looks like he's always smelling something bad, that Jacques. Fascinates some women. They think source of the smell is them."

David said in a humoring way: "That *pleases* them?"

"Lot of women can only go for a man they disgust. Moment you hold your nose they begin to breathe hard." Paul's eyes followed Masson and Emma as they walked around the ramp. They came to Emma's bedroom. Emma raised her face to Masson, looked at him for a second; she seemed to shrug. She went inside. "I had to hold my nose with the fish-stall girl. She was insulted."

Masson returned to the dining room door. He stopped, looked at his watch, then over to David and Paul. He rubbed his eyes hard with the palms of his hands, shook his head as though to clear it, went inside. In a moment the clacking of his typewriter began.

"Come on, who wrote that letter?" Paul studied his cigarette. "When Ortega mentioned it you didn't even blink. You wrote it, Paul." Paul picked a piece of tobacco from his lip and examined it. "I checked the photostat. It was done on your typewriter, the k is out of line and the w—"

"Lousy security system we got here. Total anonymous strangers

walk right in and use typewriters. Listen, why would I become suburban correspondent for the cops?"

"You tell me."

"Let me tell you about my zebra. I mingled with a vengeance
tonight. No, with a zebra. I went to bed with a stripeteaser with
strips, a stripteaser with stripes, tonight. A Stalinist stripteaser who
never heard of Stalin. She belongs to the stripteasers' union. She
couldn't see me. I wanted her to see me, you see? But I forgot to
take off my whiskers. She had her stripes on and I had my whiskers,
and there was thirty centavos in the bank. No. Twenty-seven. Some
voluminous mingling." Paul pulled his handkerchief out and wiped
his sweated forehead.

"What the hell are you talking about?" David said.

"Look. She's a stripteaser, she strips in stripes. I pick her up at
the tent show and we go to her room. The stripes are still on, she
can't wash all over between shows, can she? She doesn't want
money for it, her body's the one thing she has to give away, even
though the bank's almost bankrupt and there's only twenty-seven
centavos in it. After, when I'm putting my pants on, I spot something on the dresser. It's a newspaper, there's a hammer and machete
on the masthead—*El Machete*. Interesting headline—*ROSTOV
PLOTS WITH IMPERIALIST AMERICAN BANDITS!*—that's
what it says. Under that another line of sweet poetry—*SOVIET
ENEMY EXPOSED AS TOOL OF REACTIONARY DIES
COMMITTEE*. This is how I learn there's been a shift in the Stalinist line about us—from the Stalinist paper in the zebra's room. How
come she has a copy of *El Machete*, I ask. It turns out she doesn't
read but she subscribes to the paper anyhow, she keeps up with the
pictures on the front page. Why does she take this particular paper?
It's the only paper that writes about her and such as her—logical.
Why, she's a member of the C.P., this little zebra! She holds a party
card! Why? Well, she was a stripper for years, see. They never paid
the strippers more than beans, or frijoles. They expected these dames
to peddle their asses for pin money. But this zebra wasn't peddling
anything—she's got a sense of dignity, she wants to keep one thing
out of the marts of commerce so she can give it away. Well. Some
people come in and start an organizing drive among the strippers.
They set up a strippers' union. The zebra signs up—these are the

first people she's met who want her to get her full rights and a living wage, so she won't have to peddle her parts. All right. These guys, the organizers, are C.P. people. So when they tell her about the party she joins that, too. These are the ones who see her as a human being and fight for her striped dignity. So she's a card holder but she's never heard of Stalin. Listen, the party ought to fight for better paint for her. Those stripes do come off."

Paul held his hands up. There were red and yellow stains on the palms.

"You know what I wanted to do? I wanted to sit right down there on the floor and cry for all the zebras, including myself. Shall I tell you what I did? I'd promised her I'd burn a twenty-peso note if I could have her for nothing, to show I wasn't looking for bargains. I kissed her with feeling and left. In the hall I took a twenty out of my pocket. I wanted more than anything to go back and put it directly in her hand but I knew she'd be mortally offended. So I got out a matchbox. I put the bill in the fosforo box, meaning— here was the bill and here was the match: let her do what she liked with them. I wanted to stick the box on her door but I didn't have anything to do it with. Then I thought of my false mustache. I was wearing one, you know. I always do on these holidays. Only way I can be myself is to be someone else. I pulled the mustache off and used it to paste the matchbox on her door. You see? I was looking for a pair of legs I could crawl into to get away from the headlines. The headlines follow you everywhere. Wear all the false whiskers you want. I can't forget that little zebra. The last I saw of her she was spread out on her cot, this Indian girl with the steady face and talk of homemade Quetzalcoatls, a thing of stripes, black puff at the center of her like a dais in the convention of stripes, licking the taco grease from her fingers: every péon on his own pyramid, leaking over the landscape. Pee on. Oh, oh, what a mingling it was." Paul rubbed at the stains on his hands with the handkerchief. He was sobering fast. "Why did I write the letter? All right. There comes a time when you have to make a move against *somebody*. Can't move against your *pals*. Bad form."

"That's why you turned the whores in? Just to be active against somebody?"

"David, comrade, trusted associate, I've been making a career of waiting. Waiting, without expecting anything. It gets tiring. . . . What's eating the Old Man? Same thing. They don't make pills for *that* kind of stomach trouble. That's where you do the big waiting, you know that? In the stomach. . . . What's your theory? What Dostoevskian sly thing was I up to?"

"Same thing you were up to with the vultures? Muscle spasm?"

The typewriter in the dining room stopped. Masson came to the door, looked out at the two guards, went inside quickly. The typing began again.

Paul let himself down with a sigh on the turret steps.

"Listen to me, translator. Can you imagine what it means to be a proletarian? To feel it in your bones?"

"My father worked in a machine shop all his life. He lost his job when the depression started. I know something about it."

"The hell you do. A lot of Americans feel the pinch right now but it won't last. Nothing lasts in your country, nothing's nailed down."

"You mean we've got a proletariat in a technical, functional sense—but it doesn't recognize itself as such?"

"It's bent on annihilating itself without waiting around for revolutions—and, to an extent, does it—dissolves itself piece by piece into the more manicured levels. . . . When the economic cycle turns up it'll start all over."

"So much the worse for Marxist theory—"

"Who said it was bad? The proletariat's an eyesore, a blot—you've got to be crazy not to want to get out of it. I'm not talking now about what you find when you begin to move up—the air may be so clogged that you can't breathe, but that's another matter. . . . The point is—you, you Americans, a lot of you *can* get out of it! You yourself did. If you decided to dive down again, with the excuse of politics—that's a matter of taste. . . ."

"What's this have to do with you?"

"What about people who're born on the bottom, and stay there, and know they're going to stay there for as long as they breathe? Can you know what events take place in their guts? You can't know what it means to be a proletarian unless you're nailed to the bottom. . . ."

"I don't see any nails on you."

"Right—I managed to pull them out early in life. But here I am on the bottom anyhow! Matter of taste, matter of taste. . . ."

"You're even lower. Underground."

"In my own custom-built hole! . . . Know what's wrong with custom-built holes? Lot harder to crawl out of than in."

"If you're pinned there it's by your own hand?"

"You ordered the hole yourself, to your own specifications. . . ."

"Paul—what's your story? I've never gotten anything out of you but hints and significant looks."

"Nobody's told you my picaresque history? It's very colorful. A saga of the worm fields. See?" Paul held out the two stumps on his left hand. "The worms keep eating, eating. . . ."

CHAPTER XIII

Europe, urban Europe's a pigsty. The worm fields. Sure, there are beauty spots, the show places, scrubbed boulevards and dressy parks, but they're the few diamonds scattered over the dung. Behind them, under them, around them are the slum rats, the tenement scum, whose life projects are all in their greasy hands: people born to the grubbing jobs and knowing they'll die at them. Nothing to lose but their chains—nothing. Crumbs of social security drop from the banquet tables, wage and hour laws, pensions, doles, paid vacations—the chains stay—slightly padded.

I'm a Bulgarian. I grew up in a slagheap section of Sofia, a workers' district; my father worked in the local slaughterhouse, carting hog quarters from the spiking department to the carving department. There was never a time in his life when he didn't have a spatter of pig blood on his shoe, over his pants cuff, his fingernails. After enough years he took on the looks of the ambushed animals he carried—skull hammered, a target for the world's knives and teeth.

There were nine in our family. My father didn't make enough to support two on any minimum human level. He was the original proletarian, my friend. Not the heroic weightlifter they write proletarian novels and draw proletarian cartoons about. The beast of burden they'll have to wipe out of history and erase from memory before we have a life one notch above the stuck-pig stage.

Very early I became Americanized. My one idea was to get the hell out of the slums and the working class. As soon as I became conscious I became political: the two were synonymous in my neighborhood. My old man was a socialist; I became a communist. I got out of the proletariat fast—through the most proletarian party around.

At fifteen I organized student strikes. At sixteen I was a singer of solidarity songs on factory picket lines. At seventeen I was organizing youth militia groups. I'd already mastered Clausewitz on military strategy. I taught my bloodthirsty wards how to tear up paving stones and build barricades, I led street fighting against the royalists.

The communist youth movement sent me to study at a Komsomol academy in Moscow. I learned languages and ballistics there. When I came back to Sofia I was a graduate roughneck.

An old Bulgarian poet used to write a satiric column in a left socialist daily. He once did an article about my street battles with the cops. He wrote, "Young Comrade Paul Teleki swarms magnificently into battle brandishing the jawbone of a toy poodle." I was very militant for some years.

And drew attention to myself. Plenty. Particularly from the up and coming Nazi-inspired Iron Guard. Their gunmen came looking for me one night. They caught me. I was held prisoner for days —a special S.S. officer sneaked in from Berlin to examine me. These gentlemen took most of my fingernails—see?—I've only got three left. See the scars on my arms here? They gave me these too. Cigarette burns. But they got no names from me.

One night they put me in a covered truck. They were changing hiding places. My comrades had got wind of it. They attacked the van and rescued me.

I had to run. The war was starting up in Spain: next stop, castanet land. The important thing was to hit *some*body. . . .

I joined up with the International Brigade. I was assigned to the Bulgarians of the Dimitrov Battalion. Our station was a forward post on the Jarama de la Morata front outside Madrid—we were keeping the Madrid-Valencia highway open against the Moor attacks.

The Moors around our base at Chinchón, there in the Jarama River valley, were wild men. There were some bad skirmishes, my unit was almost wiped out. I was wounded too—here on the leg— you can see the shrapnel pits. When I got out of the hospital I was assigned, because I knew some English, to the flanking American unit, the 17th Battalion of the 15th Brigade—you know it as the Abraham Lincoln Battalion.

It's ironic, how I picked up my English. I learned the rudiments in Moscow, at the Komsomol school. Back in Sofia they'd offered to make me a paid party executive but I was too idealistic—I felt you should devote your time to the movement selflessly, without salary, and make money to live on outside. So I studied English some more, and some of our fellow traveler intellectuals got me translating assignments from publishing houses. I did the Bulgarian versions of several American and English best sellers. . . . With the Abraham Lincoln Battalion I learned to speak English like an American.

Two big things happened in the next months. The Moscow Trials, and a St. Louis Negro named Sheridan Justice. Today the Moscow Trials mean Sheridan Justice to me and Sheridan Justice means the Moscow Trials: opposite sides of the same dirty joke. Let me see if I can explain this.

We were taking a terrible beating in the Jarama valley. There came a day when our company commander got it—bullet through the head. He had to be replaced. Who was it to be? I was the one with most experience—the men wanted me. I wasn't looking for rank but I accepted when they voted me acting commander.

Orders came from above, from Brigade headquarters: the next commander had to be Sheridan Justice. Nobody was bucking for the label of troublemaker in that army. Sheridan Justice it was.

Still it was peculiar, picking this guy for a job that meant full control over a lot of lives. Sheridan was an absolutely bottomdog Negro. He'd come up to St. Louis from some small town in Alabama only five years before. He was almost completely illiterate. His head was filled with superstitions from a thousand dusty years back—he still carried a rabbit's foot under his cartridge belt, tucked away in the pages of Stalin's *Marxism and the National Question,* and he refused, on the grounds of unfriendly hexes, to be the third man in any line or formation.

What had brought Sheridan into politics? This was before the love-everybody People's Front line. The party was very leftist in those days. Its ultra-leftist program for the "black proletariat and peasantry" of America was a thing of beauty. The Negroes were a national minority, weren't they? Stalin's program for all such was self-determination, wasn't it? So the party's answer to the "Negro Question"—which nobody had bothered to ask them—was the slogan, *Self-Determination for the Black Belt.* And the party was very clear on how the Negro ought to self-determine himself. He should aim for a separate Negro Socialist Republic, a free and independent Black Belt to be carved out of the South after the revolution.

This thought fascinated Sheridan Justice: it meant his overalls could sometime give way to tuxedos. He joined the St. Louis Communist Party. Seeing visions of himself as Paul Robeson playing Emperor Jones, this was how he pictured the Self-Determined Black Belt. He learned to read a little. He listened hard. He heard quotes from Marx and Lenin and memorized them even when he didn't understand the words. When they began recruiting for Spain he was one of the first to step forward. Anything was better than sweating for his seventeen dollars a week, he, the Emperor Pretender, heir to the throne of thrones, in a paper bag factory.

Why'd they pick this pitiful, subnormal fellow to be our unit commander? You can see the logic. It would make telling propaganda back home: the pictures and articles about Hoch Kommandant Sheridan Justice, in his snappy officer's get-up, would have its effect on other Negroes in Harlem, Chicago's South Side, and so on. But it wasn't only that. The political masterminds of the party hadn't been able to locate a romanticizeable proletarian in America: the proletarians were hiding out in the middle classes. So, to fit the bill, they'd taken up the romanticizeable Negro. They'd taken the lowly Negro so emphatically to their breasts, in fact, had so over-fondled and over-petted him, they'd fooled themselves into thinking *The* Negro, and therefore, by royal lineage, any concrete Negro, especially any concrete Negro who was a card-holding party member, simply *had* to be some kind of superman, ready for anything, muscle-packed, all-powerful, all-knowing or all-intuiting—all-good. They'd fallen as deep into the trap of stock racial images as had the worst Negro haters. All because the bottommost had to be established as topdrawer material—as a matter of principle.

Terrible, what the promotion did to this fellow. He was too recently out of his overalls and mental vacuums: suddenly there were men under him, lots of men—white men! We treated him scrupulously as our equal, but he couldn't reciprocate. What did we mean, pretending he was our equal? He was our better! He was the best there is! Emperor Jones wasn't going to be the great democrat on his first day in office—the first day he'd been allowed in any office on this earth. . . . Some bottom elements can make big trouble when installed on top.

Sheridan got a fine gabardine tunic somewhere, acquired a peacock blue Ascot that he wore outside his lapels, located a pair of dandy riding boots and assigned a man to keep them immaculately polished. His off-the-record orderly would get the hell bawled out of him when the boots weren't mirror bright. Sheridan even got himself a riding crop and carried it with him wherever he went, slapping it stylishly across his thigh with each imperial step.

What does a commander do? He commands! So Sheridan began to bark orders. More often than not they were meaningless, or contradictory, or downright suicidal—but they kept coming. "Keep yo homing asses out of sight, you men theah! Dig in!" But we couldn't: we were lying face down on a basalt table, besides, we didn't have any shovels. "We gone to doublebank them mothers now: mortah fyah at one-minute intervals until oh-five-thutty." How? Oh-five-thirty was an hour away; we had exactly seven mortar shells left. . . . Soon Sheridan was upped to the rank of major. He got Ascots of other colors.

Day after day the Moors cut us to bits. I began to feel I was an automaton swarming magnificently into battle brandishing the jawbone of a toy poodle. This time under orders. A rich Alabama baritone trailing irrelevant quotes from *The Eighteenth Brumaire* over my eggshell head.

It had to end in a vileness. It did. There came a time when many units of the 15th Brigade were mustered for an attack in force. The Franco armies were strongly entrenched at Villa Nueva de la Cañada; our job was to soften up the approaches to the city, in preparation for an all-out offensive later in the year—the famous Brunete central front offensive of July, '37. We were taken in trucks to an assembly point. Sheridan Justice went off to a headquarters conference and brought back a precise plan of action for our unit. He showed us our objectives on a map. We were to take an olive grove on a certain hillside back from the road. There was only a token defense force on this hill. It would be a mothergrabbing cinch.

It was not a cinch. For one thing, there was supposed to be—according to Sheridan—a strong detachment of anarchist troops going in before us; they never showed up. For another, the Moors were dug in on this hill in strength—machine-gun nests, mortar emplacements and other light artillery. We were caught in a murderous crossfire. In less than fifteen minutes we lost close to seventy percent of our men.

What went wrong? Sheridan Justice, who'd gotten no training in map interpretation in the Alabama backwoods and the St. Louis paper bag factories, had misread his instructions. He had simply picked the wrong hill on the map. Ours was the one next door.

This was a suicide hill. Those anarchist troops weren't supposed to go up this impossible road *ahead* of us. They were supposed to go up by themselves—and not come back. Because Sheridan couldn't read very well, we'd taken their place.

Finding us in their assigned position, the anarchists had turned off and proceeded up the next hill, the practically undefended one— ours.

Six survivors, including me, crawled to a clump of olive trees at the bottom of the ravine. For the moment we were shielded from the machine guns lining the gorge on both sides. One of the six was Sheridan Justice.

Out in the open, only thirty or forty feet away but too far to get to, one of our men was lying. A Brooklyn fellow, a cutter in the New York garment district. His whole abdomen was open, half of his intestines were out on the ground. He was still conscious, his eyes were open and looking straight at us in the grove. I remember this well.

"Sheridan Justice," he called out. His voice was deep and full of echoes, as though already coming from the grave. "Sheridan Justice. You said it would be easy. You said there were no Moors. You said we would march over the hill standing up straight. Sheridan Justice, you shit. You one lump of military shit. You shit in your shiny boots." As he spoke, almost in love whispers, he was beginning, very slowly, as though with a thought-out system, to masturbate. He died that way.

Sheridan looked around at us. We looked back. He knew what was in our heads: the same words the dying cutter had spoken but which we, bound by our disciplines, our over-sympathy with the colored oppressed of the world, could not bring ourselves while our guts were still inside us to speak. He knew that if he could not pull himself together this minute and take command he would never again be able to command anything. He'd be the last man in all lines again.

He stood, making sure there was a tree between him and the

machine guns. The bullets were hitting all around us, scraping the trees. He looked around wildly with his lips going and said, more like an incantation than a military order:

"Men! Now you listen! We got to locate those machine gun nests and wipe them out! You heah! I want a reconnaissance party to go on up theah and get the picture! You—and you—and you—get yo dragging asses up theah, now!"

He pointed to three men, myself among them. It was demented. He was talking just to make noise.

Nobody moved. Nobody wanted that sure a death.

"This heah is an owduh!" he yelled.

Nobody moved. It was the low point of his life.

"You gone to not obey owduhs?"

Nobody moved.

"Yeah!" he said. "See it now! Call yoselves combrades and all that soft talk—the prayssure come on—just because the colaw of my skin is. . . ."

He'd forgotten about those Moors up the slopes, pumping bullets down at us with their fine new German and Italian guns—they were *black* men. We, the mutinous whites, were shoving him back into the gutter, not the Moors.

He made a funny gesture. Standing there frozen, looking like a falling man into the faces of the standing, orders in his mouth and begging in his eyes, he absentmindedly raised one foot and wiped the boot with his sleeve—there was a smear of mud there. Then he pulled out his revolver—I thought for a moment he was reaching for his copy of *The National Question,* in just the way that Brooklyn cutter had reached for his member—there are all kinds of magic.

"The book say what I got do with Fascist runouts," he said. His teeth were making noise. "You obey or I give it to you good."

Everybody stayed quiet. Sheridan turned his head to look at me— a man down the other end jumped him from behind. The revolver was knocked out of his hand; the other three men piled on. In seconds they'd beaten him half unconscious.

We knew what we had to do. There was some tall grass running along one side of the open field, enough to give us cover. We made it on our bellies through the grass, pulling Sheridan with us. We managed to get to some more trees—there we were safe. We had pretty good cover going from that point to the rear.

On the way back we met an anarchist outfit heading toward the position we'd just vacated. They'd taken the neighboring hill, the one meant for us, without losses, heard the heavy fire down our way, and come around to help us. I took their commander aside and warned him that this hill was swarming with Fascists, he was walking into a death trap—I didn't say a political word to him, it was all in terms of so-and-so-many guns on such-and-such a terrain. The man thanked me and turned his troops back.

We six got into a safe wooded section and stopped. Here we held a war council. There was one question on the agenda: if Justice came back to our lines with us we were in trouble, he'd bring charges of mutiny and his word would be taken over ours—he was the Black Hero, we were shits and nobodies. Rank discrimination, but there it was. It would be the firing squad for everybody. Sheridan's head was clear now. He was sitting in the middle of the circle, looking up at four men who, with their rifles on him, were deciding that the only reasonable thing to do was kill him.

Four, I say. I couldn't believe this was happening. I tried to talk to the men: this fellow was not our enemy, I said, just an incompetent. He couldn't be held responsible for the political forces that had raised him, still blinking, to command level.

The others laughed at me. They were in an ugly mood, for weeks they'd been seeing their friends go one by one—partly through Sheridan's fucking up. They weren't thinking about politics now, just about survival. To them the logic was simple: kill one man, Justice, here and now, or go back with him and have the five of us killed. One against five, a matter of arithmetic.

The vote was four to one for getting rid of Sheridan.

"We're going to do it, Teleki," John Vascos, a Pennsylvania coal miner, told me. "We're going through with it. Every man here puts his hand on the gun, you too, so it's a group action."

They took Sheridan over to a tree and tied his hands behind it. He began to make noises, it sounded like he was trying to swallow but couldn't. His eyes never left us.

I began to scream: "You can't! Do this and all our talk of betterment is a joke—we're pigs reducing the whole world to pigs!"

"You've got it full wrong, Teleki," John Vascos said. "We're reducing the pig population of the world by one. Didn't we sign up for the fight against oppression? Who's our biggest oppressor in this man's army?"

They were beginning to make jokes. The prospect of getting rid of Sheridan Justice once and for all affected them like red wine.

I kept saying I wouldn't do it. They didn't listen. The miner took his rifle and raised it to a point a few inches from Sheridan's stomach. The others all put their hands on the rifle stock—all but me.

The miner looked at me. I shook my head. I began to attack the men with my fists.

They grabbed me. Vascos got out Sheridan's revolver with his free hand and put it at my ribs.

"You get your delicate hand down on this rifle and share responsibility for gutting this pig," he said, "or you get gutted too. You know I mean it."

The others took my hand and forced it down on the rifle with theirs.

"Now, comrade Sheridan," John Vascos said, "we're going to shoot you, boy. Understand? You've been trapped too long in this bad life that's too much for you in all departments and we're going to let you out of the trap—you'll thank us for it. Only we don't want to let you out too fast, you're not used to freedom, the change might be too hard on your nervous system. I'll just aim at your lower gut, see, that's the slow way, inch at a time, no quick jumps from thesis to antithesis, it'll be real slow and transitional, Sheridan."

I was thrashing around and howling but the men held me and kept my hand in place on the rifle. The miner, talking in that soft reassuring tone all the while—with Sheridan staring, eyes bigger and bigger, and mumbling his meaningless folk singer sounds—the miner pulled the trigger. He was careful to aim low, where the bleeding is slow.

Sheridan screamed.

I don't know if I can describe what happened next. It stays in my mind as a fog, the leftover scum of a nightmare that you sense on waking without being able to pick out details. I do remember this much. Sheridan was screaming. Rather, first he screamed, then made a series of low grunts, then screamed again, repeating the cycle over and over. The men cut him loose and he fell to the ground. He was holding on to his belly where the blood was spreading slow over his freshly pressed tunic, making those up-and-down sounds. This was when the men began to do a wild Indian war dance around him.

They danced. Yes. They danced. They shuffled around in a circle, flapping their hands over their mouths to make those yipping Indian sounds, leaping into the air, crouching, always making the battle cries. Every so often one of them would jump at Sheridan, pin him down as he rolled with the pain, and maul some part of his outfit. One ripped his flashy neckerchief to shreds. Another tore the major's band from his arm. Another got out a jackknife and slashed the shiny boots. The fourth pulled the riding crop out of Sheridan's hand and broke it and rammed the pieces into Sheridan's moaning mouth.

I fell down and buried my face in the dirt. Maybe I ate some. Pity for Sheridan Justice? Oh, yes. But pity for these insane men, too. Pity for myself, above all, hopeless tears for myself for being a man and no more.

When before had I looked at a human being, another or myself? Politics is a disguise. Here I was looking at my comrades and myself naked, the politics dropped away. Some sight. Very instructive. The human being is filled with all sorts of potentialities.

There was good reason for minds to break here. We were too full of the unspoken knowledge that we weren't fighting fascism—we were pawns in a scheme of Stalin's to provide a testing ground for his untried weapons and to smash the Spanish revolution because, with so many anarchists and socialists here, he couldn't keep it under his control: we were the butts of his amok centralism. And: we were helping him to drive a bargain with Hitler. We'd heard the persistent rumors about the emissaries going from Moscow to Berlin. Those rumors, of course, were stamped by our agitprops as Rostovite and Fifth Column slanders. But if they weren't true—why did Stalin send us just enough arms to go on fighting but not enough to win? . . . We had the sense of being juggled, used. But how could it be faced and said openly? It would mean an open break with everything we'd put our emotional stakes in.

Sheridan Justice, the cartoon of a commander, out of *Alice in Wonderland* more than Clausewitz, was a fine substitute target. Easy to let loose at his stupidity and close the eyes to the criminal intelligence over and behind it. He was so handy. A tangible stomach to aim at, not a mystically remote apparatus.

It took him close to an hour to die. The war dance went on until he took his last breath. Toward the end the men were exhausted, hoarse, their faces dripping. They moved as though their feet were in wet cement—still they hopped, staggered, lurched. They took to singing *The Internationale:*

> *Arise, ye prisoners of starvation,*
> *Arise, ye wretched of the earth,*
> *For JUSTICE thunders condemnation—*

Over and over. Each time they reached the last line they leaned close over Sheridan and bawled the words into his terrified face, saying, "Arise, why don't you! Up with yo dragging ass, up with yo homing ass! Arise, you homing bah-stid! That's an owduh!"

I've never been able to hear that inspirational song since without gnashing my teeth.

Just before he died Sheridan stopped rolling and intoning. He raised himself on both elbows and looked up at the dancers and said from far down in his throat, in his rich, untutored levee baritone, a voice formed on blues and work songs, on misery and labor and anonymity, he said, rather, he crooned, with a lilt, a singsong, again a fieldhand back in the cotton fields—he said:

"Doan like the colaw of my skin, cain't stand the colaw of my face, rising up and rising up against the low and down black man."

Then he fell back and his trial was over.

To the last he hadn't grasped the meaning of the event. These were the first white men in the world to give him color parity. They'd gutted and bled him as a plain shit, not as a Negro shit; not once during the whole cannibal ceremony had anybody noticed that this squirmer and wailer had a complexion.

We got back to our lines all right. Nobody knew we'd bungled our mission. Headquarters was amazed to hear of our casualties, of course, but John Vascos, now temporarily in command, explained them: they were due to the anarchist troops from the next hill running away and letting some Moorish machine gunners get through to *our* hill. Headquarters was happy to have the facts.

They were staggered to hear of the loss of Sheridan Justice, of course. But it eased the blow when they learned from Vascos how Sheridan had died—heroically leading our charge against the Moors the cowardly anarchists refused to stop.

Sheridan Justice became one of the Brigade immortals. Proud obituaries were published in the world press about him, especially in the States. Non-party journalists were just as impressed as party ones by the brave tales told them by our agitprops. They flooded their dispatches, and later their novels, with hot tears for Sheridan Justice.

From that moment I was in a bad spot and knew it. I'd been the one man against the killing. I could talk if I wanted to.

The other four men kept away from me but they watched me.

I kept my mouth shut. The Brigade was overrun with GPU people. Sure, I shut up. I'll tell you something else—I would have deserted and sneaked off to Barcelona—the Stalinists were weak there, the anarchists and socialists and POUM people were in charge of things, I thought I might join up with one of their militias. But the GPU was all over Loyalist territory. I knew that without proper travel papers I'd be nabbed before I got out of Madrid.

Then came the big news from Moscow. More Moscow Trials.

They'd already had one big Trial, in '36, about the time the S.S. agents in that Sofia cellar were loosening up my fingernails. Old Bolsheviks I'd grown up thinking of as heroes—a couple of them I'd actually shaken hands with in the Komsomol academy—were suddenly in the docket, heaping filth on themselves, confessing abjectly to the most incredible crimes, assassination, terrorism, sabotage, wrecking, plotting with Hitler—all supposedly under instruction from V.R. in exile. I knew there was something monstrously wrong in all this. These men couldn't be guilty. If they were, then everybody was guilty. But I tried not to think of it.

I was an activist, you see. A street agitator. I had my poodle jawbone to keep busy with. I ran from the Iron Guard cellars to Spain to avoid thinking—to bury my doubts in the front lines. But this thing with Sheridan Justice unnerved me: it was like a small and parodied Moscow Trial right in our own back yard. I was shaken.

Now, suddenly, a second mass trial came up in Russia—I couldn't turn my mind from it. Again, top Old Bolsheviks dousing themselves with garbage.

Here in Spain the revolution was going wrong: non-Stalinists being given suicide missions at the front, being killed by the dozens and dumped in gutters at the rear—Moscow centralism was now going international. The Moscow Trials meant something was going terribly wrong with the revolution over *there*—and the failures in Spain could be traced to the failures in Russia, had to be. Sheridan Justice was one pint-size sign of these large failures. Our men wouldn't have felt such a need to kill that poor wretch if they hadn't found their whole world collapsing about their heads, from Moscow outwards. They were so horribly done-to—they wanted to do something to somebody else and so preserve the illusion that they were important actors instead of just pawns.

I was terrified by the new Trial. I wanted to shout in somebody's face—dirty lies! But the trenches were not the best forum for free and open discussion.

The men around me, all but the hard-core fanatics, were as jolted by the Trial as I was. Their heroes were again being buried in muck. They whispered their worries to each other. But when they tried to draw me out I clammed up: any one of them could be a GPU provocateur.

During these bad days the eyes of John Vascos and the other three were on me.

Vascos began to take over the bull sessions, laying down the Moscow line with a sledgehammer. His eyes never left me. I always moved away. If I shut up about the Trial, they'd know I was disciplined enough to shut up about Sheridan Justice. If not. . . . That's how I figured it, anyhow. It didn't occur to me that they might actually *want* me to shoot my mouth off, were *encouraging* me to blow up.

I had to ask myself: what the hell was I doing in Spain? The fight against Franco was obviously hopeless. I'd seen Stalin run down an anti-Fascist struggle once before. He'd cleared the way for Hitler in 1933 by insisting that the real enemy of the German workers was the Social Democratic party, not the Nazis: that was centralism, one-partyism, applied to Germany. He'd even welcomed Hitler on the theory that Nazism would speed up the triumph of socialism in Germany. . . . The Western powers had been too cowardly to intervene for the Spanish Loyalists, even though Hitler and Mussolini were helping Franco. That left the field wide open for Stalin—he stepped in—centralism went on another rampage—our official line here was that the anarchists and socialists were as much our enemies as Franco. . . . What did *I* hope to accomplish here? To keep myself busy. To keep from slowing down enough to think, I suppose.

But here I was in the Jarama trenches, thinking furiously, thinking hot thoughts every minute—with John Vascos eyeing me.

One morning, about two hours before daybreak, I was awakened by Vascos. I was assigned to special detail, he whispered, I was to come quietly with my rifle. I followed him to a rendezvous point some distance back of our trench. Nine other men were there, all with rifles. We were ordered into a truck and driven four or five miles toward the city, to an old bombed-out church. Vascos led us down into the basement.

A tough-looking, husky Basque in civilian clothes, wearing a beret, was waiting for us. This man, whose name was Ramón, took over. He told us that security had rounded up a bunch of Fifth Columnists in the city during the night, men who were receiving weekly instructions from Franco headquarters. It was our privilege—that was his word for it—to shoot them. Ramón was apparently a specialist in the liquidation of Fifth Columnists and others who could by any degree of phony stretching be labeled Fifth Columnists.

We were lined up. The traitors, some twenty of them, tied together, were led in.

I began to shake. Most of them wore the uniform of the anarchist militia, with the usual red neckerchief. The others were socialists, POUMists, two or three were even Rostovites.

How did I know who these others were? They told us. They stood there with hands tied behind their backs and yelled it at us. They raised their heads and bellowed it out.

Then the first condemned man, an anarchist, was led before us to be shot.

I noticed something. The boss here, Ramón, kept looking at me as we prepared our rifles. So did John Vascos.

Clear enough. The four men who killed Sheridan Justice had denounced me to security. I didn't know the details of what they'd said but I could guess—I didn't defend the Moscow Trials, I took an evasive position about Russia, I was an unreliable and worse. So I was being given the acid test—the opportunity to shoot other unreliables. My stomach felt like it was filled with dry ice.

The first victim was tied to a stone column. He spat at the man who offered him a blindfold. He looked straight at us and shouted:

"Comrades! I am not of the Fifth Column! My whole family— my wife, my three children, my parents—lie in unmarked graves in Brunete—shot by the gangsters of the Falange! I fight Franco and all swine who try to grind down our people—I fight the swine Stalin as I fight the swine Franco!"

The other anarchists were lined up against the wall to our right, waiting their turn. They began to shout with the first man. Obviously they had rehearsed this, their last demonstration. They began to chant:

"Now you shoot revolutionaries! Now you shoot the militant workers! Now you shoot your own!"

Then they began to yell one word, over and over. It still rings in my ears. All together they yelled, in a jargon that ordinary citizens would find only nonsense syllables but that spoke volumes, collected works, five-foot shelves, to our trained Marxist ears:

"Kronstadt!"

"Kronstadt!"

"*You* are the traitors to the revolution!"

"*You* kill your own, your best, in Kronstadt after Kronstadt!"

"This is how you live—by Kronstadts!"

"You are Stalin's Fifth Column against the working class! Long live the Kronstadt martyrs!"

"Kronstadt!"

"Kronstadt!"

Ramón ordered us to raise our rifles. We took aim.

He gave the signal to fire.

For ten activist years I'd been avoiding the word, Kronstadt. I couldn't avoid it here. It was exploding all over in my head.

The others fired. The anarchist dropped to the rubble. I kept my unfired rifle in the air and wept and shivered.

Ramón and John Vascos looked at me. They came over to me

and Ramón said quietly, "You have soft feelings for anarchists? Come with us."

I was led from the church under guard. They put me in a car and drove me to a small villa not far from Madrid. Here I entered the orbit of the GPU and smelled George Bass.

Ramón was Bass's strongarm man, the one who did the dirty work. Bass had another associate, a woman who operated for the most part in Barcelona against the anarchists and POUMists and Rostovites there but who occasionally was on assignment in Madrid too. This, nominally, was her villa. Her name was Cándida Baeza de Rivera.

The only one I knew about was George Bass. He was already a legend in our movement. Nobody had ever seen him but the stories spread: Philadelphia cab driver, married to the daughter of one of Stalin's closest pals, power in the GPU, world creeper, always out of sight, pulled strings inside the Kuomintang in China, built pipelines to the Japanese general staff, kidnapped White Russian generals in Paris, promoted juntas in South America, more lately overseeing the purges in the International Brigade in Spain.

Suddenly I was sitting in a pleasant villa outside Madrid and George Bass was opposite me, asking me polite questions—in appearance more a meek filing clerk than a fearful conspirator who hopped oceans and toppled regimes.

He was small, packed tight, with angular and cut-down features. He moved with wooden-soldier jerking gestures, he was always working his fingers over something in his jacket pocket. He seemed, on the whole, subdued, even friendly. We had an insane discussion the first day.

"On the surface you had a good fighting record in Sofia."

"They didn't ask me to shoot workers there; only Iron Guardists."

"When did you first sell out to the Iron Guard? How long before they pretended to kidnap you?"

"They kidnapped me because I wouldn't sell out. As you know. I shot Iron Guard people. As you know."

"You had to go through the motions, of course. For camouflage. You were an Iron Guard agent in the Party ranks." But it wasn't an accusation: an almost admiring statement of fact, a well-done. I almost wanted to agree with him, he was so sure.

"That's why they tortured me?"

"They pretended to torture you. To cover you for giving them the names of your associates."

I held up my hands.

"They pulled out my fingernails because I gave them information?"

"Who is to say where fingernails go? Maybe you had the habit of biting your nails." The subject seemed to bore him. "How do you get your instructions from the Falange?"

"Through you and Josef Stalin."

"We want the names of your associates in Madrid."

"Sheridan Justice, George Bass, Josef Stalin."

"Confess: you are Victor Rostov's agent. You were sent into the Brigade by Rostov."

"You're the author of these fairy tales. You sign them."

"It is through Rostov you get your regular orders from the Falange, as the POUM does."

"The Falange doesn't need me. Not when it has you and your organization to crush the Spaniards."

"If you are not a Rostovite-Francoite Fifth Columnist, why do you refuse to shoot Fifth Columnists?"

"Militiamen who refuse to kiss Stalin's ass and applaud when he kills true revolutionists—that's no Fifth Column."

"If you are not a Franco agent, why do you lure anarchist militiamen away from their front-line posts during an important offensive?"

Ah. John Vascos had sharp eyes.

"For you. So you can shoot them in the rear, where it's safer."

"We have documentary proof that you received communications from the Franco lines. They can be produced in court."

"Will you also produce your forgers?"

As I say, he was bored. Not just with my answers. With his own questions. He knew he was reciting fantasies; obviously I knew that he knew. Then what was he up to? Why this insane interrogation?

It became clear in time. Moscow centralism had arrived in Spain with too many bangs. The Communists were moving in to take over the top military command of the Loyalists; one of the main reasons for that Villa Nueva de la Cañada offensive had been to wipe out as many anti-Communist forces as possible—centralism will use all available shears to trim its runaway edges down. . . . Now Stalin was furious about Catalonia. For all the GPU's hard work in Spain they hadn't been able to make any real inroads in Catalonia and its capital, Barcelona. There the anarchist and POUMists—I knew about the POUM people: Marxists who'd broken away from the Comintern to form an anti-Stalin revolutionary party—were still very much in control. Directives had come from Moscow to stamp out these elements in Catalonia and push the C.P. to the top. They were already far along in their plans. Cándida Baeza de Rivera was among those handling the preparatory work in Barcelona.

Later, on May 3rd, 1937, you remember, they were to attack anarchist and POUM headquarters in Barcelona, as well as the central telephone exchange and other key buildings; then, having forced an armed conflict, they would march into the city with the Civil Guards and put down this "Fifth Column insurrection." But they had to set things up for this maneuver. After the "insurrection" they would have to hold a trial of the anarchist and POUM "traitors." The job would be to prove, with fake documents, that these men were taking orders from Hitler and Franco—through Rostov. All this, it goes without saying, would help enormously to whitewash the Moscow Trials, which were finally not sitting well on some liberal stomachs.

My arrest was one small item of these preparations. They wanted to be able to show, at the proper time, that the Fifth Column "plot" presided over by V.R. reached clear across Loyalist Spain. They wanted a confession from me, among others, linking my "treason" on the Madrid front to that of the anti-Stalinists of Barcelona. I was a good showpiece for a frame-up trial—youth leader of the party, sold out first to Hitler's Bulgarian Iron Guard, then, naturally, to Franco: all under the aegis, naturally, naturally, of Victor Rostov.

The Moscow Trails had come to Spain. I was, by a weird accident, one of the first victims. You see how, once you let a little Kronstadt happen, it reproduces like rabbits—bigger and bigger Kronstadts keep popping out. I don't know why. Maybe it's just that Kronstadt is an easy habit to form—I'd seen the process on a small scale with Sheridan Justice. What Vascos had started with poor Sheridan he was enlarging with me.

They kept me in that villa for over a week.

For the first three days only George Bass confronted me, patiently, abstractedly, playing with objects in his pocket. He was completely disinterested in anything I had to say. He repeated: Rostov, Franco, Hitler, Fifth Column, sign, confess, sign. It was routine. There was almost a gentleness in his tone. He wanted, his manner suggested, to make things easier for me, to end the tensions, relieve my mind. The only thing he neglected to mention was that the charges against me, cut-and-dried as they might be in his book, were fantasies.

They tried a new tack on the fourth day. The gentle Bass retired to the background and Cándida Baeza de Rivera came in.

"I have a son not much older than you," she said right off.

"He must have jumped full grown from your eyebrows."

"He was wounded last month in the Villa Nueva de la Cañada offensive."

"A son of yours runs up the wrong hills too?"

"I mention this not for sentimental reasons but to clarify your situation here. If my son were sitting where you are sitting now I would do to him what I am about to do to you. We work for large things. In these matters there is no consideration for persons."

"Now I am oriented I will not take it personally."

She was one of those fierce women demarcated by bone—the Spanish furnace type, the type that makes passion, rather, the Vesuvial bangings that can be taken for passion, her trademark. But true women in that hothouse of a country, even when their emotions are too loud and spill too dramatically, still manage to hold on to a certain womanly quality, a—a softness an inch down below the trademark. Cándida was fierceness all through, or did a good job of pretending to be. She was the Spanish lady spitfire caricatured to the point of—manhood.

Bass the feather, Cándida the sledgehammer—maybe they used this alternating treatment regularly with balky cases, I don't know. It's quite effective. You can somehow take the hardest blows from the world so long as you know that somewhere in an odd corner is another atmosphere, feminized, comforting, boned. Suddenly a Bass and a Cándida reverse all your hard and soft values: the man soothes and offers ease and sleep, the woman storms, threatens, bellows. Where's the refuge, then? Faced with a Cándida Baeza de Rivera in full rage, most men, I think, would break down and sign anything, even their own death warrants. Later I learned that in the Lubianka prison in Moscow, during GPU interrogations, just such lady ogres were used with particularly tough cases. That might help to explain why some of the strongest Old Bolsheviks got addled enough to sign their insane confessions.

Cándida didn't make vague references to incriminating documents; she produced them. What documents! There's a special terror in seeing wild lies about yourself in black-and-white, with the signatures of real men at the bottom. It gives you the queasy feeling that the whole world is ganged up against you—for a moment your brain shivers and you have the panicky thought: maybe I actually did these impossible things and they've just slipped my mind? There they are in cold legal writing, signed and notarized.

A letter from a Falangist colonel acknowledged the valuable data sent: addressed to Paul Teleki. A statement said I'd been undermining morale in my unit by attacking the Moscow Trials as phony and accusing Stalin of digging the grave of the Spanish Revolution; obvious Rostovite wrecking tactics; this was signed by the three men who with Vascos had danced around Sheridan's body. (I hadn't said those things, only looked them.) Another paper revealed that I'd been involved in a Rostovite plot to keep Sheridan Justice out of his command position and get it for myself, the better to carry on my Rostovite activities. Who signed that one? A Hungarian Communist, one of the Brigade's top political commissars. But I'd never said two words to the man. What could he have against me? Just this: he'd been the man behind the headquarters decision to make Sheridan our unit commander—and he knew the others wanted me, had elected me acting commander. His document also said I'd conspired against Sheridan because my Falangist superiors wanted me in the post. . . . Still another affidavit proved I was viciously anti-Negro. Dated: two days before Sheridan Justice's death. Signed: Sheridan Justice. They'd done the signature well. It was the scrawl of the illiterate Emperor.

I almost forgot: there was a paper accusing me of shooting Sheridan Justice in the back as we charged the Moors outside Villa Nueva de la Cañada. Signed by an eye-witness to the murder: John

Vascos. Apparently he'd dropped his story about Sheridan being shot by the Moors. There were no Moors around to frame.

These documents Cándida Baeza de Rivera read to me in her judge advocate voice. I was obviously finished. This was my post-graduate course in what centralism means in practice: an amalgam, a careful packaging job. You wrap up all those not devoted to the center in one compact bundle; try the bundle; shoot the bundle.

I couldn't sell myself that short, could I? I showed her my mauled fingers. I rolled up my trouser leg and exposed the shrapnel scars— my first loyalty was to them, I said. My scars would never forgive me if I signed those papers, I yelled. My scars would vomit.

This was at the end of the seventh day, I think. I'd had three full days of Cándida. It was sunny—the sun dropped yellow gangrene on everything, a universal pus. We were sitting at a table on the lawn. George Bass stayed in the far corner of the grounds, polishing some small object with a cloth. Ramón was at the gate.

"You are so proud of your wounds?" Cándida said.

"It's not a matter of pride. Just acknowledgment."

"Ramón can give you more to acknowledge for your friend Rostov."

"I'll tell him. Be good enough to give me his address."

She got up and went over to Bass. They talked in low voices for a minute; she seemed to be arguing for something and he was holding out. At the end he shrugged and handed her the thing he was holding. She came back to me and put the object on the table—it was a lens, the kind you find in optical instruments. She waved to Ramón and he came over and efficiently tied my hands to the slatted table, palms down.

"Confess you worked with the POUM to hand Spain over to Franco," she said.

"You have been doing the job too well for me to interfere."

She handed the lens to Ramón. He sat next to me and raised the glass over the knuckles of my left hand. It was a bad moment. By moving the glass up and down he got the rays of sunlight focused accurately on a spot just below one of my knuckles. Almost immediately I felt the dot of concentrated light begin to glow. Then it burned.

In another moment I was in agony. A knife of fire was stabbing through my hand to the bone. Smoke began to rise from the skin.

I thought: the blows come from all sides—left and right and left again. Who can understand it?

At this point George Bass turned and went into the house. He's a man who genuinely dislikes violence, I think. I'd have been grateful to him for the display of sensitive feelings if I hadn't remembered that he was boss here—and that this glass came from him.

You know, I believe, I really believe that none of these people enjoyed making me suffer. Not only Bass—Ramón and Cándida too looked as if this was something unpleasant they had to get through. It was an assignment, they had nothing against me. It really was impersonal. They didn't want to hurt me. . . . But V.R. didn't want to hurt the Kronstadt sailors either. . . .

"Confess you work for the Hitlerite Rostov," Cándida said.

I was shaking all over but I managed to say, "Confess you eat your own droppings."

More smoke was coming up from my hand. Fire was licking through my hand, my teeth were grinding.

Ramón moved the glass. Another spot began to burn near the next knuckle.

This was when Ramón began to sneeze—twice, then twice again. He turned his face away to avoid the smoke.

I managed to say: "Sorry my smell doesn't agree with you."

Have you ever smelled live flesh when it's burning? Especially your own? The smell's actually rather nice—something like fine sirloin smoking over a charcoal grill.

The pain, though. It's something, the pain.

Sun's so benign in small doses. But too much of it at one time— it bares its fangs, becomes a branding iron. . . . Ever since that sunny day I've been afraid to get an overdose of anything nice and warm. . . .

So I became one more meat sacrifice in the long history of meat sacrifices. But on what altar? I didn't even have a name for it. The only name I could think of was my own.

I sat there with my mouth open all the way and howling irrelevantly, "Paul Teleki! Paul Teleki! Paul Teleki!"

Why the self-advertisement? I suppose for the same reason the garment-district cutter had lain there near the olive grove with his intestines running out, jigging with the bullet impacts, trying furiously to masturbate.

There are times you can think only of yourself. Maybe it happens with double intensity when your person is being rapidly punctured or is going up in smoke. It's just a last attempt to get your outlines back intact.

"Confess. You shot working class fighters at the front, while you pretended to be a loyal anti-Fascist."

I managed to get these words out, though my voice kept breaking: "Confess you started killing your own people at Kronstadt and now you can't stop." More smoke rose from my hand: more sneezes from Ramón. "Confess you pig centralists have to kill everybody who goes one inch from your pig center." More smoke, sneezes. "Confess you want to make a centralized dungheap of the whole world." The smoke curled up beautifully, in honor of my private amalgam, my Moscow Trial, my very own Kronstadt.

"Confess you shot Sheridan Justice for the Falange."

"Confess Stalin is licking Hitler's boots in Berlin this afternoon."

Then my mind left the context of the patio and the GPU and politics and with great pride I was screaming my name for nothing again.

That's how it went. Each time she demanded a confession to one or another charge I threw it back in her face—and Ramón shifted the lens another half inch. There was a row of holes across the back of my hand, I saw the raw flesh inside. See? These two rows of shiny spots are the scars from those lens burns. Ramón was very neat, even as he sneezed.

It's bad enough in any case to be tortured. But when your torturers aren't even involved—when they're—*middlemen?*

I don't know how far the woman would have gone—she was beginning to hint that the next target was my eyes. It was George Bass who stopped it. He came back into the yard, carefully not looking at my hand, and said, "That's enough. This one won't talk if you burn him at the stake, I told you." Ramón quickly handed the lens back. He looked relieved.

I was out of my mind with the pain, my hand felt like red hot spikes had been driven through it. Still, absurd or not, I felt almost grateful to Bass for these words. I took them almost as a special commendation, a badge of merit.

I was of no use for the coming frame-up trial at Barcelona. They couldn't bring a witness into court who hadn't confessed and been completely broken. They knew all this from their experiences in framing people in Moscow. More than a few wouldn't confess and had to be shot without trial—we were never told about *them*.

But they weren't going to shoot me. At least, not in Spain. I was, after all, a fairly well-known youth leader. A few people might ask questions over my corpse. Such functionaries, when they fell into disgrace, were often as not sent to the fatherland for final processing.

That's what happened to me. They gave me an injection of some sort and piled me into a car. Before I passed out I saw that they were taking me south, toward the coast.

When I woke up I was in some kind of wooden crate. On both sides of me, and underneath me too, were cold hard objects, heavy oblongs of metal. I couldn't move, my arms and legs were tied and there was a gag in my mouth; the lid of the box was nailed down tight. I heard a lapping of water, ship's horns sounding, the clank of heavy chains.

After some time the crate began to move. It went up, swinging back and forth. After a time there was a thump, the crate settled again. Pretty soon there were voices and footsteps, somebody was prying at the top, it came away with a whine of wrenching nails. Light flooded in.

The metal objects around me were gold bullion: this was one of many such crates, the entire gold reserve of the Spanish Loyalist government was being shipped aboard this Soviet freighter to Russia. Russia, I found out eventually, had insisted on getting this gold for safekeeping and as a guarantee of payment for the Russian arms sent to Spain. Stalin sent certain minimal supplies to Spain, oh, yes. With an itemized bill. His bookkeeping overrode his Marxism. Anyhow, I was honored to be in such distinguished company.

No need to prolong the story. I was put in a prison cell in Moscow. For two or three weeks I was interrogated, but only mechanically; then they forgot about me. This was the fate of many middle-echelon Stalinists who'd gotten into trouble in Spain and been shipped off to Russia. The GPU people were working around the clock just then to complete plans for their staged "insurrection" in Barcelona. Those of us who didn't fit into those plans were of no interest.

Several hundred of us were sealed up in a freight train one day. Where do you think I wound up? The only place that gets as cold as Siberia—Siberia. Vorkuta slave labor camp. Noted for its low temperatures and high mortality rates; the thermometer there drops to fifty below.

Sofia to Madrid to Moscow to snowy Vorkuta in less than four months. And that dry-goods peddler Masson thinks *he's* a tourist. That's globe-trotting, eh?

I dropped more odds and ends at Vorkuta. Several of my toes— and two fingers. We worked in the coal mines, you see—it was cold, some of my fingers turned black. When the prison doctor was hacking the first finger off I said, "Sorry you can't have the nails too, comrade. Adolph Schickelgruber got them first." I guess I shouldn't have opened my big mouth. To this day I think only one of the fingers was too far gone in gangrene to save, the other could have been treated—but the doctor didn't like the wisecrack, he sawed off the second one too.

In Siberia I got a lovely present. The first honest-to-God handout of my life. Not from another human being, that would be asking too much. From Mother Nature with the prize-winner tits—she's no barking Cándida, that soft girl. Three months after I arrived there was an earthquake. Imagine that. The seismographs wanted to make their quotas too. Several of the administration buildings burned to the ground.

I took a long, long chance. I marched up to the camp commandant's office and said I was due for release, they had only to look at my record. There were no records, they'd gone up in smoke. They let me go—in the administrative confusion several prisoners got away through that dodge. They even gave me a train ticket.

I rode, then I walked, hiding by day and crawling along at night. All told, let's see, I traveled twenty-two hundred miles, more or less. Right under the barbed wire at the Turkish frontier and on to the peppermint-stick minarets of Constantinople. Why Constantinople? Victor was in exile near the city.

I'd accumulated a big bag of grievances, you see, I wanted to fight back. Now it wasn't only Hitler and Franco I wanted to hit; I had another target, Stalin. Victor was leading the fight against the bastards who'd done me wrong. Besides, didn't they all say I was an agent of Victor Rostov's? Didn't they burn holes in me because I was supposed to be his good right hand? I figured I might as well get to know the man.

Another thing: I wanted to get close to George Bass again. I wanted that very much. At Vorkuta the word had gone around the grapevine that George Bass had been separated from GPU work in Spain and put in charge of a big new project—to get V.R.

I arrived at Victor's house May 3rd, 1937, the day the Basses and the Cándidas drowned Barcelona in blood. . . .

I know what you're thinking. I could have headed for some neutral place and become some neutral thing. I don't know—a chimney sweep, a ballet dancer. Something less confining. Maybe I'm partial to walls, you're thinking?

But listen, my first walls are my skin. And it's covered with scars —just count them! I thought I owed my scars something.

But it looks as if I was just asking for more? If the worms ate so much of me—maybe on some occasions I offered them free dinners? I know, I know. . . . Me and my poodle jawbone. You don't take on the whole world with so limited an arsenal. . . .

You get the joke? Here I am in sunny Coyoacán—back in jail! Only this time I can't bust out of prison. I agree with the prison chief! I ran twenty-two hundred miles to find him! I support his program! He's out to get the pigs who threw me into jail the other times—*against* my will! The warden's my pal!

What a joke! I run twenty-two hundred miles—straight to the arms of the one man who, more than any other, is responsible for Kronstadt. Does that make sense? We Marxists like to believe that man's a rational creature, that politics can be, and is, conducted sanely and logically. . . . Lies! A man lets his innermost motors run wild in politics—especially revolutionary politics—even more than with a woman. . . .

I sit here nights and hear those anarchists screaming at me from the church cellar—Kronstadt!

I wake up with Sheridan Justice mumbling in my ear in his

throaty Alabama folk tones—Kronstadt, doublebank the mothers, Kronstadt. . . .

And V.R. sits by the petrified forest and reads us his limping paragraphs on Kronstadt. . . .

There go the damn cops again. Life's an excuse to sing, in their view. They're happy tonight—not in mourning for their lost whores any more. Whores are as replaceable as jails. . . . It's really a nice, comfortable jail we've got. I could be happy here. Only one thing wrong. The warden doesn't want company now. Wants to open the doors wide, throw us out, invite the whole world in. . . . You want the truth? I'm more scared now than I was in the Iron Guard's or Bass's hands. . . .

Me leave my hole? Circulate in the open? I know exactly nothing about the things that grow and move around in the open air. Look at that tree. When we moved in the fruits were small and green. Good, I said—it's a lime tree. In a month I looked again and they were yellow. Ah-ha, I said: tricky. It's a *lemon* tree. A month later I took another look and what do you think? Those things on the branches were *oranges*. . . .

What's eating me?

Ortega thinks he knows. His theory is that I'm afraid when they get the Old Man they'll get me too.

I'm not so sure. Maybe the thing I'm most terrified of is that when they get him—I'll be left behind.

I'm afraid—yes—of being evicted.

I've about run out of jails. Except for my own skin. . . .

CHAPTER XIV

Sergeant Guillermo was concertizing again, in lullaby mutes.

Masson came out and stood on the walk looking over at David and Paul. He lowered his eyes to his watch.

"So: why'd you write the letter to Ortega?"

"At a certain point—your corpuscles take over. I'm reaching now, reaching, for no matter what. That means I'm becoming something I'm not acquainted with, an openly hungry man. Me, disciplined me! . . . I turned those pigs in because I couldn't have them. Now you know."

"I was asking today why anybody works for a thing he'll never taste or feel. . . . You gave up all tasting and feeling. . . ."

"Get a big enough hate going in you, *that's* something you can taste and feel. It's all over your mouth."

"Enough to kill the other tastes?"

"Except at moments. Sometimes whores laugh too much, guitars get loud. . . ."

Masson came down from the walk and approached the door.

"You're up late," David said.

"I just finished the release."

"You missed a story of high adventure," Paul said. "It would have delighted your tourist heart." He yawned, reached out for Masson's arm; the man stepped back. "Take it easy, I want to look at your watch." He held Masson's tensed wrist up. "Almost three. I'm dead on my feet. . . . How'll we work the shifts tonight?"

"Why don't you get some sleep?" Masson said. "I'm wide awake. If David gets tired—"

"I came back so there'd be no question of your standing guard," Paul said. "I don't think you're suited for this work."

"He doesn't have to relieve me," David said. "I can last the night —I got a good rest this morning."

"You're sure? I could split it with you."

"If I get too sleepy I'll wake you, that's a promise. But I'll be all right."

Paul yawned again. "Well. . . . Remember: the door doesn't open for anybody. *Anybody.* Until I come on at eight."

"I think I know the rules by now."

"Follow them. . . . If anything happens, anything at all, wake me. . . . Maybe it'll be a quiet night."

He turned to go. "Paul." David took a step toward him. "Sleep well."

"You stay awake well." Paul started toward the house again.

"Paul—I told the Old Man tonight I'm leaving the movement. Going back to school." David came closer.

"What convinced you—that business at Teotihuacán?"

"Not just that. . . . V.R.'s manuscript. . . ."

Paul opened his collar and pulled off his tie. "*There* was a voice from the top of the pyramid."

"The best that was ever up there, maybe. But—he's not up there any more. Why's he have to go on talking as though he were?"

"To prove the pyramid was good—when he built it and occupied it. To prove the trouble with it now is—that he's not in occupancy. . . . What a thing it is when your whole program becomes—consistency!"

"He can't give proofs that Kronstadt was a plot. Any more than they give proofs in the Moscow Trials. . . . And if they didn't have proofs, absolute proofs—how did they dare. . . ."

"Maybe the pyramid was too high. Even in 1921. When they looked down they couldn't see faces, human forms—"

"Only—a dull, gray mass."

"Making trouble." Paul pulled his jacket off, then his shirt. "Go on home, infant. You're a lousy bodyguard—maybe you'll be a good linguist."

David smiled. "No reproaches? I'm not a renegade?"

"Because you pay attention to your corpuscles? . . . Listen. What I told you about that letter I wrote, it was all talk. Now I'll give you the truth. I wrote the letter because—I'm stuck here. I've fastened myself on the Old Man the way Emma's fastened herself on that bastard over there. Something from the outside has got to happen. I need an explosion to knock me loose. . . . Only one thing terrifies me more than the prospect of being evicted from here.

The possibility that I may *not* be evicted. . . . Trust your corpuscles, translator. Listen to their guitars."

David had nothing to say. He reached up to touch Paul's shoulder, lowered his hand again.

"If I snap at you sometimes," Paul said, "forget it. It doesn't mean anything."

"O.K."

Paul patted David's arm and went off toward the house. He climbed to the walk and entered his room.

David returned to the door.

"Chilly tonight," Masson said. The guitar outside stopped. "How does it get so quiet? It's unnatural. . . ." He put a cigarette in his mouth. David offered him a box of matches. "No, no, it's all right. I've got my lighter. What stopped the concert? Think I'll see what's doing with the cops." He mounted the steps to the turret and looked out. He worked his lighter and held it to his cigarette, letting it flame as he stared into the street.

"Better not stay up there," David said. "It upsets the cops, they think we're spying on them."

Masson climbed down. He hunched his shoulders, made an exaggerated shivering movement with his body. "This place is an icebox at night. Some tropics." Looking around the patio, he noticed his raincoat hanging over the back of a chair at the dining table; he went to get it and draped it over his shoulders.

"Finally got a use for it?" David said. The guitar started once more. David rubbed his eyes as he listened. "How do you feel after this afternoon? Scared?"

"I don't think so. . . . It's the waiting that's the worst thing." Masson looked at his watch again.

"Ask Paul to tell you about waiting. He's the authority."

"I think I know as much about it as he does."

"You waiting for something now?" Masson looked at him questioningly. "You keep looking at your watch."

"Oh—just a nervous habit."

"I've got a case of nerves too. Everybody has but the cops. They don't care whether they die; it makes living a lot easier, I think. . . . What's that?"

"I didn't hear anything."

"Sounded like a car stopping." David picked the machine gun from the step and ran up into the turret. *"Two* cars. . . . Three. Two down the block; the third one's parking right in back of yours. . . ."

"It must be the relief for the police."

"Yes, they're police. . . . Funny—they don't usually change shifts until four. It's just past three. . . ."

"Ortega might be increasing the guard again. It could be a reinforcement." Masson kept his eyes on David.

"That's probably it. . . . They're going toward the guardhouse. Guess Ortega's taking no chances, after what's happened." David kept looking out. "I wonder if I ought to tell Paul."

"He needs his sleep. If you wake him just to say there are more cops. . . ."

"Eight—ten—twelve of them. . . . They're in the guardhouse now. . . . Seems all right." David came down and put away the machine gun. "Ever hear of El Día de los Muertos? The Day of the Dead?"

"I—don't think so. . . . I haven't picked up much Spanish. . . ."

"It's a national holiday. People pack box lunches and take their kids out to the cemeteries. They dance around on the graves and eat cakes and candies in the shape of death's heads—the dead are supposed to be having a reunion with the living and sharing in their feast."

Masson was alert, listening for sounds from the street. "Share and share alike. Yes, I've heard about that."

"They're careless—couldn't care less. Death's nothing special to them, just a change of address. . . . They don't sit up all night on guard against it."

"This conversation's getting too morbid for me. I'm going inside."

David was absorbed in his thoughts. "You know, when I read the morning papers for V.R. it's not the political news that holds me, it's the front-page pictures. Ever noticed them? They must have the world's highest rate of traffic accidents here. Motorists drive like fiends, pedestrians stroll the streets like sleepwalkers—dozens of horrible deaths almost every night. And each morning the tabloids are splashed with pictures of mangled corpses. The more the merrier.

Each morning another Día de los Muertos, courtesy of General Motors—"

"Listen, it's cold out here."

"Maybe—it's the only thing the general run of people can recognize and understand in the news. Politics, the business of government, foreign affairs—all that's conducted way over their heads, remote as money. But death, blood, mangling—that's familiar. Something they knew about. It's like—seeing your next-door neighbor in the papers. Maybe it's even reassuring—suggests the nameless people make the biggest news after all. It must be their answer to the bureaucrats of the world. As though they were saying—here's our common denominator—you've got the same limits we do. . . . Or maybe their meaning is—death's the one thing that escapes the monopolists. It's the péon's communal property, the one belonging he's got the most of, the one thing nobody steals. . . ."

"I said—it's cold. Your necrophilia will keep, I'm going in." Masson moved away.

"Jacques. Is Emma all right?"

"She's fine."

"She's been looking terrible. I noticed—she's got some bruises on her arm."

"They're nothing; she had a fall."

"She ought to be more careful."

"That's what I told her."

Lying in her dark room, tired inside her bones, curled against thoughts that came fast in the shape of needles, Emma listened to the frogs croaking.

This plain had once been overrun with wild Chichimecs. Now—with derision bloated frogs.

The countryside laughing at her.

She had lied to Marisha. Lied to herself. Wanted him. How she wanted him now.

She became aware of the sound of automobiles, several. Braking easy. Seemed to be stopping close by—on Londres?

Police?

The four-o'clock shift. That late?

Four o'clock—and still awake, bloated with thoughts. Bloated with derision—at herself.

Had this absolute conviction that he was the abomination in her life—wanted to be filled with him now!

A sudden jangling emptiness in the air.

She realized what it was: Guillermo's guitar had stopped dead. Only the frog humor left.

New police shift coming on: naturally Guillermo would put away his guitar. Who could put jeering frogs and thoughts away?

Thought with a nasty wave of heat, prickliness over her skin: how she froze tight with the soft easeful men, how thawed out and simmered with the first icy, brute one!

To be filled with him now, bloated with him, violated, contaminated—bastard! The bastard.

She was sick with the thought of herself collapsing against his chest and begging, come, Jacques, come, now, if you would. . . . Coarse frog insistencies in her. . . .

What? What was that? Knocking on the door?

Impossible. Why knock? There was a bell.

Get up? Make sure Paul there? Wake him if sleeping?

No—David on the door. Jacques there to help if. . . .

She thought: if only she were pretty and knew it! If prettiness, a conviction of having it, of some rosy desirability plated over all of her like a cosmetic, were a sure fact in her head. Then when he looked at her like she was dirt she would not shiver and agree with him and so be beaten from the start. Then others would turn their eyes to her with yes votes and she would look back steadily in agreement with *them,* not asking for crumbs, some small affirmation, based solid inside and able to look out coolly from that fine and safe strength. . . .

More lies!

There'd been some of the softer and safer ones who looked her way with full approval. She'd dismissed them—as incompetent witnesses—biased. . . .

Voices? She thought she heard low voices far off.

But she was burning, full of the stagnant hotness, her frog of a hand hopping at the center of the hotness, needing to put it out and be cool again, to cast him out, show she had no place for him and his dirt accusing eyes, too focused, too consumed to think about the voices in the patio, oh, he was the abomination, she and her wretched hand, oh, she had need for him inside, she and her abominable hand, oh, there were spaces that ached for the filling, and the hand croaking with each move what a nothing and not wanted and having to give to herself she was and would always be.

Voices there? Voices, low?

She thought she might go and see it was all right, go and see Paul was there, but she was crying silently to herself, abominably looked after, listening to the mass laughing of the neighborhood at her and her one friend the hand, and crying quietly, listening to the waves of heckling, wondering about the whispering voices in the patio, she drifted off into noisy sleep.

Masson stood just inside the door to the dining room. He was leaning against the wall, panting, straining to hear. He took out his gun and checked the clip. His hand was unsteady.

A knock at the street door, very soft.

Masson's head jerked. He put the gun inside his belt and looked out into the patio.

David was frozen at the door. Masson watched. In a moment David hesitantly opened the peephole.

"Yes?" David said. "Who is it?"

"Colonel Vásquez," a voice from outside said. "The aide of General Ortega."

Masson could just make out the voice.

"Why did you not ring the bell, colonel?" David's voice was tight.

"And disturb the entire house? I have only to see Señor Rostov. I have a message for him from the general."

"I will have to take it. This door is not to be opened during the night."

"I am instructed to speak with Señor Rostov only."

David looked around uneasily. Masson pulled his head back.

"I regret it, colonel. I have my orders too. . . . What is wrong? The general was here only this evening."

"Señor Justin, this is official business. It cannot wait."

"Well. . . Can you hold on a minute. . . ."

"Señor, if you do not open immediately I will be obliged to arrest you for obstructing the police. Those are my orders from General Ortega."

"I am sorry. . . . I must consult the other people here. . . ."

David walked away from the door. He stopped in confusion.

Masson took a deep breath and went out. He hurried down the ramp into the patio.

David seemed to have made up his mind. He was starting off again when he saw Masson standing in the path. He stopped and said tensely, "Get Paul. Hurry up."

"I thought I heard somebody at the door," Masson said. "The voice sounded familiar. . . ." He moved past David to the door.

"Didn't you hear me? I said—*get Paul.*"

Masson looked through the peephole.

"Oh—hello, Colonel Vásquez. . . ." He faced David. "There's no need to bother Paul. I know this man. I've met him in town with General Ortega." David looked bewildered. "In a restaurant. Don't you understand? I was introduced to Ortega in a restaurant, this man was with him. . . . It was in Prendes, the steak place. I had a long talk with him. . . ." David still looked doubtful. "Use your head—how do you suppose he got through our police if he's not Ortega's man?"

"All the same. . . . Guillermo's not with him—I don't see him anywhere. . . . Guillermo always brings visitors to the door himself. . . ."

"Guillermo's probably sleeping in the guardhouse! You heard the guitar stop. . . . I tell you, I know this man! If he says it's important it is!"

Masson made a movement toward the wall buzzer. David grabbed his hand.

"No! There's something wrong about this. His accent isn't Mexican—it sounds Spanish—and something else. . . ."

"You're making a fuss over nothing!"

Masson wrenched his hand away. He reached for the buzzer again. David clutched his lapels with both hands, they began to struggle.

"What the hell are you—"

Masson reached the buzzer and pressed it.

The door swung open.

David broke away from Masson and made a lunge for the machine gun. Masson dived after him. The raincoat slipped from his shoulders.

"No wonder you were watching the time! You lit your cigarette so slow! You—you dirty—"

But Masson's hand was hard over David's mouth, the words were muffled.

They fell to the ground, locked together.

George Bass, dressed in a police colonel's uniform and wearing a thick mustache, rushed in. Behind him were two more men in uniform.

These two men took hold of David. One clamped a hand over his mouth, the other, Ramón, brought a revolver butt down on his head.

David slumped to the ground.

Bass went to the open door and gestured. Several more men rushed in, all in uniforms, all carrying machine guns.

Bass now spoke to Ramón, pointing to the body at his feet:

"Apúrate. Finish him off. Limpiarlo."

Masson had risen to his feet. He was bent over, patting the dust from his trousers. At Bass's order he whirled around.

"No!"

"It's him or you, idiot." Bass made a sign to Ramón. Ramón drew a knife from his belt. "Use your head—"

Bass had not meant to come this far. He had filled Ramón in on how to handle the cops and the guns. He had coached Tomás point by point in the handling of the door. It had been his plan to give the boys a last briefing and then wait for them at the assembly point. But about ten o'clock, after leaving the Teatro Cine, he'd made his scheduled call to the New York center. The conversation had been upsetting. Bass gave the coded announcement: "We're able to make the delivery tonight." The man at the other end said: "You'll be going along?" Bass said: "No, no, that's not it. I've given the men careful instructions. They know how to handle the goods. I'll meet them when they get back and get a full report—don't you remember the plan?" The man answered: "Not good enough. We've heard from our overseas clients. They want you to see the delivery all the way through, they were very clear on the subject, they insist."

Bass was staggered. This had never before been a condition in any mission. And this New York nobody, he was just an errand boy—laying down the law to *him!* He said only: "They don't trust me? I've had it all worked out for weeks—you all knew that." The man said: "You're the only one they do trust. That's why they want you personally handling it." For the first time in his career Bass permitted himself a note of complaint: "It sounds like they want one man to hold responsible, in case anything goes wrong." The reply to that was more disturbing still: "See to it that nothing does go wrong. This one's all to your account."

The New York man had never taken that tone with him. Bass outranked him. The man had always been, if anything, too friendly, oily. So there was a certain change in the climate. Rather, an intensification of the change. Nothing to be fooled with. Probably this meant that Molotov and von Ribbentrop were winding things up in Berlin, the Pact was close to being signed and they weren't in a temporizing mood about Coyoacán any more. Still, that didn't explain a subordinate taking such a short tone with him. That sounded like more than Pacts.

Bass had put on the colonel's uniform meant for Ramón. He had come to the door and conducted the conversation with Justin himself, against all his inclination. He had stepped through the door when it opened, against all his custom. Now he had to stand over Justin's body and give this order in person, against all his trend and taste, he was more the backstage worker, the first time in his life he had been there with the men, all the way through—

"Use your head," he said to Masson. "He knows who you are now. He can tell the whole story."

Ramón was holding his knife, looking to Bass for the final directive.

"You can't!" Masson said, almost hissing.

A moment Bass despised. He was facing a temptation of an order all the way out of Ramón's world, say. He would much prefer to let this nothing of a boy live. He could, after all, inform on nobody but Tomás. What could then happen to Tomás? Most likely, oh, almost surely, the people here would kill him in a second, before the police got there. If not? If Tomás lived? The police would take him. No danger there: he would keep his mouth shut—to protect Cándida. Nobody, absolutely nobody, would be exposed but Tomás. And if he threatened to make trouble in prison? They could get him there too, if absolutely necessary. The party had its people in the prison administrations. Justin could live.

"You can't! You can't!" Masson repeated.

It would be a beautiful way to get rid of Tomás without endangering the organization. Bass wanted to see Tomás definitively out of the action. Now—they were inches from Rostov—the job was almost done, it couldn't fail—now there was no further need for Tomás. It was a temptation. Yield to the fellow's soft pleas for Justin —and by the gesture wipe him out. But the conversation with New York had been bothersome. If the New York man was turning unfriendly it meant "overseas" was turning a little unfriendly too— more so than before—these things always came down the line. If there was a cooling-off as regarded him, Bass, he had to be careful. Take no chances, none whatsoever. Tomás would have to be kept alive for another period. That meant getting rid of Justin—

He flicked his finger at Ramón.

"Hurry it up. Anda, anda."

Ramón knelt and drove his long blade twice into David Justin's back.

David's body quivered, the legs doubled up, jerked in the air, went dead.

Masson turned away with his hands over his face. Ramón rolled the body under the turret steps, out of sight.

Bass pulled Masson around. He pointed to the bedrooms in the far wing of the house, one after the other.

"Rostov—Teleki—Emma. Right?" Masson nodded dumbly. "Get inside. We'll fire high in your room. . . . Keep the girl down." Masson ran off. He disappeared into Emma's room. Bass addressed his waiting men in a whisper: "Posiciones. Rápido."

The men hurried into the garden. They took positions along the edge of the raised walk, two of them outside each bedroom door. Ramón approached the study, removing two small objects from a pouch at his belt.

Bass waited until all were in place. He stayed near the turret steps, in shadow. He checked: everybody ready: he raised his revolver.

The stone statues were staring.

Ramón lit a match and applied it to the stub of a cigar in his mouth. Bass lifted his head questioningly; Ramón puffed twice on his cigar, held it up and nodded.

Bass took careful aim at one of the naked light bulbs hanging over the patio. He fired. The bulb exploded.

The statues blinked, changed expression.

He fired twice more. The other two bulbs went out. The patio was dark.

Simultaneously, before the sound of the first revolver shot had died away, the machine gunners crouched at the ramp's balustrade began to pump bullets into the French doors of the bedrooms. Ramón straightened the wick projecting from one of the objects in his hand and applied the lit end of his cigar to it. The wick began to fizz. He heaved the metal ball at the study door, it crashed through a pane.

Shouts from the rooms. Bass was able to distinguish the voices:

Teleki: "V.R.! Keep low!"

What? Teleki here?

Emma: "They're everywhere! God!"

Rostov: "Paul, don't come out! They're all over!"

Tomás: "Don't get up! Emma, stay where you are!"

Rostov's wife: "Victor! Victor! Away from the door! They are at the door!"

Teleki: "I can't get out! I'm pinned down! Try to hide, V.R.!"

Where'd *he* come from?

The machine guns went on pumping. Glass was splintering in all the doors. Ramón lit his second bomb and threw it into the study.

Woman's scream from Rostov's room: "Victor! Oh—Victor!"

Good: no more noise from Rostov: very good.

Emma and Teleki kept crying out. No danger. The fire was too intense for them to move.

A last piercing wail from Rostov's wife: "Ahhhhh. . . *Victor!*"

No more from that room.

Everything according to schedule. Bass examined the luminous dial of his watch: the whole operation had taken slightly over three minutes. He put both hands to his mouth and called:

"Vámonos, muchachos! Pronto, pronto! Ándale!"

The firing stopped. Ramón vaulted the balustrade and ran doubled over along the walk. He stood to one side of the Rostovs' door and sprayed the whole room with one long burst. The insurance.

The clouds broke and the moon came out. All the statues blinked once, in unison.

Crouching, all the men, including Ramón, ran for the door. Bass led them into the street. They ran for the cars, jumped in, in a moment they were careening around the péon's lot on the corner, past the Packard, moonlight over everything, Bass got a glimpse of the Packard as they sped past, looked like the rear compartment door was open, oversight, maybe should go back, no, what could it matter, too late, they were going seventy down Cortés. . . .

Paul Teleki crept from his room, bent low. He was dressed in a T-shirt and shorts. He moved warily, his gun ready.

Sound of motors being gunned in the street. Sound of cars roaring off.

Dead silence.

Hugging the wall, Paul inched his way toward V.R.'s room.

"Victor! Can you hear me?"

V.R.'s door slammed open. Marisha appeared on her hands and knees, in a long nightgown. She held a derringer. She whispered over her shoulder, "No! Stay! I will make sure!"

"Paul!" It was V.R. behind her. Marisha stood up, trying to restrain him. He took her hands firmly and put her to one side. He came to the doorway, pulling on a robe over his pajamas. "Paul—you're all right?"

Paul stood and rushed to him.

"What about you?"

"Safe! Both of us!" V.R. turned back to Marisha. "Yes? You're all right?" Marisha nodded. V.R. noticed a sputtering light from the study. "Look—"

"They've started a fire," Paul said. Masson and Emma rushed up, both holding guns. Paul addressed them: "Fire bombs! Get the water buckets, hurry!"

The two ran off. In the rear alleyway leading to what had been the servants' quarters they stopped and took the buckets hanging from the wall. They ran back, followed Paul into the study.

The incendiary bombs were hissing on the floor. Some of the floor boards were beginning to catch fire.

Paul took the bucket from Emma and barked to Masson, "Get the other one." Each emptied his pail over one bomb. The fires flickered out, smoke rose from the floor.

Paul switched on a floor lamp and carried it through the doors to light up the patio. As he came outside the frowns on the statues curved up into grins. He looked around carefully. He slumped against the balustrade and wiped his forehead.

"Bastards," he panted. "They had me pinned down. I couldn't see. . . ."

"You're not hurt ?" Marisha said to Emma and Masson.

"Not a scratch," Emma said.

"Marisha pulled me under the bed," V.R. said exuberantly.

"There were sounds," Marisha said. "They woke me."

"She shook me awake and shoved me under the bed." He kept brushing back the wild tufts of his thick hair; he seemed in fine spirits. "Marisha, Marisha, you're the hero of this affair! The bullets were hitting the mattress over our heads. . . . She tried to cover me with her body. . . ." He bent his knees experimentally, making a face. "I'm getting too old for schoolboy acrobatics."

"When you stopped shouting," Paul said, "I thought. . . . Then, when Marisha screamed. . . ."

"They thought the same thing," V.R. said. "Marisha put her hand over my mouth. . . . She screamed very convincingly. . . . How did you think so fast, Marisha?" He looked into her eyes. "I see. . . . I understand. . . . Yes. . . . You worked out a procedure a long time ago. . . . You had a plan for such emergencies. . . ." He took her hand and kissed it. "You're stronger than I suspected, Marisha. You pressed my lips so hard, they feel like two pieces of liver. . . ."

Paul was looking around the patio: "Where's David?"

"He must have gone after them," Emma said uncertainly.

"How'd they get in? David was at the door. . . . I'll see about the cops, maybe he's with them."

Paul hurried down the ramp and went outside.

"They miscalculated," V.R. said. "Mass attacks are hard to coordinate."

Masson was trembling. He had on pants but no shirt, a jacket was thrown over his bare shoulders.

"Are you all right?" Emma said.

"It's nothing. . . . The excitement. . . ."

"I'm proud of you." Emma turned to the Rostovs. "When I woke, when the shots woke me, he was at the window, firing back. He emptied his whole clip at them." Her eyes met Marisha's. She turned away.

"You have courage," V.R. said. "Did you see David from your door?" Masson shook his head. "I hope he's all right. It's strange. . . ."

Paul came into the patio with Guillermo. The sergeant was rubbing his mouth.

"No sign of him," Paul called out. He picked up the tommygun from the turret steps and examined it. He looked grim. The others went down to join him. "Hasn't been fired. Not a shot." He put the gun down. "Quite an operation. They drove up in three cars.. There were about twenty of them, twelve were in police uniforms. . . . Three cars! Twenty men! Didn't David notice? He was under strict orders to wake me if anything came up. . . ."

"We cannot tell, Señor Paul!" Guillermo said excitedly. "Only those in the uniform came at first, they look to us like more policía, how can we know! Then they are in the little house and the others not in uniform come and we are look in their guns and they are tell us to shut up. They tie us good, everyone, and put the handkerchiefs in the mouth. . . ."

"How did they get David to open the door?" V.R. said.

"Some kind of funny business, I think! From the small house I cannot hear good but I hear the man in uniform of colonel, I know it is his voice because he talk with funny accent, I hear him, he say, open, I am colonel, and Señor David say, no, is not permit, and they are talk back and forth and other voices too, I think, some voices. Then, like this, I hear the bzz-bzz for the door. . . ."

"They presented themselves as Ortega's men," V.R. said. "They may have shown some credentials."

"He knew the rules," Paul said. "Credentials or no credentials." He looked at Masson. "Didn't you hear anything from the study?"

"I'd gone to our room," Masson said. "I didn't hear anything."

"You went to bed with your pants on?"

"I wasn't sleepy. I was reading."

"That's right," Emma said. "The shots woke me up. He was at the window, shooting back."

"You know," Paul said, "the door to your luggage compartment is open. What does that mean?"

"The door? To my. . . ."

"Your car."

Masson raised his hands, dropped them again. "I can't imagine. . . . Just my samples in there. . . ."

Guillermo was calmer. He had begun to look around the patio. He spied something under the turret steps and bent to look.

He grunted. He reached in and pulled David's curled body into view.

Silence.

"No," Marisha whispered.

"David, it's David," Emma said.

V.R. and Paul bent over the body.

"In the heart, twice," Paul said. He stood, V.R. remained kneeling.

"Oh, the pigs," Guillermo said. "This good boy."

Paul raised both fists. "I told him and told him." He was almost shouting: "Don't open! Call me! Never—open! I made it plain! Him and his five languages!" He gestured violently, his fist struck the wall, the bottles of cognac on the wall shelf rattled. He took hold of a bottle by the neck, looked at it, then at Guillermo. "Why did he open!" He heaved the bottle against the wall, it splintered.

V.R. straightened up. His face was tight.

"He was going back to school." He threw his shoulders back and raised his head. "Jacques: call Ortega. Emma—we must prepare a full statement about this. Paul—find out where David's people are. I must send them a wire."

Masson was standing still, trembling. Emma took his arm with both hands.

"They killed the wrong man," she said slowly. "Somebody on their side is in trouble now. . . ."

Masson looked quickly at her.

"Jacques!" V.R. said. "Do you hear? Pull yourself together, there's work to be done!"

Masson made a visible effort to get hold of himself. He nodded.

"Twenty men to kill you," Guillermo said wonderingly. "They kill this boy, only. They are so stupid?"

"Only careless," V.R. said. "Who would try such a thing with an army? Men who have become used to working with armies—to getting things done with brute strength alone. Consider it proved: these are people who came recently from Spain. . . ."

"He wished to taste and feel everything," Marisha said. She noticed Masson's raincoat lying on the ground nearby. She went to get it and came back to David's body. She looked at Masson; he nodded his agreement. When she stooped to spread the coat over the body, her nightgown forming a small pool of silk on the ground, Masson bent over to help. "We had no more sons to give them," Marisha said. "Now they must be satisfied with schoolboys."

❦DIOSDADO

He was sitting on his heels at the doorway of his hut, cutting strips from the tire. Across the street, by the small wood house, the general of police and the sergeant of police were standing and looking over at him, and he wondered if he might lose his land and his house.

This had been his home since 1910. In that year he had marched singing into Mexico City with the others, behind Pancho Villa. Serafina was with him. She had been with him through the last year of the campaigns.

Pancho Villa went away to the palaces of government. The men and their women ate from the food stalls in the markets and slept in the parks, the courtyards, the anterooms, waiting for Pancho. Most in Diosdado's company were from the neighborhood of Parral, like Pancho. They were those without land, who worked on the land of others. They had marched with Pancho because they wanted some of the land they worked on. Pancho had gone to the palaces to see about this.

He came back to them with a long face. There was a trouble of papers, he said. Those in the palaces said it was not right to take the land without the proper papers. Those who owned the land, who had run to hide when the ones without land took up rifles, those were coming back now and showing their papers to prove the land was theirs by law. The new ones in the palaces could not tear up these papers. It was not the way of a government. The new ones in government asked for time to study the papers and the situation. They thanked the brave péons who had fought so well and asked of them now that they behave and not make trouble and wait for the situation to be studied. Pancho did not understand this talk of the papers. He was returning now to his small farm there by Parral. His head became like a top when he was in the palaces too long. Have patience, he said. Wait for a time. If they did not get their land and their rights he would be with them again. He would always be with the boys who worked the land but owned none.

Diosdado had no small finca by Parral to go to. Could he go back to work on the large fincas of others? Now, when the bosses were full of hate for the péons who had taken up guns against them?

Somewhere it was necessary to find land and build a house. Serafina was carrying a child, their first. It was time to settle in one place.

The new government of the revolution was in trouble. There was no money in the treasuries. The government needed money and so it began to print some.

Diosdado and his friends learned the place of the printing. On a certain night they followed some policía who carried bundles away from this place. They pointed their rifles and stopped the policía before they could get in their truck. They did not harm these policía but only took from them one of the bundles. They believed this was rightfully theirs. Did the government not say that to get the land one must have the paper? Good: here was the paper. It was made by the government and they, the péons, the campesinos, had made the government—clear, it was their paper. The clean new bills from the bundle they divided among themselves.

With his money Diosdado went to look for land to buy. It had to be close by. Serafina was near her time and could not travel. Far out, in the less than a village that was then Coyoacán, on a burro path not yet called Londres, he found this corner of land wanted by nobody. His notes were enough to pay for it. He built his adobe hut and this was his home. Ten children had been born here, three had died here.

Now, squatting at his doorstep, cutting rubber soles for the eight pairs of huaraches, he had the worry that he could lose this place. The tar and the cement were coming in, and the troubles that followed. A general and a sergeant looking too long at him from across the street. Men in the uniforms of policía coming in the middle of the night and shooting with machine guns in all directions.

The business of two nights ago. The shooting in the pink blue house. Trouble with guns was coming to Coyoacán, behind the tar and the cement. If the shooting came across the street could he defend himself and his family with one old Enfield rifle and no cartridges?

Since the shooting this general with the gold ropes on his cap and his shoulder was going here and there in the neighborhood, asking the questions.

Diosdado did not like to be asked questions by those in uniform. For two days he had been away on the sugar plantations.

Now, so early in the morning, the general was coming across the street with the sergeant. Straight to Diosdado.

"This is General Ortega of the police," the sergeant said as he approached. "He has some questions."

"I will answer all I can, boss." The general was looking too hard at the tire and the machete. "I do not steal, boss. This tire is not stolen goods. It is given to me by the owner." Diosdado looked to the sergeant. "You were there, boss. You saw the man give it."

"I am not interested in your tire," the general said. "We looked for you yesterday and the day before. You were not at home."

"It is as my woman said, boss. I was in the country, in the cane fields. Some days I cut the cane, boss."

"You heard the shooting of Friday night?"

"Yes, boss."

"You saw the men who came in cars?"

"The police, yes, boss. Most were the police."

"They were in the uniforms of police, yes. Where were you?"

"There behind the hut. I did not wish to be seen by those."

"Why? If you thought they were police?"

"Who wishes to be seen by the police if it is possible not to be seen, boss?"

The general and the sergeant exchanged looks. The sergeant shifted his head to study the goat.

"You heard these men talking? You heard the names they called each other, the languages they spoke?"

"I heard nothing, boss. They worked fast, as with a plan, and I think they did not speak."

"You saw them go to the hut of the police, then to the door of the big house?"

"I saw this, boss. First the ones with uniforms, then the others."

"Think carefully, it is important. Did you see how they made the people inside the house to open the door?"

"Three of them stand and talk with the ones inside. I cannot hear the words. Then the door opens and these three go in, then many more. Soon, the shooting. This is all I know."

It was not all. The street light by the big house was a bright one. The faces under that light it was possible to see from a distance. Diosdado had seen two faces come into the small door of the big door. First the young one with light brown hair, then the tall and too quick one, the one of the Packard. But were these facts to say now? Diosdado knew the rule in talking to those in uniform: offer nothing that is not directly asked. Tell more than is asked and they think you talk too much of one thing to hide another thing. The general did not ask if there was one face, then another face, in the little door. He asked only of the door's opening. Of this Diosdado knew nothing.

"There is nothing else you can tell us? Think, man. A thing however little?"

A hard question again. The ones in uniform had gone to the small wood house, then the ones not in uniform. Then three in uniform had gone to the door of the big house. But before this the three in uniform had gone to the Packard, to the place where Diosdado had earlier replaced the spare wheel. These had opened the door there with a key and removed the guns, no blankets but all the guns. Two had brought the guns to those in the small house. Then the three had gone to the door.

Were these things of importance? Diosdado thought quickly. Now to mention the guns could make trouble for the owner of the Packard. This man had been a friend to Diosdado. He had given him the tire, plus money.

Also—around each of those guns had been wrapped a serape. Better to avoid all talk of serapes.

"This is what I know, boss."

"This car," the general said, pointing to the green car, "this Packard. After the false police went away the door in the back of this car was open. You saw those men open this door?"

"I was behind the hut, boss. From this place I can see the front of the car, not the back."

The general and the sergeant were looking at him with hard faces. Their faces said that they knew things of him that were not good.

He remembered the letter. They could have heard about this letter. He wanted to show them that he could be an honest man. Also, it would be good to change the subject.

"Moment, boss," he said. "I have it in the house. I will get it, I have no use for it."

They seemed surprised. He hurried into the house, motioned to Serafina to keep quiet, that all went well. He got the letter from behind the picture of the refrigerator, went out and offered it to the general.

"I do not wish what is not mine, boss. I only keep it for those who wish it, when they come to ask."

General Ortega opened the letter and read its contents. His face became soft. He began to smile.

"This is 122 Avenida Londres?"

"Yes, boss."

"Your name is Diosdado? You have a woman named Serafina? You have seven kids?"

"Yes, boss. Seven alive."

"Then the Ministry of Social Security writes to you." He laughed harder. "You will need much social security." He handed the letter back. Diosdado heard him say in a low voice to the sergeant: "He is like all of them, this one. I know them well, I too marched in 1910. They are difficult but they are good fellows. . . . I must go. They wait for me at the National Palace."

Diosdado heard the mention of the year 1910. He thought: in 1910 I was with Pancho and I was shooting at the generals like him with the gold ropes on the cap and the shoulder.

"You have much use for this letter," the general said in a friendly way. "It is worth many, many Packard tires to you."

"Boss," Diosdado began to say rapidly, "I speak the truth of this tire, boss. Truly, I did not take it from this car, the man of the car, he is a good man, he gives—"

But the general and the sergeant were walking away to the pink blue house.

CHAPTER XV

The President stood at his office window. Below, the midmorning traffic lavas edged about the National Palace.

Across Avenida Emiliano Zapata, the sunken square with its excavated ruins, all that was left of the tall Aztec teocalli once the seat of government of this over illuminated plain; to the left, there facing on the Plaza, the Zócalo Cathedral, built by the first conquistadors with stones taken from that pyramid.

What centuries and worlds those building blocks had leaped in crossing the street! From jaguar cult's sharp edges to resurrectionist filigree—progress!

They had reshuffled the teocalli into a soaring piece of Holy Roman embroidery, yes: from a calendrical fascism presided over by azimuth ratios to messianic imperialism under the sign of the Cross and the rallying-cry of *Espíritu Santo:* altar sacrifices gave way to the Inquisitional autos-da-fé brought in by the Iberian crossbowmen: yes—progress?

At least the art of government—not to mention the science of police work—had been simpler and more direct under the full-feathered Aztec priests. Civic order had been easier to preserve when Moctezuma was an Emperor rather than a beer. Enemies presented themselves in full sight—a blessing. The Chichimecs, barbarians or no, came, not with machine guns in the dead of night, but galloping down from the northern mountains in visible and noisy swarms: no sly burrowing. Those the regime wished to pack off were dismembered, not in Dachau gas chambers and Lubianka cellars but on the jasper block with an obsidian knife—not for a Third Reich, not for the Proletarian Fatherland, for the greater honor and glory of Huitzilopochtli, the serpent-braided and pearl-studded hideous deity. Had the sacrificial gods had a true face-lifting since? Were they more photogenic today?

In the vaults of that teocalli across the way Hernán Cortés and Bernal Díaz found, piled neatly as cans on a grocer's shelf, one hundred thirty-six thousand human skulls—there was police action!

They installed the Virgin Mary and instituted a regular program of *Te Deums,* quite so. But with the razing of the blood-veneered old teocalli, as the Gothic lacework spires went up, the Dog Peoples went underground. Since then, so many creepers and belly crawlers.

Some stubborn filigrees lasted after their coatings of Christianity wore off. Clogging all areas and airs. A few Moctezuman hard lines in them would help!

When Rubén Viedma came back into the room his face was gathered in worry.

"Things were simpler in '11," he said. "We got on our horses and rode out to them."

"We had the inconceivable luxury," General Ortega said, rotating his cap on his knee. "People still fought in the open, here and there."

"Let me be frank, old friend. This affair has repercussions."

"Too many."

"The boy Justin was an American citizen. Yesterday I had two calls from Washington to ask what progress was being made. This morning—an official visit from the American ambassador."

"A boy was wantonly murdered, Mr. President. I am as interested in finding the guilty ones as the American ambassador."

"Two days have passed! The world press is full of agitated questions! So far—no arrests, no clues."

"We have the preliminaries to a clue, Mr. President, The two prostitutes."

"They remain preliminaries. You get exactly nothing from them."

"It takes time. They will talk."

"There must be a break in this case, Fidel. I insist on it. Permit me a cliché—the honor of Mexico is at stake."

"A certain question, Mr. President. How quickly these women talk—depends on how far you wish me to go with them. . . ."

"The affair must be resolved. . . . Use any means short of torture: there we must decline to imitate them."

"Then I can promise you: these two will talk."

General Ortega stood. The President walked with him to the door.

"You would like to be back on your ranch today, eh? With many tomatoes and no GPU's?" The President put his arm around the general's shoulder. "How goes it there in the country with the seeds and shoots?"

"Well. We are working now on a strain of maize that resists parasites and fungus. The first results are good."

"Tabasco—the land reform is well along there. I have been meaning to ask you—the reallocation is trouble for you?"

The general shrugged.

"Who knows how it can end? The péons of the district have much hunger for the land."

"We know this hunger from '11. It was not new then."

"I have not waited for government expropriations: last year I divided up twenty percent of my properties among the péons and the land of the village I deeded to the village in perpetuity. Some days ago I heard from my manager that the péons want more still: everything. Their appetites get bigger when they are fed."

"If the entire estancia is broken up into small farms the péons will not grow experimental plants—they will grow what they eat. . . . Listen, Fidel. If there is serious trouble—let me know. Perhaps I can do something."

"Why did we fight side by side with the péons in '11? So that now I can ask my old comrade the President for help *against* the péons?"

"This research work is needed. It will benefit the péons too."

"Thank you, Rubén, but no. I will do what I can."

"As you wish. . . . Remember: I expect some developments. Quickly."

"You will have them, Mr. President."

In the anteroom General Ortega asked to use the secretary's phone. He called his own office.

"Well? Nothing more about the women?" He listened intently. His face quickened. "Finally! Ceuta—ah, good, very good! Bring her to my office immediately. That one, Sovietina. I will interrogate her myself. And Jaime—see to it that Captain Cherni is standing by. We will have need of him. . . ."

"After ten, Cándida. We must start."

"When you tell me where we are going."

"How can I tell you the place? Be reasonable. If we are stopped on the way—can I be sure you would not talk? In your present frame of mind? . . . Cándida. We are going to meet George. George will be there. Save your questions for him."

"The one I want to see is not George."

"You will see Tomás too. You will see him."

"He will be with George?"

"Tomás will *not* be with George. Not when you *arrive*. I am to bring *you* to George. Then I go to meet *Tomás* at the Tres Quetz— at a certain cantina. Then I bring *Tomás* to *George*. At twelve-thirty exactly. You will see your darling Tomás at twelve-thirty—if you will be good enough to get in the car now. Come, Cándida. It is a long drive. The traffic will be heavy at this hour. Come."

"You have changed your tone since the big night, Ramón. There is not so much rooster in your voice, you say an occasional please. . . . What is this trickery? Why am I to go to one place and Tomás to another?"

"Woman: if we told Tomás to come to George by himself he might not come—he has much temperament now about George. So I tell him only to meet me in the cantina. There I will inform him his momma is with George. Now you understand? Tomás misses no rendezvous with his momma."

"Twelve trained men go in with guns—they get one harmless schoolboy—with a knife! Allow Tomás a little 'temperament'—he knows what this bungling can mean. . . . What will be his orders now, Ramón? What will George—"

"In the car, Cándida. Please. We must go. It is far after ten. . . ."

"And so?" the Hindu girl said. She had slipped off the bed coat and was lying back nude on the cot, abundant in thigh, slack in breast; she regarded him with eyes half sullen, half mocking. "You want only to look?" Her body had an obscured patina, as though buffed and then lightly dusted: copper vessel toned down by handling. "To look is not cheaper."

He stayed in the chair. He hardly knew why he had followed her into this crib. He had been walking the streets for hours, he'd found himself going through the stale morning hush of Organo Street, there was this girl at the door with her unwashed face, camisole parted on her breasts like the entrance flaps of a circus tent after the crowd has gone home, red caste mark on the forehead, droning out

the words, "Here, man, you want to be kissed all over?"—he'd
turned back and gone in with a sleepwalker's looseness.

"Look, then. The price is the same."

He had been almost out of his mind with agitation for two days
and nights. His stomach was a pressed ball of silver foil, he could eat
nothing. He sweated all the time, trickles came coldly down his
sides from his armpits, at times he would stop wherever he was on
the street and lean against a wall, shivering. Emma made it worse.
Now she was friendly. Now! At night she left the door to her bedroom open, when she retired she gave him the inviting cow look—he
could not bring himself to go in, the thought of touching her made
him want to shout and wash.

This morning he had got up from the sofa and slipped out of the
living room at sunrise, to wander the streets again and think about
Ramón. Why would Ramón want to see him? What was in their
minds now? What new orders, what—? He did not dare to for-
mulate any answers but there was no way to stop the avalanche of
questions. With each quick step he took to get away from the questions, another question.

"Pass me a cigarette, then. I will smoke while you give your eyes
a meal."

On the rough brick floor beside the cot, a radio. It was turned
on, a marimba band was playing. A woman's voice, high, minored,
began to sing: of love that is a jail, a crooked jai alai game, a
crucifixion.

His feet knew what they were doing when they took him to
Organo Street. Oh, indeed. His feet understood the nature of the
problem. Why, in times of trouble, did he always go to the whores?
His troubles came, always, always, from one black source—his
mother of stone. He was tied to her with a chain. He could not
break the chain but it was slack and at times he could back away,
pulling the chain, as far as the whores—his feet knew the way. The
chain reached just, just exactly, as far as the whores—those to do
anything with, at a price. No stones there.

Twelve machine guns—they got not even one tarántula on the
wall! Bastards!

She sat there on the mountain, black and immovable—stone!

"No? Then I can live without the cigarette. How long will you wish to look, your highness? I charge for looks by the hour."

Stone! Here!

He got up from his chair in the corner. He fell upon the girl with his full weight. As he pressed himself upon her she made no moves of bored endearment with hands or legs, she did not step up her breathing by the amount the payment called for, no cutrate groans, no bargain sighs—only a peculiar distending of the heavy mouth, the lips held hard together, a tensing of the muscles around the lips. Holding back a yawn! This was before opening hour for Organo business, she was tired out from last night, filled with the need not for him or anything so cursory as a man but simply to yawn—politely she held it in. Thank her!

He wanted to smash that inaccessible mouth, batter that on-sale and unavailable body.

He strained, he struggled. He summoned himself. At this moment, for the first time in his life, he felt himself wholly incapable with a woman.

He wore terror now like a tight scarf. Suddenly it pulled tighter and grew tassels of mucus.

It had never before bothered him that the bodies he held and used under him were articles of commerce and less to be reached and roused than manipulated. Even better when they were inert: obscurely it proved something, stepped up his potency. Now he was filled with a rage—stone here too!

In him—no stone.

He raised himself, resting on his knees. Taking hold of her massed black hair with one hand, he began to slap at her face with the other: palm on one cheek, knuckles returning on the other, systematically, slow motioned, the hand behind keeping her head in place.

"Let me," he whispered against his teeth. "No fight. Let me. Pay for it. Twenty pesos. Big bonus. Hurt goes. Pesos heal." The caste mark on her forehead moved with the blows, to the left, to the right, clocking his violence; a third, minor eye, she looked up at him with three expressionless but held eyes. With the slaps, in lovemaking rhythms, he said to her softly: "Bones hard." Twelve machine guns! "Wake you more than the fuck." What could Ramón want! "Pay you." They sit in black and will not soften! "Be so hard." Not even a tarántula! "Pay well." Cándida, black Cándida. "No more yawns." What could Ramón want.

The upper half of the street door was ajar.

Through the opening came, incomprehensibly, a very large saffron and deep gray butterfly, bringing no news from the morning unemployment of Organo Street.

It flitted here and there without messages, dropped for an exploratory moment onto the pillow, hopped up to the girl's caste mark and found no bounty there, lit on the pillow again.

"What does he want! Hard all through! What can the bastard want!"

As he spat out the words he was pounding on the pillow rather than her face.

The thin voice on the radio was finishing its song: love is a spider's web, love is a room without a door, love is seventeen kilos of quicksand.

"Thing of worms, thing of refuse."

She could hardly have reference to the beating. She had no doubt been in business too long, from Rangoon the long way to Tampico, to be surprised by any of the everyday quirks in her customers—impotence, foaming brutishness, high garrulity. But this was certainly the first time a man had squashed a butterfly on her pillow.

She had raised her head and was looking at the smear on the pillowcase, the yellow mash of the butterfly's spilled substances, bits of wing membrane stuck in this ooze and still jerking—some fleck of life in the débris yet. Her thick and reddened face was twisted as though she was tasting this mess.

"You thing of scabs. How much do you pay for *this?*"

He did not hear. He was still straddling her body but he had let go of her and his hands were up to his temples, pressing. His face was exploding with a laughter that was close to coughing or throwing up.

A man's voice coming from the radio:

". . . . *Hitler's troops into Czechoslovakia last night. . . . And what of Spain? An Emergency Defense Council now governs the central part of Spain—the only territory remaining in Loyalist hands. For the past week General Miaja and Colonel Casado, President and Defense Minister, respectively, of the Council, have been suing Generalisimo Franco for a negotiated peace. But Franco sneers at the overtures—at this moment he is mounting a strong new Nationalist offensive to crush Madrid, the last Loyalist stronghold. He will meet little opposition. Russia has sent the Loyalists no arms for many months. The important Communists have long since been spirited away from Spain to safer places. The end is clearly a matter of days. . . . Spain—Czechoslovakia —now Stalin's international objectives become very clear. Now we know why one month ago, early in February, Stalin signed an agreement to sell Russian oil only to Italy and Germany and their friends. Now we understand why only last week, on Friday, March tenth, Stalin spoke his first words since Hitler annexed Austria and the Sudeten lands—words containing no comment on Hitler's actions—only vilifying the Western powers for plotting to "poison the atmosphere and provoke a conflict" between Germany and Russia—a conflict for which, he emphasized, there are "no visible grounds." Now we can appreciate why, as far back as January of 1934, Stalin addressed himself to Hitler with these placating words: "With Germany, as with other states, we want to have the best relations. . . . Fascism is not the issue here, if only for the reason that Fascism, in Italy for example, did not prevent the Soviet Union from establishing good relations with that country." . . . Yesterday—three hurried days after Stalin's denial of any differences between himself and Hitler—obviously a go-ahead signal for the Nazis—Hitler marches into Czechoslovakia. Can anyone doubt this move was undertaken with Stalin's prior knowledge and agreement? . . . Spain is finished, because Stalin long ago, in orientation if not in writing, threw in his lot with the Rome-Berlin axis. Now—Czechoslovakia. . . . This morning it is reported that the secret negotiations in Berlin for a Nazi-Soviet Pact are almost concluded. . . ."*

The Hindu girl stared up with her mouth open. Masson, still on his knees, held on to his ears and laughed or coughed harder, gagging.

General Ortega did not look up when his aide brought in the woman. "Sit," he said, studying the open dossier on his desk. It was a full minute before he brought the folder shut with a slap and raised his eyes.

"Your superiors let you be arrested," he said abruptly. "Why? They thought they could trust you not to talk."

"What superiors?" The woman did not bother to smile. "I have no pimp."

"They trust you. That means you are very good at not talking. . . . Now: let me see, it is just past eleven—before noon, I intend to make you talk. Before the clock strikes twelve I expect to hear much gossip from you, you will babble. . . . Your name is Julia Duarte?"

"As it was yesterday. As it was the day before yesterday."

"Why are you known to your friends as Sovietina?"

"I have told you: some of my friends are close to politics and give me this name for a joke. Nicknames are against the law?"

"This nickname is more than a joke. You were in Spain."

"Was it against the law for a Mexican citizen to go to Loyalist Spain? I did not know this. I was told that in all the world only one country outside of the Soviet Union, only Mexico, gave support to the Loyalists and sent them guns. I represented my country in a friendly democracy. I was a good-will ambassador."

"You are a remarkably well-informed whore. . . . We sent guns, yes. We were the only ones, outside of Russia. We can take more pride in this than the Russians: we sent as much as we could, they sent as little as they dared. . . . Why did you go to Spain?"

"I do much business with soldiers. In Spain there was war: many soldiers."

"You had more complicated business in Spain. You worked in the administration of an unofficial GPU prison—under George Bass."

"Listen, general, why do you keep saying these initials and names to me? I work under men, yes, it is my business, but not in prison, in bed. . . . I did certain office work in Madrid because I was drafted for it."

"More than office work. And not always in Madrid." The general opened his dossier and scanned the top paper. He spoke out with strength: "For seven months—August, 1937 to March, 1938—you were in Fascist territory—North Africa—Ceuta. You were a whore who catered to high ranking Franco officers. For three months you were the favorite of a colonel named Dionisio Ochoa. A very important fellow—said to be a protégé of Franco himself."

She showed no reaction but her fingers were gripping tight over the seat of her chair.

"You collected military information from your officer friends," the general went on. "Data on garrison strengths and troop movements which you transmitted to George Bass's headquarters in Madrid. I have full documentation on this. Bass arranged your escape from Ceuta when Ochoa became suspicious of you. To keep Ochoa from talking you and your associates killed him with cyanide pellets discharged with force into his abdomen."

"Who makes up such stories?"

"Among the refugees from Spain are more than a few who were friends of your movement and now are not your friends. They get in line to tell their stories. I have many rich documents—with names, with dates, with addresses."

The woman stared at General Ortega for several seconds. She shrugged and recrossed her legs.

"I knew a Colonel Ochoa in North Africa, yes. There was no politics in this—in my work I go to many places and meet many officers, of all colors. . . . I will tell you the truth. I was in love with this Ochoa. He had a nice face."

"As you were in love with Nico Silva?" She stared harder. "You were the unofficial wife of Nico Silva for four years before you went to Spain. I will refresh your memory. Nico Silva is head of the Trade Union Committee of the Communist Party of Mexico."

"I have been in love with more than one man in my life. You want me to confess? I confess: there is no party politics in my bed."

"Love? Love?" Her head jerked up at the peculiarly tight tone in his voice. He stood and went around the desk to her, his hand raised in a fist. "You speak of love? You think you know love? What you know is mucus. You have dealings with men that are mucus, one mucus to another mucus, and this is your love." He leaned against his desk. His fist was trembling. He lowered his face until it was close to hers. "A woman? No—a mucus machine. Sovietina. You are a whore with a corruption they do not know on Organo Street. They would stone you and drive you away if you went there.

You and those like you say you work for a glorious end—love everywhere in the world—you claim exclusive ownership of this end. Then you say—such a shining end justifies all means. Then you make all things in the world your means—including, first of all, love. Including, even, your bodies. You dispense your vaginas as you dispense slogans! This is a vileness and a depravity, but you call it program and important work! Do not speak of love and dirty the word for good! You are the expert on mucus."

He was still smarting over his summons to the National Palace, of course. It was an indignity to have the President stepping into an investigation supposed to be in the Police Chief's hands. That the President felt it necessary to tell him of the importance of the case and the need for quick results—this was a slap in the face. But more than humiliation had brought on this outburst. All the revulsion rising in him these past months over the Rostov business, the shadows of the GPU, the world and way of life hinted at in all this—this revulsion had suddenly, at this moment, reached its boiling point. He craved the most searing sunlight—here were darks in a fester.

The general's aide could not know all this. He stood to one side listening and hardly believing his ears. He had always known his chief as a modulated man with a modulated voice.

"You liked Spain?" General Ortega said without transition. "You would like to return to Spain? Tomorrow?" He was not waiting to see her response. He signaled curtly to his aide. "Bring him in. We will help the lady make her travel reservations."

The aide went into the corridor. In a moment he came back with a bulky, swirl mustached man wearing the trim blue uniform and braided cap of a ship's captain.

"Captain Cherni," the general said, "tell this lady the name of your ship."

The captain took a long draw on his fat dun cigar. Exhaling the smoke in a connoisseur's slow cloud over the woman's head, he said with a pleasant air, "The S.S. Bahía. Panamanian registry. Oh, 12,000 tons, more or less. A freighter, but with some passenger accommodations, quite nice ones." He spoke smooth Spanish, with a vague accent of Central Europe.

"Your cargo?"

"Bananas, sisal, copper and tin ore, cocoanut oil. But, as I say, we have a few staterooms. We carry some passengers too: the cuisine and service are excellent."

"Tell what kind of passenger."

"Well, general," the man said, "each trip we arrange to put in at one port or another of Franco Spain—Barcelona, Ceuta, a place like this. We carry certain passengers back to Franco Spain from the Latin countries, you understand? Communists who ran away when Franco came too close—fellows Franco would like to see again. Naturally, these people do not book passage on the Bahía themselves. Oh, no. They do not care for ocean voyages at all."

"The police arrange the reservations for them?"

"The Latin police decide that certain of these people are too big a nuisance or a trouble and they think—maybe Franco would like these people more? But it cannot be done officially, you see, these countries do not have relations with Spain now. So it is a thing arranged unofficially, by the police more than the passenger. Usually the passengers are so strong against ocean trips that they are brought up the gangplank kicking and making much noise. They have to be carried aboard but the police are willing. Does this answer your question?"

"What is your precise interest in these passengers? Explain to the lady."

"Oh, general, do not get the wrong impression. I have nothing against these poor souls I take back, truly, it does not give me a good feeling to think what must happen to them in the hands of the Franco police. But what alternative do I have? You see, I am a small business man, the Spanish police pay me one thousand excellent American dollars for each head I bring that is on their wanted list. This is very important pay for a modest export trader like myself. Money is Number One on *my* wanted list. Also, I take some satisfaction from the knowledge that I help law and order in the Latin countries. I have all my life loved and cherished the Latins. I owe them for many past favors. It pleases me to do for them a service they cannot do themselves."

"When is your next sailing?"

"Tomorrow morning. From Vera Cruz."

"Your first stop?"

"Barcelona."

"You have your passenger list? Tell us if there are any women on it."

The captain drew a piece of paper from his breast pocket and unfolded it. "One, my general." The cigar wobbled between his teeth as he read from the typed words, holding the sheet down so that the woman could see: "Julia Duarte, alias Julia Silva, known as Sovietina."

"One thing more. How do you know the Franco police are interested in this woman?"

"Oh, general, let me assure you, I do not accept passengers unless I know with a certainty that they are wanted very much over there. It would be bad business, very risky, there could be heavy losses—you can understand this. I have made sure the lady is in demand. I have had an exchange of cables about her case." He took some yellow sheets from his side pocket and held them out politely to the woman: she did not move. "She seems to be high up on their list, near the top. In a case like this one I have high hopes to get a bonus."

"You can wait outside."

The aide showed the captain out, then took up his position at the door again.

General Ortega now addressed the aide: "You are to take this woman to Vera Cruz tonight. Keep her under heavy guard until she is aboard the Bahía. She is not to be out of your sight until the ship sails. Go and get her ready for the trip."

The officer went to the woman and indicated that she was to get up. She shoved his hand away. Her face was white.

"You only talk," she said in a low voice. "You will not do this. That piece of shit delivers Spanish refugees to the Franco butchers —I am a Mexican citizen."

"Generalísimo Franco seems ready to overlook that technicality, in view of your distinguished record."

"No, you lie. You lie. Our government is against Franco. It does not send people to be killed by Franco."

"There, dear lady, you are not in full possession of the facts. Since I have been Chief here I, personally, have sent several people back to Spain via Captain Cherni's convenient shuttle system. Have you not heard in your circles of certain important ones who disappeared into thin air? The disappearances were prearranged—by me. I will be happy to give you the names. Not many, but some. So far they have been only Spanish subjects, you are right. Like Franco, I am willing to make an exception in your case."

"Then you are a butcher too! Fascist butcher!"

"Point of information: at this precise moment, according to intelligence reports in my hands, Stalin is transferring to Hitler hundreds of prisoners from the Siberian labor camps—German refugees. Hitler will be happy to get these anti-Fascist fighters—Communists, most of them. . . . You see, this dirty work, though unofficial, is accepted international practice. Nobody talks of it, but many do it. I learned the procedure from Mr. Stalin."

"You know how Franco treats anti-Fascists!"

"Certainly. As Stalin knows how Hitler will treat the German anti-Fascists he gets from Russia. In very much the same way they are treated in Russian labor camps. . . . You talk to me of butchers? You and your friends butchered a boy two nights ago in Coyoacán! Let Franco do what he wants with you! . . . Take her, Jaime."

The woman pushed the officer back fiercely.

"I am a Mexican citizen! I have friends! They will tell the country how you serve Franco!"

"Be realistic. Your friends will never know what happened to you. You go down in the police books with the missing persons—a simple case of kidnapping—unsolved. Once you reach Spain, what can we do for you anyhow? We have no diplomatic relations with the Franco government, we are helpless to protect our nationals there. . . . You begin to see? The Chernis perform a valuable function for us feeble Latin democracies. They step in where diplomats and even police fear to tread. You will have to pardon us for the unorthodox procedure, madame: it is one of the few ways we have to make the struggle between our people and your people less unequal. . . . I will waste no more of my time on you. Take her, Jaime."

The officer pulled her to her feet. She did not resist. But as she allowed herself to be led toward the door her head was turned and her eyes stayed on General Ortega.

She let herself be guided almost over the threshold. Suddenly she broke free from the officer and threw herself back into the room. She screamed:

"All right! All right! I think you lie, I am almost sure you lie, I feel you will not do this, but I cannot, I cannot—all right! What do you want to know!"

She dropped in the chair. She put her face in her hands and began to rock forward and back.

"If it can be any comfort to you," General Ortega said crisply and evenly, "I will tell you this: I most certainly, oh, most certainly meant to send you with the lovely Captain Cherni. You need have no doubts on that score at all. . . . Now: names and addresses, please. I want to know your associates. I want the identities of at least some of the men who took part in the machine-gun attack. . . . You can begin: I advise you to be accurate. Cherni makes a trip every three months, and there are other Chernis. . . . Names, please. Names!"

"There was Marcos Guaro," she whispered convulsively through her fingers. "He brought us money and instructions. He had the apartment over us on Londres. I do not know where he could be now. . . . Antonio Derdergo—lieutenant of police in the San Angel station. He is the one who bought the police uniforms. I overheard some talk of this. . . . A man named Ramón, a Basque. I do not know his last name, I have never seen him but often he telephoned. . . ."

She talked for twenty minutes, voice shaking, hands over her mouth. General Ortega asked precise questions, making notes on his pad. When she had told it all she dropped her hands to her sides and sat listlessly, lips loose and turned out, as though she was falling asleep. The aide lifted her and, supporting her dead weight with both arms, led her out.

When he returned a few moments later he burst out: "Bravo, bravo! You did it, my chief! We have them now!"

"Some of them," the general said quietly. "The burros and pack horses of the job. You will notice there was no information as to the whereabouts of Mr. Bass and other dignitaries. I doubt she was holding back." He stood looking at his notepad with a frown. He tore the top pages off and handed them to the aide. "Send out all available men. I want these people arrested and brought here within the hour."

"Cherni asks about his money."

"Yes, yes. Let me see: he loses one thousand dollars—have a department check made out to him for that sum. Charge it to—traveling expenses." The aide turned to leave. "Jaime—listen. Keep a careful dossier on everything relating to Cherni and his operations. Get as much on him as you can. There may come a time when we have no more need of him—then we can pay him off as he deserves. . . . The filth. The animal. . . ."

The aide went out. Slowly the general walked over to the wall near the window, stopped to examine the framed photograph there. It was an old and faded monotint showing the general and Rubén Viedma as young officers, astride horses; between them their leader, point-bearded and melancholy-eyed Benjamino Madero, also on horseback: a memento of the campaigns of '10, when they rode out boldly to them.

"What grows above ground now. . . ." he said aloud to the young and sunny faces of '10. "Where are the horses. . . . What is happening to me. . . ."

"You look terrible. Still running around nights?"

"I want to know why you called me here."

"It's a nice little bar. Mink carpets and mother-of-pearl chandeliers, you can keep them; give me zinc counters and plenty of sawdust on the floor—proletarian simplicity. Wonder why they call it the Tres Quetzals? I could think of other birds to name it after. Queerer birds come in here—George, you, me. . . ."

"I asked you a question: why did you want to see me?"

"Finish your beer, Tomás. This Moctezuma's an excellent ale. . . . You really do look run down, you know. Have you given up sleep entirely? . . . Too bad things went wrong the other night. I thought for sure we got him. . . . You want my theory? We got a little spoiled in Spain; George, especially. You can get in the habit of barking orders at troops, solving everything with guns—"

"Either you answer me—"

"Drink your drink, why don't you. . . . Some momma you've got. You should have taken more after your momma. There's a cool operator; I know, I was on some jobs with her. She's got a real grip on herself. . . ."

"Where is my mother now? How is she?"

"Here's my thought: two kinds of people get into our work, basically. Hotheads and cool heads. We don't trust the hot ones—too unstable: might explode at the worst moment. Only we need them for certain things. For example, who could we get to go on a suicide mission? Who would do an unreasonable thing like that? A man with a cool head wants to keep his head; it's the only professional attitude. But a hothead, who lets his feelings get the best of him, he'll stop at nothing, sometimes. If you heat him up enough."

"Why do you keep bringing up my mother? Is anything wrong? . . . Ramón, what's George planning now? Is he—"

"You may have to pay one more visit to that house, Tomás. It is a possibility. That's my feeling about it."

"How can I go back! If they start to think about how that door got opened—"

"Thinking takes time. . . . That door's got to be opened once more. . . . You see what was wrong with Plan A, Tomás? Too many hands in the pie. Including some lousy amateur hands. . . . What we need in our business, Tomás, is professionals, right? Professionals like you and me, right?" He poked Masson humorously in the chest; the younger man shrank from the contact. "Too many hands. So now we have to do the whole job over again. With only one hand." He took Masson's hand from the table and held it up. "One hand's easier to control than twenty."

Masson jerked his hand away.

"Not mine. They'll have to find some other way. . . . I can't. . . ."

"Can't? You *can't* want your momma to take that boat ride, *can* you, Tomás? You *can't* kill your own momma, *can* you? Don't you know that's illegal, to kill your own momma? . . . Good. Now you're acting like a professional."

"You're saying these things to torment me. . . . George couldn't be thinking of using me again. . . ."

"No? You forget some details, Tomás. Days ago he gave you some presents. A nice raincoat with a loop inside, a certain manuscript. Didn't you stop to think what was the meaning behind these articles? You'd rather leave all the thinking to us unstylish fellows?"

"It wouldn't work. . . . They'd stop me this time. . . . George has sense enough to realize that. . . ."

"He realizes you'll make it work if you're serious enough. . . . I don't actually know what's in George's mind but I can guess. I'll let you in on some gossip. George is in a spot. How do you think they feel about him back home this minute? They hold him responsible for the other night, nobody but him. There are those high up who always had it in for George anyway. They'll use this failure against him for all it's worth. . . . George knows he's in trouble. You can tell—he puts on a show of being lighthearted—that's a sure sign with him. If he's called to account, you think he wants to face them as a failure? No, sir. He wants this job done right, and fast; no more misses. He'll use any means possible to get it done. The only means left—is you. . . . Of course, that's only one man's opinion. I could be wrong. In any case, don't get all worked up. Cool off that hot head. Even if you're the one it may not have to be a suicide mission. George's clever. He may have another way. . . . Come on. We have to get over to his place. That's the reason I was sent to get you."

"You sit there and talk—as though you were playing with matchsticks. No! It's my life that's involved. . . . I'm not going anywhere. I'm through being used. . . ."

"I'll let you in on something else: your momma's there waiting to see you."

"There? Now? How do I know you're telling the truth?"

"Look—you don't take a step without your momma, George knows that. And right now—I think, I could be wrong—George wants you to take a big, big step. . . . She's there all right. It's no trick. I drove her into town myself, just before I came here. Come on, Tomás. Let's get moving, man. We're due there at twelve-thirty. You know George doesn't like to be kept waiting. . . ."

"Señora Rostov? General Ortega. I am sorry to disturb you—I have something to tell your husband. Would you be so good as to call him to the telephone. . . . Thank you, señora. . . ." He waited.

"Yes, general?"

"Señor Rostov—seven of the attackers have been arrested. I have them here at headquarters."

"Excellent. Who are they?"

"I have the list on my desk. . . . Antonio Derdergo: lieutenant of police in San Angel, member of Communist Party, until last year a

political commandant in the Spanish International Brigade. . . .
Marcos Guaro: Communist major in Spain, formerly an organizer
of miners in Hostotipaquillo, member of Trade Union Committee of
the Communist Party. . . . Fernando—"

"No need to read them all, general."

"You are not interested? I thought you might care to come to
headquarters and examine the prisoners yourself. . . . These are
the men who tried to kill you!"

"*Seven* of them. Behind them are others whose names you don't
have. And behind *them*. . . ."

"I will get them! Every one!"

"You'll work hard and intelligently at it, I know. But your efforts
will be wasted. . . . I have no interest in talking to your prisoners,
general. Is there anything else?"

"The same question: the failure was not only on our side, it was
in your house, too. My prisoners are of no help. They say they do
not know how the door was opened and I believe them. They say
Bass kept them too far away to hear. It sounds like the truth."

"General, there's no reason to go through it again. It was a very
human failure: Bass tricked the boy somehow."

"You are a military genius, señor. This is well known. How much
military genius have you used in organizing your household? I have
even wondered—if you care. . . ."

"If you suspect any of my associates I must ask that you be
specific."

"You are entirely sure of them?"

"Entirely."

"These are not accusations—only intuitions. I know only that
David Justin was instructed to keep the door closed; and he opened
it. . . ."

"He was an intelligent boy but inexperienced."

"Where do you think they will try next time?"

"I can only say this. . . . Major operations are approached from
two directions. Plan A is put into motion first; Plan B is carefully
organized and kept in reserve. All we can be sure of is that B will
be utterly unlike A."

"They will rely more on brains than brute force this time?"

"The first attempt was military. The second may be—more subtle in nature. . . . It will come from the most unexpected quarter. And this time, I think—police or no police—they won't fail."

"You say that, señor—almost with relief."

"I am a historical materialist, general—I know how to reconcile myself to the inevitable."

"Try this. . . ." George Bass was leaning against the wall. He pulled at his lower lip as he dictated. *"To whom it may concern: In Belgium, during my student days, I became a fighter against social injustice. Later, in Paris, I joined the Rostovite circle. . . ."* He began to move about the room, searching for words. He was studying his feet. *"In October 1938 I was summoned to Mexico for consultation with our leader, Victor Rostov. These meetings shocked me, for Rostov wished to smuggle me into Russia to carry out sabotage and assassinate top Soviet leaders, beginning with Josef Stalin. I found my 'hero'—quotes around 'hero'—a bloodthirsty, vengeful man who cared as much for the working class as he did for his undershirt. . . ."*

The typewriter keys went fast under Masson's fingers.

They were in the Moorish-style living room of a small house set back some distance from the street and hidden by a row of firs. This was in the district out past Chapultepec Park, not far from El Toreo Bull Ring. Ramón sat in a corner, flipping the pages of an old *Life.*

"Like the touch about the undershirt?" Bass said.

"Inspired." Masson did not look up.

"Homely touches are important. Show sincerity and strong feelings." He clapped Masson on the shoulder. "Get into the spirit of the thing! This is exciting; here we are, writing history *before* it's made! Of course, I'm no Ernest Hemingway but I think I've got some neat phrases there." He began to tour the room again. "Now. Let's see."

"Shouldn't you get the new Washington line in?" Ramón said from his corner.

"Right. Right. Here: *Rostov spoke to me in the warmest terms about the work of the reactionary Martin Dies Committee in Washington. I was stunned by his enthusiasm. He said this red-baiting group of the American Congress was doing a fine job of suppressing Communist workers. It filled me with revulsion to realize that his*

*activities against Russia were under the direct guidance of the most
ruthless wings of American imperialism. The conclusion was in-
escapable that all of Rostov's projects, all of them without exception,
are being financed, and handsomely, by Dies and his degenerate Wall
Street supporters. The money Rostov offered me to go to Russia was
undoubtedly tainted Dies money."*

The typewriter worked steadily.

"What's missing is the love interest. . . . *Finally*—write, write—
*finally, to show what little concern he had for anything which did
not touch him personally, I will add that I am engaged to a young
woman whom I love with all my heart, because she is good and
loyal. When I told him I could not go to Russia because I wanted to
get married, he became upset and ordered me to break off with 'this
little tramp.'* Quotes around 'this little tramp.' . . . By the way,
what's her schedule for today?"

"Who?"

"The girl. Emma. The tramp in question."

"She's staying out there with Paul. She wanted me to join them
—I said I had too many appointments."

Bass nodded. "Take this down: *I cannot live without Emma. It
is because of her, and only because of her, that I have decided to
sacrifice myself by getting rid of this enemy of the working class . . .
In case anything should happen to me I demand publication of this
statement. Signed, Jacques Masson, March 17, 1939, Hotel Molinas,
etcetera, etcetera. . . ."*

"Nice twist," Ramón said. "You've killed not only for politics but
for love: most unprofessional motive."

"Petty-bourgeois intellectuals," Bass said, "always look for personal things in politics. We have to oblige them. The bobby-soxers
will be crazy about you too: all the world loves a lover!"

It took Masson several seconds to finish typing. He put his hands
down and hunched over the machine, reading the last words he had
written.

"In case . . . anything . . . happens . . . to me. . . ."

"This document gives a first rate explanation of the corpse," Bass
said. "Now all we need is the corpse. This afternoon you deliver it
and our work is done."

"When this was over I was supposed to take a trip—with my

mother. . . . I take a trip. Oh, yes. Only not with anybody. Not this trip." Masson looked at Bass for the first time. "You can stop playing games. I didn't agree to anything. I said I wanted to talk with my mother and then I would see. You said—"

"Leave your mind open, take this dictation, see how you like the plan—I know what I said. Well—you like it?"

"You also said—it could be handled so that I'd get out all right. . . ."

"I said maybe. There was a chance."

"You're not planning on my getting out! *In case* . . . *anything happens*. . . ." Masson rose with a quick movement and went toward Bass. Ramón dropped his magazine and sat up alertly. "Something *is* going to happen, isn't it? It's your whole premise."

"Why all the gloom?" Bass said. "People are supposed to feel good when a job's near the end."

"Your plan calls for *two* corpses today. You're *counting* on it. And you expect me to oblige. . . ."

"Stop seeing the black side of things, young fellow. It's not a Marxist attitude." Masson remained standing. His lips were moving. Bass dropped his bantering tone. "Let's talk seriously. Sit down."

Masson did not move. "You planned everything. . . . Why did I have to get friendly with the Rostovs? Not just to open the door. . . . You gave me a raincoat with a loop: what for? You wrote an article for me. *What for?* . . . You plan everything. . . . That statement is meant to be found in my pocket. After I'm dead. That's part of your plan too. . . ."

"You never figured out you'd have to be B in case A didn't work? A bright fellow like you?"

"Because *you* bungled things, *I've* got to pay. . . ."

"Somebody's got to. *I* can't; it's not my line of work."

"You really think I'll do this, to save your dirty neck? All I said was, I'd consider it, I'd listen—if there was a way for me to get out afterwards! I only said it because I wanted to see my mother and that was your condition! . . . I'm not giving my skin to protect yours, oh, no!"

"Tomás: who can say what might happen out there? There's a chance you can get away, yes. But there are no guarantees in these things. . . . The statement *has* to be on you. In case. . . ."

"In case nothing! You *expect* me to get it out there! You *want* me to! If *they* don't take care of me, *you* will!"

"You can depend on it—if you don't do the job and do it right."

"You give me a nice alternative! If I do it I'm a corpse; if I don't do it I'm a corpse—you'll see to that!"

"Then don't let your death be wasted. Do this job for us. . . . You've already been paid for it."

"Paid! You animal—*you* were paid too! All you did was shoot up the woodwork a little! *You're* in trouble too!"

"Yes. I may be in trouble. It's possible. Draw the conclusions from that: it should tell you I mean to have the job done right. And you're the one to do it." Bass shook his head. "You get so personal about everything. . . . I remind you: a third party is also in some trouble."

Masson froze. His lips came together. "Where is she? I'm finished with this insane talk—where is she?"

"I've had new instructions, Tomás. If things don't go right today, they want her back immediately. . . ."

Masson sagged. He did not try to resist as Bass took him by the shoulders and pushed him down into a chair. He only said in a whisper, "Is she really here? I must see her, I must. . . ."

Bass leaned over and began to talk quietly:

"Believe it or not, I was once so bourgeois as to have a momma. . . . For my momma I drove a cab twelve hours a night through the postcard streets of Philadelphia: she had to eat. That's momma's role: to keep us soft and regular. Momma's boys punch the clocks and drive the cabs, they don't make revolutions. . . . So I threw momma and her strawboss mouth out of my head. I stopped being a yessir-nosir chauffeur to the world. I began giving the world orders. . . . I learned languages, I became the owner of passports. I slip names on and off like cigar bands. I have money in the bank, I've been to Cambodia."

He straightened up and stepped back with a sigh.

"Listen, Tomás, the first law of power is to keep it. That's what our business is here; the rest doesn't matter. I'd give my own two-bit life tomorrow, like I'd walk into a drug store, if it helped us to keep power."

"Easy to say. . . . Nobody's asking you. . . ."

"That's the thing that makes us strong and to some point: to be connected with a structure of power. . . . What do you imagine Rostov'd be doing this minute, if he'd had sense enough to fight Stalin seriously instead of with popgun words—if he'd fought to win and won? What we're doing now against him he'd be doing against us; and he'd be right. These are the life and death matters. There are no personalities here. . . . But you: you're probably going to die today—because you're a lover in kneepants." He made a face. "A patsy. You've got to make a personal story out of everything."

"I won't die if I don't go! You can't make me go!"

"You'll go."

"I don't move until I see her."

"I know. You don't go for a haircut without momma. . . . I'll be back."

He signalled to Ramón to stay. He walked to the door and went out.

"You ought to cool off," Ramón said. "Maybe you'll come out of it all right."

"That would bother him more than my not going. Once I've taken care of Rostov I've just one value in George's eyes—I'm a mailman. He wants his letter delivered."

"Well—look at it this way. It's hard to find people for a job like this. You were born for suicide missions—it's your biggest talent."

"I thank George for taking such a personal interest in my career."

Then Masson sprang to his feet.

Bass had come back into the room with Cándida behind him.

CHAPTER XVI

Unusual activity this morning on the péon's property. Three times Diosdado had gone to the river to fill his water buckets. Alongside the chicken coop his wife had set up a large pail and in it scrubbed the children one by one. After that the young ones, who usually ran around in rags or nothing at all, had been dressed in what looked like party clothes, the boys in immaculate white cottons, the girls in crisp print dresses. All heads of hair were combed, some braided. All, even the father and mother, had put on huaraches, making a big fuss about it. Now a big open truck, filled with passengers similarly scrubbed and dressed up, big ones and little ones, had stopped in front of the place and Diosdado was helping his family climb in the back.

From across the street Paul and Guillermo saw most of this.

"Rich country, Mexico, no?" Guillermo said. "Any small thing you plant, it grow. Plant one little rubber tire in the hand of one little campesino—some crazy crop! Whole plantation of the huaraches!"

"Why the truck? Where can they be going?"

"So many? With the hair in the place and the feet in the huaraches? They go some place to dance and get drunk."

"Why? Is it a saint's day or special holiday?"

"This is big saint's day! They got to celebrate the big crop— today is feast day of St. Huarache!"

"David tried talking to that Diosdado—several times. None of his languages would work. . . . How many did headquarters say they arrested? Seven?"

"Maybe more by now. They do not stop to look."

"But nobody knows how they fooled David. . . . You don't either. . . ."

"Why you keep on to say this thing, Señor Paul? If I know something you think I do not tell unless for some goddamn bottles? Then keep your bottles. David, he was friend to me."

Paul held out the cognac bottle. "Take it. Take it. Drink a glass
to him." Guillermo hesitated, Paul put the bottle in his hand. "A
death doesn't bother you much, does it?"

"Everybody die, Paul. Some sooner, some later. I am sorry for
all, even for myself, a little. When I think of this."

"But some make a main event out of it."

"Better, I think, to make the events before."

"Dying is supposed to be hard; you make it sound easy. Most
people can't think about it that way."

"Sure. The ones who have the time to think."

"Do you want to die?"

"What for? Then I cannot to be in the line on payday."

"You wouldn't need any more pay."

"I got to have the pay check, Paul! I need my pay to buy new
strings for the guitar!" The sergeant's face darkened. "David was
my good friend, true. He ask me last week can I give him lesson
on the guitar."

Paul tapped the bottle in Guillermo's hand. "This stuff doesn't
do much for me. Maybe I could take up the five-string guitar to
keep my head from thinking."

All the members of Diosdado's family were up on the overloaded
truck now. The children were whooping and beating sticks on its
slatted sides.

The truck drove off.

"Seven, Marisha! Don't you think this hurts Bass?"

"To the degree that he can be hurt."

"He can be! He is! This is a setback for him."

"Victor—you have had no answer from David's family?"

"Not yet."

"What did you say in the telegram?"

"That the boy died bravely. That Stalin will one day be exposed
and this will be David's vengeance."

"So many sent telegrams to us in Turkey when Leon was killed.
With assurances that Stalin would pay. Condolences in the language of political forecasts—I did not read them. . . . And David's

people are not political as we are. . . . And David—was leaving politics. . . ."

"But politics overtook him."

"Ours, not his. He was with us as a passer through, a boy with too many questions. . . ."

Paul entered the study.

"The body left the airport this morning," he said to V.R. "Guillermo found out. His father's meeting the plane in New York."

"If I could talk with the man. . . ." V.R. said. "No words could comfort him now—but I would like to make him understand. . . . He hasn't answered my telegram."

"For people who have appointed themselves spokesmen for the whole working class," Paul said, "we don't have very much to say to most workers. We convince those who already agree with us—"

"How can Stalin pay?" Marisha said. "What payment is there for a son?"

"I get the impression sometimes," Paul said, "that we make oratory to the entire human race—in order to talk to ourselves."

"Can you design words to fit all ears?" V.R. said.

"Of course his father won't answer," Paul said. "Most workers die a little more each day at their miserable benches; even when they're well paid: the indignity of being a small cog among big cogs, with all your muscles in harness, is too much. They can't understand their sons dying a lot, all at once, for things not remotely connected with questions of bread and butter. . . . Man does not live by bread alone? Most of the bottom ones do. Bread—and whatever alcohol they can get—to help them forget the centralist regime of bread."

"There are words this man would understand," V.R. said. "These: seven of them have been arrested! You've heard the news? Seven of the gunmen—"

"Guillermo told me. They called him on the police phone. . . . David's father won't get worked up about the news, I'm afraid. He probably thinks *we're* responsible for David's death too. . . ."

Marisha rose from her chair.

"You make the walls high with your bags; they walk under them," she said. "Through the wall as though it were paper. How hard you work and try—such a waste. . . . You have been our best and closest friend. Oh, you have, good Paul. But your work is over. Stay and you will go with David. . . . Emma insists on doing the marketing: I must help her with the shopping list. You will excuse me?"

"A last visit with the condemned man?"

"You are wrong, son. The condemned is in Coyoacán."

"Then what *is* the word for me, mother? We must not have any terminological misunderstandings over my corpse."

"A man who shapes the world instead of being shaped *by* it. . . . A man who imposes his will on the world, to make it move in his direction. . . ."

"I want the world to move *away* from me! Far away! I want it to leave me alone—stop pawing at me! . . . *My* will is to live, simply that! Any way I can! In a dung heap, in a pig sty: only to live! . . . This afternoon my job is to do George Bass's will. *Against* my will!"

"Tomás: there is meaning in our work. We are changing the world. That is our will and it must be yours."

Masson made a half turn and impulsively seized both her hands.

"A 'better world'! I'm for it with all my heart! Only—I have a blind spot: I don't see why anybody should die to bring your 'better world' into being! Neither does Ramón: he laughs at those who die for things—without getting a taste of them. . . . What's to be won in a suicide mission? Except the sneers of you people who are smart enough to stay alive! . . . Tell me, mamacita! Why? Why?"

She turned her face from him.

"If a man is not prepared to die for something—what is his life worth?"

"If this 'better world' is to be built on my bones—if I'm never to smell it, hold it in my fingers—I spit on your better world. . . ."

"Yes. That was always your program. Spit on what eludes your fingers. . . ." She pulled her hands away. "Two years ago, at the Madrid front—what did those brave milicianos have in *their* hands? While they were dying like flies?"

"I was there too."

"For three weeks. Because I shamed you into it."

"Did you shame me into this?" He had moved back his sleeve to expose the lower arm.

"A scratch. Others lost eyes and arms and did not want to leave."

"Others lost their lives. With your help."

"You had to run back to your real home: the whorehouses. Why did you never return to the militia? You were too busy holding *your* better world—your job lot whores—in your hands. . . . But you were not satisfied only to hold, were you, Tomás?" She brought her fingers together to make a tight fist. "Sometimes you had to *squeeze*. You liked to *beat* the girls. . . . I heard the stories."

"You're sentimental about the brave defenders of Madrid. How many of them did Bass have shot in the *back*—while they were being so brave at the *front*? How many did *you* have shot; you, personally? . . . Maybe that's what I was trying to forget with the whores."

"We were assigned to the hardest front. Against those on our own side who disrupted our fight."

"Disrupted! How? By being in the majority? By refusing to let the Basses take over? . . . Who disrupted at Barcelona? I heard you planning that 'uprising' for months. . . . Franco's thanking you now for those services. He should put up a monument to your people."

"The job is to eliminate Victor Rostov, not quote him."

Masson rose and took several steps away. He came back and in wild agitation dropped to his knees, clutching at her elbows.

"Mamacita, I'm afraid! You can save me! You were always so strong—help me!"

"My strength was a loan from George. He has taken it back."

He looked up at her imploringly. Her face was set, her eyes would not meet his.

He got slowly to his feet.

"Tell me as a mother: should I go this afternoon?"

"Find the man in charge of history, the chairman of the board: ask him."

"Do *you* want me to go? *Do you?*"

"You insist that I be the least of things—a mother. Not a central fact—a sentimental little joke around the edges. . . . It is sentimentalists who drink and chase girls. Men who cannot fill their heads with events and so must fill their hands with sensation. . . . And cry, momma this, momma that. And beat their whores—for not being events."

"That was why my father drank himself into the grave? Because he was a sentimentalist—who found himself married to an event?"

"A disappointed man: a petty-bourgeois: he wanted for wife a piece of brainless putty."

"Or, just possibly, a woman. . . . Do you want me to go? Yes or no."

"I will not make your decision for you."

"You will die unless I die to save you."

"Do your work because you believe in your work."

"I believe what my fingers tell me." He took hold of her fiercely but his voice remained even. "I feel you now, this minute; you're alive. You must stay alive. . . . You tell me you are events—you feel like a woman, my mother, who must stay alive. . . ."

"You are hurting me." But he did not release her. "Why do you mistreat women, Tomás? For whom are the blows intended: the whores? Or me? Why must I be kept alive? So that you can go on hitting me—in other women?"

He let her go.

"I'll go to Coyoacán. Only to keep *you* from being killed. I can't bear the thought of . . . ."

Now he lost all his control. He dropped to his knees again and buried his head in her lap, weeping.

"No!" Both her hands were made into fists. "If I have to go to Moscow do you think it matters to me? I do what I am ordered—because I believe in the program behind the order: only for that reason!" She took hold of his hair and pulled his head back. "What you do today must have its right meaning—you understand! If it is not *your* will that does the killing, if *their* will"—she pointed toward the door—"moves you like a robot: then you do your work out of weakness, not strength! Then you are truly the victim, the condemned! Do it right—or not at all!"

"I will die only for you." He might have been reciting statistics. "Mamacita, mamacita, only for you. If I must die, let me die for you."

"You intend to give me this afternoon a present of my life? The thing I hold least dear? I refuse it! I will not let you make even your death into a mockery of me!"

"You think I hate you that much." His voice was a whisper.

"I think that even in your death—you would like to slap a woman."

His eyes were closed. He said almost hypnotically: "I'll do it—for you. For *you*."

The door opened. Bass came in ahead of Ramón. He looked at Masson with distaste.

"Do it for anybody you like. Greta Garbo, if you like." He went to the typewriter and pulled the piece of paper from its roller. *"Put this in your pocket first."*

For the first time Cándida's iron hold on herself seemed to go. She looked into Masson's face; her lips began to move, she threw her arms around him.

"For you," Masson said. "For you."

"You have a bad effect on him: he's beginning to repeat himself," Bass said to Cándida. "Wait upstairs."

Cándida held tight to her son, her head nodding in some obscure agreement. She turned his head back and tried to speak; no words came. Ramón took her by the arm; she stood; Masson remained where he was. Head down, strangely hunched, Cándida allowed herself to be guided to the door. Masson's eyes did not move from the rattan mat.

At the door Cándida hesitated and looked back.

"Not for the programs," Masson said. "Not for the butchers for the programs. For you. Because I was once inside you and you were my whole world."

Cándida said almost inaudibly: "And because you can never forgive me for that."

Ramón led her out. For another moment Masson remained on his knees; then he stood. He was still looking down.

Bass held out the paper. "Here." Masson took it. "In your pocket." Masson folded the paper and put it away. "Where's the article?"

"Home."

"Make sure to take it along."

The phone ran. Bass indicated that the younger man was to answer it. Masson picked up the receiver.

"Bueno? . . . Sí. Momentito." He handed the phone to Bass.

"Quién habla? . . . Sí. . . . Sí. . . ." Bass's face was serious. "Siete? . . . Y los otros? . . . Tenga cuidado. Mucho cuidado. A las nueve. . . . Con el capitán Cherni, si." He hung up. "Ramón really botched things. Ortega's traced the uniforms and other things too. I don't know. Maybe the girls talked. I don't think so, but maybe. . . . Seven arrested. The police have been all over Coyoacán since early morning but they're leaving now. . . . We've got to move fast." He frowned. "You have your gun?"

"It's at the hotel."

"Emma raised the question of Rostov checking the article?"

"Days ago."

"All right. Pick the gun up when you go home, along with the article." Bass took a long knife from his pocket and pulled it half-way from its sheath for Masson to see. "I'm giving you a choice. Gun or knife. There's a loop inside your coat, this will fit tight into it—carry it there. Put the gun in the pocket of the coat." He stopped to think. "Make sure you're behind him. Wait till he sits—he must be reading your article. I don't want you going for a moving target, or one that's looking at you—you're too nervous as it is. . . . *He —must—be—reading the article*. Repeat that, please."

"Sitting—reading," Masson said dumbly. "Behind him."

"Remember that. Get him to sit. Stand behind. Pick whichever weapon feels right. *And make it count*. You won't get a second chance. . . . As soon as you get home, call Emma. Tell her Rostov must see the article—must—this afternoon. You want it published immediately. Because of the attack."

"The article. . . . The attack. . . ."

"Wait: she may give you a choice of times. You should have a definite hour in mind. . . . Doesn't she go marketing in the afternoon?"

"Around three-thirty. . . . I don't know if they're following the same routine since the attack. . . ."

"Ask if she's going out. If she is—that's the only time you can make it. . . . This is important, Tomás. Very important. If it's possible to have her out of the way, arrange it. Emma's so proud of this article—and your stock's so high with her now—if she's in the house she may want to be there when the big man reads the script. She shouldn't be anywhere near. She makes you too nervous. . . ."

"I'll try to arrange it."

"All right. . . . Remember: script, knife in loop, gun in pocket—

call Emma. Better get moving now." He clapped Masson on the arm brusquely. "Do a good job."

In the corner of the patio V.R. was feeding lettuce leaves to the rabbits.

Marisha and Emma were busy under the orange tree. The older woman was dicing baby stringbeans; the younger was peeling potatoes over a large pan in her lap.

Sounds came from the room that had been David's: furniture being moved, papers being rustled. Paul was putting the room in order.

". . . . with you to Chicago?"

"I don't know. . . . I haven't asked him yet. . . ."

Emma watched V.R. as he shredded more lettuce. She thought: suppose *he* had been her father?

"Your family may find him—not what they expected."

"What do fathers expect in any man their daughters bring home for inspection?" Her own father would ask: what's the fellow's line of work? V.R. as father would want to know: what are his ideas? "They look for a younger edition of themselves. So they can admire the resemblance—while they envy and sneer at the youth." Yes, father, he has good business connections. He's in a very good line. He also happens to have what you well-connected ones never bother to acquire: an orientation larger than money, concepts to surround his money, some very up-to-date ideas. "My father would be surprised by one thing, though. He never expected me, with the kinds of friends I have, to bring home a businessman."

"I am told Jacques is a better than average one."

Hard to picture V.R. as a father. Father—in her experience it meant a monologist on the subject of money and its ramifications: a generous but heavy, work absorbed, unimaginative man who, driving his Cadillac along the lake front or seated at the cholesterol rich dinner table, spoke to her of the daily headaches at his paper mill, hagglings with the union, rising costs, market ups and downs, government meddlings—all the while begging her with tired eyes for some sign of validation for him and his enterprises, some pat that said he was not merely pushed and pushing but worthy, some cradling without conditions. . . . He had money and made money, didn't he? Then why the complaints about the accompanying needles

—which came, not surprisingly, from other people without money who wanted a few more cents for themselves. *They* were the ones who needed the cradles; but he went on asking for them, for a monopoly on the world's soft treatments, with his eyes. Maybe that was one reason she'd gravitated toward a politics of the left. If she had to live in an atmosphere of steady complaints it might as well be among people who had some right to them: the workers. . . .

"He certainly is. He can talk for hours about hard currencies and reciprocal trade agreements—my father would be bowled over."

V.R. as a father? Impossible. All spread-eagled cerebrum and nothing else: no cradling and no asking for cradles. On a level of consciousness, of scope, of concern, miles higher than that of her money perpetuating and money reproducing father: at table, driving, picnicking, sightseeing, talked not of labor costs and plunging markets but of the remaking of worlds after sensational blueprints— politics *his* business. Differences between the things men are busy with. . . .

"Then let them meet. They may get along well."

Still, V.R. had been a father. Young Leon had not gotten along with him. Paul knew some of the story. Leon had often told his mother that Victor was highhanded, opinionated, too much the final authority—a voice from the mountain: Marxist but still a mountain. Had, in fact, taunted Victor more than once with acting the power invested parent after having as a young man fought his own parents for their heavy hand.

"Life would be simpler for me if they liked each other. It certainly would."

There was the sobering fact: V.R. breathed, ate, slept politics. His one son, Leon, had turned his back on politics. Why he'd chosen to stay behind in Moscow when his parents went into exile. Assumed that as a completely nonpolitical man, a simple research chemist, he'd be safe. The worst part of his death at Stalin's hands was that, to distinguish himself from his noted father, only for that reason, he'd had no political bias, he'd been consistently bored with politics, neither for nor against Stalin.

David had raised the question whether certain people don't have to make a career of opposition. To anything rooted and bulky enough to be opposed: starting with the parents just because they're there.

If her own father had been V.R. might she not have blossomed into a Liberty League Republican—

"Damn it!" She dropped her paring knife and sucked on her finger. "It's nothing. . . ."

But change *was* needed in the world. David had said that, too. People with non-compliant personalities, opposition minds, were needed to make the changes. But if the career oppositionists were not so much drawn forward as prodded from behind—wreckers rather than overhaulers—mightn't the changes they brought about be too hasty amateur demolition jobs rather than—

"You must do what you think best, of course," Marisha was saying. "If you believe now that you can have a good life with him. . . ."

Against all logic she was pleased, and knew it, with the knowledge that her father, Republican that he was, all but Liberty Leaguer that he was, would nonetheless be more than a little impressed by her fiancé's grasp of the sterling areas and the tariff problems. . . .

Another ineptly sliced potato peel dropped into the pan.

So many world builders with trembling fingers.

In this fringe world of world makers nobody questioned her manual dexterity. . . .

"I know what you're thinking, Marisha. The other night Jacques showed his good side, yes; but doesn't the bad side remain and isn't that the side I'll have to live with? I've tried to look at it from every angle. . . . I really think I was too harsh on him at times—pushed him too much. . . ."

"I don't suppose the pushing is ever entirely on one side. . . . These things are collaborations. . . ."

"Maybe at moments he *was* a little—extreme with me. . . . But the other night proved a lot. I really think so. When he can become really involved in my involvements, fight side by side with me—he feels he has a place at last and his shakiness goes. . . . He's been the soul of consideration these last two days. He's kept his distance—but I think that's remorse. And his being so upset about the attack. . . . I'm very hopeful now, really I am. . . ."

She had not thought it possible but the knife slipped again and went into her finger, deeper this time. Marisha did not notice.

"Yes. He has his good points."

Without meaning to she raised her injured finger to stroke her upper arm, where the black-and-blue marks had been. They were almost gone now. So was the image of him pressing down with the axe in his hand—vivid in her thoughts now was the newer picture of him, spoiled, yes, too touchy, yes, but nevertheless standing up to the French doors with guts and answering them shot for shot, emptying his gun at them. . . .

The phone in the study rang. Emma jumped up.

"I'll get it," she called out to V.R.

She ran up the ramp and into the study.

"Yes? . . . *Hello.* . . . Yes, of course I remember it. . . . Is anything wrong, darling? . . . I just mean you don't *sound* it. You say you're keyed up about finishing it, but your voice sounds flat. . . . Fine! I think that's a wonderful idea. . . . This afternoon? I don't know. He's pretty busy—the Kronstadt chapter. . . . I can *ask* him, sure. . . . The market? About three-forty-five—it's all arranged with Guillermo. When can you come? . . . Oh—then I won't be here, chico! What a shame! I'd like to. . . . Well, if it's the only time. Hold on, I'll ask him. . . ."

She hurried out to the rabbit cages.

"Victor—it's Jacques. He's calling about the article he wrote— you remember I mentioned it?"

"Yes—of course."

"He's brought it up to date—he's anxious to get it printed. He wants your opinion very much. . . ."

"Strange. I asked him about the article just the other day. He said he'd put it aside. . . . Can he come tomorrow or the day after?"

"Could you possibly spare a few minutes this afternoon? He doesn't want to waste any more time. . . ."

"I was hoping to do more on the chapter. . . . No matter. Tell him to come by all means. When does he want to make it?"

"About four."

"All right. That time will do as well as any."

"Thanks, V.R.! You'll be pleased—it's a very good article!"

She ran back to the study.

"Jacques? . . . Listen, chico, it's all right! Come around four. . . . Will you wait until I get back? There's something I want to talk over with you. . . ." She saw a spot of blood on her finger and licked it off. "It'll keep. It's about Chicago—you'll be pleased. I've been thinking a lot about it, I want to tell you. . . . Wonderful. Goodbye, darling. . . ."

". . . Chica—it's finished. I've put the facts about the attack in. I had some free time, one of my appointments was canceled, I've been slaving over it since noon. . . . No, of course not. What could be wrong? I'm just tired. . . . Could he possibly make it this afternoon? I'm anxious to send it off tonight. . . . Well—let's see. Are you going to the market today? . . . Too bad. I was hoping you'd be there. . . . That's the only time I can make it, four, yes. I've got to get back to see some wholesalers. . . . Sure. Go ahead. . . ."

He had the raincoat over his knee. While he waited his fingers worked with the knife, forcing it into the loop, pulling it free again. He reached to his inside pocket and touched the manuscript: script all right, knife all right. Missing: the gun. Get the gun.

"Fine. I'll be there. . . . What is it? . . . What about Chicago? . . . All right. Tell me then. . . . Goodbye, chica. . . ."

He hung up.

Coat—script—knife—get the gun.

He went to the closet and began to feel about under the sweaters on the shelf. He stopped. There was something on top of the sweaters, something heavy. The ice axe.

He looked at it for a time. He reached up. He put the raincoat over his shoulder and grasped the axe in both hands, weighed it experimentally, lifted it and brought it down in a chop. He studied it another moment.

Could he—

It felt right.

Certainly the gun was out. A shot would be heard for blocks. Paul would come running, cops would come running, Marisha would come too, even she had a derringer—not a chance.

The distance from the study, it would probably be the study, the distance to the door and then outside to his car could be covered in ten seconds, provided Paul was not in the way; and he might be able to take care of Paul. His life depended on his having ten seconds. . . . It seemed to him that if only he went at this with care, if only he kept calm and handled himself just right at each step, he would stand a chance, a certain chance—if he could have these ten seconds to get out and away. If it could be done without a sound, to give him the ten seconds. . . .

But not the knife. The thought made him shiver. The hand would be just above the blade, the hand would have to drive the blade the full distance in, the hand would come into contact with the back of the man, have to touch him. Ramón's hand driving the blade all the way in had certainly touched David—

He would lose his senses if his hand touched the back.

But a long-handled axe. . . .

Maybe.

It seemed to him for a reason he could not name that the farther away he could be from the man's back the better he could do it and the bigger his chances would be.

If there had to be a bridge between himself and the man for that infinite second, and there would be if he used anything other than the gun—a long handle was better by far than a short handle.

He knew his hand would not be able to drive a knife in.

He studied the axe for another time.

He withdrew the sheathed dagger from the loop and dropped it into the lefthand coat pocket. He found the gun on the shelf and placed it in the other pocket. Next he tried the axe handle in the loop on the lining.

If only it fitted. He could not stop now to sew another loop, his hands wouldn't do it. . . .

The handle went in easily. The axe hung from the loop by its metal prongs.

He tested it: perfectly secure.

He tried slipping the axe out: it came easily.

With the axe in place he folded the coat over his arm: no telltale bulges, the axe was completely covered. He experimented with the coat, changing its position, smoothing out its folds.

Coat—script—gun—knife—axe.

He looked at his watch: two-forty-three.

As he went for the door he repeated to himself: sure he's sitting, get in back, sure he's sitting. . . .

". . . . time will do as well as any."

". . . . You'll be pleased—it's a very good article!"

He watched her hurrying up to the study. He heard her voice saying excitedly, "Chico, it's all right! Come around four. . . . It's about Chicago. . . ."

He pushed more lettuce bits through the chicken wire fronting the cages. He thought: rabbits make no effort to distinguish themselves from their class or from each other. Even the male could very easily be taken for the female—he was able to tell them apart simply because George was in the left cage, Varvara in the right. Set them free in the yard and immediately they are mirror images of each other: hopping alike, hunching alike, nibbling at lettuce leaves with the same generic daintiness. Let out of their cubicles—untagged— one white mass.

As for people—

Emma came out of the study and walked back toward Marisha, smiling, face flushed and full of lights.

". . . . talk to him this afternoon," he heard the girl say. "I've made up my mind—I'm going to. . . ." Then she took up her pan of potatoes and her voice dropped too low to hear.

As for people: no two alike! Marisha and Emma side by side, two women meshed in the same fabric of ideas, immersed in the same world perspectives—totally different species. Bound together by politics—at opposite poles as women.

Marisha going at her stringbeans evenly, expertly, given without reservation to the work at hand: the quiver was in her thoughts, in her private presentiments, but her doer's fingers remained steady. Emma slashing at her potatoes with a bad aim, impatient with trivia, dismissing the chore in her mind while her hands under forced labor went through the motions with an open disdain—a woman called permanently away from the immediacies and their petty assignments to chaotic inner conventions, thinking always of the overblown inner issues. . . .

Yet stringbeans had to be sliced and potatoes peeled!

Set these two loose from this absurd suburban cage and?

The one would continue to contain her sorrows and embrace the workaday world again: make another shopping list. The other would unleash more of her private ferments upon the surroundings to hound them still further away—and find more Massons to dramatize the alienation: and lose more weight to make her face still thinner.

They carried their labels wherever they went.

Men were said to be identical when they inhabited the same program cage—adhered to the same party. It was only a convenience—to make the discussion go faster. They were identical only in the dimension of politics. They echoed each other for only so long as they remained in their political cubicles—and kept their unpolitical quirks to themselves.

Let them run loose—no gray mass! No undifferentiated masses. Each unit a unique piece of work.

Out of the revolution could come a general who fired all his salvos through a dictaphone. . . .

Yet it was the first need in politics, in formulating measures and commitments and defending them, to see the mass without the differentiated faces in it. To talk of this sparkling golden mass and that dull gray mass—how easy to render political judgments in the gradations of the chromatic scale!—when the very idea of a mass was a lifeless abstraction, an instrumental fiction.

There had been faces at Kronstadt. . . .

Scheming, trivial, self-serving, get-rich-quick, White Guardist faces? Some, no doubt.

And as to that: there were faces like those everywhere, even among the Bolsheviks: there had been Stalins around and behind the Lenins: behind the Stalins, Basses. . . .

But they had not all been hoarders of grain and wearers of bell-bottoms at Kronstadt. Not even many of them. The faces of the others? No grayness in them. . . .

Yet for political reasons—politics knows parties and alignments, not persons—it had been necessary to see them as a uniform drab mass and to deal with them as such. When a whole garrison rose with all its guns how could the regime fighting for its life give differential treatment to those behind the guns—separate the gold from the gray?

The grimmest reality, the reality of the taking and holding of power, had made necessary the use of the worst, the most falsifying fiction. . . .

The fiction that two women who attacked their mounds of dinner

vegetables from opposite life principles, one getting it unobtrusively done, the other taking total stands, were comrades because
they shared an ideology. . . .

As for faces:

The night it was finally over at Kronstadt, the night the garrison
had been stormed and won, he had come back to his apartment at
Petrograd more exhausted, more fundamentally drained, than he
had ever been in his respites from the many Red Army fronts. Tired
in his marrow and in his thoughts. Marisha had looked at him with
a tight face that said: then it is over? He had nodded. What was
there to say but—yes: done: now we live with it? But Leon was
awakened by the rattle of dishes as Marisha fixed tea. Leon was
fifteen that winter. He had come into the kitchen in his night clothes,
blinking sleepily, and said: "You took the island? You killed them?"
He said to the boy: "You think it's easy to secure a new regime,
Leon?" Leon said: "It isn't easy to say no to a regime either. Not
when people like you are the regime." Marisha had tried to make
the boy stop and go back to bed but he refused to move. "They were
your best friends," he said. "Mine, too. They were wonderful to me
when you took me out there, I used to love our trips. Uncle Anastas
let me climb all over the battleships—the sailors gave me rides in
submarines—because I was your son. They loved you and everybody
with you." V.R. said: "There are moments in life, Leon, when you
must destroy some of the things you love—for the sake of other
things you love." Leon had replied to this with a rush of tears:
"What could you love more than Anastas? What happened to Uncle
Anastas? Tell me! Him too? All of them?" Anastas Yiko, whom the
boy called Uncle: the red-bearded giant, landless muzhik from the
Georgian steppes, first gunner on the Sevastopol, organizer of V.R.'s
personal guard, loud and clear voice in the Kronstadt Soviet, good
friend, a vital man full of jokes—V.R. could not bring himself to
say what had happened to Anastas. The boy finally stopped crying.
He said: "I've made up my mind what I'm going to study, father.
I hate politics and everything to do with politics. You don't kill just
some things for the sake of others—you kill them all, in the name
of politics—your kind, at least. *Politics* is all you people love. Anyhow, nobody's going to make *me* choose between those I have feelings for, and feed one group of friends to the other. I'm going to

study mathematics and organic chemistry. Tonight is a good time to tell you why. Because in science maybe I'll find some facts that people like you can't twist and abuse so easily. Because mathematics and chemistry are the farthest things from you and what you are that I can find."

The young, too-serious face turned with all its trouble and indignation up to him at that moment: his own face, age fourteen, organizing farm workers against his own father.

One fourteen-year-old championing muzhiks (Anastases!) against his kulak father: one fifteen-year-old standing with Kronstadt sailors (Anastases!) against *his* commissar father—in what terms shall the one denounce the other!

Leon's seething face in the kitchen that February night—familiar!

The face of David Justin looking steadily at him and saying, "It's what you owe the Kronstadt sailors. To stay alive—and stand against new Kronstadts."

Faces of the rebels against the rebel.

No dull gray mass. Each making his own kind of fists and programs. . . .

Problem: to root out the class origins, somewhere in the social relations of production governing the capitalist order in and around Chicago, U.S.A., circa 1920–1930, of those paper-miller's daughter's hands now mauling harmless potatoes under the orange tree! Find them!

Another face:

His nervous friend Adolphe Yoffe: how he was remembering all the old ones now! Yoffe, scholar, diplomat, fidgeter, who'd carried such weight in the Brest Litovsk peace negotiations. In Vienna, when V.R. had first set eyes on him, Adolphe was having nervous breakdowns: entered psychoanalytic treatment with Alfred Adler—the fidgets hung on. Until 1917. The man had come together and developed a new hardiness in the great revolutionary days; V.R. was to write of his brilliant friend later: *The revolution healed Yoffe better than psychoanalysis of all his complexes.* An easy Marxist affirmation of the outer world's primacy over the inner—but had it been true? In 1927, when V.R. was expelled from the Bolshevik party, Yoffe committed suicide—*in protest against the treatment of Rostov.* A highly personal interpretation of the responsibilities of friendship!

Others of V.R.'s friends, equally devoted to him, had *not* committed suicide. Then there had been a special shadow at the center of the man—a potato rejecter—which had not been derived from the prime social relations of production—and which had not, after all, yielded to the revolution's magical balm.

If politics only allowed time to examine these undersides of people! Their fidgets—their fumblings.

But only their faces could be considered. In their political, mass, colorless, faceless aspect. . . .

How the young ones, the boldest of them, the Anastases, insisted on growing one-of-a-kind faces!

Leon. (In the spirit of his father. . . .)

David. (With Leon now. . . .)

Paul. (Making a start. . . .)

He remembered his troubles in the Odessa realschule. Now he was remembering his schooldays! His expulsion for hissing and booing one pompous teacher; his reprimand when he refused to write compositions for another on the grounds that the students' exercise books were never returned. (And David had told the story of how *he* staged a demonstration in the classroom of a New York high school against the "anti-Semitism" of *The Merchant of Venice:* he'd been suspended for a month, without doing any lasting damage to Shakespeare.) Later V.R. wrote in his autobiography regarding his turbulent student years: *Such was my first political test, as it were. The class was henceforth divided into distinct groups: the talebearers and the envious on one side, the frank and courageous boys on the other, and the neutral and vacillating mass in the middle.*

That gray mass in the middle!

Even then he had been quick to think in terms of groups and masses!

He had said further: *These three groups never quite disappeared even in later years. I was to meet them again and again in my life. . . .*

But what social relations of production, what prime class forces planted courage in one ten-year-old, envy in another, vacillation in a third—fidgets here, a refusal to cope with potatoes there!

Even then he had been making judgments about the individual qualities in particularized persons, about those features in single faces which eluded the social forces—phrased in the easier jargon of class judgments.

And later—at Kronstadt.

The trouble was: the best ingredient in a movement of social revolt was the young spirit of rebellion, discovered in the depths of personality but directed outward against the pressures that stifle personality—refusal to be a group echo and reflex—the resistance to that social determination of self which was the first principle of Marxism! If that youthful fire could be kept at maximum flame— Anastas's, Leon's, David's—his own! But the revolution spends most of its fine nay-saying in its own struggle upward into institution. Then at a certain jelling and stabilizing point—what little is left of its ferment about the edges—shall it say no to itself?—is seized upon and brought back to life by the wildest and most bubbling elements—the *frank and courageous,* the perpetually youthful ones. This was what the best of the Kronstadt sailors had done, assuredly. They had appropriated for their own the revolution's first fires— relit them where needed. But when the revolution's original rebelliousness fell into those hands, to be turned against the revolution in its institutionalizing phase, the revolution then had to rear up and become the stern parental authority, the hard stifling pressure from above, *against* its own best and most incorrigible perpetuators. He had praised the *frank and courageous* ones, yes. They were the ones who made revolutions. But they were the first ones to be cut down by revolutions. . . .

He was thinking along these lines for a reason. He had dictated another section of the Kronstadt chapter this morning; he planned to go on with it later today. The theme he was trying to develop was that of the degenerative shift in the garrison's social composition—from the bold (proletarians)—to the vacillating (peasants)—to the talebearers and the envious (White Guardists). For this he needed, needed desperately, some facts: and there were no facts. David had had people digging in the libraries of a half dozen cities—no facts! He was putting down his own remembered observations and impressions and intuitions, as honestly as he could. (But was he? In his text so far there was no mention of his blank and drained feeling that foul night; the faces in the gray mass that were anything but gray; the last strangled cries of Anastas Yiko the red-bearded; the revolution's growing need to turn on its *frank and courageous* makers; Marisha's white face over the tea cups; Leon's tear-streaked face and raging outburst, his flight into organic chemistry. . . .) Impressions and intuitions were not good enough. The too-ready critics would chorus: no literary speculations, please—where are the facts? He had to *prove* the garrison had turned reactionary and restorationist. He was only stating it. Without the facts —no chapter. Without the chapter—no book. The ranting critics would say: if you cannot prove, prove with iron facts, that the suppression of Kronstadt was justified, what right have you to criticize Stalin's suppressions now? They would say: one more of the loud and gaudy altercations between pot and kettle. They would broadcast more of their jibes about the morality of Kaffirs, the fine ethical stance of the Hottentot—

"Oh! Damn it to hell!"

Emma: she had dropped her pan of potatoes on the ground.

Marisha was reaching for the pan; she was going to do the job herself.

When would the girl learn to hold things properly!

In his annoyance V.R. dropped the head of lettuce he was holding.

Here came Paul from David's room, carrying a large manila folder fat with papers. Down the steps toward the rabbit cages: eyes notably bright, face with a high color as from blushing—cunning in his face, mystery, excitement. Approaching as to battle.

The face of young Leon in the kitchen. . . .

"No news from Ortega?"

"None," V.R. said. "His prisoners haven't revealed anything yet. He still can't make sense of the business with the door."

"It *is* a question: why they had to kill David."

"He must have seen something. Perhaps Bass himself."

"Maybe. Maybe. That's enough of a puzzle by itself. When it's put together with the Packard—"

"I've told you—they were in control of the area for a moment; they wanted to be thorough. There was the offchance they'd find papers or some such thing in the car—perhaps my manuscript. . . . What's that you're holding?"

"David's folder on Kronstadt."

"He accumulated that much? He never mentioned it."

"He had a reason for keeping it to himself. . . . Victor." Paul's eyes were too bright, too sharp. "David's summed up in some notes, you should hear them. . . ."

"Let me see."

"I'll read them to you. He had a lot to say, he was thinking harder than anybody knew, he drew up a kind of chronology—let's sit by the table, I'll read them. . . ."

V.R. did not move. He gave Paul a queer look and said again:

"I said—I'd like to see the notes."

Paul opened the folder and drew from it some typed sheets. V.R. took them, glanced at the top page quickly.

"I know what intense pleasure you get from reading aloud. To me. It's become your first amusement. . . . You'll have to forego the fun today. I'm aware of these notes—I saw them on David's desk."

Paul said with a false casualness, tension just below:

"And? Your comment?"

"David was mistaken: end of comment."

"He says—Kronstadt could have been stopped. He piles up the facts—to show it could have been stopped." Paul inhaled slowly, deeply. "He says, over and over—*you* could have stopped it. . . . You've nothing to say to that?"

"It could have been stopped—by the sailors. . . . Today, apparently, you're *not* to be stopped. . . ."

Paul took the sheets from V.R.'s hand. His own hand was unsteady, the papers rustled.

"You need quotations for your chapter." His voice, too, was shaking. "David gives some quotations, I'd like your views on them."

"Didn't you hear me?" V.R. said loudly. "I said I'd read these notes."

Paul paid no attention. With fumbling fingers he flipped the pages, found his place. He began to read:

> "*The Tenth Congress of the Communist Party was taking place at just that moment in Petrograd. Did Lenin bother to keep up the White-Guard-plot nonsense in front of his party faithful? Not for a minute. Not for a second. In his speech about the Kronstadt*

*sailors he told the delegates frankly: 'They do not want the White
Guards—and they do not want our power either.'*

. . . You don't have a few words to say about this quote?"
Paul's eyes were echoing the question. Loudly.
"Many. None you would not jeer at—since your hobby now is to
jeer."
"You *killed* those people for being White Guards!"
"No: for being taken in by the White Guards. We couldn't stop
to open heads and see which ones were only tricked. They *all* had
guns—the trickers *and* the tricked. . . . Are you quite through?"
"Not yet. . . . One more quote. . . ."
"Quote too much—you will end quoting the Bible. The Bible and
nothing else. . . . A fascinating document—but meager in its politi-
cal formulations. . . ."
"This isn't from Moses, it's from you. From the memoir you wrote
just a few months after Kronstadt."
"Ah—I'm to be offered in evidence against myself now. . . . You
won't mind if I go on feeding the rabbits?"
Paul read again:

> "*V.R. acknowledges that Kalinin, Kuzmin and Vassiliev may
> have bullied the sailors too much. . . . He allows that the basic
> demands of the sailors were modest and justified, after all the
> years of suffering and privation; he admits that the New Eco-
> nomic Policy, put into effect only a few months after Kronstadt
> went down in blood, gave many concessions to the people that
> were no more than the sailors had been after. And he adds: 'Sim-
> ply because it had been guilty of a political error, simply because
> some of its less polished representatives may have blundered in
> dealing with the sailors, should the proletarian revolution really
> have committed suicide to punish itself?' . . .*"

Paul looked up. He was breathing hard.
"How many times do I have to tell you?" V.R. said. "I've read
these—"
"Read them! Read them! You *wrote* them!" Paul's lips were
quivering, as though they held more words than they could expel.

"You've no comment? David had one. He said . . . Let me find it —here. . . . *Apparently certain guilts can't be kept permanently under cover, even in such a brilliantly organized and disciplined ideologue as V.R. . . . Don't think he'll use this telltale quote. . . . No man wants to confess twice. . . ."*

Paul closed the manuscript and put it back in the folder. His breath was coming in audible jerks.

"Now I'm through," he said.

"Definitively, irrevocably through." V.R. was examining the head of lettuce in his hand. "When will you be leaving my house?"[1]

"Any progress, Jaime?"

"None, my general. You were right—most of these are the burros and pack horses. Derdergo and the others know nothing, I feel it."

"And Marcus Guaro?"

"A more special case. I have the impression he was on a some-what higher level—perhaps the liaison between Bass and Ramón and the rank-and-file people. . . . He has a close mouth. I will keep on with him."

"Do not give him a minute's rest. . . . What picture do you get of the operation?"

"There is no explanation of the Packard. The door remains a mystery. My prisoners saw nothing of what happened at the car or the door. They went into the guardhouse to disarm the police and tie them. Their instructions were to remain in the guardhouse until guns were brought to them. . . . One of those who brought the guns was the man called Ramón, the other—possibly Marcus Guaro."

"Concentrate on the compartment of the Packard and the door. We must get these things explained. . . . You have paid off Captain Cherni?"

"Not yet, my general. He comes back this afternoon for his check."

"Hold back the check. Tell him he is to stand by for the possibility of another job tonight. . . . If you do not break Guaro down by evening—we will use Cherni on him."

"Then he will find his tongue, my general."

"Señor Colón is still in the waiting room?"

[1] For the complete text of David Justin's notes on Kronstadt, see Appendix, p. 371.

"I will send him in, my general."

In a moment a man with heavy shoulders and a dark face entered General Ortega's office. He was carrying a wide brimmed country sombrero of cream color, on his feet were dusty ankle boots. The two men greeted each other with a warm abrazo.

"It is good to see you, Eusebio."

"Always a pleasure, Fidel. . . . I wish I could bring you better news."

"The news is bad?"

"The experiments go well. You did not read the report on our last trial crop? The H-strain maize is very good against the fungus, according to first tests. . . . The péons, the péons are the headache."

"Ah. They press their petition."

"More. It has gone beyond the paper stage. The village has sent a delegation to the Ministry of Agriculture to demand that the whole estancia be broken up and handed over to them. . . . That is why I am here. There will be hearings at the Ministry this week. I am called to testify."

"Then you will testify: no problem."

"It is a problem, Fidel. A big problem. The estancia does good work, it helps all the people in the long run, it must not be destroyed for the sake of an abstract social principle. A social principle is included on our side too. . . ."

"You take it too much to heart, comrade. Do not blame these people so much. True, the estancia does work that will benefit them over the years—but what do you expect? They must win and become used to the benefits of the moment before they develop the vision to see the benefits of the decade or the generation. They have not yet had the time and the luxury to learn that there are sights beyond their stomachs—that is the problem."

"You know, Fidel, what I think? They have been too long with the head down. We never understood this. We thought the head was low out of courtesy or respect to the high ones, but we were wrong. You know what they were doing? They were studying the land—our land. They were estimating which parts of the land they wanted and how much. When at last they raise the head to look us in the face they are ready with the figures—to the final square millimeter."

"Precisely. And you wish to discuss with such men?"

"How? Their heads are too full of the figures they have added up over the centuries when their heads were down. We talk to them of agronomy and animal husbandry and horticulture—they say, hand it over, so many kilometers wide, so many kilometers long: without a sir, without a please."

"To the extent they do this, Eusebio, to this extent they learn the lessons of '10. Can we oppose it? We helped to draw up and teach them this lesson." General Ortega made a turn about his desk, hands clasped behind his back. "Listen. Let me tell you this story. You read of this man Rostov some tried to kill the other night? From 1905 to 1917 he, with Lenin and others, taught the Russian workers and peasants to keep the head up. Then he and those with him came to power on the shoulders of the workers and peasants. The ordinary ones, in a place called Kronstadt, continued to hold their heads up as they had been taught. Lenin and Rostov cut those heads off. Now the world reminds Rostov of this, and laughs, and he has no answer. He will have to die to avoid answering. . . . I will not be so inconsistent."

"Life works out in strange ways, Fidel. The city has too many fingers in the country now: bad. The country was always, before, a place to get away from the city. . . . We were with them in '10 because we wanted the people to go ahead. Now those we taught in '10—wish to destroy a fine thing you have made for the people. . . . And we refuse to interfere: because of '10. . . . We are prisoners of a date."

"What would you have me do? This is a matter for the Minister of Agriculture."

"It is not for me to tell you how to run your affairs, Fidel. I had only this thought in coming here—you are of the government. You know many in the government. You have a reputation. Could you not speak—"

"I will not ask special treatments. This is not what we fought for."

"We did not fight for the destruction of a valuable agricultural research center either."

"No. . . . We will prepare a good defense for the Ministry hearings. . . . Forgive me now, dear friend. I have pressing business."

"Goodbye, Fidel. . . . We miss you much in the country."

"I have had enough of the city, Eusebio, too much. Here nothing gives: concrete and more concrete. I would like to be among green and straightforward things again; I know how to fight fungus! . . . Goodbye, Eusebio. Goodbye, old friend."

"You've *got* to say something! You *owe* it to me!"
"They all speak in the tongue of creditors now. The whole world writes dunning notes. . . . You'd have me debate with a dead boy? David was absolutely sincere—he was wrong—no more."
They were sitting at the outdoor dining table.
"You know this about me," Paul said. "I'm by temperament an activist. I don't read books and mull over theories: I prefer to cope with the approving present and forget about the mocking past. So I never tried to dig deep about Kronstadt. . . . Now, this afternoon, at one-fifteen exactly, a body somewhere over Georgia or South Carolina reaches out from its coffin and burns words into my activist brain: He could have stopped it. He could have stopped it. At every step along the way he could have stopped it. . . ."
"There are no doubt certain exacting critics who read *Oedipus Rex* today and say: He could have stopped himself from killing his father and marrying his mother. . . ."
"The Greeks wrote plays of that sort to dramatize the blind forces that push people forward. Isn't that why Oedipus puts his eyes out at the end, when he finds out what he's done? Simply to dramatize the fact that he's been blind all along, driven by the hidden things in him? . . . But the Bolsheviks placed themselves before the workers as the most conscious, most deliberate, most knowing force in history! They claimed to have their eyes wide open! If you now say Kronstadt was inevitable. . . . And suppose it was? Then you must have sensed its mechanism in advance. Then—you could have quit! You didn't have to take the first seat on the juggernaut. . . ."
"Quit? Easy to say. . . . Blind or all-seeing—and I will grant you they saw less than they imagined: *we* can see that: *now*—the Bolsheviks were the tide of history. You rode with the tide—or went to sleep on the sidelines and canceled yourself out as a member of events."
"That's easy too. . . . The commonest human pastime: to in-

dulge in all the excesses and then, by way of a whitewash for your-self and your indulgences, to draw up nice tidal images. . . ."

"You dare to suggest the Russian revolution was a whim? . . . It didn't take place by accident. And it was no accident that the Bolsheviks led it. . . . There were many liberal, left and revolu-tionary parties in Russia. All the colors of the rainbow. All the other parties, all but the Bolsheviks, were too cowardly, too muddled, too palsied to do what was necessary: withdraw the country from the stupid war, take a stand for the desperately needed reforms. And it was no accident that these parties were so soft and paralyzed."

"Soft. You use the word 'soft' as an epithet. Your worst."

"A determined fist was needed to smash all this inherited rotten-ness! The Bolsheviks provided the fist. . . . They did not create the need. . . ."

"All the more reason to quit! Don't you see—either you believe things are determined, or you believe in the role of forceful individ-uals—you can't have it both ways! If the Bolsheviks were an irresist-ible tide—then they didn't need you! To the extent you say you were needed—you say they were *not* a tide but rather a hope—a bid—an effort! . . . And if they *were* inevitable—if you weren't needed —what were you doing with them in the first place?" Paul's hands were shaking as they gripped the edge of the table. He leaned over. "You were satisfying your own needs, not history's! Don't you see—don't you see—David was right—it's finally not a political matter! You think there are runaway appetites only on the bottom? They get pretty spectacular up on top, too—they've more elbow room there! It was *your* petty appetites that came out at Kronstadt! *You* were the hungry one!"

"Come back to your premise, please: I should have withdrawn. . . . What do you suggest, with your hindsight, I might have done?"

"You had to feel you were playing a big part in the middle of a big pageant of history? You couldn't just retire? You needed to play a *hard* public role—that was your hunger? All right! Then—you could, for example, have become the spokesman *for* the Kronstadt sailors—*against* the Bolshevik tide! *There* was a way to prove your hardness!"

"Ortega resigned from the revolution here. . . . He wound up, softly growing soft vegetables."

"Maybe that's not the worst thing. People can't live on a steady diet of history: Kronstadt's the best proof of that. They need vegetables too. . . ."

"Let's allow that a leading Bolshevik might have deserted his party and become a spokesman for Kronstadt. What, exactly, would you have had him say?"

"Look what you were saying by your *refusal* to leave the Bolsheviks. To stay with them through such a dirty farce meant: their victory *isn't* guaranteed—they *need* your assistance. And if their victory wasn't a sure thing—if you'd done the inconceivably bold thing and gone over to the sailors—then, maybe, maybe, it might have swung things their way. Or at least kept the Bolsheviks from their worst excesses. With your great weight at the time. You would at least have given Stalin fewer precedents to go on. Without Kronstadt, Stalinism might have been slowed down a bit—if not stopped altogether. . . . The greater weight a man carries in public affairs —the less right he's got to invoke passive hands-down images of tides that can't be stopped. . . ."

"Interesting: you are tired of looking hard at the dialectic laws of historical movement. Your eyes are strained: you prefer to close them and abandon yourself to a static sentimentalism. A bath of warm, proper, ennobling feelings—nothing's nicer, nothing's easier. . . . But observe: along with this indulgence—you were speaking of indulgences?—you lose your analytic vocabulary. You retreat from the language of a realistic politics to—the language of theology. That is what you are moving toward now. . . . Say it: you have now decided that I should have appointed myself a saint and given myself over to all the scintillating lost causes."

"And—*your* cause isn't lost? . . . There's something suspect about a saint, absolutely: nobody's that clean. But at least the saint's loyalties are constant—haven't you talked about consistency?—he starts with the despised and ends with the despised. . . . Listen! Just listen! Openness, ferment, free space—that's what most of the Kronstadt sailors were fighting for! The same things you say you're fighting for today against Stalin! The very same things you fought for against Lenin—before 1917! You wouldn't even *discuss* them with the sailors. . . . Why? That's the question David asked himself. His last thought was: this is the first question, the question of questions. . . . Look here."

From the manila folder on the table Paul extracted a large writing pad.

"You're going to show me David's letter to his fiancee?" V.R. said. "No need. I've read that too. . . . I won't discuss Beethoven and butterflies with you."

"There's more involved." Paul had the pad opened. On one side was a compartment holding envelopes and stamps. From this space Paul drew some folded papers and opened them. "This was a note he made and put away here—maybe that last night. What's in his letter to the girl is just an echo of it."

Paul began to read:

"*Compulsive freedom fighters! Compelled to do battle against compulsion. . . . Nice paradox.*

"*Joseph Conrad: 'You revolutionists . . . are the slaves of the social convention, which is afraid of you; slaves of it as much as the very police that stands up in defense of that convention. Clearly you are, since you want to revolutionize it. [Meaning: if you were truly free of this social order, truly indifferent to it, you could just turn your back on it and walk away.] It governs your thought, of course, and your action, too, and thus neither your thought nor your action can ever be conclusive. . . . You are not a bit better than the forces arrayed against you—than the police, for instance. . . . The terrorist and the policeman both come from the same basket. Revolution, legality—counter moves in the same game; forms of idleness at bottom identical.'*

"*Key word: idleness.*

"*Conrad, further: 'The way of even the most justifiable revolutions is prepared by personal impulses disguised into creeds.'*

"*Key word: impulses.*

"*Problem: the nature of V.R.'s idleness? The forms of his impulses? (These terms will do as well as any.)*

"*Clue: V.R. at seventeen, standing in that Nikolaev garden raising wine glass and thundering at poor Marisha Shvigalovskaya, the soul of daintiness: 'A curse upon all Marxists, and upon those*

*who want to bring dryness and hardness into all the relations
of life!'*

"*Marxism hard and dry, certainly; but Marisha? Delicate, soft,
liquid woman; as she is now; why else would he marry her? Then
—why the malicious attack on her? And why did he couch it in
the peculiarly unpolitical terms of hardness-softness?*

"*This silly garden scene a paradigm of his whole career? He
was the one being hard and dry!*

"*At heart a soft, passive, compliant, dreamy boy? (His idleness.) With a burning need to disguise this 'weakness' in him with
extreme show of activity and belligerence? (His strongest personal impulse.) Makes sense. Could lead him to become a revolutionary. (It did me.) In the revolutionary movement met others
making still more spectacular show of toughness: the Lenins.
Drew back from them in some fright: maybe they were the real
things and he the counterfeit? . . . The early attack on Marisha:
was he accusing her associates of being stony monsters because
he was afraid, in his tremulous teens, that he didn't have capacity
to be as tough as they, that he was making feeble try at it (strike
he organized against father, his violent set-to's with teachers) and
only showing himself up as a ridiculous, babyish fool?*

"*Burning social problems in Russia. People suffering terribly.
Yet critical public matters can't explain why any given person—
V.R.—myself!—dives into the gathering revolution. Particularly
that far in advance. Particularly when he himself feels no economic goad. . . . Terrible social conflicts call out the revolution.
Severe internal conflicts drive the individual, particularly the well-
off individual, into this revolution: hard side fighting soft side.
. . . Sympathy? Humanitarianism? Social conscience? Self-con-
gratulatory words—tell you not why people do things but why
they'd like to be doing them if they could be instruments of pure
intellection. . . . Is it sympathy that leads a seventeen-year-old
to trick a warm-hearted girl into coming to garden party so that
he can insult and berate her? With extreme hardness—for her
hardness!*

"*One thing sure: V.R.'s attack on Marisha Shvigalovskaya in
that garden was least of all political. No creeds there. . . .*

"*The idle—impelled to much busyness. . . .*

"Once he becomes a Marxist, why does he fight the toughest Marxists, the Bolsheviks, so tellingly? Maybe senses the threat in concept of iron centralism—to him. If he accepts the Bolsheviks' centralism, puts himself fully under its discipline—his show of hard self-sufficiency exposed as flimsy lie. Apparatus over him will be harder than he, or any individual, is or can be. (It openly announces its intention to be just that; Lenin's centralism was nothing if not frank.) Will be surrounded by people like Lenin who have impressed him with their steel; they may be so hard as to make him look very soft; and he has powerful drive to appear anything but soft. Submission to this machine impossible for him—maybe because he wants so much to submit: what his soft and compliant innermost self cries out for. . . . This is the man who, from 1904 to 1917, composes the profoundest exposés of centralist philosophies in political history! (Exposing that side of himself he could not abide—his need to be dominated.) Which just shows: you have to be very close in spirit to an enemy before you can truly, with infallible intuition, understand his guts. . . .

"1917: joins the Bolsheviks. Obviously wanted all along to give up pretense of fierceness and yield softly to them, but until then had no workable excuse. 1917 provided the excuse: anybody with sense could see the Bolsheviks were going to take power any day: wave of the future. V.R. could disguise his delayed spurt of sub-missiveness as simple realism—all the more so because Bolsheviks came round to his very hard and very fierce doctrine of perma-nent revolution. . . . What's more, if he turned soft and passive vis-à-vis Lenin, he could make tremendous show of being very tough and aggressive in other directions: could organize whole Red Army and lead it on nineteen fronts. V.R.'s organization of Red Army one of most fantastic exploits in military annals. Had to be. He had to direct a war over one-sixth of the earth's surface to prove there was no easy yielding in him. . . . Some need wild façades. How impulsive the idle can be.

"Came the end of the civil war. V.R., with his acute political eye, saw what was needed. People were exhausted, cold, starving. Had to be a relaxation of tensions and pressures, a new air of easement, tolerance for petty appetites too long denied: a pre-occupation with food, clothing, deep breathing, the viscera. Soft-

ness had to be given some leeway, after the terrible overdose of hardness. . . . 1920. Almost a full year before Kronstadt. V.R. alone among the Bolsheviks stood up and proposed that the period of War Communism, of ruthless requisitioning of all supplies and absolute domination of all life by the Red Army, be officially declared at an end. In its place, he argued, a new economic philosophy must be introduced, encouraging production and consumption, ending restrictions, letting people make and exchange goods for their deprived bellies and backs. Best side of V.R. speaking here—his clearest-seeing, most realistic, least subjective, least impulsive side. . . .

"Bolsheviks shouted him down. All, including Lenin, voted to continue the harsh regime of War Communism. Perhaps not for the highly realistic reasons they professed. Perhaps, more than anything, because they'd gotten used to the absolute centralism of War Communism and didn't like the idea of giving it up, loosening the clamps on people. . . . It was the extension of War Communism into peacetime, the intolerable restrictions, the rigid military disciplining of all phases of life, that produced all the explosions of the following year; the many peasant revolts and factory-worker stirrings; the Petrograd strike movement; finally, Kronstadt.

"V.R.'s role in all this? Moment his plea for a new, gentler, more relaxed policy was voted down as being too soft and conciliatory—he reversed his direction, leaped to the opposite extreme, became the harshest of the harsh. He took on job of reorganizing the ruined railways; was absolutely ruthless about it, refusing to deal with unions, throwing their leaders into jail when they tried to protest about impossible hours and wages and rations of railway workers. Basic question came up as to what role of trade unions should be in proletarian dictatorship. Many argued the unions should be private organizations as in the West, representing workers in their dealings with the state employer, retaining freedom to oppose the state when abuses arose. V.R. took opposite position: unions must be part of state apparatus, their job was not to bargain with the state but to transmit state's decisions to workers and see that they were carried out. (This idea put into operation most effectively since: by Hitler and Mus-

solini.) *V.R. went still further: wanted work battalions organized under command of Red Army: a full militarization of labor—no idleness! (Hitler and Mussolini can thank him for this suggestion too.)*

"Why this fantastic turnabout? Overnight? No political speculations, no matter how sophisticated, can explain it. Something profoundly personal involved. . . . In moment of maximum clarity and sanity, V.R. had proposed a 'soft' policy—and been denounced, in the toughest Bolshevik language, for his 'softness.' A charge he was extraordinarily sensitive to. Set out to prove he could be harder than the hardest Bolshevik. . . . Made no difference that he had been absolutely right. His impulses, his compulsions, at this point profoundly personal, not political.

"V.R. never for a moment forgetful of the eyes upon him. He was recent convert to Bolsheviks. Many oldtimers suspicious of him. Envious, too: by virtue of his brilliance the latecomer had leaped over all their heads to position of top leadership with Lenin. They thought him one of the 'softs' who'd signed up only when they, the 'hards,' had taken the lead. They were continually watching him for proof he wasn't a 'hard.' Always under scrutiny by the envious and resentful ones—those who considered themselves so hard they'd given themselves names like Molotov—'hammer'—Stalin—'steel.' . . . But V.R. didn't have to prove his toughness only to the others. Had to prove it to himself. Had submitted spectacularly to the Bolshevik-Leninist centralism he'd once so effectively exposed. . . . When his courageous demand for a new economic course was shouted down he aboutfaced with amazing speed and took the harshest position possible on the trade union question and the militarization of labor: became the supreme centralist.

"But: a paradox he could not escape. In becoming the hardest of the hard—he exposed himself as the softest of the soft. Because in so doing he was submitting cravenly to a Bolshevik idea of hardness that was alien to him. . . . What he truly believed in in his best moments, openness, roominess, humaneness, he'd expressed in his campaign for a new economic turn. In abandoning this program under the attacks of the worst Bolshevik diehards, he was abandoning himself, his best ideas, his finest—because most *rational and least impulsive—identity. The centralism he then took up with a latecomer's self-proving passion was the final monument to his absolute submissiveness, under all the fireworks. . . .*

"*Came Kronstadt. He knew with awful clarity that the sailors' revolt was only a demand for the things he'd advocated a year before in his call for a new course. He knew that if his program had been adopted, this revolt, and the flarings of unrest before it, could have been avoided. Wasn't all this in his mind when he proposed that peace negotiations be opened with the sailors and that an ultimatum be issued only as a last resort? . . . But he also knew that the eyes of the other Bolsheviks were on him every minute now, waiting to see if he would acquit himself in this worst of all crises as a 'soft' or a 'hard.' . . . He abandoned the idea of peace negotiations as hurriedly as he'd abandoned his call for a new economic course. He went across the ice of Finland Bay and proved to everybody—everybody but himself—that he was a 'hard.' Thereby proving for all time his very fierce—submissiveness.*

"*Few months later Bolsheviks did their own aboutface and adopted in every last detail the New Economic Policy. Became the law of the land. Russian people officially exhorted to produce, trade, consume, fill their bellies, be as petty as was humanly possible. After the Kronstadt sailors had been slaughtered for allegedly enriching themselves—they hadn't: most of them were for a democratic sharing of privations—the official slogan, addressed to small farmers and businessmen everywhere, actually became: ENRICH YOURSELVES!*

"*But the Bolsheviks never said one word about this being exactly what the Petrograd strikers and the Kronstadt sailors had been asking for—even an exaggeration of it.*

"*V.R. too said very little about it. Except in that one unguarded moment: 'Because we made a mistake. . . .'*

"*From Kronstadt to today V.R.'s been the most passive of men, the softest, the most idle. He fights Stalin, that final triumph of Bolshevik-Leninist super-hardness? Yes—but how?*

"*Why, from the terrible moment of Kronstadt on, has the military genius of the Red Army allowed nothing in his arsenal —but words?*

"*Pacifism? Or—the last phase of submission? To the last and greatest wave of all—extinction?*

"*Two things I know:*

"*(1) The human nervous system was not built for sustained heroism. Neurally untenable posture. Nerves designed for protection, not impulse displays. Big dash—big backfire; the broad sweep has in it the germs of general collapse; after the impulse gush a total idleness, paralysis. . . . That may be what people are really after who make a career of spectacular hurtlings and dervishings: the snap back and total stall after the leap's spent itself. Exactly the opposite of what they pretend to want, of course. But so many hard programs end in a fatty mess. . . . Every over-bold enterprise—rather, every enterprise, however good, when approached with too much showy boldness—over-reaches itself. Because the lie behind the boldness, the mush just under the hard façade, breaks through. . . . Quieter, more limited projects, conceived with less totality and dramatics, may stand a better chance of getting somewhere and sustaining themselves; at least of not backfiring. . . . How many of us join the revolution because we secretly smell its built-in Kronstadts?*

"*(2) In the face of danger normal protoplasm contracts. The natural protective hunch, to offer the minimum of surface. So many compulsive rebels, facing danger—expand! Puff themselves up to make a still bigger target! How can you trust the rebel warrior who, when he sees trouble coming close, breathes in instead of out, bulges instead of pulling tight—demonstratively enlarges his surfaces! What's he a rebel against, finally—his nerves' proper work, Nature, self-preservation?*

"*Was it any accident that V.R. at seventeen took as his key polarity the hard-soft—and later made a career swinging between these poles?*

"*The danger in being too idle. You get too impulsive. . . .*

"*Hardest thing of all, to be soft. . . ."*

V.R. was holding the head of lettuce in his hands. He looked at it carefully, turned it about, studied it again.

"No," he said. "The hardest thing—is to find psychological formulas that will topple a Tsar. Such playful formulas are soft. Tsars are very hard."

"I think Kronstadt could have been avoided," Paul said. "I think you've come to feel this too—with one half of your mind—and can't say it. How recall the policy? You can't recall the corpses. . . ."

"Psychologists see all the problems, all—except the flesh-and-blood Tsars. Who trample on everybody. Including psychologists." V.R.'s strong fingers closed on the ball of lettuce; it shredded, fell in two parts. "When will you be leaving?"

"I never dreamed this could happen." Paul's voice was shaking. "Not this way. I thought—lose your politics—this means demoralization, shame—you've sold out. Then why do I feel as if a dingy veil's all of a sudden been lifted from the world—everything's shining for the first time? You say—dull, gray, petty mass—no dutiful political cogs in my head start to turn—I think: that's the definition of bliss! I want to be dull! I want to be an undistinguished gray! I've a craving for the petty! It's true—I've no values left. I'll take anything that looks like a valid sensation—that promises to be moving. . . ."

"I repeat: when will you leave? There's no place for you in this house. You've become my enemy."

"*Your* enemy? Nothing that pinpointed. I've become, I think this is it, an enemy of all grandiosity, including my own—though what's to be substituted for it I can't say. . . . You have to have the grandiose touch to make history? Fine. I'll make something else—something pocket-size. . . ." Paul stood up, his eyes feverish. His fingers closed tight on the manila envelope as though to keep it from being snatched away. "I'll leave as soon as I can arrange it. I'll take these notes of David's with me, if I may—they're my best passport. . . . Thanks for evicting me, V.R.! Many thanks! I should have gotten you to do it sooner. . . ."

Emma and Marisha came past them, crossing the patio to the street door.

"Is it wise, Emma?" Marisha said.

"I have to do some shopping or there'll be no dinner." She raised her voice: "Paul! How about it? I'm ready to leave."

Paul hurried toward them, carrying his folder. He looked out the peephole and said: "Guillermo—she's ready." He buzzed the door open, the sergeant stepped in.

"I do not like it," Marisha said.

"The señorita is totally safe, señora," Guillermo said. "I go with; I take three of the men."

"Stay close to the sergeant," Marisha said.

"He'll take along his guitar," Paul said. His cheeks were red, there was sparkle in his eyes. "Tell him if you have any request numbers."

"Don't forget, Jacques's coming at four," Emma said.

"For a literary consultation. . . . I'll let him in."

Paul opened the door again, Emma went out with the sergeant. The door closed.

Paul pressed his bulging folder to his body with both hands.

"What are you holding?" Marisha said.

"My passport, Marisha! David stamped all the visas in it; Victor put the official seal on!"

"I am not good at riddles, Paul."

"I'm sorry—but I'm shaking inside, Marisha, I can hardly find the words. . . . All along I thought: Victor's the way he is because his premises are getting too hard to defend. Mine, I thought, were in a bad way too—since they were his. I never once looked at *my* premises—they'd vanished! I've got no premises left—my pockets have been picked clean—I've been robbed and I feel wonderful! I feel light as air!"

"Some hunger for the last chapter," Marisha said. "And you? Perhaps the first. . . ."

She went across to the rabbit cages. V.R. was cleaning out the compartments and putting in fresh layers of shredded newspaper. He spoke quietly to the animals: "There, George who looks like a Varvara, all right, Varvara who looks like a George." He glanced up at Marisha and acknowledged her with a too ready smile. "They won't eat a thing today. All the world has appetites—they're on a hunger strike. I thought I'd change their mattresses."

"Bass has turned *their* stomachs too." V.R. laughed, too deliberately. Marisha was carrying a white sun hat; she handed it to him. "The sun is hot today. Put this on."

"You think the sun will cook my head?" He pulled the hat over his thick hair. "How would you like it, softboiled or hardboiled?"

His joking tone got no response; his face sobered. "Understand. Understand, please, Marisha. I didn't want David here. I would give a great deal to take his place. . . . Leon—I wanted to take *his* place. . . . No one asks for volunteers. . . ."

"What is wrong with Paul? He sits for a long time with you: now he talks wild talk of passports and visas. . . ."

"At least you can set your mind at rest about Paul. He will be safe. . . . Paul's broken with us, Marisha. He's agreed to go away. . . ."

"He broke with us long ago," Marisha said. "He needed the courage to let his body go after his mind."

"Well, they'll soon have a reunion. They'll be dancing the rumba together in the streets. . . ." He took the lighter tone again: "I feel rested today. You know, I slept very well last night."

"The waiting is almost over. It was the waiting you could not stand."

"What, Marisha? We've been granted a miracle and still you look sad?"

"A miracle, or—"

"Or?"

"Or—only a reprieve?"

"All right. But a reprieve is something."

"These days I think often of a line from Pushkin: from *Boris Godunov.* Do you remember it? *One more chapter and this story will be finished.*"

"Have you ever thought that if we'd remained in Russia we'd have died in our beds in the Kremlin long ago? No matter what the next chapter is, we're better off here. . . ."

"Speaking of chapters: you wrote more on Kronstadt this morning?"

He nodded vigorously. *"That* story is almost finished—and Gaspodin Josef Vissarionovitch Stalin won't like it! . . . Shouldn't Jacques be here by now?"

Marisha looked at her watch.

"It is a few minutes to four. He will be here."

"It's a nuisance having to read his article today but it must be done. We owe him something for the other night."

"Emma has changed her mind about him—she told you?"

"I sensed it. There's color in her face again. . . . She's a girl who blushes when she's happy—as though shame were close by. . . ."

"She thinks they can have a future together. She has decided to bring him to her family in Chicago."

"She intends to marry him? That sounds a little extreme."

"She feels that he rose to the occasion when Bass came. She thinks there may be a worth in him she did not see."

"But marriage can't be a series of Bass attacks. In between the crises. . . . No—it's wrong to discuss him this way. Their life together is their affair. He did behave well that night." He went on adding paper strips to the rabbit cages. The doorbell sounded. "Ah. The budding author."

Paul opened the door. Masson stepped in, carrying his coat. Marisha went to meet him.

"Paul: Marisha." He looked around. "Where's Emma?"

"She went to the market," Marisha said.

"Oh, yes—she told me she was going. I hope she's safe—"

"She's got four cops with her," Paul said. "She won't fall down."

"When will she get back?"

"Half an hour or less."

Masson looked at his watch. He followed Marisha over to the orange tree, mopping his forehead.

"Wretchedly hot today," he said. "I suffer in this sticky heat."

"You do not look well. Shall I get you a glass of water?"

"No, no, I'll be all right. This filthy sun always affects me this way."

"But you do not expect this 'filthy' sun to last."

"What? What do you mean?"

She pointed to his coat. "You expect a 'filthy' rain to chase it away. You have been expecting rain for over a week."

"Oh! Yes! Well, you know how the weather is here. These afternoon downpours, even though they only last for minutes—I catch cold so easily."

"I see. Then: today you shall not catch cold."

V.R. came up.

"You're late, young man. . . . Would you like a cup of tea?"

"I've no room! I ate late and I can still feel my meal there. . . ." He jabbed at his throat. "It's choking me."

"You're not feeling well? Your face is pale. . . . You've let the attack upset you too much, Jacques. It's time to think of other things."

"And take better care of yourself," Marisha said. "I think you neglect yourself. Emma will have a sick man on her hands." She had taken a bowl of grapes from the circular seat; she offered them to Masson. "Would you like some grapes? They will ease your throat."

"Thank you—yes. I will have some." He pulled off a bunch and began to eat rapidly, stuffing his mouth. "Forgive me for troubling you with the article, V.R. But I'm so anxious to get it right. . . ."

"It can be very helpful. What are the main points in it?"

Masson thought, then began to speak in a rush:

"Well—I've analyzed the attack, of course. That comes at the end. I trace the plot to—ah—two motives. One, Stalin doesn't want your biography of him published. Two, he's wiped out most of the Old Bolsheviks—now he wants to finish the job. . . ."

"You've left out the most important thing."

"What's that?"

"Stalin is preparing his pact with Hitler. Molotov and von Ribbentrop are meeting in—"

"Pact. . . . Yes! He's destroyed the Spanish workers; now he's about to desert the democracies altogether and join with Hitler. . . . He can't allow you to remain alive and—and expose these manures. . . ." His mouth was full. He burst out with explosive laughter; bits of grape flew from his mouth; he began to choke. "What am I saying! Manures! Did I actually say that? I meant *maneuvers*—what a silly thing!" He coughed harder. "Forgive me! Grapes—down wrong way! . . . Silly of me. . . . I'm sorry. . . ." The attack eased off.

"Come: we'll talk in the study." Masson followed V.R. toward the ramp. In the corner V.R. stopped to peek at the rabbits. "These two are quite sick. This one, George Sand, and this one, Varvara Petrovna. . . . See how swollen their bellies are?"

"Swollen? A pity. . . ."

"It came on after the attack. George Bass's music was too loud for them."

"Ah." Masson began to cough again. V.R. looked at him sharply. "More casualties—for—Bass."

V.R. had opened the cage on the right. He took out the rabbit and cradled it in his arms: "Have faith, Varvara Petrovna. The belly will get better. There'll be good days again."

He led the way up to the study, stroking the animal's fat back. He seated himself at the desk.

"The manuscript. . . . You've brought the manuscript?"

"Here it is."

Masson pulled the papers from his pocket and laid them on the desk.

"Varvara and I will give it our expert editorial eyes."

Patting the animal's soft fur, V.R. leaned over and began to read the typed pages. He gave them his full attention.

Masson stepped back and fumbled with his coat.

"The sentences are awkward, young man."

Masson started. V.R. went on reading.

"An imprecise sentence is the shadow of an imprecise thought. . . ."

Masson drew the axe out. He held it with both hands. His face twisted, he threw the raincoat over his shoulder. When he turned his body toward V.R. he kept his face to one side, as though his eyes refused to see what his hands were doing.

He raised the axe over his head, his face grew more distorted; his whole frame was trembling. The axe might have been caught on an invisible hook in the air: he was struggling to bring it down, all his muscles involved in the effort, without being able to make it move.

His eyes closed tight. The axe came down with full force.

V.R. made a high, wild noise.

The rabbit leaped to the floor and bolted through the French doors.

Masson stood paralyzed. At last he raised the axe over his head again.

"Victor!" Marisha's voice from the patio, raised high. "Victor!"

Without rising, V.R. turned in his chair and reached toward Masson. He pulled the man's arms down, got a hold on the axe with both hands. He struggled fiercely, wrested the axe away; it dropped to the floor.

V.R. made the noise again. He was supporting himself on the desk with both arms, looking up at Masson. Blood was beginning to run down his forehead and nose into his mouth.

Masson backed off to the wall. His fingers fumbled in the pocket of the raincoat and pulled out the revolver. His eyes on V.R., he raised the revolver.

But the gun seemed to be moving by its own design. It did not stay pointed at V.R. Slowly it turned in Masson's hand until it was aimed at his own chest.

V.R. fell from the chair to his knees. He managed to get to his feet. Bent almost double, he lurched toward the doors.

Marisha was rushing up the walk, hands to her cheeks.

"What is it? Victor?"

Paul was racing along the other leg of the walk, gun in hand.

"What happened? What happened?" Marisha said as she came up.

V.R. said without anger, sorrowfully: "Masson."

He fell and lay still. His eyes remained open.

Paul stopped for one second at V.R.'s body, looked in the study. He rushed inside and leaped on Masson. He tore the gun from Masson's hand and forced him back over the desk. He began to beat Masson brutally with the butt end of his own gun.

Outside, Marisha was making a cradle of her lap. She placed V.R.'s head easily on it. She dragged the shawl from her shoulders and wrapped it around his chest.

The doorbell rang.

"Marisha, I love you."

"Be quiet, my darling. My dear."

"In there. . . . I felt, I understood what he wanted to do. . . . He wanted to—again. . . . I stopped him. . . ."

The sky had darkened. A few drops of rain splattered on the walk, the bougainvillea on the far wall squirmed, the leaves of the nearby orange tree rustled.

Marisha tried to see inside the study. Masson was covering his face with his hands, crying out in anguish as Paul's gun struck him. Paul beat him to his knees, then all the way to the floor.

"What are we to do? Paul is going to kill him!"

"No. . . . We must make him talk. . . ." With all his remaining strength V.R. sat up and shouted his orders to Paul: "Make him talk! Paul! Don't kill him! He must talk!"

Paul heard. He went on beating the man but less viciously, with spaced, systematic blows. Masson groaned each time he was hit. He was only half conscious now.

The doorbell rang again, twice.

"Before I kill you you're going to talk! Who—sent—you? . . . The—GPU—sent you! Admit it!"

"No! It's they, they!"

"They! You mean—the GPU!"

"He made me do it! They've got something on me! They're keeping my mother a prisoner!"

Paul hit him harder.

"Liar! Liar! Confess—you're the one who opened the door!"

Masson was begging: "Kill me once and for all! I don't deserve to live! It wasn't the GPU—but kill me!"

V.R. had fallen back into Marisha's arms. He tried twice to say something. Finally the words came:

"If they take me to the hospital—I don't want them to undress me. You do it for me. . . ."

She could not speak. She nodded and bent low to kiss his lips.

The rain was coming harder now. The doorbell rang insistently.

Paul let go of Masson. The man slumped to the floor. Paul looked around, noticed the axe close by. He picked it up and stared at it.

He grabbed Masson by the collar and dragged him outside, past Marisha and V.R., on along the walk and down the steps into the patio. There he flung Masson to the ground. He went to the door and looked out through the peephole.

He opened the door. Emma stepped in, carrying her loaded shopping basket.

She saw Paul's face and stopped in confusion.

She looked to her left and caught sight of V.R. stretched out on the walk, head in Marisha's lap. She froze in terror, her eyes came back to Paul.

"Who opened the door for them?" Paul was panting. *"Him! Him! He* was the one David saw! *That's* why they had to kill David!"

Emma looked to where Paul was pointing. Masson lay with his face in the dust, trying to raise his head.

She dropped her basket, both her hands rose in the air.

"He's done the job over again! He did it fine today, Emma, fine! With this!"

He held up the blood-tipped axe.

Emma screamed.

The rain began to fall in a rush. Something white flashed across the garden. It was the freed rabbit, Varvara Petrovna, unused to space, frightened by the sudden downpour, rushing here and there around the neutral-faced Aztec carvings.

CHAPTER XVII

Marisha sat by the bed holding his hands. His head was wrapped down to the eyebrows in bandages. Two rubber tubes, running from a large oxygen tank behind the bed, were taped to his nostrils.

"Yesterday you said I needed a haircut." He spoke with difficulty, spacing the words; he tried to smile. "Now they've shaved my head."

"I had a bad feeling when he came. . . . I said to myself: there he comes, with his raincoat."

"I felt something too. . . . He laughed when there was nothing to laugh at. . . . He ate the grapes so fast."

"Paul was right. He said: seal the doors."

"I couldn't allow it, Marisha. . . . Stalin would have boasted to his drinking companions in the Kremlin: At first I wasn't strong enough to put him in prison—now I've made him lock himself up, six thousand miles away."

"We *were* in a prison. With faulty walls we would not fix."

"It's not the last chapter yet: there'll be more to this story. . . . Where is Emma?"

"General Ortega is holding her. To keep her from hurting herself."

"Hurting. . . . She tried. . . ."

"After the ambulance came. Paul stopped her."

"Their latest victim. . . . They feast now on schoolboys and sad girls."

"If she had not her appetite for misery . . . for defeats. . . . She invited this."

"We couldn't see it. . . . Politics narrows the vision—so does—mathematics. . . . It doesn't let you see when a man eats grapes too fast. . . . The part of the world I liked best to look at was you, Marisha. But I had little time for it. Other parts called too loud. . . . I love you, Marisha. . . . I brought complications home—from all the fronts—you wouldn't let them stay. . . . You had the lost talent, Marisha—simplicity—quiet. . . ."

"We expected others to arrange their lives just as easily: we were

impatient when they looked inward. To us, the private things—
when they were allowed to appear on the outside—were in bad taste.
Intrusions. . . ."

". . . . How Yoffe twitched and cracked his fingers—there at the
conference table at Brest Litovsk. . . ."

"Intrusions, yes. But they were also signs that there were whole
people behind the programs—people moved by more than programs.
. . . I have loved you too, Victor. My dear one. I wish—we had
had more naive days together. . . . Inward days. . . ."

"To call you hard. . . . Hard, dry. . . . You, the softest. . . ."

His eyes were almost closed. He appeared to be dozing.

The door opened: Paul appeared.

"General Ortega," he said softly to Marisha. "Can he—"

V.R. opened his eyes with an effort.

"I'm awake. Tell him to come in."

Paul stood aside. The general entered and approached the bed.

"How are you feeling, señor?"

V.R. strained to rouse himself: "Better now." He indicated with
his finger that he wanted the general to come closer. Marisha rose
from her chair and stepped back to join Paul at the door. Ortega
bent over; V.R. whispered, tapping his chest: "I feel there . . . it's
the end."

"From the most unexpected quarter. With the most unexpected
weapon."

"You have your final proof: my death."

"I have other proofs. . . . One of the prisoners was made to talk
—we have our ways. . . . Masson is not a Belgian. His mother is
an old associate of Bass's—from Barcelona. Bass directed the affair.
He was keeping the mother prisoner to terrorize the son. . . .
Things are clearer now. The compartment of the Packard—the machine guns were stored there. . . ."

"Of course. . . . No matter. . . ."

"When you and I examined the house after the attack—you remember?—something bothered me a little. It did not fully register,
it came only to the edges of my mind. The bullet holes in Masson's
room—the girl's room—were all high; some distance over the head.
They were not so in the other rooms. . . . I might have weighed
this fact in my mind and drawn some conclusions. All of us might

have. But you were so sure of the people in your house. The thought came close—I pushed it away—because of your certainty. . . . If we had thought carefully about those bullet holes—then about what Justin had seen that made them kill him—then gone back and thought again about the Packard—perhaps. . . . Why did you refuse the evidence of your own eyes, señor? Why did you blind the eyes of others? Why?"

"Interesting questions. . . . I'd like to discuss them with you at length. . . ." V.R.'s voice was almost inaudible.

"I know two things. . . . There is a GPU, whose hand can reach around the world with an axe in it. . . . You, señor, were one of its founders. . . . For the rest of my life I will ponder these two facts."

"The most interesting question of all. . . . I have a busy schedule today. . . . We'll have to postpone the discussion. . . ."

"You fought as you could. Sometimes on the battlefields I know. . . . Goodbye, señor."

Marisha followed the general into the corridor. Paul closed the door.

"Heads—fragile as eggs. As empires." General Ortega seemed to be speaking to himself. He turned to Paul with sudden energy: "You, with your silly sandbags—you were at least trying! At least you pretended you had some regard for your life! . . . That head in there—one of the fantastic, dreaming heads! It dreamed over continents, over centuries! Down to this nightmare—see how dreams can stampede!"

"How is Emma, general?" Marisha said.

"Under sedation. She is being watched."

"Say to her, please—Victor and I kiss her. We think of her."

"I will tell her. . . . There are things here I do not understand, señora." General Ortega pointed in his distress to the closed door. "He warned that in a revolution people must not lay down their weapons too soon. Permanent revolution—permanent vigilance. But he—did he not lay down *his* weapons? For Stalin to pick up?" He stepped closer to Marisha. He spoke with great emotion: "He fought a runaway GPU with—speeches, pamphlets. The words were often good: but were they meant to win? Or only to be the dignified wrappings for a defeat?"

"There was no reason to fight them," Marisha said in her quaver, "if he had to become like them."

"I must ask, señora, I must. . . . He would not stoop to their means. But how is filth to be fought except with filth? To draft eloquent theses against the bubonic. . . . And against Kronstadt—he used more than theses. . . . He called me a dilettante; was he not the worst dilettante of all? . . . These questions are never out of my mind now."

"The plague needs a precise antitoxin. We have not yet found the antitoxin. . . . We have our morality too. . . . Not all means are permissible."

"He used *all* of them in the revolution; revolutions—like police work—are impossible without barbarities. . . . Why not *after?*"

"Let the terror become casual . . . matter-of-fact . . . it grows into a way of life."

"Then it amounts to this: those who use all means will win, those who reject some means will lose. There is no remedy. . . . This is why I abandoned our revolution when it was won."

"Then explain, general—why you bothered to fight it at all. . . ."

"But he *stopped* fighting! At the George Basses—he hurled ringing phrases! . . . Had he seen too much blood? Was his stomach turning with the blood? . . . He fought with magnificent *words*. The will to win was gone. . . . Was he only inviting the grand end? Because the big questions had become too hard to answer?"

Paul had been standing to one side, listening. Now he stepped in to say: "This is not the time for a cross-examination, general."

But Ortega ignored the interruption. He was still looking to Marisha: "Señora—forgive me—I think you speak *his* answers to me. I wonder what your own answers would be."

"When I married him, general, I married all of him: his answers too," she said quietly, with her delicate head very high, although her voice was thin and unsteady. "That is my understanding of a marriage. . . . Will you excuse me? I will go in to him now."

She opened the door and went inside.

"What will you do now?" the general said. "You have no training in being alone."

"I don't have any plans," Paul said.

"All sights do not have to be spectacles. . . . Events can be small and still be worth something: do you know what important events there are in the sprouting of a grain of corn? . . . Go somewhere and run a gasoline station! Learn to build suspension bridges! . . . Your skull is still intact."

"Come up from the hole? All the way up? . . . Breathe fresh air? . . . That's the wildest, most revolutionary program of all." Paul put his ear close to the door, he listened for sounds inside. "I suppose I'll have to try. . . ."

General Ortega shook his head in some kind of fury and strode away.

He walked the length of the corridor, turned left and entered another wing. Halfway down this passage he came to the barrier of heavy steel bars that marked the entrance to the prison ward. A guard opened the gate for him; he passed through and continued on until he reached a door outside which Sergeant Guillermo stood with three other policemen.

These men saluted. He went inside.

His aide, Jaime, was standing at the window. On a chair in the corner, to one side of the cot, Masson sat stiffly. His head was bandaged along one side; his face was bruised and puffy; there was a wad of cotton taped over his left eye.

"I regret having kept you waiting," General Ortega said. "I was visiting another man with a bandaged head."

Masson stood with a nervous motion and pressed his back against the wall.

"Would you like to know the results of your handiwork?" The general picked up the ice axe from the table. "You use your tools expertly. Rostov will not live through the night."

Masson cringed.

"You are no longer a man who was careless with an axe. Tomorrow you will be a murderer. . . . I will give you one more chance to answer. You opened the door for George Bass?"

There was fear in Masson's face but he said: "Who is George Bass?"

"You admit you are Tomás Baeza de Rivera?"

"I am Jacques Masson of Brussels. That's in Belgium."

"The Belgian consul has made inquiries. The home address you gave in Brussels does not exist. The 'distinguished' Masson family does not exist."

"Maybe our house burned down. I don't keep in touch with my relatives; they might have migrated to the Congo."

"When you thought you were going to be killed by Teleki, why did you shout: *They have something on me, they are keeping my mother a prisoner?*"

"How could I speak of my mother? She's been dead for fifteen years."

General Ortega said meaningfully: "You know that we captured seven of Bass's men?" Masson pushed his shoulders back against the wall but did not speak. The general walked closer to him. "Six of them know nothing of your part in the attack. They do not know you are in Mexico; perhaps they never heard of you. Apparently your Plan A people were not told much about Plan B. . . . But one of my prisoners is a native of Madrid. He is well acquainted with your mother; he was one of those guarding her in the mountain house near Dinamos. He knew you in Madrid, in Barcelona. . . . His name is—Marcos Guaro." General Ortega was watching closely for a reaction to his words: Masson's face twitched. "I see: you did not know Guaro was in Mexico. . . . Guaro identifies you from your picture as a drunken brawler—Tomás Baeza de Rivera—son of Cándida—longterm associate of George Bass."

After a moment Masson was able to say: "Who is George Bass?"

"Hold your left arm out." Masson did not move. General Ortega took hold of his hand violently and pulled the sleeve back. "Shrapnel wound: Madrid front. Guaro knows what he is talking about."

"I received this wound mountain climbing in the Swiss Alps, two years ago. . . . You have my story, general. It's all in the statement you took from my pocket."

"I see. You were a Belgian student, a follower of Rostov. You killed out of disillusionment—and love. That is the story you will tell in court?"

"That's the story—I must tell."

Ortega considered him. He turned and nodded to Jaime; the aide at once left the room. Ortega turned his back on Masson and crossed to the barred window.

Very soon Jaime and Sergeant Guillermo came in, supporting

Emma Sholes between them. She walked with head down, noticing nothing; her feet dragged. The policemen led her to a chair and she slumped down in it.

Masson shrank against the wall:

"What have you done, general! What have you done! Take me out!"

"Oh, no," General Ortega said. "Oh, no. I do not think I will take you anywhere. This is your fiancée, is it not? Surely at such a time of trouble you wish your fiancée close to you, this *good and loyal* girl. . . . Señorita Sholes! Raise your eyes, please! Señorita! There is someone—"

Victor Rostov was going to die. The Old Man would die. No more V. and no more R. The long and pointless vigil was over. Walking through the midnight streets Paul told himself these things in a factual way: more data of the surround, like the oxygen in the air, the ingathered moon, the huddled péon figures in the doorways and along the curb. Breathe: avoid the bodies: V.R. would die tonight.

He had not wanted to leave the hospital but Marisha had insisted: "What can you do here, Paul? The walls are broken through, all of them, for good. Go for a walk—get these iodoform fumes out of your head."

Were fumes of anything but iodoform left in his head? His head was at last in the market for content, one sort or another. *Its* walls were broken through: all entries spread wide and begging. The world gave him no openings and made him no offers: only sleeping bodies to step around—

As in the doorway just ahead. This one was not stretched out like the others. In a sitting position, knees drawn up and chin resting on them. A woman. A girl, in loose country clothes. Her head moved as he came closer.

He speeded his step. These were not the offers he wanted from the world tonight. What run dry gas stations or sagged suspension bridges in her "You like some fun, mister, two pesos?"

He stopped two steps past her. She had not said a word. She had not even looked his way: her eyes were directed to a spot in the street where the paving was sprinkled with sand.

He saw that in her dark, thrustboned face there was not solicitation but some profound waiting: not for him.

He went back.

"You look for something?"

"My father."

She wore the ankle-low falda wrap over her hips, the full huipil for a blouse, both embroidered in brilliant purples; over her head and shoulders a black rebozo; from her shining tightpulled hair came the slight sweet smell of oil of mammee: styles of the Indian. But her face had solidities and depths of shadow that were not typical Indian and there was some voweled fullness in her voice that could not be named. She could not be twenty.

"Where is your father?"

"Gone with the white truck with the loud bell. They went before I could get in with him."

She had not raised her eyes to him. She was still giving all her attention to the sanded area beyond the curb.

"Why do you look there in the street?"

"My father was there."

He noticed that tracks ran along this narrow street. The sanded spot was alongside the nearer track.

He went over to look. When he brushed some of the sand aside with his shoe he saw traces of dried blood, the sand was dark with it.

He returned to the girl. "There was an accident? Your father was hurt by the streetcar? He was taken in the ambulance?"

"He told me to take care in crossing the streets of the city," she said from far back in the throat. "He did not take care."

She was not asking his help, she asked nothing of anybody, she meant only to wait at a distance and be ready for what came. But he got her to talk: step by step the story came out.

She and her father were from the south, from the Pacific slopes of the Isthmus country, there in Oaxaca. A wild portion with few people: rising from hot lagoons along the coast to cramped sierras and steep, knifing tors behind. So far away and uncovered were these stony, crumbling lands that high up, in the highest peaks, were people who still lived naked in caves, with hair to their waists. She and her father came from a small sierra village called Chochutlán, where the people kept sheep. They were a branch of the ones called the Chontal, people who had their own language not like any other, not like that of the Zapotec, the Mixtec, the Chinantec, the Huave, the Mixe, people who stayed apart from the other Indians, feeling themselves to be not like any others. Less than one-quarter of the Chontal who lived in Chochutlán could speak any words of Spanish. At certain times of the year the people of this village traveled down to the lagoons of the Huave tribe, to find the tiny sea shells fastened to the coastal rocks there. These snails were necessary to the life of the Chontal. When their excretions were squeezed on hanks of yarn, spun by the villagers from their own sheep, this yarn became a special purple, a purple that moved, swam, hurt the eyes. The cloths made from this dyed yarn were called by the Syrian and Lebanese traders who came to buy them royal purple, imperial purple, Tyrean purple of the shade once used, it was said, for the robes of kings in a far-off empire on the Mediterranean called Tyre. The Chontal brought their purpled yarns back to the sierra and from them wove blouses, faldas, serapes—things much in demand in the markets of the city because of their color. The Chontal of Chochutlán were grouped together to make a business of this, all based on the hair of the sheep and the waste products of the small snail of the Huave lagoons. Twice a year the finished faldas and huipiles and serapes were taken by burro down the mountain paths to Tlalcotihuaya, to the railroad, then carried by freight car to Mexico City, for the markets. The girl's father, alcalde of Chochutlán, was of the group for this business. This year he had been selected to go with the shipment and to collect the money from the traders in the city. He had brought his daughter with him because her Spanish was good and his less so. But he was not used to the streets of the city, he had not the habit to take care against the streetcars. . . .

"You speak well," Paul said. "You have been to school?"

"For a time I was in the advanced school of Guelatao. Today my father took me to the normal school here, to enroll for next year. He wished me to become a teacher."

"You cannot find your father if you sit. Why do you not go to ask for him?"

"He told me to talk with no one. I wait for those of the white truck to come back."

Both her hands pressed against her breasts.

"Your father gave you something to keep?" She stared straight ahead. "Listen to me. I will help you. What you have, what your father gave to you, I have no interest in. But if it is money, there is a way to make it safe—only send it by the telegraph to your friends. This can be done. I can take you to the telegraph office and you can send the money now—if it is money."

She looked at him now: with full eyes, for a long time: a fuller test than any he had been put to in all his years, he thought.

She slid her hand under her rebozo, to her blouse, and drew from there a folded manila envelope. She held it out to him; he opened it; inside was more than eleven hundred pesos in bills of large denominations.

"Thank you," he said with absurd enthusiasm, "thank you very much. Come, we will send this money, then we will find your father."

He would organize a fine telegram, the century's best manhunt! He would put all of his considerable organizational genius to work on it! Find your gas pumps and arching bridges where you may. . . . He felt the wildest surge of gratitude to this girl for letting him participate in her worries.

They came to a boulevard, Avenida Ribera de San Cosme. Here, after some minutes, Paul found a cab. Ten minutes later they were at the all-night Western Union office south of the Alameda.

"There is a telegraph office in Chochutlán?"

"No. The nearest is in Tlalcotihuaya."

"Is there one in this place you trust?"

"The alcalde, he is the friend of my father."

"Good: we send this money to the alcalde there, to hold for your village."

He explained the matter to the clerk and handed over the money. He composed a wire to the alcalde of Tlalcotihuaya, detailing the circumstances. What was the girl's name? Donaji. An old Zapotec name that had been taken over by her people; she thought it meant Cotton Flake, or perhaps the daughter of Cotton Flake, she was not sure. Paul signed the wire Donaji of Chochutlán.

"Now," he said, "I will use the telephone to look for your father."

There was a phone booth here. He called the hospital: Guillermo was on duty and available. Paul outlined the problem: Guillermo said he would check with police headquarters and call back.

Paul tried to make small talk to pass the time. "So, Donaji. The other girls of your village marry, and you wish to become a teacher?"

"When I reached sixteen," she said, "a weaver of the village wished to marry me. My father was opposed: a teacher is needed for our village, so our people can learn to speak and write Spanish and do figures and be able to deal better with those on the outside and make a better business. I went to school to become a teacher."

"You gave up the weaver?"

"We were together in the night for three years, until last year, only without the marriage. For the reason that girls who marry are not taken in the higher schools."

"Your father was not against this?"

"He wished me to have the life of a woman, like the others, but also to go to school. But the weaver tired of this and did not want to wait longer for a family. Last year he married another."

The alphabet comes in: the first Bohemians appear: next—loud politics! He saw something: the alphabet can be a true enemy of monoliths. . . . But all he said was: "The alphabet has complicated your life."

The phone rang: Guillermo. Headquarters reported that the Chontal countryman who had been hit by the trolley in the Tlaxpana quarter had been picked up by the ambulance at eight-forty-three, had died in the ambulance at eight-fifty-two, had been taken directly to the morgue. He gave Paul the address. Señor Rostov? The same, the same.

"I have found your father," Paul told the girl. "We can go there now."

In the cab he said, "Are you strong? Can you take bad news?"

"I know he is dead," she said.

He blinked at her. "You know?"

"I knew before the white truck came. I saw in his face that he would die. He knew this too. He told me."

"He died before they could bring him to the hospital." He took her by the arms. "I have lost a father today too. When I saw you I was walking just to walk and telling myself I must find the way to live without fathers."

She was puzzled. 'They die; those who are left live without them."
"Or find others to take their place. Some need this. . . . This is
why you wished to find your father? To bury him?"
"To bury him with his own people, in Chochutlán. He asked this
of me before they took him." She looked into his face with the same
steady eyes. "When this is done, when all is arranged, then I will go
with you to your house, if this is what you want. We have enough
mushrooms to eat." She held up a small cloth bag. "We will eat
the mushrooms and I will lie together with you: then I will go
home."
"Schoolteacher!" he said. "Snail gatherer! Your father is dead!"
"Would my father wish me to be dead too? That would be a bad
father."
"You are alive, sierra girl! Your words are purple—a purple that
jumps!"
"If I please you, only if this is so, truly, we will eat the mushrooms. We will lie together. We will see the good pictures—"

Impossible to breathe.
Rubber worms in nostrils.
"Anastas," he said.
In. Suck. In. Suck. In. In.
"Breathe," he said.
From a place over the seas, pulsed with winds: "All right, Victor.
I am here. It is all right."
Breathe, Anastas! Breathe, dear friend!
Yakorny Square. Snow everywhere. Soldiers in white sheets run-
ning. Some still coming through the gates, some still dropping from
the walls. White soldiers everywhere. Firing as they came. Sailors in
blue uniforms falling back from arch to arch, from doorway to door-
way, returning the fire. Bodies lying in the snow. Bodies falling.
White sheets throwing themselves on blue uniforms, cursing, firing,
flash of bayonets. Screams. Easy to breathe. Clean, freezing air to
slash at throat and surge to lungs. Under one arch the general,
breathing hard, panting, automatic in hand, watching the battle.
Breathing. Gasping.
In. In. Maximum effort: air!
"Try, Anastas! Breathe! You can do it!"

From the other side of the world: "Do not speak, Victor. Save your strength, Victor, my dearest."

Who? With such pulse in voice? From what planet?

General stood there under the arch. Gun icicle in hand, air icicle in lungs. Watching the giant half a block away, in the doorway there. Giant with wild red beard. Uniform of blue, round hat with first gunner's stripes. White sheets coming at him, at his back, from down the street. Paying no attention to white sheets creeping. Staring at the general under the arch. Raising rifle. Bellowing: "You there! Victor Rostov! Come to see the sights, have you! Nice things you build!" Three white sheets approaching his back, bayonets ready. "You eat everything! I kept you alive for this, for this! Now I'll fix—"

"No. . . . Save. . . . Anastas—behind you. . . ."

From the clouds: "Victor—try to sleep."

Sleep! He needed to breathe! Where was the air!

"Anastas! Turn—"

The man could save himself. Had only to turn. Soldiers not on him yet. Would not turn! Too busy taking aim at the general. General standing still by the archway, not taking cover, gun hanging point down. Shouting across square to giant: "Anastas! Behind you!" White sheets on the man, over him. Rifle torn from his hands. Arms holding him. Man would not struggle. Hands limp at his sides. General running toward him, trying to make the soldiers hear: "Do not harm this one! I order you—" Did not hear. Too busy holding the man as he bellowed: "Make holes in everything! What's there to save in this garbage! You build a garbage!" Taunting the soldiers but with eyes on the running general, bellowing with his bull voice loud enough for the general to hear: "Finish it! I won't stay alive in the same world with shit like you! I killed twenty of you this night! Let me live and I promise you, I'll keep on killing you, all I can! As long as I breathe! Go on! Finish your good work!" Defiant. Mocking. Watching the general as he came. Soldier in front raising bayonet. General leaping toward him: "Not this one! I am Rostov! I order you—" Bayonet driving in. Big man falling, eyes on the general. General on his knees, embracing the man: "Breathe, Anastas! I'll get the doctor! You must not. . . ." Big man trying to breathe, whole frame trying, lips sucking. "Good to get out of this.

. . . One regret. . . . Can't take you with me. . . . Like you for comrade on this trip. . . ." His last words.

"Too hard. . . ."

In. . . . In. . . . Nothing. . . .

"You must not speak, dearest one."

"Hard. . . . No. . . ."

She pressed his hands tighter.

"Anastas. . . . Breathe. . . . Try, Anastas! Breathe! . . ."

"All right, Victor," she said. "I am here. It is all right."

To breathe: it was why she had come to the revolution. As many of her generation did, out of horror, out of revulsion, out of suffocation. A world of pain, brutes, stifling—it had to be swept away. But there was more horror in the days of insurrection: bodies piled up everywhere, the statistics of bodies could not be held by any ideas. No clean air here. She was incapable of taking part in this, her whole body began to shake when she listened to the guns in the streets, she could not breathe. There had to be a building, a preservation, to balance this blood; she had to breathe. Victor traveled to the fronts; she organized the committee to preserve museum and art treasures from the looting mobs. The more she read the military news, the casualty lists—the more she stifled—the harder she worked at the museums. . . .

"Breathe! You can do it!"

"Do not speak, Victor," she said. "Save your strength, Victor, my dearest."

So he was back in Yakorny Square now. (What a long way round.) Imploring Anastas Yiko, Uncle Anastas, to take a deep breath. Too late—Anastas Yiko's lungs had become alien to air, the night of March 17, 1921. . . . That night she had been short of breath too. Thinking of what must be happening there on the island. When the Kronstadt trouble began she had, without thinking of the reason, only filled with the need, renewed her work in the museums. The night of March 17th she worked later than usual in the museum vaults. Thinking of Kronstadt, filled with a fever to work. Until late at night she remained with the other women, storing old illuminated manuscripts and monks' pieta paintings in the underground vaults. (Thinking: fingers had once had time for this!)

Victor came home only an hour after she did. There was little talk between them. Her face asked the terrible question, his face gave the terrible answer. Done: is there a place to go from here? She felt she was in a world without air. Making the tea, she tried desperately to inhale deeply, could not. Leon came in. He said, over and over, wildly, tears running over his face: "What of Uncle Anastas? Him too? What happened to Anastas?" The lack of answer was the worst answer of all. She was able to get the boy off to bed, finally. She said no word of Anastas. . . .

"No. . . . Save. . . . Anastas—behind you. . . ."

"Victor," she said, "try to sleep."

They lay in bed as the sun came up. At last he was able to talk. He told her about the last moments of Anastas Yiko, first gunner, personal guard, friend, uncle to Leon. He had pointed his rifle! Taken aim! Victor had known of his fury—it was known that Anastas had made the radio broadcast from the garrison announcing that hundreds of Communists there were tearing up their party membership cards—had spoken of the party of "the butcher Rostov"— Victor knew all this: but there he was, in the flesh, taking aim with his rifle! Refusing to defend himself against the approaching soldiers. His comrades lying all about him in the snow. He was finished with the world. He had goaded the soldiers on deliberately, in a frozen fury. He did not want to live any longer in the same world with Victor Rostov. He had said so. He was ashamed of himself for having worked so hard to keep Victor alive. . . . All this Victor told her, lying beside her in bed. Said: "This was my friend. A man I loved. He wanted to die as a demonstration—against me. I needed to explain to him. I needed him to listen. Who was ever closer to us? He aimed his rifle at me and I could not protect myself. I could not step back to cover, my pistol refused to come up. He could not breathe, Marisha. He lay there for ten minutes and choked. He looked up at me, trying to breathe, and when he could speak he said only: *You feed on blood—I finish with you.* I wanted to explain. He would not listen. Do they think it's easy, this business? Guns— the vileness. He tried to breathe, he could not breathe. . . ." All that morning she held him in her arms. He shuddered, shuddered. For a long time he wept. This man they called so callous, so fanatical

—he wept, she rocked him in her arms, he begged for comfort and could not be comforted.

As he lay now with the rubber tubes in his nose, full of the picture of Anastas Yiko, begging for comfort and finding none, begging for air and finding none. . . .

"Too hard. . . ."

He craved air! How he sucked and begged for air! She had no air to give him.

"You must not speak, dearest one."

"Hard. . . . No. . . ."

"Breathe," she implored him. "Try."

"Take axe . . . to butterflies. . . ."

These were the last words he spoke.

"Señorita, there is someone here. I want you to look at him."

Emma's head came up slowly. She looked about with glazed eyes, trying to focus.

"I must ask you some questions. Both of you."

Her lips began to move: "What did you say, general?"

"I have bad news. Señor Rostov is dying."

"I don't understand. I remember. . . . I think. . . ."

"Rostov is dying. I must ask you some questions."

She said dully: "I don't know. . . . It was a long time ago. . . ."

Her eyes moved aimlessly from side to side. They came to Masson; they rested on him with no expression.

General Ortega signaled to the two policemen: unobtrusively they moved closer to the girl.

She seemed to be waking up.

"Dying. . . . Who is. . . . Hard to breathe in the mountains. . . . Chop with the sharp end. . . ." Her eyes widened. She came fully to life, sprang to her feet. The policemen took her arms. "Because of their tin cups? Why chop them?" She was suddenly hysterical, screaming as she strained to break loose. "You! Traitor! . . . Assassin! Assassin!"

Masson shivered.

"No, general, please! You must take me out!"

An expression of ultimate animal rage had come over the girl's face. As Masson babbled she tore herself from the restraining hands and leaped across the room. Her fingers were at Masson's face, clawing.

"Murderer! Assassin! I'll tear you to ribbons without an axe!"

Ortega and the two policemen got hold of her. She struggled with a fury, pulled a hand free and snatched the axe from the table. She tried wildly to swing at Masson; Guillermo finally got the axe away.

They had to half carry her across the room. She sank back into her chair, bent over, weeping.

Ortega put his hands gently on her shoulders.

"Forgive me, señorita. The confrontation is necessary. He maintains you were the victim of Rostov's intrigues—that he killed for you."

She raised her head again. She stared at Masson.

"He killed for the GPU. He made love to me—for the GPU."

"He says Rostov tried to prevent your marriage."

"Obscene. . . . The GPU learned I was friendly with the Rostovs. He was sent to make love to me—because I could open the door." She screamed across the room: "Dare to say it isn't true! Don't lie, traitor! Tell the truth for once, if it costs you your life!"

Masson whispered: "General. . . . Don't make me stay here. . . . I beg you."

Emma was listless again. Head lowered, she said: "His money came from the GPU. His love came from the GPU."

"Thank you, Señorita Sholes," General Ortega said. "I regret I had to do this." He motioned to Guillermo to take her out. "See to it that someone is with her at all times. She is not under any circumstances to be left alone."

Guillermo and Jaime took the girl by the elbows; she allowed herself to be lifted to a standing position. Her body was drooping but she looked up once again and said: "You wish to protect me against myself, general? You're condemning me to life? That's worse than a death sentence, to me."

The general said in a voice full of pity: "You say that *now*, señorita."

"I'll say it for the next forty years. . . . For the next forty years, every minute of every day, I'll tell myself. . . . He kissed my hand because I could open a door. . . . He danced with me and made me laugh because I could open a door. . . . I wasn't a woman to him. . . . I'll remember the lies in his eyes when he looked at me, the lies in his hands . . . when he *touched* me. . . . All the nights he touched me . . . because I was a door. . . ."

She allowed herself to be directed toward the exit. Masson was cowering close by, in the corner. She stopped near him.

"He touched me. . . . *I let him touch me.* . . ."

She shuddered terribly. She raised her eyes and looked squarely at Masson.

"You . . . *touched* me."

Her face made the movements of wild laughing. She pulled almost free, leaning close to Masson and looking into his eyes. She spat at his face.

The policemen led her out.

Eat the mushrooms, she had said. See the good pictures. What? Before he could ask her meaning they had reached the morgue. The attendant had pulled out a long drawer from the wide wall refrigerator, with the air of a clerk opening a file cabinet, and inside was the prime datum of all, a man, source and subject of all dossiers, lying at rest in a collarless pink shirt, body wrapped in coarse cotton sheet: thick black hair closely cropped, sketchy mustache neatly clipped, the face Indian in its self-turning but with something vaguer and more distant in its dustiness and heavy bone curvings. Cold in this room, very cold for Mexico. Donaji stood by the side of the steel drawer and looked down at the body, nothing in her face but concentration. "Yes," she said. After a time: "We will go home and you will have a purple shirt. You will go into the ground in a serape of good purple." She took her father's hands and arranged them, not in a pious overlap at the chest but straight along the sides, as though to be ready for work and effort again. Paul noticed that at the tips of the man's fingers, along the cuticles and under the nails, were traces of a vivid purple stain. Donaji turned and walked to the door. Without turning. It did not seem an effort for her to go erectly and without a backward look. She was aimed to her own work and effort.

It took some minutes to make arrangements for shipping the body to Tlalcotihuaya; there it would be put on a burro to be brought home to Chochutlán.

Soon they were back on the street, walking.

She said: "He did not eat all the mushrooms. There are enough."

But his mind was on something else. The most impossible service stations and waterway spans: so many hands purple with such variety of purpose. . . .

"Tell me of the work in the village," he said. "Each family has its own designs for the huipiles and serapes? The same, year after year? Some are in more demand than others? Tell me how the business is done. . . ."

She explained. Yes, each family had its own patterns for the weaving. The pattern was a tradition for the family, from hundreds of years. Yes, the market was not to be predicted. In some years the demand was much for certain patterns, in other years for others. Yes, this meant a lack of sureness for the individual weaving family, it prospered when its designs were wanted and it faced bad times when the demand went to other types. No family starved, of course. The village was organized as a cooperative, the profits were distributed for all. But the changes in the demand made worries. Often there were not enough of the things in demand, while the things not in demand were in great number. A family might weave for a whole year its different cloths, then find no buyers for its goods in that year; the unwanted articles were put away and forgotten.

"Wrong!" Paul said. "Wasteful! You see this? A cooperative is organized to share the profits—in your village it is as much to share the losses. If many things are made that are not bought, that stay in the corner—this is a loss."

"My father spoke often of this. He said that if the demand could be known in advance only the wanted designs could be made and there would be no cloths left over. Many in the village do not accept this thinking. The design is a mark of the family, they do not like the idea to give up some designs when the strangers on the outside decide they do not want them. They do not like to be told what to do by strangers. . . ."

"Is it better to be told what to do by the dead? . . . Your father argued with them about this?"

"He worked with me to make a list of all who buy or might buy our goods here in Mexico City. Tomorrow he was going to see the buyers to ask which designs they wish for next year. He wished to tell the weavers which designs were wanted, and convince them to make only those."

"Your father was right! You must manufacture for the market, yes, even for total strangers, since they are the market—this is the way not to be poor! It is not a danger to the family. A family is more than a design invented seven centuries ago, by those who did not have to bother with strangers and markets. . . . The dead are strangers too! The most demanding of all!"

"To plan, this does not mean to take orders from strangers and put the village in the hands of strangers. It means only to make the strangers a help and no more a danger. My father said this."

"When the village suffers by the strangers' desires—and does nothing to fit itself to these desires—then it is truly in the hands of the strangers! To look after itself as the strangers look after themselves—this is the way not to be the slaves of others."

"I believe this," the girl said. "The need is to learn the language to talk with the far ones, and to do a better business with them. . . . The dead ones buy no blankets."

"That is the strongest need, Donaji," Paul said. "Everywhere. Hard, to find the language. Too many prefer a bad business. . . . Some listen too hard to the dead, and see more strangers than there are. . . . The important thing is that the buyers should be consulted in advance. They must be shown samples of all the designs, then allowed to order for next year as they wish. Then the weavers must weave accordingly. Then there will be no waste of yarn and labor—the village will be free of the dictates of strangers for the first time, by recognizing and studying the strangers. . . . You spoke of a list? This list exists?"

Her hand went to her bosom and drew out several sheets of paper folded together. Paul opened them and under a street lamp stopped to read: it was a compilation of perhaps a hundred names, some of trading firms, some of retail outlets and individual middlemen, written in a neat, overlarge hand.

His scanning eye lit on a marvel.

There under the M's.

In carefully rounded letters, the words: *Jacques Masson, Hotel Molinas.* . . .

That rumba dancer's fingers had been purple! With what purposes!

The man of affairs. The businessman. . . .

At this moment he knew that he wanted to be in the purple serape business, involved to his ears with the Chontal and their sheep and their snails, as he had never wanted anything in his life.

"This was my father's hope," the girl said. "To show the samples, to take the orders, to allot the designs to the weavers each year. But he saw many troubles, even if the villagers agreed. This needs much work: Letters must be written. Visits must be made. . . ."

"You cannot work with the letters? You read and write very well."

"I have good penmanship and can spell. But can I make the trips to the buyers? To make the many plans. . . ."

Paul stopped again and said to her in a tight voice: "I am a very, very good salesman. I can keep the books. I know how to travel, I know languages. I could make connection with the markets even over the seas, I could find other products for the village to make so it will not depend on only a few things. . . ."

His knees were shaking! He was applying for his first job!

She looked at him for a long time before replying.

"You would do these things?"

"If the village wished me to—yes. Gladly. You know how many I can speak with in the world? I know all the important languages of Europe! I am on close terms with many strangers, it is my business!"

"Our people do not like strangers. . . . You are not only of another place. You are of another color."

"Your people sell their goods to those of other places and colors. They must learn to speak and work with them too."

"If first they can be made to see this. My father is not here to give them the arguments."

"You are here."

"Could you take the place of my father? I do not know—"

"Take care, Donaji! You say you know how to live without the father—good: then do not look for one to take his place!"

"I could talk to the villagers. It would take time. . . . You would like to spend time in Chochutlán?"

"I would like it very much."

"Then I will talk with them. I will do all I can. . . . You will be able to come soon?"

"I think so. Very soon."

"I will try. I think too that it is better to come together to share profits and not losses." Now she held up her cloth bag again. "This night we will be together? We will share? You want me to lie with you?"

"You want this?"

"I want to be together with you, yes."

"Donaji. Donaji the serious: the things I did for you were little things and you want to pay for them with a big thing. I want no payments."

"It is not for the payment. It is to have something good from this night, to balance the bad. It is for me. I do not lie with all. No. In all my life I have been together with only one, the one I wished to marry. Since he married another, for one year, I have been with no man."

"Shy Bohemian!" he said. "Reluctant avantgardiste!"

She paid no attention: "But I want it with you. It is for me, but only if it is for you also."

"Why do you want this with me rather than with another, Donaji?"

"You know how to do the things without a big talk. You do not make the many faces, like others of your color. You keep the one face. That is the way of our best men. My father was this way."

"I make the many faces when I have the many thoughts. Oh, yes. My head is empty tonight—that is why my face stays asleep. . . . Why do you carry the mushrooms?"

"This was for my father. He left many. There will be enough for you and for me too."

"I do not understand: why should we eat mushrooms? It is not possible to lie together without mushrooms?"

"You do not know of this? It is not the ordinary mushroom. This is the 'nti sheeto, in the Mixeteco name, which is also our name."

"What does this name mean?"

"Divine mushroom—holy mushroom—the food to bring many pictures to the eyes from inside."

"Does everybody eat the mushrooms in Chochutlán?"

"My people eat the 'nti sheeto since long before Cortés."

Now Paul remembered. In his voracious reading young David Justin had come across some mention of these mushrooms. When Cortés first came, David had explained, he found the Aztecs of the central plains eating mushrooms too. Among the Aztecs the magical plants had been known as teonanacatl—God's flesh. After the Cortéses appeared—they no doubt ate faster. . . . And the Indians of the South, those who knew some Spanish, said of these mushrooms, according to David—*Le llevan ahí donde Dios está.* . . .

"They carry you there where God is," Paul said. At least, where Cortés is not.

"That is the saying. Where is God? I do not know. I know only that the pictures come from inside and look more good and more clear and more real than the pictures from the outside. If the saying has a meaning, it means that God is on the inside but must be made to wake up from his sleep and show himself."

"Why did your father eat the mushrooms in the city?"

"There are too many things to be seen in the city. They make a confusion. Many of the pictures from the streets are not good. My father ate the mushrooms to have the good pictures in his eyes when he was away from home and among bad sights."

"He ate them tonight?"

"In the night, and the whole day before. This, I think, is why he did not see the streetcar. He was busy with better pictures from inside."

"He was killed by the mushrooms. You wish now to eat them with me?"

"He was killed by a bad thing of iron and noise that would not respect the mushrooms. We will eat them in your bed where there are no iron things to run over us. That is the place for the good pictures, all that can be seen."

"Donaji—do you know why people of my color make so many faces? Because they see too many pictures of trouble—Cortéses everywhere—all from the outside, they think."

"This is the reason to eat the mushrooms. They will bring to your eyes the more friendly pictures from the inside."

"Try to see this: pictures from the inside are what my people fear the most. We try to drown them with faster and faster pictures from the outside. Then we make faces at these pictures."

To himself he said: And now I know the definition of politics.

"We go now to eat the mushrooms together?" the girl said. "You will wake up the friends inside—maybe this will be what they call God in your language. When you look from the inside to the outside again you will see me—another friend. I wish for this."

"I do too. But bad things have happened; bad pictures from the outside are still on my eyes. And some from the inside too."

"Then when you come to Chochutlán?"

"We will eat mushrooms together and I will try to find out if some of the things inside me are my friends."

It was marvelous, to be talking this language. So far from program—possibly, just possibly, it was reasonably close to corpuscles! Whatever it meant. . . .

He found a cab. They went to the railroad station and he bought her a ticket to Oaxaca; from there she would take a bus. He gave the cabdriver twenty pesos to stay with her and see to it that she got safely on the train.

He said to her: "I have to go to the hospital. Another man is dying there."

"Your father?"

"The only father I have, or thought I had. I do not know what color his fingers are. . . . I will try to take leave of him as well as you took leave of your father. If I cannot make his hands ready at his sides—I will try to make mine so. . . . No need to say goodbye. When I come to Chochutlán we will be together. We will see if we are good together."

"May it be soon."

"It will be."

"May the business of the serapes go well."

"It will. . . . May we be good together."

"We will be."

He did not know what was in these words, if she could have a meaning at any point touching on his, if her understanding of good and rightness had some erotic content, some echo of the corpuscles, or had reference only to hallucinogenic mushrooms, pretty dream pictures, but at the sound of her solemn words there was the spurt of exultation in him, many doors swinging free inside, many flowers opening fast all through him—and for the silliest and most childish of reasons: the world had through this serious girl made an uncalculated bid for him! For him!

Possibilities!

He saw somewhere over the rooftops, spread there across the calm and contained constellations, a condition in which no man would have a thought of following him, sounds would not be warnings, false mustaches could be thrown away. . . .

"Shy Bohemian!" he said. "If there is a place where God is, we will try very hard to find it! We will eat what God's flesh is available!"

To himself he added: may I do a few things reasonably well; may I not make too many faces.

He held her for a moment, kissed her on the dusty, high, bulge-boned forehead.

"We will sell many serapes of Tyrean purple, schoolteacher! Cotton Petal and daughter of Cotton Petal!"

She put the bag of mushrooms in his hand: "Take them and eat them. They will show you there are pictures inside which are your friends."

When he came to the hospital again he saw there was a large crowd outside and he heard their singing:

> *Señor Rostov pensó en Méjico,*
> *Este suelo hospitalario y grandioso,*
> *Para vivir muy dichoso. . . .*

He ran as fast as he could up the steps, the cotton bag swinging in his hand.

It was a common thing in those days for people with nothing else to do, people without the necessary funds to underwrite projects, to wander the streets of Mexico City playing guitars and making up songs. These sung poems were for the most part about the names and events in the day's headlines: musical editorials which brought the front pages to life for those who could not or did not care to read. Essentially without point of view, these corridos, as they were called, dealt with any and all matters that got talked about—wars,.

elections, taxes, killings, maimings, couplings between the famous, deaths of notables, mishaps among the frequently mentioned. Most of these street ballads were heard in one or another pocket of the town for a day or two and then died out. But now and then one of them so captured the quality of a special happening, and so caught the mood of the people about it, that it sped along all the grapevines of the city and in a matter of hours was echoing, against a rich vibrancy of strings, from all the quarters of the capital. The ballad had originated almost by accident in the mouth of an aimless promenader whose mind was most likely on his next meal or his next girl, a man who sang as he lived, indifferently, absentmindedly, marginally, improvisationally, trying to pass the slow time by calling out a footnote to the remote parade, a haphazardly rhymed addendum to the undersides of doings; but it could become, for one high moment, the voice of the city.

What could move, first a few streetcorner serenaders, then whole slum communities, then an entire city, to raise voices at certain unpredictable moments? Maybe it was just that so much was happening, marvels, catastrophes, that they knew and saw little of. While the world went along with its spurts, heavings, false starts and stampedes, they were, and knew it, permanently nailed to one overlooked and inconsequential spot, never consulted. Nobody likes the sensation of large and whistling events taking place way above his head, where they can be neither observed nor influenced. The feeling of being permanently locked out of everything is annoying. Maybe these people made up songs about the big doings only to slow a few of them down and bring them closer.

Who knows, finally, why people sing? Maybe they feel a vacuum around them and want to fill it.

In any case, the people of this city liked to sing about this or that item of news.

Few of the ones gathered outside that hospital on the night of February 17, 1939, knew who Victor Rostov was. They had a dim idea, picked out of the air, that this was a man with a beard, that he had been chased by somebody in some parts of the world, that he had come to live in Coyoacán as the country's guest, that somebody, identity unknown, had opened his skull with an axe, that he lay now in a room of this hospital, a room there on the third floor where figures went back and forth in a businesslike way across the lit window; that he lay there badly off, sinking. They had a picture of an axe and a man with a beard. They knew nothing about where the axe had come from or where the beard might have been going.

Minutes after the event, news seeped into the crowd that this man was dead of his axe wound.

No one could say how the word arrived. Maybe a hospital orderly, coming out on the steps for a smoke, whispered it in somebody's ear; maybe somebody looked up and saw the shocked white face of a nurse in that third story window. Whichever way it happened, the bulletin hurried along from mouth to mouth: Row-stowf is dead. Row-stowf is finished. The axe has killed the beard.

Nothing happened at first. The news had to be digested, the final touches put to the picture.

Then one man placed fingers on guitar and sang tentatively:

> *Señor Rostov pensó en Méjico.* . . .

Somebody else swept a chord from his guitar and added the line:

> *Este suelo hospitalario y grandioso.* . . .

The first man, possibly it was the first man, had an idea for the next step:

> *Para vivir muy dichoso.* . . .

Somebody else finished it off:

> *Bajo el techo de este cielo.* . . .

A rough but workable first stanza, enough to build the picture on, had been put together. They tried it again, more voices joining in:

> *Señor Rostov pensó en Méjico,*
> *Este suelo hospitalario y grandioso,*
> *Para vivir muy dichoso*
> *Bajo el techo de este cielo.* . . .

So much for the foundation. It would hold a structure. Now came the story. One of the singers tried to build higher, to encompass and hold the full picture:

Un zapapico alpinista. . . .

A knock on the door. Sergeant Guillermo opened it; a policeman stuck his head in and said something in a low voice. The sergeant went across the room and whispered to the general.

General Ortega nodded. "I thought so. The singing. . . ." He looked at Masson and said flatly: "Twenty minutes ago you became a murderer. Perhaps you deduced that from the street musicians." He stayed at the window, looking down at the crowd. He listened as they began to sing again. "You are a famous man now. . . . They sing about you in the streets."

He regarded Masson. The prisoner sat rigidly in his chair, looking at his fingers.

"*El Gran Corrido de Señor Rostov y el Cobarde Asesino.* This seems to be the name of the song. . . . Ah. I forget. You are a distinguished Belgian, you do not know our language. . . . I will translate for you: *The Grand Ballad of Señor Rostov and the Cowardly Assassin.* . . . They begin again: Guillermo, tell him the words they sing about him."

Guillermo listened. He said: "*Señor Rostov pensó en Méjico . . . .*"

The general said: "Señor Rostov thought that in Mexico. . . ."

"*Este suelo hospitalario y grandioso . . . .*"

"On this soil hospitable and grandiose . . . ."

"*Para vivir muy dichoso . . . .*"

"To live very happily . . . ."

"*Bajo el techo de este cielo. . . .*"

"Under the roof of this sky. . . . ."

"*Un zapapico alpinista . . . .*"

"An alpine ice axe . . . ."

"*El cobarde asesino llevó. . . .*"

"The cowardly assassin carried. . . ."

"*Y al estar solo con Señor Rostov. . . .*"

"And being alone with Señor Rostov . . . ."

"*A mansalva le arrancó su existencia. . . .*"

"Risking nothing, snatched his life from him. . . . Now you are famous."

"There are risks that street singers don't know," Masson said.

"And some they do." General Ortega walked over to Masson. "Why do they sing? Do they know who you are? Do they know who Rostov is? They know this: one man went around in back of another man and sank an axe in his head. Can you imagine why this moves them? I will tell you. They have strong feelings about bullfighters. Bullfighting is a matter of sharp weapons and resisting bones too. But the bullfighter faces the bull. He waits for the bull to see him and come toward him. This they call, perhaps too dramatically, since the man does not have to be there—this they call the moment of truth. It is the bullfighter who is forbidden to move, not the bull. This makes all the truth of the moment. If the bullfighter crawled around in back of the bull and without being seen thrust his sword in, they would not admire him. A mansalva! A mansalva! You see? Risking nothing. . . . Our people have a sense of style, you will note. They have contempt for the moment of truth that is made into a moment of absolute falseness. . . . What moves them now is not the death; hardly that; they are used to deaths. It is the false manner of the killing. . . . They sing of a torero who was too cowardly to face the bull and give him his last run. . . . They know a torero is one thing and an assassin another. . . ."

General Ortega stopped with a certain sense of confusion. Somewhere, somehow, in slightly different words, he had had another discussion like this. Recently. He had tried to say these same things another way, in a different setting; he had not found the right words.

He remembered: the conversation with Rostov at Coyoacán, hardly more than a week ago. When he had come to protest Rostov's press statements and stayed to debate the techniques of making history.

When he, Ortega, had expressed contempt for secret police, all police, had he not been trying to say that he wanted no part of a history made by those who gave the bull no run, worked from the back?

When Rostov had accused him of being a dilettante had he not really meant: you, Ortega, wish a history made by toreros—an adolescent's proud and rosy dream—the facts are less theatrical and more brutal—this is not a stylish game and there are no rules except to win?

So it came down to this:

Is the world run and altered by proud swords?
Or by cowardly axes?
Were the movers to be crusaders—or crawlers?
Day parades—night schemes?
And the question was answered.
The evidence was in.

"You have taught me something," he said. "I am an amateur as a policeman. Perhaps—a dilettante. . . . I want no contact with your world of slime. None. Not even as the executioner of such as you. The danger of contamination is too great."

He took a seat near Masson and lit a long brown Vuelta Abajo panatella.

"I am retiring. But first I am going to take you to court and convict you: as Tomás Baeza de Rivera, or as Jacques Masson. . . . There is no death penalty here in the Distrito Federal. The maximum you can get for murder is twenty years and a day. . . . I promise you, on my honor as a general of Madero: I will get you your twenty years and a day."

He stood, walked once around the room, came back.

"You will get out in—1959. You will be—what?—fifty-three, fifty-four. What will be waiting for you? . . . From today forward you are another David Justin to your superiors: you can talk. *They* will be waiting at the prison doors twenty years from now, Masson. Think of that—every day, every night, for twenty years. *That* is the inconceivable present Victor Rostov gave to you as he lay there and gave you back your life. He gave you a thought to fill your mind for twenty years."

He leaned very close to Masson and began to speak with an icy rage:

"Begin to think, you dirt! Think of the Basses who will be waiting at the gates! Your friends with no faces—they will be there. . . . *Think* of it! You filth. . . . You slime. . . ."

He struck Masson's face with all his force.

He had shot a certain number of men in battle, men with guns in their hands and free to shoot back, but it was the first time in his life that he had struck another human being, armed or unarmed, with his open palm.

Outside the singing was louder.

"Since when do you get orders direct? Your orders come through me."

"This time they came around you, George."

They were both dressed in field clothes and sombreros. They walked along without looking at each other, talking in low voices. Some paces ahead the woman strode tall and insubstantial in her white nun's habit, a head on a column of laundry, face screened off by the flaring starched shields of her headgear.

"Since when do I get bypassed?"

"When did you get the cable, George?"

"A little before eight."

"All right: since a little before eight."

The news about Rostov, George Bass speculated, must have reached Moscow at five-thirty, thereabouts. They must have been sitting at the Commissariat waiting for it. Right away, in a matter of minutes, they must have dispatched coded new instructions to the New York center: instructions maybe drawn up in advance. From New York to Mexico City came his new orders at exactly seven-fifty-two: *GOODS NOT NEEDED NEW YORK WAREHOUSE REROUTE HOME OFFICE FASTEST.*

He was not due back in Moscow for months. This Mexico City situation had to be cleaned up absolutely. Then he was scheduled to spend some time in New York putting the new Dies Committee-Wall Street line in operation for the States. That was the way Erzhov had outlined it to him when he was last in Moscow: Mexico, New York. Why the sudden recall?

Were they angry because Tomás remained alive to face trial? A trial like this was bound to cause some harm, granted. All the same, the big job was done. Besides, Tomás staying alive by a fluke couldn't be laid at *his* door. Besides, Tomás and the trial could be handled too. They were beginning to handle it right now, tonight. It should be *his* job to stay and handle it—

"I stay on here and see after things," Ramón said. "Don't go after me for it: those are my orders."

Some kind of playfulness, needles, in Ramón's tone. Echo there of the smart-aleck note in the New York liaison man's voice three nights ago.

Something else. This afternoon—when he'd been dictating the

"suicide note" to Tomás. At a certain point Ramón had cut in to suggest: "Shouldn't you get the new American line in?"

Remarkable, come to think of it. Ramón giving political hints to *him*. As remarkable as Ramón getting new orders *he* knew nothing about.

"Just who do your orders come from?"

"Never mind the intermediaries, George. The one they start from is—Rachevsky."

Rachevsky! That crossed the T.

Rachevsky—First Deputy Commissar—one of the second-line ones in the Commissariat who'd had it in for him, Bass, all along.

"You forget: *my* orders come from Erzhov. My last orders from him were: see it to the end in Mexico, then—New York." Erzhov was Number One, the Commissar: the name made no alterations on Ramón's composed face. "I'll get to the bottom of it, I can tell you. I'm calling New York tonight for a full explanation: I don't move from here till I get it."

"What's the sense, George? It's throwing away good money. You'll find your friend up there is gone—he's been called home too. There's a new man in the center who takes a strong attitude about you—one of Rachevsky's men."

Suddenly Ramón knew everything and he knew nothing. Suddenly Ramón was with the ones against him and he was with—nobody. You feel the sidewalk dropping away from your feet—

"I begin to see. You've been sending back bad reports about me? You?"

"It wasn't on my initiative, George. I do what I'm told."

"Who told you—Rachevsky?"

"Rachevsky is the one: right."

"You know Rachevsky was always against me—because I had Erzhov's backing. You got a lot of happiness from writing them lies about me? Did I treat you so bad? . . . What did you tell them about me?"

"George, to be frank, they asked my evaluation of Plan A. It was absolutely clear to me the thing was slipshod, that you'd gotten careless after Spain: I had to tell them so. . . . The way it worked out, I was right."

"You had better ideas? You could have told *me*."

"You didn't ask me. . . . Rachevsky did."

"One small thing you overlook. I got it done."

"I think they have the impression, George, that it was more my doing."

"Ah. . . . What's Rachevsky planning now? Why's he calling Erzhov's top men back? How does he get the authority? You know that too?"

"I know something about it, George. . . . Rachevsky's the next Number One. He's already acting head. Erzhov was arrested last week—it's been kept quiet so far. . . ."

And there it was.

Finished! The moment Ramón said it in his teasing drawl Bass knew it was so. The man was incapable of making up a story like that.

"Erzhov too. . . . They dare to. . . ."

Of course they dared. They didn't dare not to. Erzhov—the man responsible for developing the slick counter-Gestapo core in the GPU. Of course he had to go now; he and the upper-level ones close to him. The counter-Gestapo side of things was bound to be toned way down. The experts on it would be offensive to their opposite numbers in the Gestapo, the ones they'd have to work with once the Pact came in.

One more sop to Hitler.

The one offshoot of the Pact he, Bass, hadn't thought of.

"Idiots! What do they think, I'm *against* the Pact?"

But before he put it in words he knew the objection was beside the point. He was identified with the counter-Gestapo side. No matter what ideas were or were not in his head—he had to go to soft soap the Gestapo. Many would have to go. Not only operatives. Diplomats, the foreign affairs people. The Litvinovs—the ones with the Entente psychology, the Versailles orientation, the pro-Wests, the League of Nations actors. Since Hitler was anti-Entente, anti-Versailles, anti-West, anti-League of Nations. Anti-Bolshevik too—but that was another matter. . . .

"What do they think I am—a Rostovite? After the job I did here?"

But he did not bother to put any spirit in the words. He knew they were beside the point.

As the policy got more twisted, more sophisticated—the personnel got more primitive. Had to. The primitives were taking over.

The Dzerzhinskis who'd set up the first Cheka under Lenin and Rostov: intellectuals, theorists, men of real brains and scope. The Erzhovs Stalin had replaced them with? Erzhov had been—a statistician, a clerk. As George Bass had been—a cabdriver—with ambitions to become a bookkeeper. Still, men who could think and sense the existence of ideas, in some ways. Who did not automatically put a match to all ideas.

The Rachevskys? Rachevsky had been—an Odessa druggist.

Ramón—a Barcelona waterfront tough.

Men who'd never faced a concept in their lives. The Rachevskys and the Ramóns had never for a minute had any thought more abstract than which plane goes to which city, which passport suits which customs, which key fits which lock.

Logical progression: the Stalins shove aside the Rostovs. From brains—to schemes.

With the Pact, the policy was getting very, very sophisticated; the personnel—mindless.

He had the wild thought: run. This minute—run for dear life, lose himself in the back alleys of this city he knew like the back of his hand. It was clear enough what waited for him in Moscow, without Rachevsky and Rachevsky's apparatus to back him up. He was naked and without props and he could not stand the feeling. . . . That night in the cab with the gun at his neck he had wanted to run too. . . .

Could not run. Now as then.

Gun at neck again.

Sophie and the child were in Moscow.

He was a good family man: they had him.

"You never married, did you, Ramón?"

"You know me, George: I don't believe in accumulating property."

There was the corpse of a smile on his lips as he said, "So that's the way it is. The old order changeth, eh?"

"It changes," Ramón said evenly. "We're the ones who should know about that. Changing orders is our business."

Disturbed, needing to give his muscles some small play, Bass put his hand into his pants pocket; as the fingers closed Ramón had a firm grip on his arm and was bringing it up.

"Better not—I'll relieve you of your plaything. You might try something you'd be sorry for. I'll just take that—" He stared at the piece of glass in Bass's hand. "That—that's your armory?" He began to laugh. "*That's* what it was all along?" He laughed harder. "And I thought . . . Ha! Ha, ha! You're a big joker, George! A—oh, no!"

"I've had no instructions about how I'm to travel," Bass said coldly. "I suppose you've got the inside information on that too?"

"I know something about it." Ramón got control of himself; he slipped the glass into his own pocket. "I take you and Cándida to Vera Cruz tonight. Plus Tomás, of course, if we get him out. Tomorrow morning you board a ship—the S.S. Bahía. The captain—a fellow named Cherni: know him?—he does jobs for us from time to time: he's reliable, we pay him well—"

"I know Cherni a little better than you do. I was with him not three hours ago. I reserved three cabins on the Bahía—for you, for her, for Tomás. . . ."

"Well, we're using the cabins. The only change is, you'll be going in my place."

"He'll lock us in, of course. Until what port of call—still Beirut?"

"At Beirut you'll be transferred to one of our ships—then home. . . . Don't try anything, George. My orders are to get you on that ship tomorrow."

Bass thought carefully.

"I suppose—if things go well tonight you'll get the credit?"

"It's possible."

"If it doesn't work I'll be held responsible?"

"If they see it that way—could I change their minds?"

"I can't get the credit—I'd like to bring it off all the same. Not for your sake, my friend. I don't want one more charge over my head if I'm going back. . . ."

He went faster. Ramón kept up with him. In a moment he was alongside the woman.

"I'll go over your instructions once more," he said to the woman. "When you get inside the building—"

"I'll handle this if you don't mind, George," Ramón said. "This isn't your last assignment; it's my first. . . ." He addressed the woman without looking at her: "We'll wait outside. You go in and ask for Dr. Alvarez—Alvarez—he'll be close by the reception lobby, waiting for you. . . . Your name is Sister Emiliana—Emiliana—remember. . . . Alvarez—Emiliana. . . ."

They were approaching the hospital. Soon they were on the edge of the crowd. The song was loud now:

Un zapapico alpinista. . . .

"You've got fifteen minutes and no more," Ramón went on softly. They were making their way through the crowd. "That's the limit Alvarez gives us. Make sure you bring him around. Make absolutely sure. There's a third berth reserved on the ship, Tomás must be in it. . . ."

The woman only nodded, stiffly.

Ramón patted her arm. She went on alone, through the singers and on up the hospital steps. Ramón and Bass pushed their way to the wall and leaned against it.

The song was starting up again:

Para vivir muy dichoso
Bajo el techo de este cielo. . . .

"Is there any profound ideological reason why you can't give me my optical glass back?" George Bass said. "It's not finished. It'll give me something to do on the ship."

"You won't have any use for it over there," Ramón said. "I know you're a big sun worshipper but how much sun gets into the Lubianka basements?"

Paul opened the door enough to see in. The oxygen tubes had been removed from V.R.'s nose, his eyes were shut. His bandaged head lay at rest against the pillow, the hive of blossoming visions and billowing blueprints at last vacated—where was the artist's mass of gray hair? Only a shaved skull domed with adhesive tape. . . . Not the general now, not the bold stormer of palaces and fortresses, rather the pushed away artist, stalled and stilled by a world he had had to engage but could not order—all the words dulled, their bite removed. There would be no more press releases, no more programs. The Old Man was gone from concern.

Marisha was sitting at the side of the bed, holding the dead man's quiet hand with both her own, nodding in some private acquiescence.

Paul shut the door without a sound. He had the feeling that he had been a trespasser in a communion that could not work but had to be tried. Halfway down the hall he found a small waiting room; he sat in an arm chair.

For the first time in his memory he felt inside himself no theses, no marchings, no tendencies, only a vacancy with minor thoughts of purple serapes floating through, but it was not unpleasant and he had no urge to change it. He, with no need to change anything!

He thought of Jacques Masson on the Chontal list of traders. There was a joiner!

He had been sitting for some time when Ortega came by.

"Things work out," the general said.

"In a way it's a comforting thought," Paul said. "There are finally no loose ends."

"You seem calm enough."

"Should I be in mourning? Too late: I mourned him in advance."

"It makes the head swim. Was this politics, ideologies? No. All of this, all of it, would have stayed on the level of impossible fantasy—if a grown man had not been too much tied to a too busy mother. . . ."

"I knew her, you know. In Spain. Not the pots and pans type."

"Nor was her son the doting offspring type. Not one to send Mother's Day cards, that one. . . . Over-energized mothers! Oversalivating sons! The only things you politicians are not trained to look for. . . ."

"Nor you policemen. . . . Isn't it nice? The terrorist and the cop are brothers—the blind jostling the blind."

General Ortega took a seat. He lit one of his oil sheened dark panatellas.

"You know what we must learn, my friend? How to live in some reasonable sort of polity without too much politics. We are a long way from it. First we will have to become beings without fingers, tongues, teeth, mouths—the acquiring instruments."

"Too simple. The essence of politics is not to take but to be taken from. . . . I give you Victor Rostov."

"But how shall we look when we stop being political animals? We

may be so radically cut down that we will no longer be men—we
will have to be called by another name."

"What would that be—saints?"

"No: the saint is something still further off. Before we become
saints we will have to be reduced to thoracic air bags and great cerebrums untainted with any thalamus—that troublemaking sac that
breeds thirsts and exclamations."

"You'd have us go that far? After decorporealizing that much,
there may be no sense to staying in the animal kingdom at all. Might
as well finish the job and join the air."

"Possibly. At the saint stage we will look very much like aerated
cauliflowers."

"Then the police forces can be disbanded—maybe. . . . *There's*
the new vegetable you ought to develop on your experimental farm."

"The péons may soon be running my farm. I doubt they will wish
to grow so inedible a vegetable. . . . You will be leaving Coyoacán?"

"I'll stay with Marisha until she gets her life going again. . . .
Then . . ." Paul sat up and looked questioningly at the general.
"Then: I might spend some time in—Chochutlán."

"Where?"

"Chochutlán. A Chontal village in Oaxaca, on the Pacific range."

"Ah—I know the region. In 1910 I passed through there recruiting fighters for Madero. The men hid from us in caves. . . . The
Chontal? You are serious?"

"Quite. I may be going into the Tyrean purple serape business."
Talking rapidly, hearing his voice rise as he went on, Paul told about
his meeting with the girl, the nature of the village cooperative, his
ideas for improving their production and marketing practices. He
described the list with Masson's name on it, sure it was important,
the key to this matter, but unable to say why. He wound up: "Don't
you see? He organized himself onto that list! As he did onto wretched
Emma's list! That's the slimiest thing of all—the son of a bitch or-
ganizes himself in and out of people's lives without a stopover! I'd
like to stop somewhere. . . . Organization—that's the trick, general! If you can do it in the open. For things you dare to mention.
Meaning it. Showing everything in your suitcase. . . ."

"Most things are organized now," General Ortega said. "Over organized. On the top—on the bottom—underground."

"Only in between, with the poor, the Emmas, are things loose, scattered around. In between it's every hand and every village for itself in the ratrace. . . . Maybe in one village I can help to change that a bit."

"You are quite sure you are suited for business?"

"Look at the things I've organized in my time—street riots, Marxist study classes, youth cells, International Brigade units, Siberian slave-camp discussion centers, Coyoacán security forces—they all fell apart in my fingers. I think I can organize a serape weavers' cooperative that'll last. Yes, indeed."

"You chaotic ones learn organization well—you need it, to contain yourselves. You become specialists in getting things in order—and—ultimately—produce George Basses. Who will organize anything. Organization machines—it is their one business. . . . You may be less needed by these Chontal than you think," General Ortega said without lightness. "The backward ones are learning more about organization than anybody gives them credit for. They too."

He was frowning. Eusebio, his plantation manager, had this evening sent over a copy of the petition the péons had presented to the Ministry of Agriculture to support their demand for Ortega's land. When he had finished his interrogation of Masson, the general had gone back to his office to read this document. It was a carefully thought out and knowledgeably drawn up piece of argument. Some of the barefooted had learned to read and to debate only too well. Behind the fighting words of this petition could be sensed plans, strategies, strong instincts for effective group blows. . . .

"One problem," Paul said. "If I do anything for the Chochutlán co-op, and maybe for others like it, I'll need a work permit."

"Amazing. Whoever worked harder than you in Coyoacán? But you never needed a permit. Such enterprises are not recognized as work anywhere in the world."

"There's not even a name for them. . . . Can I get the permit?"

"Young man: before you become the serape entrepreneur you should perhaps know a few things about the Chontal."

"What's there to know? They make good serapes."

"But they are more than talented fingers. They are not Indians in the true sense, you know. Their language has nothing in common with the Indian ones, though they have borrowed some words. The Indians in the Zapotec regions are considered to be derived from Indo-Siberian migrants, but the Chontal—they are suspected to be Australoids. By the Indians themselves, who are strangers to our world, the Chontal are considered to be strangers. Even by *themselves* the Chontal are called strangers. Do you know what the word Chontal means? *Strangers!*"

Paul stared. He stood up. He began to laugh:

"I'm very much at home with strangers."

"You think of tropical Oaxaca as a luscious place of sun and loofas and tapirs and bananas? Some of it is, yes. In the valleys Nature is lavish and the people are warm and with sunny, open dispositions; the vallistas are famous for this. But Oaxaca is a place of malaria too, of intestinal parasites and smallpox, the place of the pinto disease that makes the skin a study in gangrenous blue, the place of the fly that blinds thousands with its bite. The lagoons of the coast are dry, feverish, swept by choking sandstorms. Where the Chontal live, high in the mountains, there are drenched rain forests that never stop dripping, and thick fogs that never lift, and vile orange and red earths to offend the eye where the land rots away and leaves open wounds. These Chontal, like other sierra tribes, are known among the southern Indians as the cerrados—the closed people. Closed. With the walls around. I would have thought that you, of all people, had had enough of walls. . . ."

"General, when a man like me wants to rejoin the human race— what makes you think he can get in any way but through the back door? . . . I don't care if the Chontal have red and yellow stripes across their bodies and wear cocoanut shells over their heads. I'll start with the strangers, and tunnel in. . . ."

"You know the kinds of craftsmen you will be dealing with? Men who still weave on the primitive saddleback loom—women who still sew with maguey thorns."

"Then I'll become a missionary of the shuttlecock. I'll preach the gospel of the Singer sewing machine."

The general stood up.

"I know this!" he said. "For once—for the love of God—you must lower your eyes to some trivial piece of ground! Get involved in some small things! . . . All right. I will use my influence to get you your work permit."

"I've never known anybody," Paul said. "I'll see if I can get to know the Chontal. . . . All the strangers. Myself included."

"And see to it," General Ortega added with anger, "that once you organize them they do not try to break you and all your work. Those you organize and teach too well can become the worst Chontal to you."

"I think I've learned how to deal with Kronstadts."

The general raised his fist violently.

"Oh, no! Oh, not at all! All you have learned is how *not* to deal with them!"

General Ortega strode away down the corridor. He was, as a matter of fact, put out with himself rather than with Paul Teleki and his extravagant plans for making his way into ordinary society through the most extraordinary back door. That was to be expected of a man who began to dream of centralities after making his home for so long on the outermost fringes: his route back was bound to be circuitous.

General Ortega had thought for a long time after reading the petition of the péons. Then he had taken a piece of paper and composed a careful note to the President, explaining that for reasons of temperament and side interests he was no longer able to hold the position of Chief of Secret Police and must respectfully ask to be relieved when the Rostov case was closed. Then he had thought again about the petition. If he retired from the government he needed a place to go and busy himself. The estancia was the one place he wanted to be; it was home, occupation, daily therapy for him, what he needed to get the many bad tastes and bad smells of the city out of his head. But if the péons were granted all his lands he would have no estancia to go home to. So, biting on his tongue, full of an uncontainable disgust for himself and for a world that pushed a man this way, he had taken up his pen again and added a postscript:

> *Dear friend, against all my inclination I force myself now to make a special request of you. I have no wish to impose on our long friendship, I have until now gone out of my way to avoid*

such an imposition, but circumstances begin to press hard and I have no choice. I remember that only this morning, during our talk, you were kind enough to ask if you might help me to preserve some portion of my estancia. There is grave danger that I may lose all of it if someone in authority does not intervene; the case is pending now at the Ministry of Agriculture, the hearings will be this week. I am told there is a better than good chance that the péons will win their case—certainly they have drawn up a most persuasive petition. All that is omitted from their brief is a mention of the positive, valuable, entirely non-profit work that is done on my experimental fields. . . . If, dear Rubén, you would find it possible yourself to bring these balancing facts to the attention of the Ministry. . . . If you can in any way. . . .

Now, going down the corridor and thinking back to this neatly penned abomination he had put his name to and dispatched by special courier to the National Palace, he bit so viciously on his cigar that the tip snapped off. He spat the piece out.

Teleki thought he knew how to deal with Kronstadts?

Who would ever learn how to deal with these daily maddening Kronstadts! In such a way that he could live with himself!

He put both hands to his visored cap to center it; he had the feeling it was badly, clownishly askew.

Paul sat for a long time without stirring.

It occurred to him that he was ravenously hungry. He had not eaten since noon.

The mushrooms! He took the cloth sack from his pocket and rummaged in it.

They were small, faintly gray, tan veined. He bit into one: not bad, though on the bitter side and rather too oily, a suggestion of something rancid. He finished this mushroom and ate five or six others.

For a while nothing happened except for a queazy beat that came and went in his stomach.

There was a certain quickening, a sense of liveliness, in and about him. The walls took on a gleam and began to flutter a little.

His thoughts speeded up and began to flutter.

He was in a glow about Donaji. Someone out there took notice!
One with no perfume of red snapper—no acne! Made offers for
him—offered herself in turn! Said he was worth driving bargains
for!

No matter that she was of another planet, an Australoid whose
chanting ancestors had come the long Pacific way in their double
canoes—she had eyes—saw him! He was aware of the ridiculous
core in this bubbling, swelling elation—the childishness of a joy
over simply being seen and commented favorably on. But he saw
too that there was nothing especially wrong, nothing shameful, in
being a child: who wasn't? A relief and a further intensifying delight to be able straightforwardly to say: I'm an infant—my club's
the jawbone of a toy poodle—no more big acts! If V.R. had once
been able to bring the essential babyishness into the daylight—and
bust out laughing at it—no more struts, struggles, squirmings, mus-
clings, Kronstadts—crack through the hard crusts!

The walls were vibrating. Sheets of gay gold and vibrating, giving
off deep guitar sounds. Fine thing, flamenco walls!

He felt a laughter in himself to be surrounded by such quantities
of rhythmic glitter.

Now here was the mistake: to live exclusively with the schisms.
Fusions were at the top of the agenda—all possible blends below
and prior to program—the most extravagant amalgams! Let the
most disparate arms entwine—Bulgar, Australoid—resigned manifesto bearer, confirmed snail gatherer! Amalgams simply for warmth
and reassuring bulk—

These thoughts seemed to come in waves from his stomach as it
pulsed in phase with the walls.

His body a mass of lead. Tons of it. But it did not weigh him
down. His true self was free of it, equipped with marvelous jets,
climbing out to tour.

Left far behind, on the chair, his baggage of bloated flesh: traveling light today, with the walls, in the walls, one with the walls and
quivering goldenly as they quivered, giving out deep guitar chords
in tune with theirs.

The ceiling some miles above became a saffron drum and began
to vibrate and then without transition he was the drum with ears
of saffron that had vibrating strings inside. Llamas in blinding stripes

of red and yellow marched across the drum's surface in perfect military columns, golden shining animals that nodded sagely in tune with the guitars and drums; they carried over their nodding heads umbrellas with stripes of red and yellow as they marched in and out of his sounding ears.

The song being played? The song he was?

Este suelo hospitalario y grandioso. . . . Para vivir muy dichoso. . . .

Then:

Mañana me voy, mañana. . . . Mañana me voy de aquí. . . .

Without body but feeling an overall skin tingle he was astride a striped llama, watching his lessening lead body in the receding arm chair, enjoying the pulse of the llama's, no, zebra's flying muscles between his legs, flying.

They came under a dome of guitar vibrancies to a pastel orange sea, ringed with magenta reeds which sported giant red ants on their tips. A striped zebra with Emma's face, carrying a shopping bag, leaped into the sea, crying, *I have lost the way to Chicago!* It reappeared again on the stained waters with Marisha's drawn face and whispered, *When there's nothing in your head but iodoform,* and went down again. It sprang up another time, sprouted, it was a great sweep curved body of a woman a hundred feet tall, rising with Donaji's face from the waters, up to her knees in the tinted waters, all purple. Pyramids of dancing deep purples rose from the waters behind her, each with an absurdly small pajama'd péon on its apex, urinating placidly in a glinting silver stream. Purple Donaji looked down and said: *All good pictures come from God's flesh, God's place, far inside.* From between her purple legs poured a torrent of sparkling pinkish and silvery waters, to make the sea. Down this cascading stream, bobbing in the bright juices, came a profusion of limes, lemons, oranges, all smiling. Sheridan Justice floated on his back down this gush, among the limes and lemons, hands folded across his smart tunic, eyes closed, a shell of white bandage over his head. He was smiling. His lips moved: *Ah now totally an permanently organizated an Ah out a reach a them all. Case they down lak the hue an cry o mah homing skin all right bah me. Was all ovuh red an yallah lak unto zebra but gone be one steady puhple fow the remainduhs.* Vultures flew everywhere above with flamenco flamingo flapping, glinted, bodies of polished aluminum, faces curved with the open maximum smile of the Quetzalcoatls. There were serpents gliding in easy inchings over Sheridan Justice's purple face, smiling. Serpents slipped and slid over the low flying aluminum vultures, vibrating like guitar strings: *Para vivir muy dichoso. . . . Mañana me voy. . . .* The high Donaji had a bandaged head. . . .

The room stopped dancing. The walls oozed off their sheen.

The guitar music stopped, his thoughts settled back in the arm chair and lost their throb.

He was aware of sandbags of tight-packed flesh walling about him again.

He knew this with a finality. His political part, that ran after gaudy quick pictures from outside, tried to stuff the outside with nervous pictures, was dead, a corpse under the dome of V.R.'s bandage there on the hospital bed, there under Sheridan Justice's tunic floating down orange waters and out to sea: another part that had no name and no outlines was left, to live on inside pictures, and there was no guarantee the supply would not run out. It was running out now. Or that they would retain their color. They were fading and freezing fast now.

He would have to provide his own pictures. If there were enough purple dyes in the inside world to give them tint.

And a danger: Too many nice pictures to look at inside and you do not see the situation coming.

In bed—no loud iron things to run you over.

But when you get out of bed?

Uphill climb from this point on, up the cragged and poisonously vermillion Chontal mountains dim in fog. Would he get over the top and down the other side? Into the valleys of some sun again?

He patted the papers in his pocket with a heavy hand: David Justin's last notes.

"Thanks for everything, David."

He was shriveled with fear. Could he find a way to exist in Chochutlán without squirming? A question. Could he adjust to a life filled with acres instead of continents, hours instead of eras? Accommodate himself to the small and immediate, live within the confines of his eyes' and ears' minute by minute data?

He was terrified. He knew with the starkest finality that if he could not manage that restriction, that pinpointing in cramped time and boxed space, he was condemned to a life suspended above the living, surrounded by men of whom only the topmost cerebrums could be seen—over-reaching blooms of gray matter—dull, dull—floating like balloons: Ortega's benign cauliflowers, forever pulsing over a landscape of permanent mists, all guitars silenced. What he was most afraid of, he saw with a constriction of his stomach, was not confinement but an existence too high up, dangling in a stratosphere of theories of human affairs, far out of reach of those below, at the bases of all pyramids, who lived these affairs through in minutes packed or vacuous; he needed some closure—walls that threw him against other warm bodies huddled close. Unspectacular sandbags. . . . But could he take the concentrated and sometimes herded way that made a finca, a milpa, a world? He was a claustrophobiac from the slagheap districts of Sofia. His father had had pig blood purplings under his fingernails. . . .

"Thanks for everything, translator. Passports don't necessarily get you there."

Marisha was coming toward him along the corridor, very small, daintily held. He stood and went forward to meet her.

"Ai, Marisha," he said. "All wasted."

Doll face, brooch of a face, end of all the noble and vanished lines of imperial Russia: now in its sad composure hauntingly and heart-rendingly like the somber face of the Chontal girl as she straightened her father's slack arms, arranged the purpled fingers, and walked away through the morgue with its chill.

Women who knew how to stand straight at all times. Hands ready at their sides.

"Paul, Paul." Her voice that found no resting places. "He said to me . . . *Take axe—to butterflies.* . . . Then he died."

He put his arms around her miniature body and held her tight. His chin rested on her marbled, unretreating forehead. Her face was at rest but inside her, he could feel it, the smallest bird—beating. He felt a little sick to the stomach, from more than the divine mushrooms.

With arm close about her shoulders he walked by her side along the corridor.

"No more waiting," he said. "No more noises to listen for at night. Come, I'll take you home, Marisha."

The steel gate banged shut behind them. They continued on along the corridor.

"Fifteen minutes maximum," he said. "After that—Ortega may come."

"I will try," she said.

They came to the police guard outside the door.

"Good evening, doctor," Sergeant Guillermo said.

"Good evening, sergeant. I am required to make another examina—"

"I was told of this, doctor."

"This is Sister Emiliana—she will assist me."

"Very good, doctor."

Guillermo unlocked the door. The doctor and his companion passed through. The door clicked shut.

With his good eye Masson watched them enter. His jaw dropped. "Mother. . . ."

The doctor raised his finger to his lips in warning; he indicated the door with a tilt of his head.

Masson rushed to her and took her hands.

"The doctor said you'd come. . . . I couldn't believe it."

They embraced. He sat on the edge of the cot, she on a chair; the doctor stood by the door, listening alertly for sounds in the corridor.

She freed one of her hands and reached out to touch his bandages. "How you have been hurt."

"It's nothing," he said excitedly. "I don't even mind this place. . . . If only I could sleep; every time I close my eyes I hear that man's scream. . . . Prisons are noisy places, especially at night. . . . But—I'm alive! That's the main thing! You see, momma—we manipulated history after all. . . ."

From the folds of her robe Cándida brought out a small paper bag.

"I looked for them everywhere, son. It is not easy to find a French confectionery here."

He opened the bag: "Licorice sticks! I'd forgotten all about them."

"You used to love them, Tomás. Every time I took a trip to Paris I had to bring a bag for you. . . . Do they treat you well?"

"Fine. Everything's *fine*. My meals will be brought in from a good restaurant; they'll send me a woman when I want one; Dr. Alvarez says everything can be arranged, no matter which penitentiary I go to. . . . All I have to do is keep my mouth shut. And be inconspicuous. . . ."

Cándida moved back slightly: "Inconspicuous?"

The street song had started still another time.

"Listen: they're singing about me in the streets. My picture's in all the papers. . . . In a year, two years, they won't even remember my name. *Then* I can slip back into the world. . . . It can be arranged whenever I'm ready. The doctor told me."

"Easily. We have our people in the prison administration."

"You'll see: they'll forget I'm alive. . . . That's the time to do it. . . . I'll send for you. We'll go to some out-of-the-way place— Perú, the Argentine. A place where we can have a quiet life, without headlines. . . ."

"That is what I live for now. The thought that you may be with me again, some day. . . ." Emotion disrupted her voice: "Chico! Chico! You do not have to wait a year! Not even a day! I can get you out of here now—tonight. . . . I have money: look." She produced a purse from her robe and opened it; she drew a wad of bills halfway out. "This is only a part of it. I have one hundred thousand dollars. Enough to see us through anything, any place. . . ."

His voice tightened: "Impossible. I told the doctor so."

"*Why* are you afraid to leave? Our people are impressed by your silence. They say favorable things about you."

"They talk about me? . . . Why don't they *forget* about me. . . ."

"Why, chico? If they think well of you they will do things for you. They will help us to go where we want: the Argentine, anywhere. . . . Chico, think! We can be together—*now!*"

Masson shifted away from her.

"I begin to see. Yes. I haven't opened my mouth but they don't trust me yet. . . . Yes, yes. They will treat you well out there—so I won't talk in here. But they're not entirely sure of me, so long as I'm out of their reach. . . ."

"You do not understand. You will be found guilty; you will get twenty years."

"And a day. Don't forget the day."

"The trial will be embarrassing for us. Things will come out that we do not wish the world to know. The public does not understand these matters."

Masson stood. He took up a newspaper from the table; his picture was on the front page.

"No. They don't understand abandoned revolutions and pacts with Hitler, either." He pointed to a headline halfway down the page: *"LOYALISTS SUING FRANCO FOR PEACE."* Near the bottom his finger stopped again: *"STALIN AND HITLER ABOUT TO SIGN TREATY OF FRIENDSHIP.* . . . I helped in my modest way to make this possible. . . . The public couldn't be expected to understand we're dropping Spain and embracing Hitler for *them.* . . . Rostov would have confused their minds still more."

She said with force: "This trial must be avoided at all costs. They insist on it."

"There are no musts for me any more. All that must be avoided at all costs is that I leave this cell too early. If they don't trust me— I don't trust them. . . ." He came close to her again, took her hand and began to plead: "Mother! For once, try to see it *my* way, not theirs! . . . There's going to be a war. That much is clear. When it begins, the world will forget Victor Rostov and Jacques Masson. That's the time for me to go, not before. . . . I'll never speak! They'll see! They'll be no danger to me—when they see I'm no danger to *them.* . . ."

"If you insist on staying it can only mean you want to reserve the *right* to talk. . . . No, Tomás. They do not want you to have this luxury. It seems to them a sort of blackmail. . . . They want you *home.* With me."

"Home? You said we could go to the Argentine."

"Later. First, we must go there. Until all this blows over."

Masson stood up and began to pace nervously. He turned back to her:

"What's happened to—Emma?"

The doctor answered from the door: "Her father is coming. He will arrange to put her in a sanitarium in the States. She tried to commit suicide."

"Isn't it strange? What I did to her—any average mother would despise me for. You—approved. . . ."

Cándida said: "I never approved. What you did, you had to do. . . . But you *enjoyed* it, I think. For that, who could forgive you. . . ."

"All those you had tortured and killed in Spain: you never enjoyed it?"

"What is necessary is not always—pleasant."

"To Bass it's pleasant."

"Not the cruelty; the organization behind it. The cruelty he shuts out of his mind. . . . Perhaps that is why he was our superior. . . . Ramón thinks even less about the unpleasantness. *He* becomes our superior now. . . ."

"It must amuse them to be sending me ultimatums in prison. They love to hand out ultimatums, in all directions. . . ." He walked about again, looking at all the walls. Again he came up to face her: "Do you think I'm a complete fool? I know what they think of me. I did a job for them; now they've no further use for me. . . . To them I just have nuisance value: I can tell tales and name names. . . . I disobeyed their instructions once, by staying alive. They mean to pay me off for this infraction of discipline!"

"They can pay you off here as well as outside. . . . If you refuse to go—they have their people all around you. . . ."

"They won't try anything here. The world would understand whose hand did it—they'd be exposing themselves. . . . They want me over *there*—where I can disappear in their cellars without anybody knowing. . . ."

"You are always dramatizing. You were so sure you were going to be killed this afternoon, too."

"In Coyoacán things can go wrong. In Moscow—*nothing* goes wrong." He leaned over and pointed his finger at her. "They're inviting me there to get a bullet in the neck." He leaned closer still: "And they send *you* with the invitation." His face was almost touching hers: "And—you *come*. Asking me to die a second time." He stood erect, held the bag of candies up. "Did they suggest the licorice sticks too?"

He hurled the bag into her lap. For a moment he stood glaring; she looked back steadily.

Suddenly his indignation caved in. He fell to his knees, he buried his head in her lap.

"Mamacita! Mamacita! I've been almost out of my mind, worrying about you. . . . I wanted so desperately to see you. . . . Now you come—with more orders. . . ."

"Fool! You think it was easy for me to come? I do what *I* am ordered!"

"I won't go. This time I don't have to take orders. I can stay here for twenty years—"

"And a day."

"—listening to that terrible scream each time I close my eyes. . . ."

His head was still on her knees, moving from side to side.

She looked down at him, her face softened. Her hands reached out to embrace him; she pulled them back. She shoved him away and stood.

"The world is for you a big lap. It is cold outside, the wind comes at your face with claws: you will not step out, you run for the lap and the kind lady who brings you licorice candies. But you will learn: build your house in a warm lap and you will be evicted. . . . You cannot make a lap out of this prison too! Life is not all warm fireplaces and nice licorices! We have our duties, there in the cold world! It was my *duty* to come here on this dirty errand! It is your *duty* to go there!"

He said brokenly: "Did I want so much from you? . . . Only soft words, the words of a mother. . . ."

There was all of revulsion on her face:

"You came into this world with one need—*not* to be catered to! To have this grudge against the world! . . . Thank me, my son. Thank me! You *needed* me for a mother. If I had not existed you would have had to *invent* me. . . . What mother ever gave a son so much—of what he needed most. . . ."

He remained on the floor. He raised his wet face. "Look at *your* history and *my* history. Who was ever more *shaped* than us? More *squeezed?* More *manipulated?* . . . But here—I've escaped their orders. For the first time in my life I'm free. I can stay here for twenty years if I want. . . ."

She said quietly: "Listening to that man scream every night?"

She started for the door. Masson reached out for her robe, hooked his fingers into its folds.

"Stay with me! Mamacita, I need you!"

She pulled free.

Slowly, helplessly: "Hold on to your 'freedom.' It comes with bars on the window. . . . All right. All right. . . ."

As she approached the doctor she seemed to falter, to lose her erect carriage. She seemed about to turn back.

For one moment she stood quite still.

Then she squared her thin angular shoulders. The doctor opened the door and she went out, her step firm.

The doctor followed her. The door closed.

Masson remained on the floor, his head down. Outside the guitars were getting livelier, the voices stronger:

> *. . . . cobarde asesino llevó,*
> *Y al estar solo con Señor Rostov,*
> *A mansalva le arrancó su existencia.*

They had put into words a full picture of the event. But the song still needed a conclusion, a rounding out, some statement of summing-up. They had had the time to work on that, too.

They sang their new and concluding stanza:

> *Fué un día martes por la tarde. . . .*

Masson said aloud, tonelessly: "It was on a Tuesday in the afternoon. . . ."

> *Este tragedia fatal . . . .*

"This fatal tragedy . . . ."

> *Que ha conmovido al país . . . .*

"Which has moved a country . . . ."

> *Y a todo la capital. . . .*

"And all the capital. . . ."

There was no reason for him to translate the words into English, of course, but he had nothing else to do.

❦ DIOSDADO

He had never known so much to happen from morning to night.

It had begun this morning, with the general. As soon as the general left Diosdado had hurried to the central square of Coyoacán. The general had said the letter was for him. Good, then he had the right to know what was in the letter. It was necessary to know.

He went to the store of the medicines. The man in the white coat was glad to read the words for him.

Many words:

> *"Dear Sir: It has come to the attention of this Institute that, while the last census lists you as residing at 122 Avenida Londres with your wife and seven children, there can be discovered in the files of the Bureau of Vital Statistics no record of your marriage. It is our earnest obligation to inform you that the lack of a duly registered marriage certificate is a matter of the utmost seriousness because, without the requisite certifications, you and your family cannot and will not be eligible for the several forms of Social Benefits now in operation under the dispensation of the Ministry of Public Welfare. In order to rectify this disparity, and with a view to completing and harmonizing our files, will you be good enough, dear sir, to call at your earliest convenience at the Coyoacán City Hall and at that place to discuss this vital matter in its entirety with the undersigned, Sr. Fulgencio Barrea, Dr. Lic., resident officer of the Federal Social Security Institute of the Ministry of Public Welfare. Rest assured, sir, of my respectful and continuing sentiments, and under all circumstances accept my word that I am permanently at your service. . . . "*

"These words have a meaning, boss?" Diosdado said.

"They mean," the druggist said, "that you better go across the square right away, to the City Hall, and see this Señor Big Words Fulgencio Barrea."

Diosdado went. A few minutes later he was sitting awkwardly in the office of a man with a black suit. This was in the building once the headquarters of the man named Cortés, who had started all the trouble around here. The man seemed very happy to see him.

"What luck that you should come today! Tomorrow would have been too late."

"What is to happen tomorrow, boss?" Diosdado became confused. He tried to think of all the things for which they might arrest him tomorrow. "That tire was a gift to me, boss, it would not be right to take me to jail for this. Now, the serape, that is another thing—"

"No, no. You do not go to jail. . . . But it is very serious that you are not married."

Diosdado immediately felt better: "Excuse me, boss, but you make a mistake. I am totally married."

"You have the proofs?"

"I had ten children, seven alive."

"They prove only that you and the woman Serafina live under the same roof and sleep on the same bed."

"Boss, is this not to be married? To be under one roof and on one bed? There is more to do with a woman?"

"Try to understand: there is no proof of a legal ceremony in the eyes of the law."

"The law? What does the law wish of me, boss? I have explained about the tire, and about that serape—"

"For such proofs, countryman, the paper is required. You follow this? The piece of paper of the government."

"I have no need for the paper, boss. I cannot read."

"It is not for you to read but for others. Others in the government, like myself. We in this department, in this bureau, in this Institute, how can we give you any of the Government Benefits for which your family might otherwise be eligible if you cannot prove that you are married and therefore, in the legal sense, a family? Our office requires this paper."

"What is this of government benefits, boss? In what way can the government wish to benefit from me and my family? From péons?" He became worried again. "If you take from us our house and our milpa, you will benefit, true, the house does not leak and the land is not bad, but how will we live then?"

"The government wants nothing of yours. Let me put it this way. Would you not like to have unemployment insurance if you lose your job?"

"I have no job, boss."

"Ah: you see? You could be collecting the insurance now, from the time you lost your job, if—"

"I did not lose any job, boss."

"You do not work?"

"Yes, I work all the time, boss. I find things and I sell things, I water my maize, I go here and there, a few days I work in the sugar cane fields. But I have not a job. I had a job in 1910, yes, on an estancia by Parral. This I left to go with Pancho Villa, since then I have no job. The government wishes to give me the wages I do not have from 1910?"

"No, no, this is not the approach. . . . In any case, you could be eligible for medical expenses when you are sick: for money to pay for the medicines."

"I do not get sick, boss. I never use the medicines. It is from the medicines that people get sick."

"Well. . . . Would you not like to have old age benefits, money to take care of you when you are old?"

"I am not old, boss. When I am old I will not need money because then I will be dead."

"Dead! All right, now—that brings us to a very important category. Suppose you die?"

"It is to be supposed, boss."

"What will become of your woman and your children when you are gone if we do not look after them?"

"You?" Diosdado was astonished. "Why would you look after them, boss? You do not have a woman and children of your own? Life must be hard for you, I regret it, boss."

"It is, at times. But I have a wife and children to lighten the load. . . . Answer me: who will look after your close ones, countryman?"

"Boss, the maize and the frijoles will grow for Serafina as for me. The things to sell can be found in the dumps and on the streets by my sons as by me. One thing will change when I am dead, there will be one mouth less in our house to eat up the tortillas and the frijoles. They will not have to grow so much."

The man in the suit seemed to be having trouble keeping his mouth together. He put his fingers over the lips to hold them in one place.

"Permit me to ask you this. Are there not things your family needs? You have your own house, you grow your own food—but clothing, for example, articles of clothing? The péons have much trouble to get huaraches for their families—do you not sometimes need huaraches?"

At last the man was saying something that had a meaning.

"That is the truth, boss, huaraches are a big need for us. For a long time I looked for them, for many weeks before the tire—"

"You see, then?" There was victory in the man's voice. He made some notes on a piece of paper. "You need huaraches. Families who cannot afford huaraches can receive them from this Department, but for this they must have the paper of marriage to prove they are families."

"Boss, I think, if I can say this, I think to see that we are a family what is needed is not a paper but eyes."

"The eyes give you no huaraches, man! For the huaraches only the paper will do."

"Then I think I would like to have this paper, boss." It was clear that the man wished him to have this paper, and Diosdado wished him to be happy. "To get the huaraches when they are needed is good."

"Fine! Very good! Now I will tell you what to do. Run home right away and get your family all cleaned up and ready."

"Excuse me, boss, but first you say I have not a family, now you say clean the family—"

"What do I care what you call them—call them your garden, your fingers—only get them ready! In three hours, in exactly three hours, no more, a truck will come to your house. . . ."

Serafina and the children were ready when the truck came. It was filled with other people cleaned up and dressed nice. They were driven into the city to Chapultepec Park and there led into a very great building called the National Auditorium. Many other families, gardens, fingers, whatever name they were to be called by, were there, all in their best clothes. There were almost five thousand families on the floor of this building, people said. All around, in the

many rows of seats, were twenty-five thousand more people. Diosdado had no idea how much five thousand or twenty-five thousand
was but the place was full, in all directions there were armies.

All afternoon and into the evening there was a grand fiesta. Marimba bands and groups of guitar players came to all the corners
and people gathered around them to sing and do dances of the
different country districts. Diosdado had the good luck to find a
group from his old home place. He had brought his guitar with
him, as had others. From time to time, when he heard a tune he
liked and remembered, he lifted the guitar from his back and played
along. He sang. Serafina sometimes sang. Twice he danced with
Serafina, while the children jumped around and giggled. Foods of
many kinds were brought in, it was a fine feast. Some had bottles
of tequila and mescal which they passed around with a neighborly
word. Diosdado had quite a few drinks during the long, pleasant
day. He was feeling very good when finally the music and the dancing stopped and on a big stage in the middle of the great room
several priests appeared, in robes of different colors, holding cruci-
fixes in their hands.

One of these priests stepped forward and made some motions
with his hands in various directions and began to half sing some
noises that sounded like words but were not words.

He sang some more.

This went on for some time.

"Now you have received the holy sacraments and you live in
grace," this priest said. "God go with you."

A man in a black suit came on the platform and spoke into the
metal box:

"Friends! Countrymen! I congratulate you on the felicities of this
important day! Now, please, have the goodness to form in lines at
the tables along the side of the auditorium. Workers from the Institute are there to tell you which lines to go to according to the
alphabet. Other workers at the tables will give you the papers. Be
so good as to form the lines and be patient! All will receive what is
theirs!"

So Diosdado went and stood in a line. Serafina stayed at his side,
herding the children along.

It was a long wait. The men at the tables had much work to do.

Bottles passed up and down the line, Diosdado had more drinks. After an hour, maybe two hours, it came his turn at the table.

He was asked his name and address. He gave them. The man in the suit looked through many cards in a long metal box. He then looked through a pile of white papers. He found one and held it out.

"Here, sir. Your marriage certificate."

Diosdado took the paper, rolled it carefully and gave it to Serafina to store under her rebozo.

The man in the suit brought out another paper.

"This is the paper for your huaraches. Go to the store at this address: give them this paper: you will get your huaraches at no cost."

"Huaraches, boss? I need no huaraches."

"I am sorry, you seem to be down for huaraches, definitely."

"How can this be, boss? I have good huaraches, anybody can see, new ones." He lifted one foot for the man to see. "My woman and my children have the new huaraches." He pointed with pride to the feet of Serafina and the children.

"I know nothing of this," the man said. "You must have told somebody who interviewed you that you needed huaraches and he put you down for huaraches. Do not make a war over this, man! Can it hurt you and yours to have two pairs of the huaraches instead of one? The second pair not homemade nothings of rubber but fine woven leather ones, for show? There are people with two pairs of huaraches, man! In many places of the world! Join the privileged classes! Learn to live in the style of the upper tenth and the conquistadors, become a friend to luxuries! . . . Next! Next, please!"

So Diosdado rolled up this paper too.

They were walking to the exit, to the trucks, when a short, birdlike man in a black suit came up and whispered in Diosdado's ear:

"You wish to sell the papers?"

"I cannot sell the papers of marriage," Diosdado said politely. "If I sell these papers we will not be married again, boss, and they will send us more letters I cannot read. These letters make me to worry, I do not sleep and—"

"Who wants the papers of marriage! Keep all such papers! Sleep ten years! I buy the papers for the other things—shirts, pants, stockings, shoes! You have the requisitions for such things?"

"They have given me a paper for the huaraches."

"Please to let me see."

Diosdado took the paper from Serafina and gave it to the man. He examined it. His eyes rolled.

"Nine pairs! Oh, then! Oh, what a paper—I will pay—let me think—two pesos the pair—I will pay you exactly eighteen pesos for this excellent paper! Agreed?"

Diosdado felt his head swimming. Eighteen pesos! He understood how much it was—ten and eight. It was very clever of the government to give papers worth such an amount.

"The boss will give us eighteen pesos for this paper," he said unbelievingly to Serafina.

"Is it good to sell this?" Serafina said. "We do not need the huaraches now, true. But the little ones run around much. The cement and the tar come now. The huaraches will wear out. Next year we will need huaraches and then we will have no more paper."

"You can get another paper, woman," the little man said.

"How is this possible?" Serafina said. "They give us the paper now because we get married. Can we get married again every year in order to have another paper?"

Diosdado felt a little dizzy but he was very excited and happy. He felt like making a joke:

"Woman, who can know? Maybe tomorrow they will tell us, get divorced and we will give you more papers for this. Now we have the ability to get divorced. We are different people, with more abilities than before. There will be more papers. We will have many. . . . Boss, I will sell this paper to you."

"Very good. You make a good business with me, I pay the best prices."

"The government sends you to buy this paper, boss? It must be so because I do not need the huaraches but I have use for the money. If the government gives me paper for the huaraches when I do not need—"

The little man had been looking around as though to make sure no one was watching. Perhaps he did not want the others to see how much the government was giving for this paper—they would be jealous. Now he took several bills from a large roll and began handing them to Diosdado: "Ten—fifteen—sixteen, seventeen, eighteen. . . . A day of happiness to you and your nice family! Blessings and a long life to the newlyweds! Good day, good day!" He hurried away.

Now Diosdado was feeling too good to go home. He did not want this unusual night to end. At the place of the trucks he said to Serafina: they could forget the truck and go for a walk to see the sights in the city, no? It had been years since they were in the city. They had the money now to take the bus back to Coyoacán in their own time. Serafina agreed and they set out. Not toward Coyoacán but in the opposite direction, along the pretty Paseo de la Reforma toward the center of the city.

They walked for a long time. Block after block. They stopped many times to marvel at the fine houses, the stores bigger than imagination. In one window was an enormous white refrigerator: the children recognized it with wild shouts: "Like ours! Like ours on the wall!" At one corner Diosdado went into a cantina to buy with one of his pesos a bottle of mescal. He had some more drinks. Serafina took a small swallow or two.

He had the feeling that they were waking up after a long sleep, to a morning that would stay.

There would be more papers for huaraches, more pesos for the papers, more days of chicken.

There would be many tires.

One day, who could tell, there might be a true refrigerator on the floor instead of only a paper one on the wall. With the wires to make it go. With many things, chickens, rice, inside it.

Today, it was said, men at the National Auditorium had been talking of it only this afternoon, a few péons even got some small milpas of land from the government in certain places.

Could anyone tell in these days of miracles? Maybe he would get a milpa. Maybe even a finca, with his new luck.

Meanwhile, the paper of marriage would look nice on the wall of his house, next to the picture of the white refrigerator.

He had the feeling of a fine waking up. He took some more drinks.

Somewhere far off, in the streets to the left, was the sound of music. Singing. Guitars, and the sound of many voices.

"It must be a fiesta in the streets," he said to Serafina. "Let us go that way. Maybe there is dancing."

They walked in that direction. After five or six blocks they saw a very large building. In front of this building was a large crowd, the singing came from there.

They began to make their way into the crowd. They did not feel bashful about it, they were not ashamed to be there, these were people like themselves, dressed like them, with faces like their own.

They made their way as close to the wall as possible. It was an interesting song they were singing, Diosdado had not heard it before. He listened carefully. A very good song. The tune was a pleasing one.

He slid his guitar around to his chest and placed his fingers on the strings.

He began to sing along with the crowd, picking out the notes on his guitar:

> *Un zapapico alpinista*
> *El cobarde asesino llevó,*
> *Y al estar solo con Señor Rostov,*
> *A mansalva le arrancó su existencia. . . .*

An interesting rhythm.

A tall, thin nun came down the steps from the large building. He could hardly see her face as she came close because of the curved white pieces on both sides. She walked very straight and with a firm step toward the two countrymen leaning there against the wall.

She stopped before these two men. They looked at her. She shook her head.

Diosdado felt dizzy but he watched the angry faces of these two. They did not have the look of péons. He watched in particular the smaller one and he thought: where have I seen this one?

He thought: the night of the guns, just before the guns, the man outside at the door of the pink blue house, the street light strong on his face as on that of the tall one inside, the dark and generous one of the Packard—

He laughed at himself for the thought. This one was a péon. That one was in the uniform of a colonel of police.

Péons do not go around in the uniforms of colonels.

The two men began to push their way down the street, the sister between them. What? Péons are not close friends of sisters—

Diosdado lost interest in these people. He turned his attention again to the singing. He raised his voice:

> *Fué un día por la tarde,*
> *Este tragedia fatal*
> *Que ha conmovido al país*
> *Y a todo la capital.*

Fine song!

He had it now. He had all the notes.

He threw his head back, far back, and struck a flourish on his guitar as he laughed out loud. He laughed again. The children tilted their heads back, unusually far, to look up into his face with admiration, and they began to laugh too. All in his family, his duly certified family, his garden, his fingers, were laughing with their heads back.

APPENDIX

David Justin's Glosses on Kronstadt

THE ANNALS

February 24, 1921. Strike movement Petrograd. Patronny munitions works, Trubotchny and Baltiyski mills, Laferm factory; spreads to Admiralty shops, Galernaya docks. Rioting workers' district Vassilevsky Ostrov.

February 27. Strike proclamation posted around Petrograd. "The workers and peasants . . . don't want to live by the decrees of the Bolsheviks . . . want to control their own destinies. . . . Liberation of all arrested socialists and nonpartisan workingmen. Abolition of martial law, freedom of speech, press and assembly for all who labor. Free election of shop and factory committees, of labor and soviet representatives." Basic demand: right to trade freely with villages. Wanted ban on food collecting in villages lifted. Reason: average heavy-industry and transport worker getting 700–1,000 calories a day.

Petrograd Soviet counters by declaring extraordinary martial law. Machine guns set up at factories and docks. Strike leaders arrested by Cheka. Intensified repressions.

At this point—not before—slogan for CONSTITUENT ASSEMBLY (that is, a convocation of regional delegates for the purpose of replacing the soviet system with a constitutional parliamentary government along Western, bourgeois-democratic lines) crops up. Note: (1) from advanced workers, not backward peasants; (2) not universal in strike wave but primarily among Menshevik workers; (3) a counter to Bolshevik absolute control of Soviets, an answer to Bolshevik-Cheka repressions.

February 27–28. Sympathy for Petrograd strikers aboard Petropavlovsk and Sevastopol warships. Spreads to whole fleet at Kronstadt and even Red Army regiments stationed there. Sailors on ships pass resolution for free new elections to Kronstadt Soviet. Kronstadt sends fraternal committee to Petrograd strikers.

March 1. Brigade meeting, Yakorny Square in Kronstadt. Called by crews of First and Second Squadrons of Baltic Fleet. Present: 16,000 sailors, Red Army men, workers. President of Soviet Republic Kalinin greeted with honors and brass bands. (Some mutiny!) No mention of Constituent Assembly in any of this. Resolution of ships' crews presented to meeting:

Demands for new elections, secret ballot, full freedom of agitation, freedom of speech and press for workers and peasants, freedom of assembly for unions and peasant organizations, nonpartisan conference of workers-soldiers-sailors of Petrograd and Kronstadt, liberation of all political prisoners of socialist parties, commission to review cases of those in prisons and concentration camps, abolition of political bureaus (whereby state subsidized Bolshevik party but no others), abolition of armed traffic squads and confiscatory units (set up and controlled by Bolsheviks alone), equalization of rations for all who work, abolition of commissars of army's fighting detachments and guards at mills and factories (let army units appoint and shop workers elect, rather than leave naming exclusively in Bolshevik hands), freedom to peasants regarding use of land and right to keep cattle, right to engage in individual smallscale production by one's own efforts. Again: the call for free food-collecting basic.

Resolution passed over bitter opposition from President Kalinin, Commissar of Baltic Fleet Kuzmin, Commissar of Kronstadt Soviet Vassiliev. Thunderous threats of retaliation from these gentlemen. . . . One sailor shouts: "Drop it, Kalinin! You manage to keep warm enough! Look at all the jobs you've got, and I expect you draw a ration for each of them!" Another yells to Kuzmin: "Have you forgotten how you had every tenth man shot on the Northern Front? Kick him out!"

Committee of Thirty sent from Kronstadt to inform Petrograd strikers of resolution. Committee arrested.

Until this point: sailors against arbitrary rule by commissar bureaucrats but clearly on side of Communist Party; considered themselves supporters of soviet system. Note carefully: no word about Constituent Assembly in March 1 resolution.

March 2. Conference of Delegates for Soviet Re-election at Kronstadt. Fiery addresses by Kuznin and Vassiliev: threaten Kronstadt "troublemakers" with strongest Bolshevik retaliations.

These two commissars detained. With ample reason. Communists had all the arms. Sailors had no access to telephone to find out what was really being prepared against them. Many other Communists present; none arrested, none. Even though rumor was circulating that Rostov was marching on Kronstadt with Bolshevik shock troops to attack meeting. And remember—one day before, the Kronstadt Committee of Thirty had been arrested in Petrograd: who was provoking whom?

March 1 resolution passed at this Conference. Presidium of Conference turned into Provisional Revolutionary Committee to preserve order and safety of garrison city, arrange new soviet elections.

March 2. Order signed by Lenin, Rostov and others calling Kronstadt a mutiny. Sailors branded "tools of former Tsarist generals who together with Social-Revolutionary traitors staged a counter-revolutionary conspiracy against the proletarian Republic." Whole thing "the work of Entente interventionists and French spies" under the guidance of General Kozlovsky, White Guard general now in Kronstadt. Martial law declared.

March 4. Proclamation of Petrograd Committee of Defense dropped over Kronstadt by plane. Announced families of Kronstadt sailors living in Petrograd being kept as hostages for Kuzmin and Vassiliev. Sailors' answer to this new provocation: "We want no bloodshed. Not one Communist has been shot by us."

Kronstadt organized for "equal rights for all, privileges to none." (Impeccable Bolshevik slogan!) Food rations equalized. Sailors, who under Bolshevik dispensation were getting more food than workers, voted to take the average ration. (More than Bolshevik bigshots would do!)

March 4. Petrograd Soviet meeting, Zinoviev presiding. Resolution passed calling Kronstadt counter-revolutionary, demanding immediate unconditional surrender.

March 5. Rostov's ultimatum to Kronstadt. Orders rebels to surrender unconditionally: "Only those who do so can count on the mercy of the Soviet Republic. Simultaneously with this warning I am issuing instructions that everything be prepared for the suppression of the mutiny by armed force. . . . This is the last warning." Most trusted divisions from the fronts, Cheka detachments, kursanti (army cadet) groups, military units exclusively Communist, gathered in bay forts of Sestroretsk, Lizzy Noss, Krashaia Gorka.

March 6. Radio message from Kronstadt to workers of world: "Our cause is just; we stand for the power of soviets, not parties. We stand for freely elected representatives of the laboring masses. The substitute soviets manipulated by the Communist Party have always been deaf to our needs and demands; the only reply we have ever received was shooting! . . . In Kronstadt the whole power is exclusively in the hands of the revolutionary sailors, soldiers and workers . . . not with counter-revolutionaries led by some Kozlovsky, as the lying Moscow radio tries to make you believe. . . . Do not delay, comrades! Join us, get in touch with us; demand admission to Kronstadt for your delegates. Only they will tell you the whole truth and expose the fiendish calumny about Finnish bread and Entente officers. Long live the revolutionary proletariat and the peasantry! Long live the power of freely elected soviets!"

Voice of White Guard generals here?

March 7. 6:45 P. M. Under Rostov's orders Sestroretsk and Lizzy Noss fire first shots at Kronstadt. Garrison can't answer fire effectively because main guns fixed in westward position.

Under attack sailors send out radio message: "Today is a universal holiday —Women Workers' Day. We of Kronstadt send, amid the thunder of cannon, our fraternal greetings to the workingwomen of the world. . . . May you soon accomplish your liberation from every form of violence and oppression. . . . Long live the free revolutionary workingwomen! Long live the Socialist Revolution throughout the world!"

Voice of grasping peasants and White Guardists?

March 8–17. Wave after wave of Rostov's crack troops, covered with white sheets, creep over the ice. Fought off. Enormous losses. Most Communists inside the garrison fighting on the fortress walls against the attackers: announce they have torn up their membership cards in "the party of the hangman Rostov." This announcement broadcast over Kronstadt radio by First Gunner Anastas Yiko of warship Sevastopol. (Yiko one of Rostov's closest friends: had followed V.R. to the Tauride Palace, to the Kresty prison, to the walls of Kazan on the Volga, had organized V.R.'s personal bodyguard. It was the Yikos V.R. had in mind when he said of the Kronstadt sailors that they were "the pride and glory of the revolution.")

Hundreds of freezing men from Rostov's units crawl to fortress, beg for mercy. Kronstadt people take them in, feed them; none hurt. Whole garrison contains less than 14,000 men—among them 10,000 sailors.

March 17. Morning. Gates of garrison forced. V.R. enters city. Slaughter. One big reason for the defeat: the Communist prisoners who had been taken in and fed betrayed those who gave them refuge and attacked from rear.

Dibenko made new Commissar of Kronstadt. Absolute power to "cleanse mutinous city." Continues blood bath.

Hundreds of Kronstadt prisoners sent to Petrograd jails. Groups marched out and shot night after night. Others sent to concentration camps of Archangel, dungeons of Turkestan.

March 18. Big celebration in Petrograd of 1871 Paris Commune (drowned in blood of French workers by Gallifet and Thiers). Turned into official celebration of the "great victory" at Kronstadt. . . .

THE HORRORS

(1) Revolt of backward petty-bourgeois peasants? Impetus came from the Petrograd heavy-industry strikers—the most advanced and revolutionary proletarians! (Petrograd workers subsequently repudiated Kronstadt? Sure: after all their leaders had been locked up, after they'd been terrorized by mass arrests and extraordinary martial law. After two weeks of a vicious press campaign by the Bolsheviks spreading all sorts of lies about the sailors. After two weeks with Kronstadt absolutely cut off and unable to refute the lies. If the Petrograd strikers had not been crushed; if they'd been able to have contact with Kronstadt and visit there—they would have been side by side with the sailors on the garrison walls fighting off V.R. After all—the sailors had only picked up the slogans the industrial strikers had been terrorized into dropping!)

(2) Bolsheviks never presented one shred of evidence to prove the sailors were involved with anti-soviet plotters. If they'd had one convincing document—wouldn't they have produced it? . . . Ex-White Guard general Kozlovsky was at Kronstadt, yes. But he'd been stationed there by the Red Army! And the sailors refused to have anything to do with him! *The Bolsheviks*

knew this. When V.R. began the attack the few Imperial ex-officers in the garrison wanted to seize a bridgehead on the mainland as a defensive measure; the Provisional Revolutionary Committee voted them down. When the S-R's offered military aid, the offer was rejected. *The Bolsheviks knew this.* True, the rightwing S-R leader Victor Chernov, then in Paris, offered food supplies to the Kronstadt sailors. But the sailors, though they needed supplies badly, unceremoniously turned down the offer! *The Bolsheviks knew all about it. . . .* Amalgam! Amalgam! The technique of the amalgam perfected here! Trick of tying your opponent in with all the worst bugaboos of the moment. Where's the difference between calling Kronstadt a Finnish-Lettish-French-Entente-interventionist-agent-provocateur-White-Guard plot and calling V.R. first a Hitler, then a Dies Committee, agent? Stalin didn't invent the amalgam! He had a rich heritage.

(3) The Tenth Congress of the Communist Party was taking place at just that moment in Petrograd. Did Lenin bother to keep up the White-Guard-plot nonsense in front of his party faithful? Not for a minute. Not for a second. In his speech about the Kronstadt sailors he told the delegates frankly: "They do not want the White Guards—and they do not want our power either." . . . Amalgam!

(4) It could have been stopped. It could have been stopped. If centralism had any tolerance for the off-center. . . . At any one of a dozen points: (a) The Petrograd strikers could have been talked to instead of smashed; some of the worst abuses they cried out at, discriminatory rationing, the ban on food-gathering in the villages, etc., corrected. (How did the Bolsheviks dare to think they were more sensitive to hunger and cold than the general run of humanity, and therefore entitled to more of the food and clothing in such short supply?) (b) The Petrograd strikers and the Kronstadt sailors could have been allowed to visit each other. The Kronstadt Committee of Thirty need not have been arrested. (That was what spurred the sailors to arrest Kuzmin and Vassiliev; these arrests, in turn, led the authorities to take members of the sailors' families as hostages: a mounting spiral, set in motion by the Bolsheviks.) (c) Martial law could have been suspended and peace negotiations opened. (Impossible to deal with traitors? But early in March even V.R. made it clear he did not consider the sailors traitors. He outlined a plan for handling Kronstadt to the Tenth Party Congress: first, peace negotiations, then, if they failed, a surrender ultimatum. Would he for one moment have entertained the idea of peace talks with these people if he'd believed they were restorationist plotters? But if the Bolsheviks had been serious about starting peace talks they would have had to create an atmosphere for them by halting their extreme provocations—arrests, hostages, lying propaganda, threats, etc.) (d) Intermediaries could have been used to calm nerves on both sides and create a climate for compromise. Alexander Berkman, the American, was in Petrograd at the time. As an anarchist leader he might have been expected to sympathize with the libertarian quality of

the sailors' demands—but he didn't: he was more on the Bolshevik side at first. Still, he commanded considerable respect among left libertarians everywhere, including Kronstadt. If he'd been allowed to go to Kronstadt his word would have carried great weight there. He begged for permission to go, to urge patience on the sailors. He was categorically turned down. (e) Time after time the sailors broadcast invitations to workers to send delegations into the fortress; such visitors could have reported the truth about whether there was a "counter-revolutionary mutiny" under way or not. The Bolsheviks could have made such inspection tours possible. . . . It could have been stopped. It could have been stopped.

(5) What were the sailors demanding that they hadn't been encouraged to fight for in the revolution? Bread, equal rights, a voice in things, liberty—Bolshevik bywords—these were the bywords at Kronstadt. Why did the Bolsheviks react to them with such snarling harshness? Because they had another byword which they hadn't bothered to popularize with the "naive" masses—centralism. The Bolsheviks wouldn't give an inch on matters of inequitable rationing and so on—centralists don't encourage pressures on the center; this led the sailors to talk of cutting down the Bolshevik absolute control of everything—without, mark this, without overturning the soviet power. This was what they meant by their first slogan, ALL POWER BACK TO THE SOVIETS, and by the later slogan, FOR THE THIRD REVOLUTION. Stood for power of soviets, not parties. For dictatorship of proletariat rather than dictatorship of one party over proletariat. That and no more. This little was too much for the Bolsheviks. Had to smash Kronstadt because its advocacy of democratic rationing, many workers' tendencies, open debate, secret ballot, etc., was open challenge to idea of one iron center. . . . This intransigent stand might well have pushed the sailors finally to idea of Constituent Assembly, as it had some of the Petrograd strikers. *It didn't.* Many lies told about this: fact is that slogan of CONSTITUENT ASSEMBLY never once appears in any Kronstadt broadcast, publication, resolution. (Nor does slogan of THE SOVIETS WITHOUT THE BOLSHEVIKS, so often attributed to Kronstadt; not even that.)

(6) V.R.'s program against Stalin today is—many tendencies within Bolshevik party, many workers' parties, open debate, secret ballot, elimination of bureaucratic privileges, etc. What's he fighting for now that he did not deny by force of arms to the sailors? . . . But then he was in the saddle! Now he's locked out!

(7) Social degeneration at Kronstadt? (a) Yes, in the year 1921 66.7% of the Communists in the Baltic Fleet were peasants. But in that year the peasants bulked just as large, or larger, in the Red Army communist cells! The Bolsheviks knew this. These were official Bolshevik figures. (b) In the Kronstadt civilian party, 30.9% were peasants: just what the percentage was in the party everywhere in Russia. Official Bolshevik figures! (c) The peasant representation at Kronstadt did not prevent the Bolsheviks from parading

large contingents of Kronstadt sailors in the May Day festivities, May 1, 1920—only ten months before the "mutiny"! The sailors were pointed out to the British Labour Mission as the revolution's showpieces, the legendary heroes who had saved the country from Kerensky, Petrograd from Yudenien. (d) Later that year, during the October anniversary—only *five* months before the "mutiny"!—the Kronstadt sailors were chosen to re-enact the taking of the Winter Palace; wildly acclaimed; no mention of their degenerated class composition. . . .

(8) The Bolsheviks betray themselves. . . . (a) April 3, 1921, V.R. reviews parade of the troops that overwhelmed Kronstadt. He says: "We waited as long as possible for our blinded sailor-comrades to see with their own eyes where the mutiny led. But we were confronted by the danger that the ice [of Finland Bay] would melt away and we were compelled to carry out . . . the attack." No gloating over a defeat of the class enemy now. Instead—shamefaced apologies. Sailors suddenly not reactionary peasants and White Guardists but—"comrades." (b) One of V.R.'s biographers reports: "Foreign Communists who visited Moscow some months later and believed that Kronstadt had been one of the ordinary incidents of the civil war, were 'astonished and troubled' to find that the leading Bolsheviks spoke of the rebels without any of the anger and hatred which they felt for the White Guards and interventionists. Their talk was full of 'sympathetic reticences' and sad, enigmatic allusions, which to the outsider betrayed the party's troubled conscience." (c) No wonder we can't find the quotes that V.R. now wants. The only people who could have had the full facts, the Bolsheviks, buried the whole episode at the very bottom of their most secret archives. Not one real trace of Kronstadt remains in the enormous Bolshevik literature. A massive literary suppression in the wake of the military one. Is silence the posture of men proud of having wiped out an enemy? Or were these guilt-ridden people who hoped, by erasing Kronstadt from the record, ultimately to erase it from their consciences? (d) The sailors were reactionary plotters? Then the honest proletarians should have been only too willing to march against them. They weren't. How carefully V.R. had picked his troops for the assault. Still he had such grave misgivings about how they would fight that, at the last moment, 300 of the delegates to the Tenth Party Congress were recruited to go along on the mission and spark morale. And even this didn't work! The most fanatical Communist troops V.R. could round up had such little heart for the march that Cheka detachments had to walk behind them with guns pointed at their backs! The most dedicated party fighters in all of Russia—forced to move against Kronstadt at gunpoint! . . . No wonder those black weeks have dropped out of the archives and been expunged from the record. . . . V.R. will have to make up his own quotes. . . .

(9) One pertinent quote does exist. From a memoir written by V.R. after the event. He acknowledges that Kalinin, Kuzmin and Vassiliev may have

bullied the sailors too much. (Accident? Or policy?) He allows that the basic demands of the sailors were modest and justified, after all the years of suffering and privation; he admits that the New Economic Policy, put into effect only a few months after Kronstadt went down in blood, gave many concessions to the people that were no more than what the sailors had been after. And he adds: "Simply because it had been guilty of a political error, simply because some of its less polished representatives may have blundered in dealing with the sailors, should the proletarian revolution really have committed suicide to punish itself?" . . . One of the most fantastic statements in the history of political struggle. *There* is a quote, if V.R. has such need of quotes. Apparently certain guilts can't be kept permanently under cover, even in such a brilliantly organized and disciplined ideologue as V.R. . . . I don't think he'll use this telltale quote that slipped out of his own depths. No man wants to confess twice. . . .

AUTHOR'S NOTES

AUTHOR'S NOTES

LEON TROTSKY lived out the last phase of his life in Turkey, France, Norway and Mexico. Many Western eyes were on him during those twelve years. Thousands of people took up his ideas, not a few came to be his friends. In the opposite camp hundreds of thousands of Stalinists were taught to look upon the nettlesome exile as the chief ogre of their hierarchic universe.

Trotsky was killed on August 20, 1940. In all the years since then, none of the people once so exquisitely aware of his presence, not one of his quondam well-wishers and not one of his old vilifiers, no one, literally not a single one, has given us a sober retrospective word about his incendiary career and terrible end.[1] I am not talking only about novels and plays, though it must be said that a truly live social movement is bound in the long run to attract novelists and playwrights who will want to write about its uppermost legends and turmoils. There has not been even a political essay or personal evaluation of lasting merit about Trotsky.[2] This fact by itself says enough about the fossilization of Bolshevik-Leninism, the form of revolutionary Marxism to which Trotskyites, Stalinists and post-Stalinists, whatever their doctrinal differences, all adhere. When a body of social thought and program loses its capacity to digest its own central experiences it is dead, no matter how much ideological lumber

[1] Victor Serge's *Vie et mort de Trotsky* (Paris, 1951) is less an interpretation than a factual review and sketchy memoir.
[2] Two useful historical studies do exist, Bertram Wolfe's *Three Who Made A Revolution* (1948) and Isaac Deutscher's *The Prophet Armed* (1954); but the one stops at 1914 and the other, the first volume of what is to be a full biography, at 1921. (In his glosses on Kronstadt, on page 373, David Justin quotes seven lines from Mr. Deutscher's book. Justin, of course, is supposed to be writing in 1939, fifteen years before this book was published. My only excuse for this extreme liberty is that the materials in this significant passage date back to the year of Kronstadt and could, therefore, have come to Justin's attention in one form or another.)

it has managed to deposit over persons and nations as its flattening legacy.[8]

In 1937 I spent eight months in Trotsky's Coyoacán household as a member of his secretarial staff. At twenty-one I was less than an astute observer of politics and personalities, but I took home with me a sense of some profound and unacknowledged crisis in Trotsky's life. Everything I have learned and thought since then has fed this impression. For a long time I wanted to work out a novel on Trotsky's last days, but I saw no approach to it until it occurred to me that his final tensions must have centered on Kronstadt as much as on any one supra-personal thing, and that, accordingly, a meaningful telling of the man's story would have to dig back to the island massacre of 1921 as it moved ahead to the crash of the Alpine ice axe that ended his life almost two decades later. The present book became possible when I saw that the GPU-sponsored blow could be taken, and in a sense *had* to be taken, as a last spasm of the corpse of Kronstadt.

But the Russian exile in the story is not called Trotsky. There is good reason for this. While Victor Rostov's record follows the main lines of the model's, and while his key political formulations are taken from Trotsky's texts (sometimes, though not always, verbatim), the fictional person and the real man are by no means identical. At important points actualities have been altered, or gone beyond, or put aside entirely. For example:

Stalin's decision to get rid of Trotsky had a good deal to do with the Moscow Trials, the Spanish civil war, and the slow progress toward a Nazi-Soviet Pact. But by 1940 the Trials and the Spanish agony were gone and forgotten and the rapprochement with Hitler was ancient history. I have therefore moved the assassination back eighteen months, to February of 1939, so that readers with no memory of those far-off times can see the historical connections rather

[8] To be strictly accurate: one "creative" work purporting to touch on Trotsky in exile did appear toward the end of Stalinism's literary heyday in the States, Isidor Schneider's *The Judas Time* (New York, 1946); it belongs to the world of letters in much the same way as a counterfeit coin belongs to the world of currency. The GPU has over and over demonstrated its deftness in the dictation of fictions; nowhere has it shown itself capable of dictating literature.

than have laboriously to reconstruct them. It was only circumstance —if not downright inefficiency—that prevented the GPU from killing Trotsky in 1939 or even in 1938. The plot took shape in and around Spain as far back as 1937, and certainly Stalin hoped to have the job over with long before it was.

The machine-gun attack on Trotsky took place on May 23, 1940, that is, three months before the assassination. In this book only one week elapses between the two attempts, to avoid the drawing out of an unbearable tension. (Torment has to be doled out in novels much more sparingly than it often is in real life.) Again, during his Mexican exile Trotsky lived first in a house belonging to Diego Rivera's wife, then in the villa which he bought and in which he was killed. The home described here is modeled more or less after the first residence, simply because that is the one I have personal knowledge of.

One bulky strand of the Trotsky story has here been pulled out entirely. Among his bodyguards at the time of his death was a young New Yorker named Robert Sheldon Harte, who presumably opened the door for the machine gunners; he was "kidnapped" by the GPU people during the attack and some weeks later his body was found in a lime pit near a GPU hideout in the Desert of the Lions. According to General Sanchez Salazar, Mexican Chief of Secret Police at the time, there are reasons for supposing that Harte was a GPU plant in the Trotsky household. I have not tried to establish a second enemy agent inside the Trotsky circle because his story would inevitably have had a tangential and muddying effect.

Another element in the machine-gun incident has here been dropped as too unwieldy. Supervising the real operation was "a man who spoke French" (very possibly the GPU operative George Mink), but the person wearing the colonel's uniform and directing the physical action was David Alfaro Siqueiros, the Mexican painter, who was then fresh from high-level GPU missions in Loyalist Spain. For weeks after the attempt, from various places of hiding, Siqueiros addressed communiqués to the Mexico City newspapers insisting that the operation had been conducted against an enemy of the Mexican Revolution and the international working class and was therefore not a crime but a legitimate *franctireur* political act. Months later, after Robert Sheldon Harte's body had been found and Trotsky had been assassinated, General Salazar led a posse into the mountains outside the mining town of Hostotipaquillo and there captured Siqueiros. The painter faced nine charges, including that of murder. He has not, I believe, ever been sentenced to prison.

Trotsky did not participate personally in the military operation against Kronstadt. (The reasons, according to him, were petty ones, having to do with inner-party frictions; but did he not breathe a sigh of relief as he backed away from the assignment?) He and Lenin, however, drew up the ultimatums issued to the sailors, and in later years he took full responsibility for the suppression and repressions. For obvious reasons it was important to have my main protagonist in command of the Kronstadt operation rather than represented there by one of his subordinate generals. But whether he was physically involved or not, Trotsky must have been in a very particular agony over the ultimatistic handling of the "mutiny." Of all the Bolshevik "greats," he was the one closest to the sailors, the one most idolized by them; and, as the ideologue who had held out so long and so eloquently against Bolshevism, he was the one who had most clearly foreseen what had to happen if Lenin's centralism came to absolute power and ran amok. Kronstadt was the cannibalism he had for fourteen years dreaded and warned against. Now he was obliged, as leader of the Red Army, to be its master of ceremonies.

As to the "authenticity" of the other people: Marisha is not meant to be Natalia Ivanovna Sedova-Trotsky except in respect of her courage, delicacy and self-effacement. (Actually Trotsky was married twice and had four children; I have given Rostov only one wife and one child in order to bypass in an already crowded story the biographical clutter so often found in the careers of revolutionaries as in those of bohemians.) The two bodyguards are complete inventions, although fairly representative of *some* of the younger people who came to Trotsky in his places of sanctuary. Emma Sholes most particularly is a fictional construct; the real Trotskyite girl who was duped by Jacques Mornard, the real assassin, has had her life blighted enough without gratuitous blows from novelists.

Much as I would like to, I cannot claim that Cándida Baeza de Rivera, her son Tomás, and the GPU overseer George Bass are exact studies of true-life models. GPU agents seldom sit for their portraits. There were people like these in the plot, of course, and they seem to have played roles very much like the ones described here.[4] Their true names are known: Caridad Mercader del Río, Ramón Mercader del Río (alias Jacques Mornard, alias Frank Jacson), and, possibly, the legendary George Mink; but little has been set down about their personal qualities and private lives, except, perhaps, in secret police records not usually available to writers of fiction.[5] I can say only that my conspirators are patterned after the real ones to the extent that anything is known—and revealed—about them. If the subjects feel they have not been done justice here, they can speak out. Two of them, at least, are still alive: the assassin is due to be released from his Mexican penitentiary sometime in 1960, and his mother was reported not long ago to be living quietly in Paris. Even George Mink, if indeed he was one of those who supervised the plot, may be alive somewhere in the world, assuming he has survived all the Stalin and post-Stalin purges in the GPU hierarchy.

Finally, Fidel Ortega does not in any way represent General Leandro A. Sanchez Salazar, the Secret Police Chief who handled the Trotsky case. I am, however, deeply in General Salazar's debt on another count: the book which he wrote in collaboration with Julian Gorkin, *Murder in Mexico* (London, 1950), remains the only detailed record of the assassination in print, and I have relied on it at many points, even down to the words of the street song about Trotsky's death. I should perhaps add that in the description of the assassination scene I have followed more or less faithfully the moving account written by Mrs. Trotsky, to the point of including some spoken lines as she recalled them. This memoir, too, is to be found in General Salazar's book, as well as in various Trotskyite publications and in the afore-mentioned Victor Serge study.

The facts, then, have been rather freely "tampered" with in this novel. That will explain, I hope, why my Russian exile is not named

[4] According to General Salazar's account of the killing, when Trotsky's bodyguards rushed in and began to beat Mornard brutally, that is, at the moment when Mornard was sure he was about to die, he screamed: "He made me do it. . . . They've got something on me. They are keeping my mother a prisoner!" My characterization of the assassin was arrived at largely by working backward from these remarkably suggestive words.

[5] A short biographical sketch of George Mink, alias Sormenti, alias George Hirsh, will be found in pages 407–410 of David Dallin's *Soviet Espionage* (Yale, 1955).

Trotsky. Much current practice to the contrary, it can still be argued that the alteration of one comma in the historical record demands that the result be presented as the fiction it is and not as "reconstruction" or "documentation."

My guess as to Trotsky's state of mind in his last days is just that —a guess, informed to the extent possible. Certainly the inner agitation, if it was there, did not come out as nakedly as I have suggested. Supremely conscious of his public face always, Trotsky would not have allowed any doubts he might have had as to his past historical role to surface; nor would his associates have raised such boldly provocative questions with him. I was obliged to take those torments I assumed to be buried deep in Trotsky and some of the people around him and bring them into the open, where they could be looked at.[6] The faltering quality of Trotsky's writings in his last years as regards Kronstadt and the over-riding questions of Bolshevik end-means morality would *seem* to hint that these self-harryings did exist somewhere in the man, but I will not pretend that this is more than speculation. All the more reason why this work cannot be called a history. It is, rather, a fiction based upon, derived from— dogged by, if you will—history.

There are certainly grounds for suspecting that *something* was operating in Trotsky that interfered with his will to live.[7] He would have been safe with adequate security measures of a sort not impossible to arrange. Even without careful physical defenses, might he and his friends not have noticed the strikingly bizarre behavior of Jacques Mornard—*if their eyes had been attuned to such "subpolitical" matters?*[8] There are those very advanced intellectuals who to

[6] In a few instances his friends' doubts *did* come out, though in half-veiled form. See the uneasy questions directed to Trotsky *from within his own circle* in the occasional discussions of Kronstadt conducted during 1938 and 1939 in the pages of *The New International*.

[7] Victor Serge reproduces this statement of Natalia's: "Leon Davidovitch had moments of dejection. 'Perhaps,' he said to me, 'my death might have saved Sergei. . . .' At times he seemed to feel a certain regret over still being alive." No doubt the purging of his son Sergei at the hands of Stalin was a terrible blow; but this "regret over still being alive" may have had other sources too.

[8] Ample documentation as to Mornard's provocative strangeness and Trotsky's heedlessness is to be found in Natalia Trotsky's reminiscences (contained

this day look upon Trotsky as a towering figure and simply that, with none of the emotional shadowings of a mortal man; confronted with the facts as to his enormous and persistent carelessness, they shrug off the problem with the sentimental formula that he was "a lonely man." They do him no honor by attributing to him soap-opera motives and nothing else. He *was* lonely—and he was also a trapped and haunted man opening his arms wide to death, I believe. His diary for the year 1935 (*Trotsky's Diary in Exile: 1935*), just now brought out by Harvard University Press, is filled with so many references to death—that early!—as to suggest a wish as well as a prediction; and in the astonishing testament appended to this volume, a document written in March of 1940, six months before his assassination, he goes so far as to reserve for himself, on the inadequate grounds of "rising blood pressure" and possibly impending "brain hemorrhage," the right to end his life by his own hand.

Paul Teleki rests his case against Rostov on the question of "indispensability." It is a burning question, because a Bolshevik leader who felt he was not absolutely needed by the revolution might conceivably have been emboldened to stand up against his comrades at their moments of excess—might, for example, have spoken out for the Kronstadt sailors; such a break in the Bolshevik ranks might have prevented, or at least mitigated, this or that Kronstadt. The 1935 diary indicates that the subject of his indispensability to the revolution was very much on Trotsky's mind. He makes this entry:

> *For the sake of clarity I would put it this way. Had I not been present in 1917 in Petersburg, the October Revolution would still have taken place*—on the condition that Lenin was present and in command. *If neither Lenin nor I had been present in Petersburg, there would have been no October Revolution: the*

---

in Victor Serge's volume). Mornard drove his car wildly, bragged of his big business deals; Trotsky several times spoke distastefully of the man to Natalia, expressing his lack of enthusiasm about seeing him. Yet when an American friend became so suspicious of the hanger-on as to suggest that he "ought to be looked into," Trotsky exclaimed, "Come! Come! What are you saying!" and refused to discuss the matter. Again, holding the dying Trotsky in her arms, Natalia murmured, "Oh. . . . Oh. . . . No one should enter here without being searched!" *Then!*

leadership of the Bolshevik Party would have prevented it from occurring—of this I have not the slightest doubt! If Lenin had not been in Petersburg, I doubt whether I could have managed to overcome the resistance of the Bolshevik leaders. The struggle with "Trotskyism" (i.e., with the proletarian revolution) would have commenced in May, 1917, and the outcome of the revolution would have been in question. But I repeat, granted the presence of Lenin the October Revolution would have been victorious anyway. The same could by and large be said of the Civil War, although in its first period, especially at the time of the fall of Simbirsk and Kazan, Lenin wavered and was beset by doubts. But this was undoubtedly a passing mood which he probably never even admitted to anyone but me.

Thus I cannot speak of the "indispensability" of my work, even about the period from 1917 to 1921. . . .

But if a top Bolshevik leader could have been dispensed with during the years of insurrection and civil war, how much more must that have been the case in 1921, when the counter-revolutionary armies were long since crushed and disbanded. Yet no Bolshevik leader of any echelon stepped forward to take the side of the Kronstadt sailors. Not even Trotsky, whose word as leader of the victorious Red Army would have carried such weight—and who by his own admission was not indispensable and *knew* it—not even Trotsky advanced one inch toward the sailors, his dearest friends. . . .

For a long time Kronstadt was all but erased from history. Now, at last, a fine and hard-headed scholarship is beginning to resurrect this paradigmatic event for us. I must express my particular debt to the studies of Kronstadt contained in Leonard Schapiro's *The Origin of the Communist Autocracy* (London, 1955) and D. Fedotoff-White's *The Growth of the Red Army* (Princeton, 1944); without their pioneering my own explorations would have been impossible. As for Trotsky's meager and impatient reflections on Kronstadt, they can be found in several articles published in *The New International*, "Hue and Cry over Kronstadt" (April, 1938), "More on the Suppression of Kronstadt" (August, 1938), and, marginally, "Their Morals and Ours" (June, 1938) and "Moralists and Sycophants against Marxism" (August, 1939). How his incisive mind began to

waver and shift ground when forced to face up to the core problems
of Bolshevik morality is devastatingly exposed by John Dewey in an
article entitled "Means and Ends" (*New International,* August,
1938). Neither Trotsky nor any of the Trotskyite theoreticians was
ever able to rebut this piece of cool argumentation with more than
mechanical invective.[9]

The Sheridan Justice incident is not entirely an invention. Such
an ill-equipped American Negro, by name Oliver Law, was promoted to an important command in the Abraham Lincoln Battalion
in Spain, and was killed in an insane orgy by some of his over-pressed
comrades. He was later glorified in publications of the Friends of
the Lincoln Battalion for his "heroic death in action," but the true
story of his end is known to more than a few veterans of the Spanish
fighting. The facts are to be found in an unpublished recollection
of the Spanish experience by William Herrick, himself a veteran of
the civil war; one of our New York publishers should have the courage to bring out this important document.[10]

The two GPU chiefs mentioned glancingly here are called Erzhov
and Rachevsky. These fictitious names are given to similar gentlemen in the late Victor Serge's novel, *The Case of Comrade Tulayev*
(New York, 1951), and I have copied them as a small homage to
that excellent and neglected work. This is the only piece of fiction I
know which captures the full horror *and grotesquerie* of the Russian

[9] The important critiques of Kronstadt published in *The New International*
during this period were: Victor Serge's "Once More: Kronstadt" (July,
1938), Dwight Macdonald's "Once More: Kronstadt" (July, 1938) and
"Kronstadt Again" (October, 1939). A particularly mindless attempt to defend Trotsky's position was written by John G. Wright under the title, "The
Truth About Kronstadt" (February, 1938).

[10] The story of Paul Teleki's liberation from a Siberian labor camp by an
earthquake, unlikely though it sounds, is based on fact. The Spaniard Valen-
tín Gonzalez describes precisely such an escape (his own) in his book *Life
and Death in Soviet Russia* (New York, 1953). It is too bad that his eloquence about the labor camps in Russia does not extend to the subject of his
own activities in Loyalist Spain as the magnetic Stalinist general known as
El Campesino. Regarding his own role in the shooting of anti-Stalinists and
"unreliables" at and behind the lines he has only these cryptic words: "I am
not pretending that I was not guilty of ugly things myself, or that I never
caused needless sacrifice of human lives. I am a Spaniard. We look upon life
as tragic. . . ."

purges and trials of the thirties; in it Serge constructed, in what was to be the last creative act of his life, a completely surrealist *tour de force* by the technique of sticking meticulously to the bare, bald facts. This novel eminently deserves to be reprinted.

What were Stalin's intentions in Spain? To answer this question you must ask another: at what point did Stalin decide to woo Hitler for a pact? The second answer will almost automatically provide the first, because either Stalin turned to Hitler as a *result* of the Spanish defeat or he *arranged* the defeat as part of his overtures to the Nazi leader. My assumption here has been that Stalin secretly faced away from the Western powers and toward Germany as early as 1934, two years *before* the civil war began in Spain. Evidence for this view will be found in the book entitled *In Stalin's Secret Service* (New York, 1939) by General Walter Krivitsky, once chief of Soviet Military Intelligence for Western Europe, especially in the chapter, "Stalin Appeases Hitler." It is Krivitsky's documented thesis that Stalin decided the West was finished, and that Nazism had created a firm and enduring power, when Hitler carried out his ruthless blood purge of the Röhm "radicals" on the *Walpurgisnacht* of June 30, 1934.[11] Possibly, if Stalin could have been sure of leading and controlling the Spanish revolution, he might not have stamped it out as brutally as he did; but the Communists were an insignificant minority in that strongly anarchist and socialist land, however artificially propped up by "Russian aid" and the GPU; and Stalin must have been perfectly willing to sacrifice a country of incorrigible anti-Stalinists on the altar of his "security" deals with Hitler.[12]

[11] Stalin was always one to appreciate a well-executed purge. As far back as 1923, during a drinking bout with Kamanev and Cheka chief Dzherzhinsky, Stalin gave his definition of life's highest moment: "To choose the victim, carefully prepare the blow, satisfy an implacable vengeance, then go to bed. . . . There is nothing sweeter in the world." . . . About Krivitsky there is this question: were his speculations too close to the mark for Stalin's taste? The general died in a Washington hotel room on February 11, 1941; there was a bullet in his head but no sure indication as to how it got there. Did Stalin that night have one of his "sweeter" sleeps?

[12] This is also the view of Jesus Hernandez, former Spanish Communist leader who was for a time editor of the party daily *Mundo Obrero* and later Commissioner General of the Loyalist armies. Speculating about why Moscow first ordered the Spanish Communists to participate in Largo Caballero's government and then pressed them to get out, Hernandez writes in his book

How sympathize with the wretched of the earth in a way that will not be merely a whitewash of old exploitation or the prelude to new? How embrace the worst-off without breaking still more of their bones? Hard questions to answer, these hard days. Worse yet: intelligence itself places road blocks in the way of a too-quick gush of warmheartedness for the people of the bottom.

For one thing, no special merit attaches to being a beast of burden, a hand of factory or field. The outermost fringes of human affairs are not where Eden lies, though some dharmatized D.P.'s of the newest literary fad, last-ditch romantics that they are, persist in thinking so. Lowliness in itself is not a commendation. There are few grounds, other than a wildly misplaced prolo-pastoralism, for making cute and over-erotized Noble Savages of Tortilla Flat discards, Neon Jungle scrabblers, Tobacco Road harelips. These have-nots and expect-nothings, humankind's true "outsiders," show up the bemused students of outsiderism for the bookish schoolboys they are. Fringe-dwellers live out their lives in cramp and blight and that is their total story.

Still the fellaheen of the world at the very least deserve a kind of straight-on confrontation which their professional admirers, too busy emitting their own dream images onto the human landscape, do not give them. Those who gravitate toward the pit for reasons of program rather than poetry, who are on the hunt for ideological rather than esthetic fixes, are the worst offenders. Intellectuals who announce a *political* solidarity with the humble masses turn out more often than not to reserve their warmest comradeship for the fierce bureaucrats who yoke the masses in the name of better worlds allegedly a-building. The communoid *clercs* coming up now in Western Europe and England seem able to recognize misery only when it has the right labels attached.[18] Prowling along in Algeria, the colonial

---

I Was A Minister of Stalin (Mexico City, 1953) that "this withdrawal would shove the Republic further toward catastrophe. And Moscow wanted to wind up the Spanish Civil War in order to get on with the negotiations with Hitler." About the terrible battle of the Ebro, where 70,000 men were lost in a two-month slaughter, this Moscow-trained observer says, "Is it possible that the Soviet military advisers did not know that pushing us into this battle was forcing us to commit suicide? They knew it well."

[18] Jean-Paul Sartre writes a passionate foreword to the French Communist editor's story of how he was tortured by Massu's paratroopers in an Algerian

Congo, Harlem or the Deep South, they feel their class-conscious gorges rising at every sign of oppression. (God knows there are plenty of signs.) But when making the grand sightseeing tour through the People's Republic of China they let their eyes skip nimbly over forced laborers, slave-camp veterans, relatives of slaughtered oppositionists and purgees. Why the flickering vision? Because in the one area there is a rotting order (so all is swinish) while in the other, nothing but building, progress, the future (so anything goes). End-means, end-means. Suffering comes to the philosopher's attention only when in the wrong, "unprogressive" context.[14]

---

prison (Henri Alleg's *The Question,* New York, 1958). What happened to this man, no matter what his politics, was an absolute abomination, and Sartre's indignation is thoroughly in order. But we have not yet had from the distinguished left-moralist any similar outburst against (for example) the torture and liquidation of many *millions* of people in GPU prisons and labor camps; and his revulsion with the not entirely pacifistic role of the Russian tanks in Budapest seems to have subsided rather abruptly, with no permanent damage to his pro-Russianism. We can ask further: would Sartre contribute an approving foreword to an account by a pro-French Algerian of his torture at the hands of Algerian nationalists (it being clear enough that both sides use such violence freely)? The existentialist answer, of course, is that it is a sign of "bad faith" to abstract violence from its living socio-economic context and pass judgment on it *sub specie aeternitatis.* Yet one of Sartre's own arguments, and a strong one, seems to have just this sort of abstract, universalist ring: he insists that the whip is as debasing and dehumanizing to the wielder as it is painful to the victim. Or does he mean that this boomeranging takes place only when the whip is in reactionary hands? If so, is there not a certain suggestion of "bad faith" in the premise that only reactionary torturers will be seared by their methods while "progressives" can lash away with impunity? The whole history of Stalinism testifies to the contrary. Incidentally, it is to be observed that most left intellectuals kept absolutely quiet about Stalin's fantastic brutalities all during his regime. It remained for Khrushchev—Khrushchev!—to reveal them to the world for his own less than humanitarian reasons.

[14] Through much of Simone de Beauvoir's novel *The Mandarins,* the advanced Parisian intellectuals debate one question: how to take the reports about slave-labor camps in Russia when they come from tainted sources? ("Tainted" here means "anti-Soviet" or at least "anti-Stalinist." Most of the survivors of these camps, having learned the hard way about Stalin's policy of making expendable industrial capital out of human bodies, *were* probably so tainted). They worry so much over the taint in the witnesses

Commitment? Engagement? Embrace of the existent? Or such resolute fixation on an abstract pie-in-the-sky vision that what is two inches from the nose cannot be seen?

It remains an icy truth that the view from the tourist's limousine is very, very different from the view afforded the man nailed down in a slave-labor gang—the most fully "committed" man of our time.

Left-bound intellectuals have arrived at such a nicety of discrimination that they can be appalled by the fate of the Hollywood Ten and other McCarthy victims but feel it not incumbent on them to so much as mention the ninety-nine of Mao's "one hundred flowers" who allowed themselves to open up, at his express invitation, only to be unceremoniously cut down. (At the risk of being accused of the worst kind of faith one must point out that McCarthy's victims lost only their livelihoods, and some not even that; Mao's lost their heads.) These latter-day friends of the lowly work with a remarkably selective social indignation which sees victimizing only when it proceeds under auspices not to their liking. (In the animal psychology laboratories this dramatic narrowing of the perception and response range is called "trained incapacity.") An on-again-off-again sort of humanism, this, operated by ideological push-button. Such people will defend the masses only against blows from the right; all blows from the left, however vicious, they will take and dress up as caresses.

The poor had better find ways to protect themselves against partisans with such a parttime morality.

What is becoming clear is that the immobilized will never find real friends among those who are free to come and go. Philosophers are notoriously peripatetic.[15]

---

they hear about that they have no time left to go out and look for some who are not tainted. Is this the vaunted existential plunge into the true life situation or the wildest kind of stratospheric abstraction? While the most sophisticated minds of Paris weighed these niceties as to sources, thousands of hollow-cheeked veterans of the Russian camps were straggling back into Western Europe. (Interviews with hundreds of them are summarized in an authoritative book, David Dallin's and B. I. Nicolaevsky's *Forced Labor in Soviet Russia*, Yale, 1947.) At that moment the population in the camps, whose existence could not be established in a philosophically satisfactory way, was at the very least fifteen million. . . . Good faith? Any faith at all?

[15] Academic people who come tardily to a politics of the left after long abstention from worldly concerns often strike the most bloodthirsty poses, as

A catastrophe: left-facing intellectuals are today rummaging through one half of the world looking for miracles, and through the other, for horrors. To the observer concerned less with faith (good or bad) than with fact, it is clear enough that on both sides the horrors outbulk the miracles. There is an essential horror whenever and wherever man exerts control over man; this barbaric condition holds on in all quarters; it needs only to be added that in the sovietized areas, where the controls are at their most brutal and pervasive, the attendant horrors are most spectacular. Any moral distinction drawn finer than this, or with more elasticity, gives evidence of a faith so corroded as to be non-existent. Besides, in this matter of allegiance to the oppressed, can the communoid intellectuals claim to have one one-hundredth of the good faith of those French and Italian worker-priests—their politics quite apart—who put away their frocks, move into the slums, and go to work in the factories side by side with the people they have declared for? Short of joining the poor and living their lives all the way, nobody has any damned right to speak in their name or their behalf; all the rest is demagoguery and humbuggery. The present crop of left intellectuals in Europe will deserve to be taken seriously the moment they give up their political tourism and differential indignation-at-a-distance, their limousine solidarities, for the sort of total "engagement" they theorize about but live not. Not before.

---

though to make up for lost time. Years ago an existentialist philosopher was telling me about the kind of bold social engineering he had come to admire. "In a certain remote area of Russia," he said, "just after the Revolution, a great deal of virulent anti-Semitism began to show up. The Bolshevik authorities understood that it would take several generations to root out this disease by re-education, and they had no time to waste. So they took all those past a certain age, the worst carriers of the infection, and shot them. Boom —no more anti-Semitism!" I do not know whether such an incident really took place; I rather doubt it. The point is that the clenched-fist philosopher *believed* it had happened—and heartily approved. Nice ends: the more histrionic means the better. . . . To his credit, this man later came to see that revolutionary politics somehow called out in him a terrible, irrational fierceness which was neither political nor philosophical in origin nor even sensible in intent; he broke off his connections with politics, wrote a telling critique of Bolshevik morality, and retired to scholarship and philosophy, in which areas, if he makes bad judgments, he can only confuse people, not help to liquidate them.

Not only is the revolutionary Marxist hand held out fitfully. When it does appear it holds ambiguous gifts.

The Bolshevik-Leninist logic leads too often to a deification of the proletarian. In his best moments Trotsky saw the absurdity in such veneration of a particular class among people devoted to the abolition of classes; in the books *Problems of Life* and *Literature and Revolution* he brilliantly exposed the ominous fatuity of encouraging a "proletarian culture" when you profess to believe that the proletarian is a vile way to live and must be thrown out of the human situation. (Lionel Trilling speaks of Trotsky's "superb contempt for the pieties of the conventional 'proletarian' esthetics.") But the exigencies of his embattled politics led him to violate this deeply humane insight. More than once he was moved to glorify the proletariat *as against* other groupings of bottomdogs; see his foundationless denunciation of Kronstadt for its "social degeneration" from noble-prolo to backward-peasant. This was not a simple human sympathy with the total mass of oppressed but a calculated maneuver to drive a wedge between blocs of them, to keep them separated and at each other's throat. The close fraternity between the Petersburg heavy-industry workers and the Kronstadt sailor-peasants had thrown a bad fright into the Bolsheviks.

Certain hammerblow Marxists will go on smiling broadly when distinctions are blurred between segments of the impoverished mass. Nevertheless all sophisticated subdividing is avoided here because it is too often undertaken by those who wish to use the different wings of the dispossessed, manipulate them, pit them one against the other —in order to perpetuate their own power pyramids. As against all this purposive segmentation there is an attempt here to raise the naivest and least "political" voice possible on the side of *all* the unmoneyed and unnoticed in *all* pyramidal societies (that is: everywhere); to produce a low-keyed hymn to the unwashed and un-catered-to of all stripes and dominions—those who huddle in the tenement and those who curl up under the rural hedgerow, those who are harnessed to lathe and those who are tied to plow, those who roam the slum and those who creep through the forest. These unsung ones can surely for once be given an overdue bow without lapsing into sentimentality and cultism—always, it seems, the precursors to manipulation. The peons of the world, East *and* West, are worth at least a wry hosanna because, whatever the state of their grammar or their personal hygiene, they still, even in these days of social freeze, are capable every so often of shrugging their collective shoulders and, in the process, of shaking the seats of the mighty for a moment. Only recently we have seen what tremors they can stir up, in the Little Rocks and Montgomerys as in the Poznans, the East Berlins, the Budapests, the Vorkutas.

Yes: in this improbable decade there has even been a wild revolt of the slaves in the Siberian forced-labor camp known as Vorkuta. The left-left novelist adores to write glowing accounts of the slave uprising led by the Roman gladiator Spartacus in 73 B.C.; the Spartacans of the less exotic but rather more relevant Siberian colonies have not yet managed to catch his eye.

Trotsky once observed that ours is an age in which politics brutally dominates the whole of life. The bottomdog shrug tends to loosen its weight, or at least shift it, for a fraction of a second. The nameless, all of them together, without thinking much about politics, with no program for a "vertical invasion of the barbarians," uninformed about the apparatuses sprouting over their heads but chafing under their weight, having no thought for the fine distinctions between their own "progressive" and "backward" components, are still capable of this periodic shrug; and they can still send shivers through the theo-techno-auto-bureaucrats on all the apexes of all the pyramids. They can still, just for exercise, just to stretch their cramped muscles, produce an occasional Kronstadt; and that, though not always world-shaking, is fine, very fine.

AFTERWORD

AFTERWORD
William T. Vollmann

1

Why should you read *The Great Prince Died*? What is its project, and how does it go about fulfilling it?

Do not expect an accurate relation of Trotsky's assassination. Bernard Wolfe informs us that "this work cannot be called history. It is, rather, a fiction based upon, derived from, dogged by, if you will—history."[1]

Whatever it is, it cannot be called great literature, either. In isolation, Wolfe's construction just quoted might be accepted as passable, if uninspired. But as one reads (and, at times, toils) through this novel, one encounters more of the same.

As if wearisome redundancies of style weren't enough, Wolfe continually undermines his own verisimilitude, eschews subtlety, has a tin ear for dialogue, etcetera.—Enough. Irving Howe once wrote about Theodore Dreiser, who *is* in fact a great writer, that "as for his faults, no great critical insight is needed to identify them, since they glare out of every chapter, especially ... his habit of crushing the English language beneath a leaden embrace."[2] If Wolfe's prose is riddled with these same faults, and meanwhile lacks Dreiser's great virtues, which left Howe "greatly moved and shaken,"[3] then once again: Why on earth should we read this book?

2

The Great Prince Died does in fact concern itself with the assassination of Trotsky, but V. R. Rostov lacks three of Trotsky's four children and one of his two wives, and even meets his death a year earlier than the original, so that Wolfe can haunt us with that cynical triumph, the Nazi-Soviet Pact: "Idea of agreement with Hitler a jolt. Had to introduce it in stages: first as plot. After that, no novelty or shock power to the idea ... Rostov working with Hitler must be in Hitler's pocket. Stalin working with Hitler must have Hitler in *his* pocket. All the badness in the idea pinned to Rostovites. Rostovites wiped out—idea remains, minus its badness."[4]

And here let me pause to temper my earlier criticism: when Wolfe writes in this telegraphic style, he can be quite effective. Moreover, some of his episodes achieve true narrative interest— for instance, the impulsive liaisons and ghastly memories of Rostov's security guard Paul Teleki, the most fully realized character.

If you have read Orwell's *Homage to Catalonia* or Hemingway's *For Whom the Bell Tolls*, you will probably remember how the International Brigades of anarchists, Communists, socialists, do-gooders, and fellow travelers were systematically undermined by their supposed ally, J. V. Stalin. The circumstances of Teleki's initiation into this truth are rather extreme. And just to make things neat—far neater than real life could be—his educators turn out to be some of Rostov's future assassins. "You know," he tells us, "I believe, I really believe that none of these people enjoyed making me suffer ... They didn't want to hurt me ... But V. R. didn't want to hurt the Kronstadt sailors either ..."[5]

At any rate, Wolfe has strong feelings; he means to paint a certain picture, and to do so he will not hesitate to alter this or that— which is peculiar, since he informs us that he was Trotsky's secretary in 1937, so that he must have known the facts pretty well;[6] he could have served them up with a sauce of hyperrealistic local flavor. And yet the closer we look at his tale (or parable, I should better call it), the greater appear his alterations.

Consider the actual mood in Trotsky's besieged fortress. In the final volume of his great biographical trilogy, Isaac Deutscher, who was not there, conveys a sad and increasingly ominous impression. Joseph Hansen, who *was* present, having been another Trotsky secretary not long after Wolfe, insists that "Deutscher's picture of the years in Coyoacán is of virtually unrelieved gloom, life ... being overcast by a hopeless battle against the Kremlin's executioners. This is not the way it was."[7] Well, then, how was it? Trotsky had hopes[8] and even successes; he sometimes achieved propaganda victories. For instance, regarding the third "great" Moscow show trial of 1938, "Trotsky, the chief defendant, succeeded in turning the tables on Stalin, becoming the chief accuser."[9] In *The Great Prince Died*, the picture is more like Deutscher's than Hansen's.

"Certainly," Wolfe admits, "the inner agitation, if it was there, did not come out as nakedly as I have suggested."[10] But in his re-envisioning, Rostov and the entourage are not merely hemmed in; they are waiting for death. And the subtext—distasteful, disturbing to be on Stalin's side!—is that Rostov might even deserve killing—for we hear a certain name on everyone's lips: Kronstadt.

3

Kronstadt is the focus and locus of Wolfe's fictional project. Rostov says the word with a guilty irritation; Paul Teleki continually needles him about it. Even the wide-eyed young American linguist overcomes his hero worship enough to make accusations. It is difficult to imagine the real life Trotsky putting up with all this. As Robert Conquest remarked, Trotsky's "ideas are notable for . . . a total lack of solicitude for the non-Communist victims of the regime: no sympathy whatever was expended, for example, on the dead of the collectivization famine."[11] Therefore, "the crushing of the Kronstadt rebellion was as much his personal battle honor as the seizure of power had been."[12]

A résumé of certain events related to Kronstadt may help a reader to judge the success of *The Great Prince Died.*

In 1917, the Romanov era finally came to an end with the abdication of Nicholas II. The curtain of the February Revolution unsteadily rose upon a Provisional Government whose elements were various and antithetical: Bolsheviks, Mensheviks, anarchists, Social Revolutionaries, Tsarists, prospective White Guards—all biding their time under the mercurial leadership of Alexander Kerensky, who thought to bridge the unbridgeable gap between the bourgeoisie and the ultraleftists. According to Trotsky, one of these myriad indissoluble globules was "the independent Kronstadt republic,"[13] the fortress where "the flame of rebellion never went out."[14]

That flame had glowed in the failed 1905 revolution. As Trotsky tells the tale, "the politically conscious among the soldiers tried to restrain the masses, but a spontaneous fury broke out." ("Spontaneous" is an adjective with labyrinthine connotations when it has been penned by a vanguardist.) "Having proved unable to halt the movement," he goes on, "the best elements in the army placed themselves at its head." And the result? "The best of the soldiers and sailors were threatened with execution."[15] Considering what would happen in 1921, those last words exude a loathsome irony.

Back to 1917. "The February Revolution was relatively blood-less," writes the historian Richard Pipes. "Most of the deaths oc-curred at the naval bases in Kronshtadt and Helsinki, where an-archist sailors lynched officers, often on suspicion of 'espionage' because of their German-sounding surnames."[16] Or, as Trotsky more romantically tells it, "In Kronstadt the revolution was accom-panied by an outbreak of bloody vengeance against the officers, who attempted, as if in horror at their own past, to conceal the revolution from the sailors."[17] (*The Great Prince Died* omits this ep-isode entirely, for it is essential to Wolfe's project to represent the sailors as heroic victims.)

As Kerensky's coalition continued its inevitable disintegration, there presently arose, "spontaneously" again, the ultrarevolution-ary demonstrations of the "July days," when hordes demanded that Bolsheviks break with the Provisional Government and establish Red rule.[18] Of course five or six thousand Kronstadt sailors took part, raising the banner "All Power to the Soviets."[19] Lenin, how-ever, hesitated, believing the Bolsheviks too weak to seize power just yet. No doubt the militants were disappointed, being "sponta-neous." "In the political sphere," explains Trotsky, "the Kronstadt sailors were not inclined toward maneuvering or toward diplo-macy . . . It is no wonder that in relation to a phantom government they tended toward an extremely simplified method of action." Although these words reveal the condescension of the politician toward the mere militant, their utterer goes on to express a fond pride: "Kronstadt stood there as a herald of the advancing second revolution."[20]

Lenin's caution proved correct, for the "July days" presently burned themselves out—except for one last manifestation: the Peter and Paul fortress remained under the control of Kronstadt sailors and other ultraradicals. Stalin and a Menshevik colleague[21] (or, to hear our hero tell it, Trotsky[22]) finally visited them to ne-gotiate their surrender, which was accomplished without violence and led to no executions.[23]

So it happened that emissaries of the Kronstadt Soviet found themselves able to travel all over Russia, urging peasants to pillage the aristocrats, persuading soldiers to desert from the frontline. Trotsky pays them this tribute: "The sailors far more deeply expressed the demands of historic evolution than the very intelligent professors."[24]

Later that year, the Bolsheviks finally did seize power in the October Revolution. Of course Kronstadt sailors were there.

4

Five years later, with the Soviet Union starved and exhausted by the Civil War, Kronstadt rose up against Bolshevik unilateralism because, as Wolfe so accurately explains, "the trouble was: the best ingredient in a movement of social revolt was the young spirit of rebellion."[25] So the sailors demanded a "third revolution"—and with good reason, for the stern measures of "War Communism," which Lenin, Trotsky, and company had applied, had grown intolerable. In his autobiography Trotsky nearly admits this: "The question at issue was really one of daily bread, of fuel, of raw material for the industries ... the thing that really mattered was the economic catastrophe hanging over the country. The uprisings at Kronstadt and in the province of Tambov broke into the discussion as the last warning."[26]

It was March 1921. A few weeks earlier the bread ration had been cut by thirty percent.[27] Joined by soldiers, workers, even card-carrying Bolsheviks, the sailors once more established their own provisional revolutionary committee. Aleksandr I. Solzhenitsyn gave them this epitaph: Kronstadt and Tambov marked the last time *in forty-one years* that the people would speak out.[28]

What the people said in this final declaration was nothing that the new autocrats wished to hear. Let me quote from one Kronstadt manifesto: "The power of the police-gendarme monarchy has gone into the hands of the Communist-usurpers, who instead of freedom offer the toilers the constant fear of falling into the torture-chambers of the Cheka[29], which in their horrors surpass many times the gendarme administration of the tsarist regime."[30]

The Cheka were already on the case. They warned Lenin: "The Kronstadt revolutionary committee clearly expects a general uprising in Petrograd any day now."[31] Lenin advised the Tenth Congress: "Now as to Kronshtadt. The danger there lies in the fact that their slogans are not Socialistic-Revolutionary, but anarchistic. An All-Russian Congress of Producers—this is not a Marxist but a petty bourgeois idea."[32]

Not coincidentally, I suspect, in this same document Lenin goes on to say: "Trotsky wants to resign ... But Trotsky is a temperamental man with military experience. He is in love with the organization, but as for politics, he hasn't got a clue."[33] After all, he had loved the Kronstadt fighters. But fortunately for his personal equilibrium, he was practiced at breaking with former allies—and the rupture must have come easier to him when the other Bolsheviks rapidly made up their own steely minds to follow Lenin's intimations.

The Great Prince Died alludes to what happened next: "Pyramids of Teotihuacán. Pointed tops: rooms of sacrifice there. Where men used to face charges. Charged with being wanted by the boss, the sun god, without delay; hearts pulled out and dropped, still pumping, on fires."[34] And again, more blatantly (this somewhat recalls the doctrine of the High, the Middle, and the Low in Orwell's *1984*): "Those who rise to the apex can't see the base ... the base will rise up one day, not seen until the last minute, and destroy the apex."[35] On the subject of Kronstadt, Rostov explains, "We had to stop their premature attack on the pyramid—in the interest of abolishing pyramids altogether."[36]

So the Cheka arrested two thousand worker sympathizers, after which the military assault on Kronstadt began. "Thousands of people" were killed in the taking of the fortress. This was not enough for the vanguardists at the apex. We read that 2,103 prisoners received capital sentences and 6,459 were imprisoned. (Considerable numbers of the latter would be tied to stones and drowned in the Dvina River.) In 1923, 2,154 civilians were deported from Kronstadt to Siberia, "merely on the grounds that they had stayed in the town through the events."[37] Meanwhile, as many as possible of the besieged who had escaped into Finnish internment were lured back and likewise dispatched to the Gulag.

"Trotsky," says Wolfe, "did not participate personally in the military operation against Kronstadt ... He and Lenin, however, drew up the ultimatums issued to the sailors."[38] In *The Great Prince Died*, Rostov *leads* the attack, and on "the night it was finally over at Kronstadt," his fifteen-year-old only son, whom Stalin will eventually assassinate, upbraids him: "They were your best friends . . . Mine, too . . . Uncle Anastas let me climb all over the battleships . . ."[39]

After the rebellion had been crushed, Lenin went easier on the general population while tightening the screws within the Party; from here on, even the most loyal and reasoned disagreement increasingly became labeled as "factionalism" and received appropriate punishment. In *My Life*, published in 1930, the freshly exiled Trotsky justifies the practice: "As a rule, solutions had to be found on the spur of the moment, and mistakes were followed by immediate retribution. . . . If we had had more time for discussion, we should probably have made a great deal more mistakes."[40] But by 1937, with Stalin's assassins closing in, he writes in *The Revolution Betrayed*: "This forbidding of factions was again regarded as an exceptional measure to be abandoned at the first serious improvement in the situation. . . . However," this "proved perfectly suited to the taste of the bureaucracy."[41]

Accordingly, in the novel we find Paul Teleki worrying that "it," meaning both bureaucratic centralism and Rostov's death wish, might have started after Kronstadt.[42]

5

The Great Prince Died stands or falls by its invocation of Kronstadt. I say it stands. In essence, the novel is a Socratic dialogue with more or less colorful interruptions. If it tends to heavy-handedness, well, so do the conversations in Plato. Wolfe's own position is clear. He argues first with Trotsky, then with Bolshevism, and eventually with authority itself. As the book progresses, the metaphor of Kronstadt grows and grows, until it stands in for any time and place in which someone employs power upon the weak in the service of a stated good.

Do the ends justify the means? This is one of the great questions of any time. We should consider it deeply and *provisionally* answer it for ourselves. To help us do so, Wolfe has simplified real life into a parable in order to present us with the following question: *If* the Kronstadt mutineers were "innocent," "virtuous," and somehow "correct" in their political line, and *if* Trotsky were responsible for their suppression, which not only was ("necessary" or not) an atrocity, but also furthered the cause of bureaucratic centralism through which millions, including Trotsky, were liquidated, *then* how valid would Trotsky's justifications be?

Paradox: If Trotsky was correct at Kronstadt, then his own murder could also be construed as right. If his murder stinks (as I most certainly believe), then he was wrong at Kronstadt, in which case his murder again becomes justified so long as he supports Kronstadt-like actions. Like most paradoxes, this one ultimately fails to hold together—but only in the "real world." Rostov is a reduction of a far more interesting and ambiguous man. But the protagonists of parables must be types, emblems, tropes. Rostov represents not who Trotsky was, but a certain principle that Trotsky stood for. If we feel willing to generalize and simplify, then this parable with its paradox does have something to tell us—for the events that haunted Bernard Wolfe reincarnate themselves endlessly. For instance, the America in which I write is a place which has weakly disavowed its late policy of torture but declines to punish any high-level perpetrators. I suspect that most of my fellow citizens would accept the continuation of torture if they believed that would make them safer from terrorists. Perhaps we ourselves wouldn't care to waterboard prisoners—but consider the following exchange of courtesies:

> *"I never exterminated my own men," jeers General Ortega.*
> *"How could you!" Rostov replies. "You ran from power the moment you had it, so others less squeamish would do the job for you."*[43]

In a sense, this is a Grand Inquisitor's answer. But that cannot alone disqualify it—or validate it.

Do the ends justify the means?

In this novel Rostov gives many other answers to this question. The assassins proffer their own answers. It is for you and me to evaluate them.

"Then it amounts to this," says General Ortega to the dying Rostov's wife. "Those who use all means will win, those who reject some means will lose. There is no remedy . . ."[44] Can it be so? Trotsky believed it. Sometimes, so do I. (That is why I prefer to lose.) Exactly here we come face to face with Wolfe's defective, unlikely greatness. His formulation must never be forgotten. It is one of the darkest axioms not only of politics but of human life itself.

Notes

1. Wolfe, 388.
2. Theodore Dreiser, *An American Tragedy* (New York: Signet Classics / New American Library, 1964; orig ed. 1935), 816.
3. Ibid., 817.
4. Wolfe, 148.
5. Ibid., 211.
6. The assassins, though they bear some similarity to their counterparts in our universe, have likewise been changed. Cándida Baeza de Riviera and Tomás are loosely modeled after Caridad Mercader and her son Ramon. I was sorry not to encounter the Stalinist painter Siqueiros, who led the assassination attempt with a machine gun. Wolfe's George Bass, who tortures his victims with lenses of his own manufacture, is a remarkable villain, but still perhaps less fascinating than the real article, Mark Zborowski, who after procuring the death of Trotsky's son and of various members of the Trotsky circle, then became an anthropologist at two American Ivy League universities (Robert Conquest, *The Great Terror: A Reassessment* [New York: Oxford University Press, 1990], 475).
7. Leon Trotsky, *My Life: An Attempt at an Autobiography* (New York: Pathfinder, 1987 repr. of 1970 ed.; orig. pub. stated as 1930), xii (introduction). The reader who wishes to get a sense of Trotsky's personality and literary style could do worse than read *My Life*. One attempt to address the central question of the man's means and ends is the "Defense of Authority" chapter of my *Rising Up and Rising Down: Some Thoughts on Violence, Freedom, and Urgent Means* (New York: HarperCollins, 2003). There Trotsky is compared in some detail to Abraham Lincoln.
8. "The life of the household was an engagement in building the Fourth International . . . All of us were committed, dedicated even, to this work . . . Everything Trotsky himself did was directed toward this goal." Trotsky, *My Life*, vii.
9. Ibid., xxvii.
10. Wolfe, 388.
11. Conquest, *The Great Terror*, 412.
12. Ibid.
13. Leon Trotsky, *The History of the Russian Revolution*, trans. Max Eastman (New York: Pathfinder, 1992; Trotsky's preface dated 1930), 401.
14. Ibid., 430.
15. Leon Trotsky, *1905* (New York: Vintage Books / Random House / Studies in the Third World Books, 1971; orig ed. 1922), 166.
16. Richard Pipes, *The Russian Revolution* (New York: Vintage Books, 1991 repr. of 1990 ed.), 303–4. "Kronstadt" and "Kronshtadt" are rival transliterations. I have used the first because Wolfe does.
17. Trotsky, *History of the Russian Revolution*, 255.
18. For one concise summary of events in the "July days," see Isaac Deutscher, *Stalin: A Political Biography*, rev. ed. (Harmondsworth, UK: Penguin Books Ltd., 1966; orig. pub. 1949), 156–59.
19. Pipes, *The Russian Revolution*, 427.
20. Trotsky, *History of the Russian Revolution*, 430–31.

21. Deutscher, *Stalin*, 163.
22. Trotsky, *History of the Russian Revolution*, 433.
23. A month later, all the various parties temporarily united against an attempted counterrevolutionary putsch by General L. V. Kornilov. Isaac Deutscher tells a relevant anecdote: "When the sailors of Kronstadt visited Trotsky in his prison and asked him whether they should not 'deal with' Kornilov and Kerensky in one stroke, Trotsky advised them to tackle their adversaries one by one" (163).
24. Ibid., 434.
25. Wolfe, 282.
26. Trotsky, *My Life*, 466.
27. Stéphane Courtois et al., *The Black Book of Communism: Crimes, Terror, Repression*, trans. Jonathan Murphy and Mark Kramer (Cambridge: Harvard University Press, 1999), 112.
28. "The flare-up at Novocherkassk was the first time the people had spoken out in forty-one years (since Kronstadt and Tambov) ..." Aleksandr I. Solzhenitsyn, *The Gulag Archipelago, 1918–1956: An Experiment in Literary Investigation*, vol. 3 (New York: HarperPerennial, 1992; orig. Russian ed. 1976), 507.
29. The secret police; forerunner of the NKVD, GPU, and KGB.
30. Robert V. Daniels, *A Documentary History of Communism in Russia: From Lenin to Gorbachev* (Hanover, NH: University of Vermont / University Press of New England, 1993), 107 ("The Kronstadt Revolt," from "What We Are Fighting For," by the Kronstadt Temporary Revolutionary Committee, March 8, 1921).
31. Ibid., 113.
32. Richard Pipes, ed., *The Unknown Lenin: From the Secret Archive* (New Haven: Yale University Press, 1996), 124 (Document 66: Summary of Lenin's Remarks at the Congress of the Delegates to the Tenth Congress ... , 13 March 1921). Deutscher took a similar line (224–25): "Their slogans were borrowed from the slogans of the Bolsheviks in the early days of the revolution. Yet ... the rising stirred new hope in the ranks of the defeated counter-revolution."
33. Pipes, *The Unknown Lenin*, 124.
34. Wolfe, 78.
35. Ibid., 84–85.
36. Ibid., 88.
37. The information in this paragraph derives from Courtois et al., *The Black Book of Communism*, 113–14.
38. Wolfe, 386.
39. Ibid., 279.
40. Trotsky, *My Life*, 437.
41. Leon Trotsky, *The Revolution Betrayed: What is the Soviet Union and Where is it Going?*, trans. Max Eastman (New York: Pathfinder, 1991 repr. of 1937 ed.), 96.
42. Wolfe, 104–05.
43. Ibid., 131.
44. Ibid., 311.

CPSIA information can be obtained
at www.ICGtesting.com
Printed in the USA
BVHW030727161220